Rolling over in the soft, fragrant hay, Rolfe pulled Marged on top of him, imprisoning her against the throbbing, swelling heat of his desire. "Now say you don't want me," he challenged.

"No—I'm virgin."

"All women are virgin at some time. 'Tis no excuse."

Marged struggled to be free of that taunting arousal, but with one swift movement he rolled her onto her back in the hay and pinned her there. How she longed to discover the dark mystery of his passion, yet such knowledge gleaned from a hated enemy was a shameful thing.

"Marged, please, be not afraid of me." His lips engulfed hers, and she gasped in surprise as she felt his hot hand against her bare breast. His touch seared her with flame. Suddenly she wanted to stroke his smooth, tanned flesh, she longed to caress, to inflame, to discover the hidden secrets of his body. Shocked by her own admission, Marged stared into his eyes, seeing desire blaze there. He knew!

"Let me show you how wonderful it can be," he whispered. "Let me love you."

TOUCH ME WITH FIRE

by Patricia Phillips, author of

JENNY and CAPTIVE FLAME

Also by Patricia Phillips
from Jove

CAPTIVE FLAME
JENNY
ANISE
MY SOUL WITH THINE
LOVE'S DEFIANT PRISONER
ROYAL CAPTIVE

A JOVE BOOK

TOUCH ME WITH FIRE

A Jove Book / published by arrangement with
the author

PRINTING HISTORY
Jove edition / August 1982

ISBN: 0-515-05908-0

Jove books are published by Jove Publications, Inc.,
200 Madison Avenue, New York, N.Y. 10016. The words
"A JOVE BOOK" and the "J" with sunburst are
trademarks belonging to Jove Publications, Inc.

PRINTED IN THE UNITED STATES OF AMERICA

Touch Me
with
Fire

{ one }

THE SUMMER DAWN was slow in coming. Marged Bowen leaned against the cold stone parapet flanking the castle's west tower, and watched the day unfurl beyond the misty peaks of the jagged Black Mountains. At this waking hour the world seemed hushed. Forested hills stretched to the brooding mountain range that formed a natural defense of the Welsh border. The River Wye lapped at the foot of Bowenford's red sandstone walls. Two hundred yards upstream, the river shallowed and the resulting ford was named Bowenford Crossing. Marged loved her wild homeland with a passionate fervor; it was deeply ingrained in her soul. Yet had she been a boy, she would gladly have left to join the gathering army of King Harry Lancaster.

A chill river breeze blew a wayward lock of hair across her smooth brow, and sliced through her red silk gown. Drawing her thin wool cloak more tightly around her body, she reluctantly turned her back on the summer-mantled Welsh Marches and went below.

Even now, Marged's father and his men assembled in the

outer bailey, preparing to answer the call for men to repel the Yorkist rebels. In this summer of 1460, the uneasy peace between the royal houses of York and Lancaster had been shattered; Richard Neville, mighty Earl of Warwick, had mustered a vast army to support his leader, the Duke of York, which was tantamount to declaring war. Generally such affairs of state were of little concern along this isolated stretch of the Marches. However, Sir Richard Bowen owed his allegiance to Jasper Tudor, the Lancastrian Earl of Pembroke, who had summoned him to Coventry, King Henry's midland seat of government.

Bowenford was an unimposing castle compared to the mighty structures of Goodrich, Skenfrith, and White, built by the Normans to defend the Golden Valley from Welsh invaders. Yet had her home been the mightiest castle in the land, Marged could not have been any more proud. The Bowens had held charter to this land since the first fortress was built to protect the vital border between England and Wales.

Marged's Welsh mother, Eirlys, had claimed descent from the warlike princes of Powys. From this Celtic strain Marged had inherited much of her striking appearance: golden, sun-flushed skin that flowed smooth as satin over her high-cheek-boned face; luxuriant hair that coiled like ebony about her dainty ears; large, almond-shaped green eyes that gazed from beneath a curtain of silky black lashes. Yet for her shapely body at its voluptuous peak of maturity, for her thin-bridged nose with its flaring nostrils, for her full red mouth suggesting passion, she must thank her smattering of Saracen blood handed down through her father's family since the Third Crusade. These noble bloods of her ancient lineage mingled to impart dainty hands and feet, as well as an unusual grace of movement for a woman far taller than average.

As she hastened down the tower stairs, she lifted her clinging silk skirts free of her shapely ankles to speed her passage. When at last she reached the stone archway leading to the outer bailey, she paused, swallowing the lump in her throat that rose at the sight of the castle soldiers arrayed for battle, kneeling bareheaded on the grass to receive the priest's blessing. Old Father Dan walked through the ranks, reciting the Latin liturgy of the Mother Church while he sprinkled the men with holy water. Accompanying him was a shivering acolyte who swung a censer, distilling the sweet smell of incense into the damp air. The blessings given, the soldiers rose and donned their helmets, and suddenly the grassy outer bailey came alive—grunts, coughs, rough voices and laughter mixed with the clang of armaments and the neighs of nervous horses.

Marged hastened to where her father stood bareheaded beside his great war-horse.

"Fare thee well, Father," she whispered tearfully as he took her within his burly arms in a great bear hug, crushing her against the cold steel of his breastplate.

"God keep thee safe, Marged," Sir Richard whispered, his voice gruff with emotion. It was unwise to display weakness before his men, so he strove to harden his heart. "We'll be home before you've even missed us," he blustered, setting Marged aside, the better to feast his eyes on her beauty. "Daily you grow more like your mother," he said, his voice breaking over the remark, for he had dearly loved Welsh Eirlys. "The transformation gives me great pleasure. When you're wed, you'll make a lovely bride."

Her father's seemingly innocent mention of marriage pitched Marged's stomach; neither was she overjoyed by his expressed pleasure over her "transformation." As a child she had been treated more like a boy; Sir Richard taught her to hunt, to shoot a bow, and to wield a sword—freedom usually denied girl-children. When she reached marriageable age, those former privileges were abruptly withdrawn. And seeing his willful young daughter's growing resentment over her new restrictions, Sir Richard regretted having allowed her such earlier freedom. Now he wished her to appear meekly subservient, the better to please a husband.

"Treat not the lads too harshly, Father, they're so young," Marged ventured, looking at her eight- and nine-year-old step-brothers, Martin and Arthur, who slumped sullenly astride their ponies. They were to ride with Sir Richard as far as Hereford, where they were to begin their training as pages in a noble household.

"You coddle them far too much, daughter," Sir Richard remarked gruffly as he swung into the saddle. "They must learn to be men—but I promise they'll be well looked after in Hereford. Now go, bid them farewell, and let us be on our way."

Marged ran fleet-footedly over the grass toward her stepbrothers. Despite their scowls, they appeared unusually cherubic with their girlish pink-white complexions and soft flaxen hair. In appearance they resembled their frail mother, a French widow whom Sir Richard had taken to wife after Eirlys's death, and who had provided her husband with two sickly male heirs before she finally succumbed to a lung ailment, worsened by the cold, wet Marches weather.

"Goodbye, Arthur. Goodbye, Martin. Don't forget me, will you? Remember to obey Father. And be brave and serve your new lord well," Marged cautioned, blinking back tears as she saw fear and apprehension rise in their pinched faces.

"We will, sister. Goodbye," said Martin huskily, speaking for his younger brother as well. Arthur was too close to tears for speech.

"Here, sweet brothers, you must wear my token for luck." Alys's shrill voice announced her presence as she jostled Marged aside to thrust a rose silk kerchief into each small fist. The boys were Alys's brothers too, and she had a perfect right to embrace them, yet Marged fought to control her surging anger at her stepsister's rudeness. She was used to Alys's high-handed behavior, but for all that, it never ceased to rankle her nerves. From the day of her arrival at Bowenford, a haughty, sharp-faced eleven-year-old, Alys had made it plain that she had no intention of lowering herself to befriend the daughter of a wild Welshwoman and an insignificant Marcher lord. Alys's arrogance was encouraged by her mother, who flaunted their ounce of French royal blood. During the intervening years, Alys had been both married and widowed, yet it had not sweetened her disposition. It was with heavy heart that Marged had welcomed back her newly widowed stepsister when she returned to Bowenford last spring. Despite her humbled attitude in the beginning, Alys soon reasserted herself, growing more unpleasant as enforced spinsterhood deepened her naturally shrewish nature.

"Daughter." Sir Richard's deep voice boomed above the din in the bailey as he signaled to Marged to come to his side.

"Is it time to leave?"

"Aye, it's long past time." He smiled down at his daughter,

reluctant to leave her in charge of his beloved property. His hand gentle on her sleek black hair, he said, "You've but a skeleton force left for defense, yet I expect no trouble." Sir Richard seemed to hesitate before expressing his next thought. "Have no fear for my safety, Marged, for we're to join de Bretayne's troops outside Hereford."

Her eyes widened at this unexpected revelation. Her father had never exhibited much love for their neighbor to the south. "But I thought de Bretayne's loyalty was still in doubt. Did he not stand for the Yorkists at Ludlow?"

"York was defeated, love. A defeat oftimes shows men the error of their ways. You forget, Sir Joce is a kinsman by marriage, being distantly related to your late stepmother. Is it not fitting that we should ride together? And, depending on the outcome of the war, he could prove a staunch friend. It's not meet to scoff at wise men who keep a foot in both camps."

His words surprised Marged, for she had always considered her father King Henry's man. What else had he withheld from her, she wondered, as she noted how his manner had changed from bluff heartiness to an alien demeanor.

"The guard is to be led by the Bretons."

René and Ardan had but recently joined her father's garrison and were not popular with the men. "Surely another choice would be preferable," Marged protested quickly, but she was swiftly silenced by her father's angry glare.

"Remember—'tis not for a woman to question men's orders!" he snapped, his face tightening. "They are experienced soldiers late of Sir Joce's service; he recommends them highly. Let me attend to military matters, you to the household. Rob will help you to govern the servants. He's a good steward and will prove useful once his leg is mended."

Duly chastened, Marged nodded. The ranks were already moving toward the drawbridge, whose squealing winch shattered the relative peace of this summer morn.

"Take care, Marged."

"I will. God speed and protect you."

Sir Richard placed his helmet on his shaggy gray head, securing the leather straps; no longer did he look familiar behind that impersonal mask of glittering steel. For a moment his dark eyes gleamed with betraying moisture before he swung his destrier toward the gate, and raced to the head of his troops.

The ranks drew up together beyond the walls as the soldiers clattered over the wooden drawbridge. A stiff breeze whipped their pennants as well as the proud Bowen standard of a broad-sword on an azure ground bearing the motto, "Shrink Not from Might." As they passed, many of the soldiers shouted farewell to Marged; they found their lord's daughter a comely, spirited wench, and many among them wished she had been heir to Bowenford, instead of her young brother Martin, who was a puny, unhealthy lad, lacking in courage.

Blond Alys stood unbending as a statue beside Marged, fluttering her kerchief. Her thin, pinched features turning increasingly sullen as she received little acknowledgment from the departing troops. She was not popular, and today the men left her in little doubt about their sentiments.

"Life will certainly be more refined without that rabble," Alys remarked peevishly, tossing her head in defiance of their snubs.

"And far more dangerous," Marged reminded her before she spun about and headed for the tower, from whose battlements she intended to watch the soldiers depart.

Alys ground her teeth in resentment as she watched her stepsister's bright red figure bobbing over the bailey. She had never liked Marged. The younger woman was everything she was not, though Alys had always considered those differences shortcomings on Marged's part. She sometimes wished she had been born a little more like her stepsister. Marged was virtually idolized by the castle servants, the soldiers, and even by Sir Richard himself, who had indulged the little fool shamelessly over her reluctance to settle on a husband. They were dolts! Far too primitive to recognize a true lady's worth, they mistook beauty, high temper, and flightiness for breeding. Alys glared hotly at the last departing soldier, who rode past in sullen silence, before she whipped about and stalked indoors.

For a long time, Marged stood watching the line of soldiers cutting through the green valley. They had forded the river, their horses submerged shoulder-deep in the swift water, swollen by an unusually cold, wet summer. She continued to strain into the distance until the column became mere black specks and was finally swallowed by the densely wooded hills.

On the morrow, the verdant countryside of the Marches grayed beneath a driving onslaught of rain. Taking the hunting hounds for company, Marged made her rounds of the castle. She found Rod, her father's steward, much improved, his shattered leg in a splint, the swelling all but gone. The red-haired steward, sensing her unease, frequently reassured her of their safety inside these walls. And though he did not dispel her doubts concerning the advisability of leaving the two Bretons in charge of the guard, his assurance of the men's ability as soldiers did much to ease her nagging fear of insurrection.

While Marged attended to the running of the castle, Alys withdrew to her chamber, where she sang French love songs by the hour to the accompaniment of her lute. At least her stepsister was not underfoot, Marged thought with relief, hearing Alys's reedy, quavering soprano penetrate the solar. Though Alys plagued her daily, Marged sometimes felt sorry for the older woman. Life had condemned Alys to live out her days as a shadowy, unloved presence within another's household. Women in her position often retired to a convent, yet Alys's viperish disposition hardly suited her to a spiritual vocation.

Marged opened the casement and leaned against the chill stonework to survey the rain-sodden countryside. Fate would eventually resolve her frequent clashes with Alys, for Marged had reached full marriage age and time was pressing. A half-dozen suitors had already been suggested, all of whom she had emphatically refused. She smiled somewhat guiltily as she pictured her father's mounting fury over each successive refusal. Someday his patience would run dry and then, to her liking or nay, he would thrust upon her the most advantageous match. To her surprise, her meager dowry had been small deterrent, for men seemed enamored of her beauty alone. It was fine to be called beautiful, and she would not have wished it otherwise. Yet for so prized an asset, her beauty had so far profited her little.

* * *

By nightfall the rain, which had abated after noon, began to fall again in earnest. Marged pulled her heavy cloak over her head as she mounted the battlements for her nightly check of the defenses. The men were at their posts, huddling against the stone breastworks for shelter. The fresh clean scent of open country blew all around her as she gazed intently into the wild night, the wind off the mountains stinging her face with needle-sharp fury; the chilly rain slashed her cheeks. She drew her hood tighter. When lightning jagged unexpectedly across the sky to illuminate the trees to the south, her heart lurched. Had that been the glint of armor? She waited for another revealing flash, but only the thunder rolled ominously in the distant hills. She cocked her head to one side, straining to hear the sounds of betraying hoofbeats; whatever danger lurked beyond the trees was hidden by the lashing rain against the stonework. Giving up her vigil, she went below.

Sometime during the night she was awakened from a heavy, dreamless sleep by a strange noise. The rain had stopped; all was quiet within the west tower. Then the peculiar rustling, scraping sound against the walls and corridor started again, and Marged woke fully. Pausing only long enough to fling a cloak over her transparent shift and slip on her shoes, she ran to the door. When she wrenched the iron handle to the right, the door groaned loudly on its hinge, swollen by the damp. Cursing under her breath, Marged realized she had just destroyed the advantage she needed to catch someone at an evil deed.

Though her eyes sharply pierced the murky corridor, she found it deserted. The cold stone wall felt damp beneath her hands as she groped down the twisting tower stairs. From the lower level she could hear what sounded like clanking armaments, and her stomach pitched in alarm. There had been no attack, nor was there any reason to expect an armed confrontation; she would have been summoned, had the sentries been challenged. Despite those sensible reassurances, she could not dispel a mounting feeling of danger.

She hesitated on the stair, listening, her scalp prickling as a bloodcurdling scream issued from the guardroom below and was quickly stifled. The betraying sound charged her into action. Racing recklessly up the narrow stairs, she ran onto the battlements to alert the guards. The cold wind whipped her garments and she slid over the slippery stonework. Her journey would have been easier, had she possessed the forethought to carry a light. At the door leading inside the east tower, Marged froze; the portcullis was being raised, the winch squealing like a tortured animal.

"Treachery! To arms! To arms! We are attacked!" Marged sounded the alarm as she burst through the tower door and headed for the main gate.

Sleepy, half-dressed guards emerged, fumbling with their weapons. Marged passed sentries slumped against the battlements, enemy daggers planted in their backs. Even as she neared the main gate, the frenzied clash of weapons and the screams of the wounded mingled with the din of the rising portcullis.

When she stopped outside the guardroom, Marged found herself seized from behind; a large, gauntleted hand silenced her shrieks. Yanked inside the room, she saw that a score of men milled about in polished steel helmets.

A heavy blow sent her reeling into the corner, where she remained conscious long enough to identify the thunder of mounted men galloping over the drawbridge, and see the glint of steel through a murder hole in the floor, before she was engulfed by a black wave.

When Marged opened her eyes, her head buzzed like a beehive. She still had the presence of mind to wrap her cloak around her body, for when she tried to sit up, she found that her flimsy shift had been ripped in two, exposing her body above the waist.

"Nay, 'tis a pity to cover so lovely a sight. I've gazed at you these minutes past, and I assure you, lady, my thoughts were not of war," said a man's voice from the gloom, amusement tinging his words.

She turned toward the sound, distinguishing naught but a steel-encased blur. She blinked rapidly to clear her vision. A man moved from the bench where he had been sitting. Suddenly the door burst open and a dozen others spilled into the room, rending the blackness with blinding lantern light. She winced and closed her eyes against the painful glare.

"My lord, all is secure," announced the man with the lantern.

"What of the garrison?"

"Harmless as babes."

"And our losses?"

"A handful."

The men around her conversed in a foreign tongue, their speech generously mixed with laughter. Marged ventured a glance at them, but they remained shadows beyond the light. Without knowing what it would profit her, she decided to tip over the lantern and set the rushes alight. Slowly inching across the floor, she kept an eye on her jailors. She was almost within reach of her goal when one of the men realized her intent.

"Beware, my lord!"

Like lightning their armored leader moved, kicking her reaching hand aside. Marged yelped, clutching her injured hand to her bosom, where she nursed it, her eyes filling with tears.

"She's a crafty wench. Take her back to her chamber. And treat her with respect—remember, she's lady of this castle."

Marged tried to resist them, but theirs was the superior strength. Still she struggled, desperate to escape as they bore her effortlessly in the air. Their leader laughed in amusement at her futile efforts, commenting about her fiery spirit before he turned back to his men.

Marged had identified their tongue as Breton, for the language spoken by her father's foreign men-at-arms was closer to Welsh than was courtly French, and she had been swift to understand it. But Marged was given little chance to translate their conversation. She was slung across a brawny shoulder and borne to the west tower, where she was locked inside her room.

In the hazy gray dawn, the leader of the invading force strode boldly inside Marged's bedchamber, rudely awakening her from sleep.

Alert as an animal, she gave him a smoldering gaze, holding the covers beneath her chin to deny him further glimpses of her body.

"So, wild one, are you well rested?" he asked pleasantly.

"'Tis no thanks to you if I am."

"There's no need to be churlish."

Marged glared at the man's broad back as he sauntered to

the arrowslit facing the river and pulled aside the leather curtain to admit a feeble shaft of light.

"By the Rood! 'Tis a cold chamber!"

"I like it."

"No doubt it suits your nature," he jested, turning from the window.

Marged did not speak to her captor, though she took in every detail of his person. This morning he wore a steel-banded leather jack over a doublet striped with orange and brown; his movements possessed a lithe grace that belied his height and strength. There was a musical ring to his voice, his foreign-accented speech not unlike that of the Welsh. The Breton was black-haired, olive-complexioned, and his eyes appeared surprisingly pale in his dark face as he studied her intently.

"Who are you, who invades my home and puts loyal soldiers to the sword?" Marged demanded angrily.

He inclined his head, freshly amused by the venom in her voice. "You find one Rolfe de Bretayne—at your service, lady."

"'Twill only pleasure me to find a de Bretayne at the end of a sword!"

He chuckled at her retort before turning back to the window, where he surveyed the water meadows of the Wye. "This castle sets fair. The river provides a natural defense."

"But not strong enough to prevent your taking it."

"We had help. 'Twould not have been possible without the assistance of loyal comrades."

"So the Bretons betrayed us! I should have known! Of course they were de Bretayne men—your men!" Marged cried, starting up, belatedly remembering to seize the bedcovers as his eyes roved downward anticipating a rewarding sight.

"Ah, you disappoint me." Rolfe de Bretayne grinned as he lounged against the wall, relaxed and confident. "Come, sheath your dagger, lady, 'twill avail you nothing. Bowenford is well and truly taken."

"Only cowards take fortresses by treachery," she taunted, pleased by the deepening flush spreading over his cheeks.

"Sometimes such tactics are necessary. I'd have preferred to storm the walls—but other methods seemed more appropriate." He came to stand beside Marged's bed. "I'm in charge of your home, lady, so you'd best resign yourself to the idea."

Marged shrank further into her feather pillow, smoking with rage beneath his mocking gaze. The Breton grinned at her as he critically studied her lovely face, golden against the white linen.

"Your treachery will profit you nothing," Marged declared in anger when he did not speak. "Once my father returns, you'll not have men enough to hold against his might."

"You're wrong. I've many reinforcements arriving on the morrow."

"I know not what rights a man possesses in Brittany, my lord, but in England there are laws to protect—"

"Seek you to *reason* with me to vacate your land?" he asked incredulously, shaking his head. "Not over seizing land for greed did I risk my life. I hold this land for Richard, Duke of York."

Marged gasped in shock at his pronouncement. "You are one of the traitors!"

"Traitor, lady? 'Tis a harsh word. Let us first examine your noble sire and determine on which side of the fence he sits, before you start pointing an accusing finger."

"I don't know what you mean!"

"Do you not?" He regarded her closely, his eyes narrowed, his face stony. "Good Sir Richard seeks to keep both York and Lancaster in his pocket by putting his hand in support of one, his mouth the other. A man cannot dither between two sides indefinitely. So, to reinforce his good intent, I am dispatched hither to claim this castle for York."

"You lie! My father is loyal to the king," Marged cried in anger. Yet in all honesty she could not wholly repudiate his slurs, for had her father not said, "It's not meet to scoff at wise men who keep a foot in both camps"? Had divided loyalty created his unease on the morning of departure? And this sudden friendship with the turncoat Sir Joce de Bretayne—her captor's kinsman—lent further support to the suggestion. Never bothering to involve himself in policy-making, Sir Richard may have cultivated both contenders for the throne in an effort to keep his beloved Bowenford.

"From now on, lady, consider yourself a hostage for York."

"What difference can it make to you, a Breton, which king

sits on England's throne? Worse, your own uncle has declared his support for your avowed enemy—Lancaster—and rides with my father."

"It makes no difference whatsoever to me who sits on the throne. That I back the winning side is my only concern. And as for my uncle—he be nothing more than a distant relative and may do as he pleases."

"You mercenary!"

His mouth quirked to a grin, but his eyes remained hard.

"Though 'twas intended as such, the name 'mercenary' is no insult. For many years men have honorably sold their swords to further a cause. Why should this cause be different?"

"My father was called by his liege lord to defend King Henry's person. Jasper Tudor fights for what he believes," she cried, choosing to ignore the accusations leveled at her father's loyalties by this upstart Breton.

"I also fight for what I believe." He strode across the room and, pausing in the doorway, said, "My heart's devotion is concerned solely with the preservation of one Rolfe de Bretayne. For that alone will I risk my life. I'm going below to break my fast—you will join me."

"The taste of treachery robs me of appetite."

"Then come below and watch me sup—but come below, lady."

The warning hovered in the air as Marged listened to him clanking down the corridor, his spurs ringing against the stone.

Presently, Bron, her Welsh maid, was sent to her, and though she had maintained her bravery before the enemy, no longer could Marged uphold her courage when she saw Bron's familiar rosy face all wan and tear-stained.

"Oh, Bron, Bron!"

Weeping, they held each other, rocking, moaning, imparting comfort with the warmth of their bodies. At last, Marged regained her composure and she gently stroked back Bron's sandy hair. "Be not afraid, Bron, we'll not be captive long."

Bron sniffled, struggling to smile, but her round face only crumpled like a dried apple as she turned aside to weep. "No, 'tis hopeless," she sniffed. "They're too strong, mistress. When the master returns, likely they'll slaughter him too!" Her voice rose to a wail of distress.

"No, you mustn't say that, it's not true," Marged cried as she grasped Bron's plump arm. "We're not defeated while we still draw breath."

Bron blinked away her tears and attempted to smile. "Aye, lady, that's true."

"That's better. You must be courageous. The other servants must take direction from you."

Bron dressed her mistress, trying to hold back tears of despair as she worked. Marged's mind seethed with a dozen half-formed plans, which she discarded. While Bron brushed and arranged her hair, she still sniffled miserably, her weakened state preventing Marged from asking how many of the garrison were dead.

"Thank you, Bron," she said kindly, patting the other woman's arm after she had curled her abundant hair within a silver fillet. "We must not let them see how sorely they've wounded us. Why think you I wear my feast gown? Those treacherous Bretons shall not find me cowed and hopeless."

But when she walked inside the Great Hall, Marged regretted donning her best raiment. The men's eyes rolled toward her, boldly raking the length of her body, assessing her finer points as if she were a prize mare at market. The periwinkle-blue velvet skirts clung sensuously to her body as she walked, making Marged feel virtually naked before the invaders' lecherous gaze. And there was no way she could distract their attention from the bodice where a gold-embroidered girdle pushed up her breasts.

"Greetings, lady, I'm pleased to have you join me," said Rolfe de Bretayne, rising from his chair to welcome her.

Marged mounted the dais to take her rightful place at the high table. "When you are done with your meal, perhaps you'll make an accounting to me of the damage both to my home and to the men under my care."

"Perhaps," he agreed, ushering her to the chair beside him.

Smarting at his insolent manner, Marged sat sullenly in her place, glaring icily at the bold men-at-arms who showed little deference to her rank. "I find your soldiers insolent dogs," she said at last, unable to endure their scrutiny in silence.

"My men have been in the field these weeks past. They are hungry for women."

"God, if you let them take—"

"So far your women have not been touched. Their continued well-being depends entirely on you."

"What do you mean by 'on me'?"

"On your not resisting us. I've been informed that you're in charge of the fortress in your father's absence."

"Aye, and a sorry showing I've made," Marged muttered, staring down at her clenched hands as tears welled to her eyes.

"Nay, lady, you could have done no more, had you been a full-fledged knight," he said more kindly, his face softening as he beheld her dejection. "Even mighty fortresses fall in the face of treachery."

Marged brought her head up, defiantly meeting his eyes. "I'll not rest until you're gone," she vowed.

Rolfe de Bretayne pushed a platter of rye bread toward her. "Here, lady, break your fast. One needs fuel to stoke such hate."

Marged refused the bread. "I've not yet attended mass."

"Nor will you, for your good priest has long since gone to his reward. Eat—you'll grow monstrous hungry ere the archbishop replaces him."

Biting her lip, Marged considered his sarcastic remark. Father Dan was dead! What harm could an old priest have caused—unless the Bretons had sought to desecrate the small chapel against the walls. The old man would then have fiercely defended his pride and joy.

The servants brought platters of sliced fowl and foaming jugs of ale. Marged smiled reassuringly at the women's woebegone faces, trying to reassure them of their safety.

The Breton poured her a cup of ale and piled her trencher with meat, over which he dripped a puddle of mustard sauce. "Eat, lady, or I vow you will regret it."

Marged picked at her food, irritated by his churlish manner, yet not wishing by her disobedience to make her people suffer. While she ate, she was aware of a dozen anxious eyes silently pleading for her to behave at her most gracious. This morning the familiar Great Hall was gloomy, the air reeking of woodsmoke and stale cooking odors. Marged resented the sight of the Breton's troops sprawled at the tables, quaffing ale and greedily devouring the castle's provisions. While she ate, she remained highly aware of her enemy. The glances she stole in his direction told her he was not a man with whom to trifle. His firm jaw, clean-shaven and sun-bronzed, the unwavering gaze of his pale eyes, belonged to a leader of men. Yet the betraying softness of his finely chiseled mouth, the frank appraisal of her appearance, told her that soldiery was not the extent of Rolfe de Bretayne's interests.

"When I've inspected the castle, you will throw open your account books to me."

Marged was jolted to the present by his unexpected request. "Why should I make your tasks lighter?"

"Because you want your women kept safe."

"And do you blackmail me to keep them so?"

"'Tis the only way you'll bend. Your people are dependent on you. A worthy lord always protects his own."

And so, when the meal was at an end, Marged meekly ushered her captor around the castle precincts, forcing herself to be civil.

Rob seethed with anger when Marged asked him to turn over the castle's accounts to their enemy. Yet, bedfast—his shattered leg paining him until he must have regular drafts of laudanum—he knew he made a poor match for the tough Breton. When she sought to speak to her father's steward in private, de Bretayne ordered her to leave, which cut short the possibility of their hatching a rebellious scheme.

Within the hour, de Bretayne emerged from Rob's chamber, well pleased by what he found. "Your father is to be congratulated for the choice of so capable a man. Do you think you can persuade him to serve me as well?" he asked, stepping forth into the sunshine to join Marged where she stood on the battlements, gazing wistfully over the open countryside and smarting under the bitter loss of freedom.

She turned toward him, her voice scornful. "You ask the impossible, my lord. Even I have not power to make him love you."

De Bretayne's mouth twitched in humor at her retort. He came to stand beside her. Marged wanted to step away from him, but she defiantly stood her ground. His striped doublet brushed against her as he leaned forward on the stonework, his blue eyes slitted against the glaring sun as he surveyed the green vista of the Welsh Marches.

"My men will be here before nightfall."

"Congratulations. Then you'll have force enough to conquer the Marches."

"Aye, if I'd a mind to waste my life here, perchance you are right."

"Have we already become too insignificant to merit your attention? Pray tell me what other important conquests await?"

"I intend to carve a niche for myself in England. Brittany offers me no further challenge," he replied, turning to face her.

Marged met his gaze boldly, growing uncomfortable when he did not look away. His large, luminous, dark-lashed eyes probed deeply. "It grieves me to learn you now consider my home worthless after you crushed it beneath your fist." Marged's voice cracked and she was forced to look away from him as something akin to fear, yet sparked by mounting excitement, gripped her soul.

"Your home is not insignificant to me. You forget, lady, I knew nothing of it, nor of your existence, until last week. I am a soldier. My order was to subdue Bowenford and fortify it for the Duke of York. The conquest was nothing personal. A soldier merely obeys his orders."

A treacherous flicker of understanding stole through Marged's mind. Thrusting aside such a dangerous weakness, she raised her eyes to his. "And now that Bowenford has fallen, what are you commanded to do with it?"

"That I cannot tell you. When I formulate a plan, lady, perhaps I'll acquaint you with it."

"In the meantime, what of my women? And of the wounded?"

"I've allowed the wounded to be nursed. The dead are to be buried this morning—you've ten men fewer in your garrison to cause me problems."

"And the women?"

"My men are only human," he answered gruffly, turning toward the Wye.

"You said this morning—"

"I said they'd not be raped if you offered no resistance. But, lady, in Brittany or on the Marches, men and women follow an age-old course. Given time, they'll couple out of choice."

"Never! The women are loyal to my father. They'll have naught to do with the enemy!" Marged spat fiercely. "If you let your men touch them, you've broken your word."

"I shall not be here overlong to stop whatever my men choose to do. So, if you are wise, you'll encourage your women to select champions amongst the soldiers who'll protect them from the more rapacious ones. Come, lady, you are a sore loser. Life goes on. The banner flown from the tower makes little difference to human nature."

At his scoffing words, Marged glanced upward, expecting to see the familiar Bowen standard. To her anger she found the Breton's blood-red banner now fluttering from the keep. Depicting a barbican with raised portcullis over a motto on silver ribbon, the banner declared in unbridled arrogance, "I Come."

His gaze followed hers, but before he could translate the Latin inscription, Marged snapped, "I fully understand your arrogant motto, my lord. I'm familiar with Latin."

"Your accomplishments know no bounds," he said sarcastically as he swung about. "Come, we will go below. I confess to growing weary of your company."

An angry retort rose to Marged's lips, but she bit it back. She marched ahead of him, head high, longing to slap his arrogant face, but too conscious of the many souls dependent on her for their safety to indulge her temper.

two

"I'LL NOT OBEY that upstart's command. Nor do I even intend to set eyes on him," Alys declared defiantly.

"Can't you see that your actions endanger others? I welcome him not, yet I am wise enough to feign obedience for the moment. Can you not swallow an ounce of your pride for their sake?" Marged demanded, her patience rapidly dwindling. For the past thirty minutes she had attempted to persuade Alys to answer the Breton's summons to attend him below, but Alys had stubbornly insisted on sewing in the solar in defiance of his orders.

"A woman of royal blood will not allow herself to be blackmailed," Alys stated defiantly, jabbing her needle viciously in the linen altar cloth. "Besides, what need has he of me—plain, impoverished widow that I am? Surely you, my lady, the pride of Bowenford, will be more than sufficient to salve his ill humor." Alys's thin mouth twitched in satisfaction as she saw the gleam of anger in Marged's face.

"You're as selfish as ever!"

"Selfish, am I!" Alys shrieked, jumping up and spilling her needlework to the rushes. "How dare you speak so to me, you . . . you . . . Welsh savage!"

Marged gasped as Alys delivered a stinging blow to her cheek. For a moment she stared glassy-eyed at her stepsister's rage-contorted face, then something snapped inside her head. Resentment for all the years of torment she had endured at Alys's hands erupted in a surge of anger as Marged snatched her stepsister's wimple from her head. Alys retaliated by grabbing Marged's silver fillet and ripping it from her hair, which tumbled about her shoulders in a dark cloud.

"I'll never humble myself to speak to that Breton dog! Besides, 'tis likely the serving bitches would welcome the attention . . ."

Alys fell backwards as Marged leaped at her, muttering a string of Welsh curses. Suddenly, Marged found herself grabbed from behind and swung off the ground. With a cry of rage she tried to beat off her assailant, but Rolfe de Bretayne held her fast.

"By the Rood! You squabbling she-cats can be heard below. Get you to your chamber, Lady Alys, and stay there!"

With a fearful parting glance, Alys seized her sewing and fled, tripping over her skirts in her haste.

"As for you . . ." Rolfe de Bretayne released Marged, who stood panting in indignation, for he still gripped her shoulder. "God take me for a fool! Why did I storm a fortress with a hellcat in residence? I curse your sire for not wedding you sooner, lady—you're more than five years past the age for bedding. Mayhap chastisement with the proper weapon would soothe your temper."

Eyes blazing at his insult, she wrenched away. "There's no man born—"

His hand shot out, cutting short her words. Marged struggled beneath his imprisoning grasp, fighting for speech. Fear chilled her spine as she wondered if she had just provided this despised Breton with a worthy challenge.

"Is that so, lady? Then perchance you've met your match," he growled, his voice low and menacing. "There are two days before I must set out to join the Yorkist troops. Think you it possible you can act as a civilized woman? Two days is but a short while. I trust it will not strain your resources overmuch."

Wrenching free of his hand, Marged cried, "How dare you insult me so! Never did I ask you to come here, nor yet to stay. Even two days of your loathsome presence will seem an eternity."

Far from exhibiting anger at her blazing taunt, Rolfe de Bretayne's stern features lit with amusement. "Tell me, would you endure that eternity any easier if I took you on a hunt? I hear you shoot straight as any lad with a bow. There are abundant deer in these forests, and I grow weary of playing soldier."

Marged blinked, trying to resolve the heated emotion coursing madly through her veins. Though she felt deep anger and resentment, the temptation of riding through the forest, of sharing the excitement of the hunt, was too alluring to deny. "You seek to hunt?" she whispered hoarsely.

"Yes. Will you join me? Or, like Lady Alys, do you intend to whine away your days in martyred solitude?"

"You've learned naught of me if you can compare me to her!" Marged retorted indignantly, not pleased to have her name linked with that of her stepsister.

He grinned warmly, revealing strong, even white teeth. Marged blinked in surprise at the transformation; she had not seen him smile in recent days. Without his usual stern, determined mien, his handsome face appeared softer and more appealing. Handsome! It was no lie, Rolfe de Bretayne was an unusually handsome man, but the acknowledgment did nothing to lessen her hatred of him.

"Well," he prompted, his lean, bronzed hand on the iron ring of the door, "shall I hunt alone?"

"I'll come, if only to show you where the best game thrives," Marged allowed begrudgingly, trying to quell her surging excitement over the prospect of being released from prison.

Bursting with infectiously high spirits, the noisy cavalcade issued forth from Bowenford in the quiet summer dawn. The huntsman, trailed by leashed dogs and their handlers, went on ahead to search out the quarry.

Marged's heart soared as the sweet scent of freedom overwhelmed her with joy; the familiar touch of warm horseflesh, the feel of the reins in her hands, even the smell of the excited animals, quickened her blood.

Though at first feeling apprehensive, Marged had easily persuaded her father's huntsman to lead the chase. Gared chafed at domesticity, receiving scant satisfaction from caring for his charges and mending leashes while he awaited his lord's return. A happy peasant, he owed little loyalty to king and earl; he could as readily lend his skill to their Breton conqueror as to his own liege lord, if the stranger kept him busy.

The lush water meadows of the Wye sparkled like diamonds in the rising sun, and the banks were stained with purple march orchid and graceful yellow iris. They entered the still forest, where each cracking twig, each hoofbeat, echoed through the canyon of trees. After riding for some time, the hunters reached a clearing where they broke fast while Gared scouted for evidence of deer.

"Lady, come sup with me," suggested the Breton, catching her arm as Marged dismounted beneath the dark trees.

She studied his face in the shaded daylight, and found that his welcoming smile triggered an unwanted emotion. The blue of his eyes was still soft from sleep; even his usually guarded expression had flown, leaving his handsome face young and almost vulnerable. His purple doublet, gaudy beneath a worn leather jack, made his skin look swarthy as a gypsy's. This morning his head was bare, and dark hair curled abundantly over his embroidered collar. A chill passed through Marged's body as she gazed at him, but it was not born of fear.

"If you command, I'll share your board," she announced stiffly, walking ahead and disdaining his guiding hand.

The servants laid jugs of ale and crusty fresh loaves on a linen cloth, offering the hunters earthenware pots of honey and golden slabs of butter; there was also a platter of sliced beef and a wicker basket of dark almond cakes studded with fruit.

While the hunting party ate their leisurely meal, the dogs and their handlers found what they were searching for. Having located a deer's spoor, Gared deftly measured the animal's size by probing its tracks in the soft ground and the gashes made by its antlers on nearby trees with his fingers. Armed with this knowledge, he approached his new master, his hunting horn bearing the animal's dung, to verify his sighting.

Rolfe de Bretayne studied the deer droppings and listened carefully to Gared's account of his finding. "Aye, he appears to be a worthy adversary. A buck that size will give us hearty sport."

Well pleased with the Breton's decision, Gared departed, calling the dogs to cut off the deer's line of retreat.

Marged had to remind herself a dozen times that as he talked amiably about the impending chase, she supped with her enemy. Again she chilled at finding Rolfe de Bretayne an attractive man. While he had been her enemy, he had been far easier to hate.

"I'm eager for the chase. The scent of the forest sets my blood atingle," he confided as he lounged full-length on the matted carpet of leaves and pine needles.

"Mine too," Marged agreed before she could stop herself. At her sharp intake of breath, he smiled, understanding the treachery of that admission.

"Come, lady, I'm but a man, though perhaps not as worthy as some. I too have human emotions. Can we not be friends for a few hours?"

How much she wanted to deny him that privilege, but so genuine was his entreaty, she cautiously relented.

"Perhaps not friends, my lord, but fellow huntsmen."

He stretched out his hand. "Shall we cement that vow with a handclasp?"

The warm strength of his fingers, clasped firmly about her own, made Marged uneasy; at his touch, a message she had no desire to hear, sped along her arm. Quickly she withdrew her hand. "Until the hunt be done, I salute you as a comrade, my lord."

"Nay, lady, did not our sires distinguish us with names? Will you not address me as Rolfe and let me call you Marged?"

Her face clouded at his suggestion, but the gentle smile he flashed, the soft expression in his pale blue eyes, dissolved her objections. "Very well—but only for the hunt," she added in warning, lest he get more grandiose ideas about this truce.

"Agreed."

When all was ready, they mounted, steel tense beneath the shadowing trees. Now Marged was glad she had lowered the barrier between them: it would be far more enjoyable hunting with an ally instead of an enemy.

Gared deployed the hounds with skill, using the lead pair of limers to drive the deer toward the waiting huntsmen. At the given signal, Rolfe raised the silver-inlaid oliphant to his lips and sounded a series of single-pitch notes to summon the huge greyhounds to the chase.

The sweeping wind tugged Marged's coiled black hair free of its confining net, tossing it in wild abandon about her shoulders, making it appear to be a fluttering, silken banner against her sapphire habit. Rolfe galloped beside her, his face alight with excitement, his nostrils flaring as they spied the red buck bolting across a distant clearing, with the shaggy hounds in frenzied pursuit.

Ducking to avoid low-hanging branches, the hunters pounded across fields and marshy water meadows of the Wye before plunging back into the forest, where thin sunlight cast the chase in a silvery haze. The valiant buck gave them good measure for their pains, zigzagging across field and forest while the hunters scattered into small groups, pursuing favorite hounds hot on the deer's trail. At one point the stag entered the Wye, but the swift current turned him back. Fearlessly the baying hounds plunged after him, swimming like fish in the shallows. Downstream, the buck changed course as, like a great thunderbolt, he plunged free, his coat gleaming silver in the sunshine.

Rolfe reined roughly in, and leaning forward in the saddle, he gazed in admiration at the magnificent beast with his massive antlers.

"He's far too lordly to put to the lance," he shouted to Marged, who had galloped to his side, her horse growing skittish beside his.

"Aye, I recognize him now. Yon stag is one we've pursued on many a morn."

"Perhaps I can wing him."

"You can try." Her eyes sparkled with laughter at his suggestion, for she recalled how many arrows had hissed futilely past the fleeing beast.

The baying of the excited hounds suddenly panicked the buck, who plunged headlong back into the forest.

"Damn him, he's too fast," Rolfe cursed, the arrow taut in his bow. "After him! He's heading south."

Marged rode hard, but the Breton's great dun stallion outpaced her black gelding. Seeing the stag come to rest in a clearing, Marged pulled her horse to an abrupt halt, and got off a shot from her pearl-inlaid bow; the twanging bolt fell short, landing harmlessly in a dead stump. Feeling disappointed, she remounted and noticed that they were far away from the main body of hunters and straggling hounds. Though the Wye was hidden by trees, she could hear and smell the water.

"By the Rood!" Rolfe exclaimed in surprise as he suddenly spied the buck's red hide plunging back into the river. "The devil seeks to trick us. After him! After him!" He got off a well-aimed arrow that sang harmlessly by the beast's proud antlers and into the dappled water. At a small wooded island twenty feet from shore, the buck pulled himself to land; his sides heaving, he seemed to listen to the pursuing dogs and horses on the opposite bank, blocked from his terrified gaze by the trees.

"The fools must have crossed the river. Did they not know he's still on this side?" Rolfe scowled in anger as he fitted an arrow into his bow.

"Let him live!" Marged cried unexpectedly as she reined in beside him, watching the magnificent beast, lathered and spent. Tears of pity for so majestic a creature, hunted and frightened, unexpectedly stung her eyes. "He's given us good sport. It's nigh on noon," she observed, glancing at the position of the sun.

"What! You plead for his life?"

"Let him live," she repeated softly, her eyes filled with tears.

Rolfe gripped her hand, understanding softening his blue eyes. "Damn you, Marged Bowen, you've got a heart after all," he said, his voice gruff.

Marged pulled free, bristling at his mockery.

Slowly, Rolfe replaced his bow, keeping his eye on the trembling wild creature. Then he abruptly turned his back on it. "Come, for I've developed a mighty thirst. Yon glade looks promising as a resting place."

Joy sang through Marged's veins as he spurred the stallion and headed for the inviting shade of a nearby mossy glade. She cast one final glance at the stag, who watched her intently, as if he understood that she had won him a reprieve—at least for the moment. "Flee now, your majesty, while you still have the chance," Marged whispered huskily, watching him.

Two brindled hounds surged about her horse's hooves and Marged whistled to them. At first, surprised to be called from their quarry, the hounds hesitated until she barked a stern command. Obediently they loped forward.

When she reached the clearing, Rolfe was stretched lazily on the grass, his head pillowed on his arms. "I thought you'd take all day," he remarked amiably.

Marged slid from the saddle and let the gelding go free. The horse cropped lush grass at the edge of the clearing, casting his eyes warily at the huge stallion viewing him with hostility.

"Christ, even the horses cannot forget their differences," Rolfe commented sharply, sitting up.

"You forget, today we are but fellow huntsmen," Marged reminded him with a smile as she offered Rolfe a leather bottle of wine from her saddle.

He rinsed his mouth with the harsh liquid, then spat it on the grass. "Is that the best you have to offer at Bowenford, or did you bring such a brew in an effort to poison me?"

"Had I intended to poison you, I could have done so easily before now."

"Aye, that's true. Though in the beginning I wondered if I might find a dagger between my shoulder blades—your hatred stung as fiercely as arrows."

Marged turned toward him, soothed by the peaceful setting and the sweet knowledge that she had granted life to a poor, hunted creature. "You assaulted my home. Surely you did not expect to be greeted with joy?"

Rolfe smiled, but he did not reply. From the distance came the plunging sound of the escaping deer. Beside them, the eager hounds cocked their ears and Marged had to remind them that the hunt was done.

Marged lay still, dozing, totally at peace for the first time since the Breton's troops had invaded her small world.

"Do you still hate me?" he asked unexpectedly.

His husky question made her stiffen, but she did not open her eyes.

"Sometimes."

"And at others?"

She shrugged. Though her eyes remained closed, she could sense his presence drawing nearer. The warmth of his hand on hers made her eyes snap open. "Then I merely dislike you," she replied coldly, withdrawing her hand.

The softness fled from his face. "Well, by God, you're nothing but honest," he snapped. He leaped to his feet and, without speaking, wrenched her roughly beside him. "Come, we must join the others."

Marged rode in silence through the cool, shadowed darkness beneath the trees, regretting her hasty words. There had been something akin to friendship blooming between them, and she had destroyed it. Unaccountably, hot tears stung her eyes. It was unfair of him to have asked such a question when her defenses were down, she thought angrily, glaring at his broad back as he ducked to enter a tunnel of crisscrossing branches.

Though they journeyed toward the sounds of their fellow huntsmen, they seemed to get farther away from them. Rolfe stopped at a low point in the riverbank and refilled his empty wine flask. Sullenly, Marged waited in the saddle, her pleasure in the hunt spoiled.

"Here." Without asking if she wanted a drink, he handed her the water.

Marged took a few swallows and handed it back. While he swigged the river water, she watched him closely, suddenly aware of the precariousness of her position. They were nowhere near the others. So far he had treated her with chivalry. From gossip whispered about the Hall, she knew he had not taken any of the women to his bed, though many of his men had been welcomed to the servants' pallets, bearing out his cynical remark about human nature. If his men had been woman-starved, what of their leader?

"How far have we come?" he asked, replacing the leather flask on his saddle.

Marged glanced around the unfamiliar territory. "We can

take the road east and recross the river at Welshford; otherwise it will take us till nightfall to reach home."

Rolfe cursed beneath his breath. "Why did you not tell me we rode in the opposite direction from Bowenford?"

"You did not ask me for directions, my lord," Marged supplied stiffly, raising her head in challenge.

Casting her a dark look, he heaved himself into the saddle and sharply turned the horse's head to the east. "This ford, is it still passable?"

"The river runs high, but we should be able to cross."

They rode in silence. The afternoon sun hid behind a cloud cover and the wind blew chill. Marged, familiar with the ever-changing weather of the Marches, smelled the scent of an afternoon storm. By the time they reached Welshford it was like twilight; heavy, threatening clouds hung low, and the trees appeared black in the hazy light.

Slowly they forded the swift water, taking it gently lest the strong current sweep the horses downstream. Marged's skirts were soaked, her boots wet, when they pulled ashore on the opposite bank. The rising wind snapped tree branches and tossed knots of leaves to the ground.

"There looks to be a squall threatening," he grumbled, glancing about for shelter. "God damn you for your closed mouth."

"Would you blame the storm on me also?" she snapped, setting off along the road skirting the woods.

A few minutes later the first raindrops pelted coldly, yet freshly, against her face.

"Damn you, listen! Hold up! We'll shelter there," Rolfe bellowed, pointing to a ramshackle building propped between two felled trees.

For a moment, Marged was tempted to defy his order, but the cold rain, which was now falling at full force, snaked a chill passage between her breasts. Spurring her horse, she pounded after him, ducking her head as they entered a dark cavern of trees. Here the foliage was so heavy that the rain barely penetrated.

"Pull your mount beneath this overhang. 'Twill help keep him dry," he instructed gruffly, tethering his dun stallion to a stake driven in the ground.

Obediently, Marged did as she was told. The chill numbed

her. Shuddering, she hugged herself with cold arms, squeezing trickles of water from her sodden garments. She looked so miserable, he grinned in sympathy. "Mayhap 'twill soon be over," he suggested hopefully, surveying the thrashing sky where gray already lightened to murky white.

"I forgot to warn you about the weather in the Marches," she said.

"So you did."

When great gusts of wind lashed branches against the roof, showering them with rain, they retreated deeper inside the hay shed. Tiring of his vigil, Rolfe sat down on the dry hay raked into a pile in the far corner.

Not anxious to join him, Marged remained at the entrance of the hut, her eyes on the stormy sky. The rain appeared to be increasing rather than decreasing. Sighing in aggravation, she turned her back on the elements to find Rolfe looking at her, a curious expression on his dark face.

"Are you hungry?" he asked at length.

"Why, are you to invite me to a banquet?"

"Nay, but I've a handful of dates in my saddlebag."

While he went to fetch the food, Marged dropped thankfully on the dry hay, wishing she could change her clothing; the soaked fabric chilled her to the bone. She struggled to pull off her kid boots, and emptied a stream of river water on the ground.

"Here." Rolfe handed her half the dates.

Marged nodded her thanks, delighting in the sweet treat. She discovered how hungry she was, for they had not eaten since early morning. Growing uncomfortable under his unblinking scrutiny, she became aware of her wet bodice outlining the contours of her breasts; her nipples protruded with cold. Marged exclaimed in annoyance at his boldness and defiantly crossed her arms across her chest, resenting his intimate knowledge of her body.

Rolfe grinned in amusement before turning away, but not before Marged was made aware of his arousal, for his clothing was plastered like a second skin to his muscular frame. Since he had tossed aside his leather jack, the drenched wool and hose left little to the imagination. An uneasy quiver pierced her belly at her alarming discovery.

"This is a rousing sendoff, seeking to drown me on my last

night," he joked hoarsely as he lounged on the great mound of hay, carefully keeping his distance.

"Where go you tomorrow?"

"I head for the main Yorkist force, which I'm told draws close to Northampton. I hope to join the Earl of March, for he is known to me. But it matters little whose right arm I aid."

"And what of our welfare during your absence?"

"I'll leave you sufficient men for defense. They'll do you no harm, nor will they rape your women," he assured her, before adding in afterthought, "'Tis the first time I've realized how few hours are left to me. Sitting awaiting the end to a storm is not what I would have chosen to pass the time."

Marged swallowed uncomfortably, declining to ask him what entertainment he would prefer. Highly conscious of his blue eyes boring into her, she shut her lids tight, choosing not to see him.

"And the poor wench whose favor I chose for this last night will lie awake thinking herself rejected."

Marged's lips tightened at his jesting remark. "I doubt she's too distraught. You flatter yourself unduly, my lord."

"You may be surprised to learn that not all women reject me, lady," he rejoined sharply.

She did not reply. Mounting tension filled the lean-to. His overwhelming masculinity reached out to engulf her, and she felt stifled by his presence. The wind suddenly changed direction and stole inside their primitive shelter, penetrating her drenched garments until she shivered so hard that her teeth began to chatter.

"I've a blanket in my saddlebag," Rolfe said, observing her discomfort. "Dare I suggest you strip off your wet garments and warm yourself in it?"

"You may suggest it, but to no avail," Marged replied stubbornly, hugging her arms about herself.

"Oh, come here, you fool woman," he snarled impatiently, seizing her arm and pulling her toward him. "Pride will earn you your death of cold."

Though Marged wanted to resist, the welcome warmth of his body was too great a temptation to refuse. Obedient as a child, she allowed him to pull her close as he wrapped his strong arms around her and cradled her against the comfort of his hard chest. She became highly aware of the steady, rhythmic beating of his heart, and of the unaccustomed scent of his wet skin, warmly fragrant in her nostrils. Possessed once more by that indefinable emotion she had sought to deny, Marged shuddered uncontrollably in his arms. She heard his sharp intake of breath, and his embrace tightened, alerting her to the insistent stirring of his body against her thigh.

"No," Marged gasped, fighting the answering beat of her own blood, which surged almost beyond control as he gazed deeply into her face. His mouth looked grim, his strong jaw tense. A thousand thoughts surged through her mind as she fought to maintain her reason within the prison of his arms.

"Oh, Marged," he breathed huskily, "you beautiful, tempting creature, wild as the storm clouds. Why was it my misfortune to meet you in such an uncharitable circumstance? Come, forget what differences there are between us. Forget who I am . . . oh, Marged, Marged."

Panicking, she struggled feebly, but his superior strength soon overcame her protests. He bore her easily to the straw, trapping her like a wild creature. Inwardly she screamed for release from this place, yet the treachery of her own nature imprisoned her beneath his body, pressing hard against hers, clamoring and fully aroused. Suddenly the frightening loss of her reason joined with the tumult of the stormy twilight, and this man, insistently demanding against her frail flesh, assumed the mystical proportions of a magnificent dream figure. And, as she often did in dreams, Marged disregarded the course that conscience and loyalty bade her follow.

"Oh, Marged, sweetheart, yield to me." His husky voice was a sacred litany of possession, sweeping her away to a wonderful forbidden place.

"No," she protested feebly before his hot lips devoured hers, bruising and igniting a fire that ripped through her frame. No longer did she repel him, but strained to meet his fierce kisses until, seizing her in a frenzy of passion, he forced her lips apart, and his hot, invading tongue released a surge of passion that rocked her limbs.

Eagerly, Rolfe slid his hands over her full breasts, fondling the chilled contours, touching her aroused nipples and shuddering with delight.

"Oh, God, I want you so," he breathed, his ragged voice against her ear, his heated mouth searing her flesh.

Marged did not remind him about the serving woman awaiting his noble service. Instead she gripped his broad shoulders, steaming beneath his wet clothing, and rejoiced in the wonderfully arousing strength of his body.

"Say you want me too," he urged, tracing his tongue tantalizingly along her cheek until she shuddered with delight. "Say you need me too," he repeated, his lean, wandering hands inflaming her breasts, her hips, her thighs.

Above the roaring blood in her ears, above the pounding of her heart, Marged croaked, "No, I'm virgin." Belatedly she tried to withdraw, gathering her fleeing wits. If she did not stop him . . .

"No, Rolfe, please . . . don't, I'm virgin . . . don't!"

"That does not matter."

"No, I can't," she whispered. "I must not." Her own panting voice sounded like a stranger's, the words more to reinforce her own flagging will than to repel a lover.

He smothered her protest with his mouth as he seized her. Rolling over in the soft, fragrant hay, he pulled Marged on top of him, imprisoning her against the throbbing, swelling heat of his desire. "Now say you don't want me," he challenged, bruising her against his heated agony until she shuddered with passion.

"No—I'm virgin."

"All women are virgin at some time. 'Tis no excuse."

She struggled to be free of that taunting arousal, but with one swift movement he rolled her onto her back in the hay and pinned her there. Thrashing her head from side to side, she cried out, desperate to avoid his demanding mouth as tears spilled from her eyes. How she longed to discover the dark mystery of his passion, yet such knowledge gleaned from a hated enemy was a shameful, forbidden thing.

"No . . . no," she protested, trying to deny the pleasure of his hands as he fondled her breast.

"Marged, please, be not afraid of me," he whispered, gently subduing her protests. "I want to love you, not hurt you."

Blinded by tears and trembling, she stared up at the dark blur of his handsome face, wanting desperately to flee, yet longing to stay. His lips engulfed hers, less demanding now as he slowly vanquished her resistance. She gasped in surprise as she felt his hot hand against her bare breast, for he had deftly unlaced her bodice. So chilled was she, his touch seared her with flame.

"For so long have I wanted to do this," he whispered, pressing his lips against her flesh.

She cried out as his hot mouth fastened about her nipple. He drew forth her heart, her very soul. Suddenly she wanted to stroke the smooth, tanned flesh revealed by the open neckline of his purple doublet; she longed to caress, to inflame, to discover the hidden secrets of his body. Shocked by her own admission, Marged stared into his eyes, seeing desire blazing there. He knew! The smile that crossed his face as he hugged her in delight told her as much.

"Let me show you how wonderful it can be. Let me love you."

"Oh, Rolfe, I don't . . . oh, Rolfe . . . yes . . . yes . . . yes . . ." she breathed, sobbing in ecstasy as he slid his hands over her full breasts, rousing her blood to dispel the chill.

"Since first I saw your lovely breasts, I've dreamed of touching you like this."

Marged smiled at his admission, no longer afraid. "Rolfe," she whispered, slipping her hands into his thick hair, finding she had wanted to do this for a long time, "I don't hate you—'twas all a lie."

He inched down her clinging habit from her shoulders, drawing away the sodden velvet to reveal her rain-chilled body of smooth, honey-gold silk. His gaze moved from her full, brown-tipped breasts, past her narrow waist and over her swelling hips to the silky nest of dark hair between her thighs. Marged was as perfect as a statue. And she was his to awaken and arouse. Never in all his dreams had he anticipated so wonderful a gift. Trembling, he swept his hands the length of her body in a fiery caress.

Watching the adoration in his gaze replaced by passion, Marged sighed with pleasure. No man had ever looked at her like this, nor had she ever felt so wholly receptive to a man's desire. "Will you hurt me?" she asked him candidly.

Rolfe smiled at her frank question. "Should I lie and say

you nay? You know the way of things, sweetheart, but I promise to be gentle. You will have no cause for grief."

"Love me, then," Marged said, stiffening slightly as she prepared for invasion.

His laughter made her eyes spring open. "What do you find so amusing?" she demanded, her swift temper roused.

"You make a poor sacrificial virgin, Marged Bowen. God, I want you not in selfless surrender, but hot, aroused, needing me with the same fervor I feel for you—and remind me not you're virgin, else I'll be forced to slap you."

Her mouth turned down woefully. "You mock me."

"Nay, I desire you."

His hot, sweet kisses reawakened the liquid heat of arousal. He stroked and caressed her, his mouth and hands driving her to the brink of insanity.

Yet still, when he molded her hand about the iron-hard swelling beneath his hose, Marged drew back, shuddering at the unexpected discovery. Forcing her hand down, he imprisoned it there, making her fully aware of his throbbing passion. "Nay, be not so modest. Make love to me in return, sweet," he urged huskily.

Rolfe helped her remove the sodden fabric, but still she gasped in surprise as the throbbing reality of his flesh burst forth. She admired him, afraid and yet terribly aroused by his body. Breathing husky love words, he eased her into her own sensual heritage, until Marged's blood ran hot as his own. Gently he probed the core of her being until, when she was ready, his hot mouth devouring hers, he invaded the inferno of her body. Her eyes flew wide open with alarm as hot, searing pain brought tears stinging to her eyes. But the urgency of his hands, the message of his mouth, drew her over the threshold, leading her deeper into that unknown world of passion, initiating her into a lifetime of fire.

Marged panicked to retain her senses, but Rolfe relentlessly drove on, strong inside her, engulfing her belly in fire. A dark cloak descended about her and Marged moaned in ecstasy as a terrible, heated wave, almost like dying, swept her away from this time and place. Then upward she soared, not knowing or caring that this man, whose magnificent body pulsed as one with her own, was her captor. The pinnacle attained, she plunged through a warm, soothing pool, carrying him with her, cleaving their very souls by this ultimate act of passion.

A bird chirped from a tree branch, and Marged blinked in surprise, slowly drifting back to her surroundings to discover that the rain had stopped. "Oh, Rolfe, my love," she whispered in wonder. "I didn't expect it to be like that."

He smiled, the tension in his face spent, and kissed her, his mouth no longer demanding, but softly vulnerable. "Nor I. Never before have I enjoyed a woman so intensely," he confided in surprise, drawing back to study her lovely face. Tear-washed and softly blurred, Marged's features were awesomely beautiful in the aftermath of passion. Her full breasts were like ripe, tempting fruit.

The sheer adoration in his dark face made Marged smile with pleasure. Boldly she reached out to stroke his smooth shoulders, no longer hesitant. She pushed aside his unfastened doublet and shirt. He obliged her by slipping the garments off. Head to one side, she thrilled to admire his broad shoulders, square set and smoothly fleshed. Dark hair tangled in a mat across his chest. Tentatively she reached out and fingered a dark nipple, smiling when he shuddered at her arousing caress.

"Does it pleasure you also to be touched there?" she asked in surprise, recalling the devastating emotion he had created with his caressing hands.

Rolfe smiled. "You've much to learn about a man's body. And, God willing, it will be my greatest delight to teach you. Come here."

Eagerly she slid into his arms, thrilling to the pressure of his long, hard body against hers. "You did hurt me," she accused softly, "and you promised not to."

"I tried not to. Did I not delight you more?"

Marged grinned at his conceit, but she nodded her assent. "Oh, so much. I thought I must be dying. Now I understand why men are so desperate to possess a woman, for if their feelings even partially match mine . . ."

But he was no longer listening. The sweet press of her ample curves against his flesh had fired him to renewed passion. Marged gazed in wonder at his newly aroused flesh, darkly throbbing with surging blood; tentatively she slid her fingers about its smooth, tremulous strength, fondling him in delight, amazed by the changes passion made in a man's body.

"'Tis no wonder I was hurt," she observed wickedly when he finally stayed her hand. "Had I but known with what you intended to reward my interest, perchance I'd have been less eager."

Rolfe grinned at her observation, lazily stroking her breast. "I was but keeping my vow," he said.

"And what was that?"

"I swore to chastise you with the proper weapon." He laughed, ducking as she swung at him in annoyance.

"Oh, you beast!"

"Shut your mouth, woman, for there's much unfinished business still between us," he growled, welding her against him.

Marged was terribly aware of the searing heat of his body probing her thighs. They slid about in the hay as he smothered her with kisses and she pretended to repel him. Marged gasped aloud in surprised delight as he entered her body in a burst of heat.

"This time it will not hurt, you have my solemn promise," he whispered hoarsely before his mouth devoured hers with bruising passion.

As Marged strived to drive him deep inside, she realized the consuming heat, the throbbing delight, were re-created, but this time all was molten pleasure, without pain.

"Oh, Rolfe, I love you so," she heard herself whisper in a torment of desire, fastening her hands in his hair, eagerly answering the fiery demands of his mouth. "Love me, love me, love me," she sobbed, unable to endure the torment of his caresses.

Grim-faced, he covered her body with kisses, seeking to delay that bursting moment of sweet release, but she thrashed so wildly beneath him, he could endure no longer.

Marged opened her eyes, wanting to see him at that final, terrible moment. His blue eyes bored into hers, darkly glistening. She clung to his broad back, raking her nails over his hot flesh as he brought her hips up from the hay, increasing the throes of her delight so that she screamed her joy and he absorbed her anguished cries with his tender mouth. Once more she lost the conscious side of her being as she relinquished herself to a dark, engulfing passion.

Later they smiled into each other's eyes, and Rolfe sighed in contentment. "You're worth waiting a lifetime for," he whispered.

"Now you are mine. Rolfe de Bretayne is my lover," she said in surprise, as if she had just become aware of that startling fact.

"Aye, for as long as you want him."

"Oh, I'll want you forever. I want you to kiss me, to touch me, to make me swoon with sweet delight . . ."

Rolfe shuddered, freshly aroused by her words. "Enough!" he whispered grimly. "Christ, woman, do you seek to make me repledge my vow yet again?"

". . . to fill my body with heat until I'm consumed by fire . . ."

Groaning, he seized her and welded his mouth to hers. "Witch," he whispered, when she smiled in delight at his actions, "temptress, 'tis exactly what you intended."

Marged reached down to fondle his rising flesh. "Your lovemaking has proved such a wondrous discovery, I can scarce have enough," she confided with a throaty giggle as his fingers bit deeply into her shoulders and he shuddered repeatedly.

"You are a she-devil, Marged Bowen," he growled, his hand hot upon her neck, "yet I'm fool enough to seek to match you at your game."

When next Marged looked beyond the doorway of the lean-to, she saw the sky laced with silver-edged clouds as the sun emerged. She stretched and sighed, rolling against him, chilled by the damp air. He smiled and, without opening his eyes, gathered her up to gently fondle her smooth back.

"Much as I hate it, we must start back," he groaned against her abundant hair. "We've many miles to go."

"Already you must take my secret route to reach Bowenford before dark," she revealed with a smile.

Rolfe's startled eyes opened, and Marged shuddered as she saw her love-ravaged face mirrored in their pale blue depths. "You did not tell me that," he said gruffly. "It was not my intention to lay myself open to such scheming."

"You're not the only one who can hatch schemes."

Rolfe smiled contentedly, still making no effort to rise. He smoothed back her tangled hair, locking his hands in its glossy depth. "Think you I schemed to seduce you?"

"Didn't you?"

"No—though I've wanted you since the night we met."

"You could have taken me by force, but I grant you it would not have been easy."

Rolfe grinned at her. "Nay, love, it was far more enjoyable and much easier to win you by kisses and soft words."

Marged punched his hard shoulder. "Was I but a game then, a fresh challenge to conquer?"

Rolling on top of her, he kissed her thoroughly, his hot mouth silencing her voice. "If you're a game, Marged Bowen, I pray God I live long enough to master the rules," he whispered.

His ardent words made Marged smile with pleasure as they helped each other dress. Their cold, sodden garments were heavy with water; Rolfe first wrung out as much as he could from the fabric before he placed her habit around her shoulders.

Afterward, they faced each other, kneeling in the hay while Rolfe gazed deep into her lovely face, his own expressing pain. "'Tis usually the way of things to have one's dearest wish fulfilled at the eleventh hour." His voice was heavy with regret.

"Eleventh hour?"

"Aye, 'tis purgatory to have found you on the eve of departure. Surely you've not forgotten—I leave at dawn."

His words delivered a sickening jolt to Marged's heart, and she felt physically ill. "Leave?" she croaked. "You're leaving?"

"But, love, you've known all day."

"But that was before," she protested. "You can't leave now! You can't go to war!"

The smile was dashed from Rolfe's dark face by her tearful exclamation. "What mean you—can't?"

"Not after we . . . not loving as we did. You can't!"

"I've not the choice."

"You lie! You care not which king sits the English throne, you told me so yourself. What possible difference can it make whether you join the fight?"

"I gave my word."

Aghast, she stared at him, all the softening aftermath of passion dissolving before his determined face. "Your word! But what of me—am I not worthy of your word?"

"Marged, speak sense. There's no comparison."

"I said I loved you. I gave you my maidenhead. You lay with me and whispered sweet vows . . ."

"None of which were lies," he reminded her sternly as he drew away and stood looking down at her. "Never once, lady, did I promise to stay with you. The depth of my passion for your body has naught to do with the war."

In that instant, Marged hated him. So fierce was the emotion that surged through her body, she stumbled when she tried to rise. "Oh, damn you, damn you!" she cried, fighting angry tears, ashamed of her womanly weakness.

"If you regret your sacrifice, you have leave to claim I raped you. 'Tis all the same to me," he said, spinning about and striding outside.

Great sobs tore from her throat, and Marged slid to the ground, consumed by grief. All the magic of their lovemaking had been destroyed. Though she hated to admit it, never once had he promised to stay with her. No word of marriage, betrothal, or any binding pledge had passed between them. But she had thought when he had taken her with such delight, reveling in their fierce union, that those vows had been understood.

For how long she stayed there in a huddled mass on the dirt floor, Marged did not know for her mind was so wracked by emotion. Suddenly the shrill note of a hunting horn blasted through the stormy lull. Raising her head, she listened again; she was not mistaken. Rolfe heard it too, for he came to the doorway, holding his stallion's reins.

"They are drawing near. Come, unless you prefer them to see you thus."

She stared at him, searching his set face for some betrayal of the burning passion that had passed between them. "Damn you, Rolfe de Bretayne! I curse the day I laid eyes on you. You lying, cheating . . . what know *you* of love?"

She scrambled into the saddle; disdaining his assistance, she sharply kicked aside his hand when he reached to help her.

"You speak so scathingly of lies you believe I told," he

growled, wrenching the gelding's bridle about, holding her there until he was done. "What of the sweet words you whispered to me? Were they lies also?"

How much Marged wanted to say "yes"! Though Rolfe was bristling with anger, his mouth set in a straight, unyielding line, memories of the delight of his lovemaking were still too fresh for lying. "That foolishness can only be termed temporary insanity," she hissed, thrusting at him as she fought to release her mount. "And if you have even an ounce of chivalry, you'll not reveal what took place between us."

"I can't agree to that. My men will know what happened."

"Have you so vast a reputation that no woman is safe alone with you?" Marged cried, her eyes flashing, "Or, by God, did you boast abroad how easily you would tame me?"

Rolfe glanced away as the sound of approaching hoofbeats reached them. "Enough of your tantrums! For your own safety, I intend to tell them what took place."

Marged gasped in shock. "Would you shame me thus?"

"Don't be such a little fool." He gripped her knee, forcing her to look at him. "I seek not to shame you. However much you pretend it didn't happen, I took you and you welcomed me in passion. Whether we repeat the experience is your choice, lady, but listen, and listen well, for we have scant time before they are upon us. For your own safety in the months to come, and for that alone, will I publicly claim you."

"If you were the last man alive, I'd not be yours!"

His smile turned grim as he increased the bruising pressure on her knee, but Marged refused to wince. "To preserve your reputation, I'll claim to have taken you by force. Perhaps nine months from now you'll thank me for the consideration, you ungrateful little bitch."

A bleak wave of misery gripped her at his angry words. Nine months from now! She had given no thought to the possibility of bearing his babe. "I'd sooner die than bear your bastard," she spat just as the thundering horde of men and horses quaked the nearby forest floor.

Rolfe was given no chance to retort, but his grim visage told Marged her scathing words had driven home.

"My lord, we thought you lost, as we've been these hours

past," called Chagall, Rolfe's yellow-haired second-in-command.

Rolfe strode toward his men. Deep in conversation, they stood at the edge of the trees. Marged sat hunched in the saddle, feeling cold and miserable. By their glances in her direction and by their surprised expressions before they broke into laughter, she knew the men were being given the story. Humiliation flooded hotly through her body and she hung her head in shame.

"Come, lady, direct us along the shortcut. And, by God, play me not false," Rolfe growled in an undertone, gripping Marged's bridle and pulling her horse about.

Chagall joined them, sweeping Marged with a suggestive glance, the knowledge of his master's conquest turning him unusually merry.

The journey to Bowenford through the twilit countryside seemed a thousand miles long. Marged was conscious of Rolfe's intent gaze, but she refused to meet his eyes. Never had she hated anyone so fiercely, nor yet had she ever loved anyone so deeply. He had given her fire and passion for one short hour, and she knew the memory would torment her the rest of her days.

{ three }

MARGED GAZED FORLORNLY at the rolling countryside silhouetted against the sunset. The summer day was dying in a blaze of crimson, violet, and gold.

Rolfe had been gone more than a week, traveling with a heavily armed troop of his best men. Poignant, stirring memories of that storm-lashed day when she had lain in his arms often flitted through her mind. How scornful she had always been of women trapped by weakness into a life of shame. Only then she hadn't known the sweet temptation of a man's kisses, nor the answering fire in her own blood.

Marged turned from the window, forsaking the panoramic view of the towering peaks, black against the fiery sky. She started in surprise when she found Chagall watching her from the doorway. Since Rolfe's departure, his young second-in-command had lorded it over Bowenford.

"Is it forbidden for me to watch the sunset?" Marged demanded, forcing away the painful emotion generated by Rolfe's memory. She hated him more than any man alive, she told herself fiercely.

"No, nor is it forbidden for me to gaze upon your beauty." As he spoke, Chagall brushed back a shock of his wavy yellow hair. He was a quiet, slender man, possessed of a soft musical voice, his manner more suggestive of a minstrel than of a soldier.

Marged smiled stiffly as she realized that he sought to charm her. "If you'll step aside, I'll retire to my chamber."

"Be not so hasty to depart. Can't you stay and talk to me?"

"I doubt much I have to say will interest you."

"Ah, there you're wrong, for one kind word from your ruby lips will be as precious to me as gold," Chagall breathed extravagantly, moving closer.

Marged warily skirted the wall. Because she assumed he was going to try to embrace her, she was amazed when he dropped to his knees in the rushes spread over the floor. Taking the hem of her scarlet gown, he ardently pressed the fabric to his lips. His thin, sun-reddened face was upturned to hers, adoration plain in his gray eyes. The unexpected discovery of his ardor so took her by surprise that Marged could think of no light remark to hide her discomfort.

"Say you'll sup with me," he beseeched, his request nearly drowned by the sharp cries of homing swallows circling beyond the walls. "Even the graceful swallow grows clumsy before you," he said, eagerness strengthening his courage. "Oh, sweet lady, have pity on me. Am I not as true a man as my master?"

His mention of Rolfe stung her. "If you seek to ingratiate yourself, don't speak to me about him," she warned sharply.

Chagall's smile turned sly. So, she cared naught for his lord! The revealing knowledge increased his boldness. Seizing Marged's hand, he now pressed his lips against her soft skin. "I swear never to mention him again. You'll soon learn that not all men ravish and plunder—some woo with kindness, praise—"

"And flattering lies."

"Nay, never lies. Come, say you'll sup with me. There's no need to stay a prisoner in your chamber. A hostage need not sacrifice the right to life."

"Yet you deny me the right to freedom."

Hope spiraled through Marged's body when she saw the frown knit Chagall's brow. One glance at his soft face and weak, dimpled chin told her he was fighting a losing battle with his conscience. Should he grant her favors in the hope she would reciprocate, or should he obey his master's orders? At times a crafty light flickered in his eyes, warning Marged not to trust him too far, yet his sensual mouth, his quickened breathing when he gazed upon her, convinced her his unexpected fervor could be manipulated to her advantage.

"What do you want that you don't have?" he asked at length, rising from his knees.

Marged smiled triumphantly, her heart fluttering as renewed hope spurred her on. "To move freely about the castle. To be able to walk—nay, ride—beyond the walls—"

"Enough!" His voice had turned gruff. "You're asking the impossible. I've explicit orders denying you access beyond the walls."

"Given by a man who took me by force!"

A quiver of guilt for her lie speared Marged's conscience as she silently beseeched Chagall to succumb to her demands.

"He's still my lord—yours too."

"He's no lord of my choosing! No man is my master!" Marged's full mouth tightened to a grim line as she regarded his wavering. "Your master wouldn't be overjoyed, were he to learn you pay me court."

"Nor that you've not repelled me."

"Neither have I encouraged you."

Chagall's soft-soled boots hissed through the rushes. He was so confident that he stepped on Marged's scarlet train to detain her. "I live in hope you'll warm to my suit," he whispered, reaching for her lustrous plaits, bound in scarlet satin.

"I might—given time," she allowed invitingly as she gazed up at him from beneath thick black lashes. Though Marged longed to strike aside his fondling hand, she stood her ground, moving only when he boldly outlined her mouth.

A shaft of waning light suddenly speared the gloom and framed her lovely face in a golden halo.

Chagall caught his breath, more than a little discomfited by the fiery gleam in Marged's green eyes. A chill, akin to fear crept through his body as he whispered, "You're not mortal! I swear you're a goddess incarnate. Some mystical Celtic deity . . ."

"Goddesses can be tempted from their pedestals," she whispered, lightly brushing her hand across his russet doublet. Then, leaving him with that tormenting thought, she swept regally from the room.

Chagall's heart raced with mingled fear and delight as he recalled Marged's inviting exit. Whatever the cost, he was freshly determined to have that woman!

When Marged entered the solar the following morning, a silver bowl of sweetmeats awaited her. The confections were accompanied by a posy of daisies, dewy eglantine, and blue forget-me-nots.

Bron chuckled as she placed the flowers in water. "The young one grows fevered," she commented, considering Chagall's wooing a great joke. "Can't you see he's calf-sick with love of you, lady?"

Marged's plan, such as it was, appeared to be working. She would allow Chagall to woo her, constantly fueling him with promises, but delivering little. He must grant her the right to move freely about the castle, and even more important, she must have permission to ride beyond the walls.

Last night as she lay in her chill tower room, listening to the Wye lapping against the stonework, Marged planned her escape. She would ride to the Brecon hills in search of her mother's kinsmen; then, protected by an armed band of Welshmen, she would go to England in search of her father. When she found him, she would give Sir Richard the story of the Breton's treachery. It would not be long before her father's men descended on the castle and wrested Bowenford from enemy hands.

During the following week, Marged continued to smile invitingly at her victim while cleverly eluding his embraces. After she complimented Chagall on his fine appearance, his dress grew brighter as he strove to be as fashionable as his limited wardrobe would allow. Marged smiled, she teased, she flattered, mustering hidden reserves of feminine wiles she had not known she possessed. After she was convinced that Chagall would not take her by force, she almost enjoyed her role of seductress. Despite his swaggering, she soon found he had little actual experience with women.

Driven to the point of distraction as he daily waxed more passionate to no avail, Chagall finally granted her first request.

On Friday morning the sentry who usually followed Marged about the castle was removed from his post.

Out of gratitude, while they broke their fast in the gloomy Great Hall, Marged allowed Chagall to feed her tidbits from his trencher. She did not even protest when he seized her hand and pressed it to his lips. All the while, as he breathed sweet love words around her earlobe, she was consumed with longing to be free. She could barely wait to finish her meal. The primrose sunlight spilling through the open doors beckoned her outside.

First Chagall consulted with his men about the orders of the day. He half rose, vastly tempted to follow Marged when she excused herself from the high table. She continued to walk toward the sunny doorway, confident that he would not abandon his duties to pursue her.

Birds chirped as she hastened over the grassy bailey. After glancing about to make sure she was not being followed, she sped toward the thatched shed where Gared, the huntsman, mended his leathers.

A mingled aroma of leather, goose greese, and lye met her as she pushed open the rickety door and peered inside the gloomy building. "Gared! Are you here?"

The huntsman, blinking in the bright sunlight, emerged from behind a shelf of trappings. "Aye, lady. Welcome. 'Tis a fine morning. Are we to go on a hunt?"

Marged smiled at the expectancy in his voice. "No. But I would discuss a private matter with you. Are you alone?"

Gared nodded, a puzzled expression settling over his blunt features. He ushered Marged inside his hovel, apologizing for the clutter. Without ceremony, Gared flung a heap of leather from a wooden bench and, after dusting the surface with his sleeve, pronounced it fit for her use.

"I need your help."

"Help, my lady? What help can I give?"

"Soon I expect to have permission to ride beyond the walls."

Gared dropped his gaze, feeling too uncomfortable to meet her eyes. Lately he had heard unpleasant gossip concerning his lady's chastity. While no one could fault her for falling victim to the Breton leader's lust, it had distressed him to hear that she openly courted the yellow-haired one.

"Things are not as you think," Marged snapped, gritting her teeth as she became aware of his thoughts.

"No . . . no, lady," Gared mumbled, still not looking her in the eye.

"I despise this Breton no less than his master."

Gared glanced up. "But they say—"

"They say I tempt him to my bed. Oh, yes, I know the slander bandied about the kitchens. Today I've won my first victory. Do you see a guard hovering on the threshold?"

Gared shook his head in bewilderment, his slow wits unable to connect the events.

"Because I've cosseted and cajoled that vain creature, he granted me the right to move freely about the castle." Marged leaned forward, her eyes glittering in the weak light, her voice quickening with excitement. "Next I intend to ride beyond the walls. That's where you can help me."

A glimmer of understanding passed through Gared's brown eyes. "You mean to escape!"

"Exactly. And I need your help."

Warming to their discussion, Gared leaned closer. "What can I do to aid you?"

"I need a guide to the Brecon hills. Someone who knows the country well."

"There's no one here from the hills."

"Think, there must be someone," she urged, leaning forward, desperate to settle her plans before Chagall came in search of her.

"Ifor's from the hills, but he's too old for adventure."

"He also has a lame leg," Marged added, recalling the falconer's infirmity. "Someone else. Someone young, with a taste for adventure. Oh, come, Gared, think. I can't entrust too many with my confidence. What about Rhodri?"

"Rhodri?" Gared repeated in surprise, hardly considering his nephew worthy of so important a mission. "Rhodri has little enough wit to find his own way to Brecon."

"But he does know the way?"

"Aye, he's been there twice since Candlemas."

"The Bretons won't know he doesn't belong to the household. We could pretend he's gone for supplies."

"Or birds, lady—sometimes he traps falcons for Ifor," Gared added, his enthusiasm mounting.

"When do you expect him next?"

"Before next week's out. He comes from the village to fetch food for his . . . his . . . mother . . ." Gared mumbled, reluctant to reveal unapproved charity. "She's lame and cannot fend for herself."

"No matter. I'll keep Rhodri's mother well supplied if he helps me flee the castle. Would he be willing to risk his neck for me?"

Gared fell to his knees on the beaten earth. "We'd all risk our lives for you, Lady Marged," he vowed.

Marged's eyes misted and her throat went dry. She patted Gared's gnarled arm, touched by his loyalty. "Get word to me when Rhodri arrives," she said hoarsely. "Tell him to pretend to belong to the household—assistant falconer, if you will. Pray God the weather holds so that I can hunt."

"Perhaps the Breton will insist on hunting with you. What then?"

She bit her lip. She had not considered that possibility. "Could a disturbance be arranged, something to delay him just long enough to allow me a head start?"

"You can count on me. But where will you go? Surely Sir Richard's not in Brecon—I was told he went to England to fight for mad King Harry."

"I intend to recruit men-at-arms from my mother's kinsmen to help me find him. When Father hears what's happened, the Bretons won't sit so securely beside our hearth."

"That they won't. Sir Richard'll dangle yon puny lad from the tower," Gared declared with relish, his eyes gleaming with satisfaction. Then his face clouded. "What if the other one returns? That one's no simpering smooth-face, lady, he's a man to be reckoned with."

"Then that's all the more reason not to delay."

There was a rising commotion in the bailey, and Marged guessed it was Chagall's search party. "Are you with me?" she asked quickly. "Take Ifor into your confidence. We'll need his help."

"You can count on me, Lady Marged." Gared had also heard the guards. "Here, this way, through the back."

Marged darted down the narrow entry behind the kennels. This passage connected with the mews where Ifor the falconer worked. Thinking to make her rapidly forming story even more convincing, Marged cut through the mews, holding her breath against the rank stench of perched birds on this warm summer morning.

When next she emerged in the sunlight, she saw Chagall and a party of guards approaching Gared's hut. One of the soldiers saw her and alerted his master. He spun about, the scowl dissolving from his fair face.

"Sweet lady, we thought you were missing," he said tactfully as he hastened to her side. "We've searched for you throughout the castle."

"Missing! How could I be missing? I've not permission to go outside the walls."

"What have you been doing?" he asked suspiciously, after he had commanded the soldiers to return to their duties.

Marged took a deep breath before she flashed him her most charming smile. "Oh, my dear, dear Chagall, let me thank you from the bottom of my heart for taking away my guard."

Some of the tension left his face. "I thought my generosity had been ill advised."

Marged looked downcast. "Do you trust me so poorly? Can I not visit my falcon without becoming suspect?"

Contrite, he seized her hand. "Forgive me for my suspicions. Come, we'll visit the hawks together. We shall do whatever gives you pleasure."

Ifor bowed low as they entered his domicile. Hurrying as much as his bad leg would allow, he went to summon Mert, the assistant falconer, to bring forth the birds.

"When you let me go outside the walls, I'll take my bird hunting. She's the best of them all."

She prattled on about the merits of her goshawk, bewildering

Chagall by her unexpected friendliness. He had never actually promised to allow her beyond the walls, yet in view of her improved mood, he was reconsidering. The little witch, it was as if she read his mind, for now she laughed even more gaily and clung to his sleeve as they entered the dark inner mews of the castle.

A window and narrow doorway gave access to the semidark, evil-smelling room where the hawks perched. Mert held Marged's fierce falcon, hooded in tooled red leather, and wearing golden bells on her feet.

Cooing lovingly to the bird, Marged leveled her wrist as Mert released the leather jess. The spotted falcon alighted gently, gripping its talons in her red silk sleeve.

"She's one of the largest goshawks I've seen!" Chagall remarked in surprise, stroking the sleek, dappled brown wings with a tentative finger.

"And fierce. She out-hunts any bird I've ever owned." Marged smiled as she whispered endearments to the falcon, pressing her cheek against its feathers. "And to think I named her Mair."

"Mair?"

"In honor of our Blessed Mother, for I received her on the Feast of the Assumption. 'Tis Welsh for Mary."

Chagall turned his attention to the two short-winged hawks held by Mert.

"These birds are smaller than I'm used to seeing," Chagall observed. He slipped on the leather gauntlet Mert handed to him.

"They're short-winged hawks, my lord, best for wooded country." The young falconer released the leather jess allowing a black-hooded bird to mount Chagall's wrist.

"I see. Yet this one seems even smaller than the others."

"He's a tiercel." Marged was appalled by Chagall's ignorance. "Males are usually inferior hunters, but he's proved acceptable. We use him for hawking at the brook. He's bagged a goodly catch of ducks from the Wye."

Chagall frowned at her speech. Somewhere, deep down, he suspected mockery behind Marged's statement. "Males are never inferior," he corrected sullenly.

"Then you don't know falcons." Marged hid a smile as she

returned Mair to her handler. "I'll give you ample chance to prove him. I've not been hawking for many a day. Who knows, the tiercel may excel."

"What makes you think I'd choose him?" Chagall grumbled as he returned the brown tiercel to Mert.

Marged's red mouth twitched with humor. "Because, my dear Chagall, worship me you might, but to be bested by me you could not stomach. You'll take the tiercel if only to prove me wrong."

In the background, Mert smothered his laughter.

Chagall stared at Marged, tension tightening his mouth. "How sure of me you sound."

"Most virile men are alike. Don't fault me for being wise enough in women's ways to understand you."

By degrees, the tension left his face. Chagall gripped Marged's shoulder, drawing her close. He would have tried to kiss her, had not Mert emerged from the mews to interrupt him.

"Will the new falcons be arriving soon?" Marged asked the stocky falconer.

"New falcons, Lady Marged?"

"The ones Rhodri's bringing from the hills." Turning back to Chagall, Marged continued confidently, "The lad's amazing. He knows exactly where to find the fiercest birds. Perhaps he'll bring a likely brancher we can train for you."

"I didn't know he was expected—" Mert began stupidly before Marged hastily interrupted him.

"Perchance Ifor forgot to tell you. Rhodri took a goodly collection of eyases this year. He'll already have them broken to command."

They entered the hut where Ifor worked, and the old falconer stumbled to his feet to greet them.

"Let me know the minute Rhodri arrives with the new falcons," Marged commanded, unusually imperious. The falconer's heavy face looked blank, for he knew better than to question his lady. "My lord Chagall would choose a falcon for his own. But he'll have to wait a long time before it's trained well enough to challenge Mair."

"Nay, the tiercel suits me well enough," Chagall snapped. "Ready the birds for the next fine day, falconer."

Marged gasped in dismay. It was too soon to put her plan into action! They must wait until Gared took Rhodri into his confidence.

"Don't you want to wait until you've seen the other birds?"

"I'm a patient man, yet sometimes, lady, my patience grows sorely frayed," Chagall snarled, ushering her from the darkened hut. His angry remark held far deeper meaning than their dispute over hawks.

While they crossed the bailey in the warm sunshine, Marged reviewed her plan. Everything had worked exactly as expected, including her gibe about the tiercel being inferior to her own falcon. Everything, that is, except the crucial timing of the hunt.

"When are we to go hawking?"

"Tomorrow, if the weather holds."

"Oh, you're granting me permission to ride beyond the walls!" Marged cried in feigned delight.

"Aye—for a price."

"A price!" Her heart began an uneven thud at his sharp reminder. "What price?"

Chagall swiftly pressed Marged against him, taking her so completely by surprise that she had no chance to elude his embrace. She quickly turned her head as his eager lips came down and caught her cheek. Angered by her maneuvering, Chagall tightened his grip, yet when he saw the challenge in her eyes—her refusal to flinch—he released her.

"You're too impatient," she snapped, making a great show of smoothing her rumpled gown. Never would she have expected him to choose so public a place for amorous adventure; they stood in full sight of half the castle.

Torn between mounting frustration and remorse, Chagall swallowed and, his face working, said at last, "A kiss . . . what would it have cost you to grant me that?"

"Kisses can be stolen. Kisses bestowed with joy are the greater treasure."

"I could steal far more from you than kisses. Sometimes I think—"

"You intended to show me how unlike your master you are," she reproached, her mouth downturned. "Are you retracting your vow?"

"Nay—but when will you yield? If only to welcome my embrace instead of standing stiff with resentment."

"In my own time. Have I not been kinder to you of late?"

He nodded, stepping closer. "Sweet, I beg you to be kinder still. One kiss of passion is all I ask."

Marged sidestepped his outstretched arm. "After the hunt," she promised, bending supple as a willow from his grasp. "If your tiercel bests my falcon."

From Chagall's set mouth issued an explosion of anger, but Marged was fleeing to the safety of the buildings, her bright skirt bobbing across the bailey turf.

Alys was waiting when she entered the solar.

"By all the saints! I've always known you were wanton, but that disgraceful display—"

"Was none of my choosing," Marged snapped, going to the open window as she caught her breath. Chagall stood below, exactly where she had left him, his face dark with anger.

"If Sir Richard were here, he would have you flogged!"

"Had Sir Richard been here, none of this would have happened."

Alys swished her skirts aside as Marged moved closer. "You're wanton! All the Welsh are wanton—little removed from savages. They couple as easy as barnyard creatures." Alys paused, for Marged had swung about, her face stormy with temper. As Marged advanced upon her, Alys grabbed her sewing and bolted for the door. "Nay, you wild creature, you'll not vent your spite on me a second time. Besides, I speak only what is true."

"You know not the truth. You speak only what you imagine to be true."

"How do you mean?"

"I despise Chagall as much as his hated master!" Marged spat, clenching her fists until the knuckles whitened. "His panting attentions will serve us well."

"Think you to buy our freedom by whoring with him?" Alys sneered. "It didn't get you anywhere with the other one."

Marged drew in her breath deeply. Twin spots of red glowed high on her cheeks. Her hand tingled to slap Alys's haughty face. "When a man forces a woman, she has little recourse," she ground out through clenched teeth.

Alys's mouth twitched in pure scorn. "Forced, sister dear? Come, I'm not blind. There was nothing of force to it. Though he be our hated enemy, de Bretayne has the looks and charm to coax favors from the most confirmed virgin—and you can hardly be called that. I imagine Welsh wanton blood and Breton run much the same."

This final taunt delivered, Alys fled, with Marged in hot pursuit.

She abandoned the chase long before the blue skirts slipped around the stone lintel at the foot of the stair. Let her go. Though Alys wounded out of spite, there was more truth than she knew to her accusation.

The castle's inhabitants had readily accepted Rolfe's story. When they stood together in the Great Hall and he pronounced her under his protection, Marged had hung her head in shame. Ready sympathy for her plight stirred within many a heart on that gloomy day, yet her loose behavior with Chagall had destroyed much of the servants' pity. Now spiteful Alys was not the only one who considered her a wanton.

Marged squared her shoulders, determined not to flinch from her purpose. Once her reason for flirting with Chagall became apparent, the condemning tongues would be stilled. What if she couldn't escape? What if Chagall, growing increasingly impatient, tired of her game and claimed his prize by force? Because of her encouraging glances, her soft touches, her inviting smiles, she would be left at his mercy. No one would come to her defense.

Uttering a ragged sigh, she rested her fevered cheek against the stone embrasure of the window. To the west, a bank of clouds was forming, crowning the jagged Black Mountains with smoky haloes. If only it would rain and delay the hunt! Chagall was not an experienced hunter—as his ignorance about falcons revealed. Surely inclement weather would dissuade him from his sport.

Eyes shut tight against the wavering light, Marged pressed her face in her hands and prayed desperately for rain.

For more than a week, strong winds and violent rainstorms raked the Marcher valleys, reinforcing the local belief that this had been the wettest summer in a hundred years.

Down on her knees, Marged repeatedly gave thanks for this heavenly intervention. Each gloomy gray day gave her one more chance for a successful outcome to her scheme.

Chagall's temper was frayed by this providential thwarting of his plans. Afraid to anger him too much, lest he force her to yield to him, Marged played a dangerous game—encouraging on the one hand, playfully discouraging on the other. Across the backgammon board, or over a simple game of chess played with dice, Marged attempted to sooth his ill humor. No longer was she able to refuse his hand-kissing or even his tentative embraces, for circumstances forced them to spend too many hours together.

At last, desperate for a break from Chagall's perpetual presence, Marged feigned illness, hinting archly that it was her woman's time and she was beset with agonizing cramps.

Unrelenting as ever, Chagall, brightly arrayed in his best doublet—kingfisher blue, dagged in purple—visited her thrice daily. Marged insisted on Bron attending her during these unwelcome visits. And though he resented the serving woman's presence, Chagall made no outward objection, understanding that it was proper for a lady of noble birth to be attended by her maid.

On a gray, rain-lashed Friday, Marged lay propped against a mountain of pillows while she listened to Chagall sing a French love ballad, accompanied by a lute. During a rare moment of genuinely warm feelings between them, the young soldier had confessed to her his youthful ambition to become a minstrel; his father, considering soldiery a more masculine way of life, had forced him into service with the de Bretayne family.

His song at an end, Chagall plucked a few lingering, plaintive chords, the notes echoing long in the quiet room.

Marged smiled in genuine pleasure, having vastly enjoyed his performance. "You have cheered me considerably," she said sweetly.

"I would cheer you far more, would you allow it."

His thinly veiled invitation made her smile. "I hope tomorrow will be suitable for our hunt. I'm weak with longing to be outdoors."

"And I grow weak with longing for quite a different reason."

Chagall came to the bed. Though his gray eyes remained soulful, he had let resentment mark his soft face. "You'll at least yield your mouth to me, whether your falcon bests the tiercel or not."

Marged swallowed uneasily, growing cautious in the face of this new insistence. "Perhaps, if you're very, very kind to me," she dismissed teasingly as she fingered his hanging sleeve. "This afternoon you've been most attentive. In case tomorrow dawns fine, I want to be well rested for the hunt, otherwise I can't endure long hours in the saddle. I really must rest." She watched him from beneath lowered lashes, hoping her tone had been convincingly languid.

With an exasperated sigh, Chagall turned aside. "Very well. I hope you'll be sufficiently rested to sup with me."

Eyes still downcast, Marged studied her linked fingers as she spoke. "I'll try very hard to join you later."

Chagall wrenched open the door, ignoring Bron, who ran to unlatch it for him. He immediately stepped back into the room as a serving woman, leading a wet, cloak-swathed figure, loomed out of the darkness.

"What's this?"

Bron spoke to the woman in Welsh. Turning to Chagall, she explained, "'Tis a poor girl come to beg sanctuary of my lady."

Muttering beneath his breath, he glanced toward Marged, who forced herself to stay supine. "Show her in. Don't stay overlong, wench. Lady Marged mustn't tire herself."

Marged waited only until he was safely in the corridor before she leaped from her bed and sped toward the door. To her disappointment, she discovered that the swathed figure was indeed a woman, and not Rhodri in disguise.

"Why do you come to me?" she asked as the bedraggled girl slipped back her sodden hood to reveal golden hair dark with rain.

"Oh, sweet lady, have pity." Dramatically the girl fell on her knees and bowed her head. "My father is dead, and so in debt were we, I've neither food nor shelter. To save myself from a life of sin, I've come to beg your charity."

The sweet-faced girl raised her tear-streaked face, her large brown eyes beseeching. Marged's heart went out to her.

"Have you traveled far?"

"From a holding across the Dore, near Pontrilas. We're gentlefolk, my lady. Father was a knight who found himself in reduced circumstances after the French wars. He was once befriended by your sire, and spoke most highly of the Bowens."

"What can you do?"

"Some dairying . . . but . . . I hoped to attend you, Lady Marged. I sew well and can sing true. I was never raised to be a serving wench."

Marged watched the pansy-soft brown eyes filling with tears. Though she had no reason to doubt her story, Marged's intuition told her this pretty wench tended to try and wring forth every last shred of pity. "What's your name?" she asked more sharply.

"Joan Vaughn."

"Are you related to the Vaughns of Tretower?"

The girl hung her head. "Very slightly, lady."

"Then why don't you seek help from them?"

The girl's dark eyes took on a defiant gleam. "Mother never married. I don't bear my father's name."

Bron signaled to Marged over the girl's head, and Marged nodded.

"Go below and we'll find food and dry clothing for you. Though I'm in no need of a maid, my stepsister has recently lost her old servant. Seeing that you're daughter to a knight, I'm sure she'll welcome you."

Sheer delight suffused Joan Vaughn's fair face. Her soft mouth quivered as she spoke, revealing small white teeth that gleamed against rose-red lips. "Oh, bless you, Lady Marged, you've truly saved my life."

"How did you come this far alone in such evil weather?"

"Rhodri guided me. We met along the way."

"Rhodri," Marged croaked, her voice failing her. "Rhodri is come!"

Joan Vaughn was surprised by the elation in Lady Marged's face. "We've been here all afternoon. Many roads are awash, but we forded them all without mishap."

After Joan had gone below, Marged paced the floor, her impatience growing by the minute. The sky already appeared brighter, and the rain had stopped. If only the storms would hold off, she could name tomorrow their hunting day. Perhaps it would be wiser to wait, yet the thought of freedom forced her to a hasty decision.

"All indications are that tomorrow will be dry," Marged disclosed as she sat beside Chagall at the evening meal.

"It's about time. I was beginning to think it does naught but rain in this godforsaken place," Chagall grumbled, snapping a pigeon bone between restless fingers. "We'd best wait a day or two to be sure. I don't relish riding abroad only to get a soaking before we've gone a mile."

"All signs point to fine weather," Marged assured him, gambling recklessly that her words would prove correct.

"It can be fine at dawn, pouring by noon, dry again by evensong, and raging a tempest before midnight. I've little faith in your Marcher forecasts."

In mounting agitation, Marged crumbled a crust of rye bread across the blue table cover. They must ride forth tomorrow. She could not endure another day's imprisonment. Nor was she sure she could continue to fend off Chagall's unwelcome advances.

"How I long to ride beyond the walls! I feel like a caged beast."

"You must learn patience, Lady Marged, as I've been forced to do." Chagall's eyes glinted with temper as he looked at her; his patience was all but spent.

Casting aside all caution, Marged plunged recklessly ahead. "Can you forgive me for playing you so sore?" she whispered penitently, her hand pressing gently on his arm. "You're a brave, true knight, and so chivalrous to have endured my whims with such good humor. You do not deserve to have been served so ill."

Chagall cocked a blond eyebrow at her speech, puzzled, yet highly intrigued. "This is certainly a change of tune. The weather does strange things to you."

"Nay, 'tis not the weather," she whispered, fluttering her abundant dark lashes at him as she drew closer. "Oftimes a woman is hard won, but you, my lord, can consider yourself the victor."

At her words, his breath rasped audibly in his throat. "Victor! Christ Jesus . . . are you saying . . . will you . . . yield?"

The smile she gave him was of purest sweetness. "Tonight, for your promise, I'll yield my lips. As for the rest—I cannot say."

"Anything. Name it."

Taking a deep breath, Marged leaned even closer, her shoulder pressing his. She was wearing her periwinkle-blue festival gown—well aware of the devastating effect her raiment could have. The low-cut bodice emphasized her breasts, the clinging skirts complimented her shapely thighs. Already Chagall panted, his hot breath fanning her cheek. Marged slid her hand in his, and after moistening her red lips, she said, "Promise we shall hunt at daybreak."

"And?"

"Tonight you shall taste my mouth."

Though such pittances would not satisfy most men, they appealed to Chagall's chivalrous soul, nurtured by a lifelong study of minstrels' lays depicting the game of Courtly Love. On such crumbs of passion did the gallant game survive. Heat surged like a furnace through his body as he seized her hand and buried his lips in her palm.

"You have my word. With what am I to be rewarded, if my tiercel bests your falcon?"

Highly aware of his gaze sliding to the voluptuous swell of her bodice, Marged laughed softly. "Oh, my lord, surely you can think of something."

He would have taken her in his arms then and there, had not Marged stayed his arm.

"Come, let us not exchange kisses before the others," she whispered, gambling that he would not take advantage of their privacy to press her to even further intimacies.

Like an obedient dog, he followed Marged behind the arras dividing the Hall. Alys usually held sway here in the evenings, where she kept her spinning wheels and tapestry frames. But tonight she was so enchanted with her new maid that she had chosen to take her meal in her bedchamber while she instructed Joan in her duties.

"Here?" Chagall breathed, his heart pounding.

"Here," Marged replied.

With flushed face and quickened breath, he swept her

against him. She steeled herself not to turn her mouth from his moist, ardent kiss. Passion made his body tremble while she remained detached, feeling nothing beyond distaste for this unwanted intimacy. So bewitched was he, however, he did not even notice.

Waxing even bolder, Chagall allowed his hand to stray to her bodice until Marged twisted away, but not before the unwelcome pressure of his fingers invaded her breast.

"You're stealing more privileges than I offered," she chided playfully as she tried to mask disgust for his panting, red-faced lust. Gone was the soft, sweet-singing minstrel of this afternoon.

"What matter tonight, or tomorrow—come," he urged breathlessly, his arms outstretched, pleading with her to yield.

Marged ignored his pleas. "It matters greatly to me. I've yet to learn whether you intend to honor your bargain. Do you swear on the Cross, if the day be fine, I can ride beyond the walls to hunt with my falcon?"

"Aye, I already gave my word," he dismissed impatiently, his temper rising as he realized she would not willingly offer more. "After we're done with the hunt, Lady Marged, I'll no longer be content with sops. You may have won your way, but the cost will prove far greater than you expect. Do you understand me?"

Marged cast her gaze to the herb-sweetened rushes at her feet. "I understand," she said.

{ *four* }

MARGED'S STOMACH CHURNED with apprehension as she peered at the overcast sky. Long before first light she had put on her sapphire-blue habit and waited impatiently for Bron to plait her hair inside a blue silk fillet. Then, her feathered chaperon secured atop the net, she went to the window and watched as black lightened to fledgeling banners of gold that burnished the distant hills.

"Oh, Bron, it's going to be dry," she whispered hoarsely, her clenched fists white with tension.

"Never before have I seen you so eager for the hunt," Bron remarked in surprise, not comprehending the reason for her mistress's excitement.

"I've never been a prisoner before," Marged said as she kissed Bron's cheek. Her hands shook with excitement as she pulled on her gauntlets. "You're a good woman, Bronwen Parry, and I love you well."

Bron blinked in surprise, her mouth turning up with pleasure at the unexpected praise. "Thank you, my lady. It's my delight to serve you."

"Wish me luck," Marged whispered as she swept from her chamber.

In the Great Hall, the sleepy soldiers were stirring in the rushes. Marged acknowledged their mumbled greetings as she walked outside into the chill dawn.

A brisk wind ruffled her skirts as she anxiously inspected the heavens for storm clouds that would wash out her plans. Satisfied that the day promised to be fair, Marged hastened across the bailey.

Outside the mews, she glanced behind her. Certain she had not been followed, she creaked open the door and entered Ifor's hut.

"Greetings, lady," said Ifor, who had been expecting her since first light. "All's ready."

On the surface, the falconer's remark seemed little more than a polite way of reassuring her that the birds were ready for the day's hunt. Yet Marged needed only to look at his stolid face to know her escape had been arranged. "Thank you, Ifor, you've ever been loyal to me and mine."

Somewhat embarrassed by her praise, Ifor colored as he backed toward the mews. "Mert has the birds ready. Rhodri's with him."

"Are the horses provisioned?"

"Yes."

With hammering heart, Marged stepped back into the bailey.

Mert and Rhodri, carrying the hooded falcons, came from the shadows between the buildings. It was the first time Marged had met the huntsman's nephew, and she was surprised to find him older than she had expected. Still slender as a willow tree beneath his Lincoln-green tunic, Rhodri possessed shoulders that branched out broad and straight, suggesting hidden strength. When their eyes met, he nodded. Gared must have confided only in Rhodri, for Mert was behaving as if nothing unusual was afoot.

Marged found Chagall and his men painfully slow about departure. There was no mention yet of the disturbance that would keep Marged's jailor inside the castle. She prayed that this vital aspect of the plan had not been overlooked.

Marged need not have worried. Even as Chagall came toward her, dressed for the chase in russet and green, an anxious soldier ran across the bailey.

"My lord, come quick. There's trouble."

"Trouble!" Chagall scowled, turning half about before thinking better of it. "There's no trouble serious enough to keep me from hunting beside my lady," he said, reaching for Marged's hand, his gray eyes brimming with expectation.

"One of the Welsh has gone berserk! We fear for our lives!" The soldier cried, his eyes dilated in fear. "Already he holds two men at swordpoint—my brother's one of them! I beg you, lord, come to subdue him."

With a growl of frustration over this unexpected disturbance, Chagall turned reluctantly to his man. "Christ, of all times! Wait, Lady Marged, I shan't be long."

"We cannot tarry. Already the sun's climbing high. Soon the game will have run to ground. Come, the trouble can wait," she pleaded, her full underlip pouting. "We'll miss the best sport. And you promised . . . you swore . . ."

Chagall muttered an oath beneath his breath, torn between lust and duty. "Can you not wait fifteen minutes? I swear, the knave will breathe his last long before then, if only in punishment for spoiling my plans," he boasted gruffly.

"Why can I not ride ahead?" Marged turned toward Rhodri, who stood holding the hooded falcon. "See, Mair's anxious to be aloft. You're such a master horseman, 'twill be but a matter of minutes before you catch us," she purposely flattered Chagall.

"I'll look after the lady till you can join us, my lord," Rhodri offered, consciously deepening his voice to more manly proportions.

Chagall glared at him, heartily disliking this assistant falconer who had emerged from the storm like a drowned hound. "I still think you should wait," he began, his voice gruff with anger. Then, seeing Marged's agonized expression, he impatiently waved her on. "Go then, lady, before you punish me for breaking my word."

Marged blinked in surprise at the mounting anger in his face. "I'll save the best kill for you," she promised throatily, reaching for his hand.

"See that you do," he muttered as he spun about and strode toward the keep.

The hunting party mounted and rode through the west gate and over the narrow moat, their horses' hooves clattering on the lowered drawbridge. They spilled into the lush green water meadows bordering the Wye, shouting, laughing, glad to be freed from duty. So much rain had fallen of late, the horses cantered hock-deep in water, splattering their riders with mud.

Marged was gripped by a surge of fierce excitement as the fresh wind blew in her face and she smelled the scent of freedom. Her gaze wandered to the distant, shadowed mountains. How she longed to ride near those jagged peaks, climbing higher, each mile bringing her closer to Brecon.

"We'll take that path," Rhodri suggested, pointing to a tangled stretch of woodland on this side of the Wye.

Chagall's men were reluctant to follow Rhodri's directions. Many of the soldiers hung back to await their leader. Marged restrained her mount fiercely, for the gelding sensed her desire for speed. When they entered the trees, the party split into small groups and she was able to increase her pace gradually. The dank, chill air trapped between these ancient gnarled trees cut through her thin habit, and Marged was glad when they finally broke into a sun-splashed clearing.

"See, lady, up there," Rhodri shouted, pointing to a white crane flying above the trees.

She galloped forward with several of Chagall's men in pursuit. When they were a few bowshots from their quarry, she unhooded her falcon, whispered soft words of encouragement, and released the bird.

Plunging through thickets of gorse, of bracken, twisting down winding paths in the pretense of reaching the riverbank, Marged led the unknowing soldiers on a merry chase. Suddenly sighting a quarry, the hounds began to bay in excitement. Marged slackened her pace, confident that the soldiers would abandon her for the pursuit.

Rhodri had already turned north and was threshing uphill through tangled undergrowth. Marged snapped the gelding's head about, ducking to avoid treacherous, low-hanging branches, and sped after him.

After a few minutes they reached a forester's hut, where

two provisioned pack animals were waiting. Rhodri smiled assurance at Marged as he indicated a narrow, branch-shrouded path leading sharply uphill.

"That's the quickest route to take, Lady Marged. Make haste. I don't know how long it will be before they grow wise to our trickery. Mert will have called in the falcon long ago."

Marged's heart pounded as she thudded after him. Her gelding stumbled and she gripped him tightly between her knees, afraid of being unseated. Though Rhodri's shaggy pony was of doubtful parentage, it maintained a grueling pace as he wound back and forth on the meandering trail, traveling ever higher up the forested hillside.

Shouts echoed in the distance, growing closer, then receding. Marged's heart pitched in alarm. Chagall must have joined his men only to discover he had been tricked. Rhodri apparently shared her thoughts, for he switched direction abruptly, choosing an even narrower trail. Sounds of pursuit still traveled sporadically on the wind as they struggled along the bracken-covered path. Their enemies did not gain on them.

The sun was already high when they finally reached the Dore. The narrow ford could be crossed by using great boulders as steppingstones. It was difficult to take the packhorses across, but Rhodri coaxed and pushed the reluctant beasts until they eventually reached the opposite bank.

When they reached high ground, Marged paused to survey the surrounding countryside. "See, aren't those horsemen?" she cried, shielding her eyes from the glaring sun as splashes of color moved among the trees.

"Aye, but they're not on our trail," Rhodri assured her. "Come, we mustn't delay. We can't go much farther without resting the beasts."

At noon they ate bread and cold fowl. Though Rhodri waited on Marged, his lack of training in a noble household was glaringly apparent in the casual, comradely manner in which he served her. At times it was as if he quite forgot she was the lady of Bowenford.

The sun shone warm on their faces as they rode into the foothills of the Black Mountains. A sea of poppies glowed blood-red amid the tangled grass; clumps of foxgloves nodded their pinkish bells beside the flinty road. Kites circled in the distance looking like black specks against the bright blue sky. Here beneath the shade of towering sycamores that sheltered serenading, sweet-voiced thrushes, the harmony of nature brought with it blessed peace. Yet as they rode ever deeper into the remote mountains, they felt increasing fear for their safety, which gradually prevented Marged from enjoying the wild surroundings.

The first night on the road, they stayed at a hovel brazenly called an inn. The rooms were small and evil smelling; the food was fit only for swine. Declining the filthy pallet, Marged wrapped herself in her cloak on the straw-covered floor, and dozed fitfully, ever alert to intruders.

The new day dawned chilly and wet. Despite the dismal prospect of traveling through drenched countryside, Marged was eager to depart. Miraculously, their baggage was intact. Rhodri had slept beside the packhorses, his hand on his dagger. With profound relief they left the primitive hostelry, which survived because it flanked a road pilgrims followed to a hillside shrine.

As they toiled to the summit of the first hill, the sun finally broke through heavy clouds. Below, the gleaming silver Usk threaded its way through the green valley. Beyond the river, the lofty Brecon hills were framed by a brilliant rainbow. This unusual phenomenon seemed so like a heavenly sign that Marged hastily crossed herself before beginning the steep descent.

Never having traveled deep into the Brecon mountains, Rhodri soon became as much a stranger as Marged. Wherever they went, he asked for directions to Dinas Cwm, the manor of Maredudd ap Rhayadr, Marged's paternal grandfather. No one could help them. The villagers viewed them with open hostility, marking their English clothing. Disheartened, they turned westward.

In a more affluent village where stone dwellings were grouped about a market square, Marged asked several goodwives if they had heard of her mother, Eirlys the Fair. Though at first the peasant women feigned ignorance, when Marged asked fluently in their language for directions to her grandfather's home, they relented and pointed to a narrow track plunging into a wooded valley.

The imposing, purple mountains were shrouded in evening

mist when Marged and Rhodri reached Dinas Cwm, the stone fortress of Maredudd ap Rhayadr.

Two huge yellow hounds bounded forth, their fangs bared at the sight of strangers. Marged's gelding shied in fright, lashing out at the hostile creatures that snapped about his heels. But, good horsewoman that she was, Marged kept her seat.

"Who comes hither?" demanded a gruff voice.

Rhodri nervously relayed their business, his voice cracking in fear as a fierce, barrel-chested man appeared. The unfriendly stranger glowered at them from under a thatch of tangled black hair. A gleaming array of knives was slung from his broad belt.

"Why do you seek Maredudd?" the man asked in English, though his heavy accent made his speech difficult to understand.

"I'm Marged, daughter of Eirlys the Fair. Maredudd is my grandfather," Marged answered in Welsh, keeping her voice steady, though inwardly her heart fluttered. She had never supposed their reception would be anything but joyous. The lengthening night shadows and the sheer isolation of this manor boded no good, for the stocky man viewed her with bold black eyes, licking his thick lips in contemplation as his insolent gaze roved over her body.

"Then you must seek him on yonder hill, for Maredudd's been laid to rest these years past," the man said at last, stepping close to her mount.

"Who is master here now?" Marged demanded next, twitching her skirts out of the man's grasp when he tried to fondle her leg.

A resonant, musical voice answered from the shadows. "I am master. What do you want with me?"

Marged sighed with relief as a man, clad in thigh boots and a russet doublet, appeared. The fierce one hung his head penitently, for he knew he had been caught with his hands about the woman's calf.

"My mother was Eirlys the Fair. I seek my grandfather or his kin. We were directed to this manor."

"Eirlys was aunt to my mother. I'm Rhys ap Morgan," said the man in the russet doublet. Curtly he ordered his beetle-browed henchman to attend to their mounts. Then he reached up to help Marged dismount.

"Thank you, Lord Rhys, for we've ridden far and are in need of rest. I'm Marged Bowen, from Bowenford on the banks of the Wye."

She found herself swung easily from the saddle. Marged pierced the gathering purple shadows to find in this man's swarthy face some resemblance to her mother. She found none.

Rhys's expression was solemn, yet when he peered at her fully, his hazel eyes softened with admiration, and twin creases framed his hard mouth. "Welcome to my home, Marged Bowen," he said pleasantly. "You speak our language well, so I don't doubt your story. Come inside and warm yourself at the hearth. My servants will prepare a meal."

Long hours in the saddle had made Marged so weary that she stumbled, her stiff legs refusing to obey her.

Rhys caught her and supported her against his strong body as he led her through the nail-studded door and into the welcome warmth of this valley fortress.

A great fire blazed in the stone hearth. The hall's low plaster ceiling was supported by thick, smoke-blackened beams, festooned with an assortment of armaments and horse trappings.

Marged stretched her weary limbs before the fire. The tapestried cushions on the high-backed settle felt like sheer bliss after the unrelenting hardness of the saddle. She had begun to grow drowsy in the warmth when a serving wench brought her a steaming porringer of leek soup, a plate of crusty, buttered bread, and a jug of ale.

After Marged had eaten her meal, she told Rhys why she had come to Brecon. And she requested a party of his men-at-arms to protect her on the search for her father.

Rhys leaned forward, listening intently to her story, his hazel eyes gleaming with excitement when Marged gave him a stirring account of Bowenford's capture. When she recounted her escape, he marveled aloud at her bravery.

"On the morrow we'll go to the village to recruit men. They'll gladly follow, for they owe allegiance to me. We didn't know the war had resumed. Here we rarely receive news from the outside world."

Rhys went to relay Marged's story to his retainers, who were gaming at the far end of the room.

While Rhys was gone, Marged let her eyes rove around the

smoky hall of this ancient fortress, far removed from the grand dwelling she had always envisioned when her mother had described her ancestral home. Though the living accommodations were Spartan, this austere setting seemed eminently suited to her toughened Welsh kinsman.

Rhys came back to the hearth. In the spilled ash he traced their proposed route into England. While he bent to his task, Marged studied his face. Softened by fireglow, his hard features were most pleasant to behold. Above wide-set hazel eyes, his craggy brows gleamed black in contrast to his chestnut hair. He was no more than average height, yet the breadth of his chest and shoulders, the knotted muscles bulging in the worn sleeves of his russet doublet, revealed great strength. Resting against the hearthstone was a longbow, which Marged guessed to be his, for Rhys wore leather bowman's straps about his thick wrists.

"You need not fear for your safety on the journey," he said softly as he took her hand and raised her to her feet. "My men are fearless fighters."

Rhys led Marged through a low doorway to the foot of the narrow stairs. "Glynis is waiting upstairs for you. Never did I expect such a lovely creature to come out of the mist. Good night, Cousin Marged."

Marged smiled in pleasure at his compliment and accepted the brotherly kiss Rhys placed on her cheek. "Thank you for your hospitality. I knew I could count on my mother's family for aid."

"You may count on me as long as you have the need," Rhys assured her warmly. When Marged caught him in a swift appraisal of her curvacious body, his expression turned guarded. "Surely no greater beauty will ever grace my hearth," he mumbled uncomfortably, not meeting her gaze.

"You're much too kind," Marged protested. "I must look a sorry sight with my gown all muddy and torn. I suspect you to be a great flatterer. But I still thank you for your gallant lies."

Rhys caught her arm as he said, "Not lies, sweet cousin, merely poetry spoken from the heart."

The sheer intensity of his expression made Marged uneasy. She had just escaped one ardent suitor; she had little desire for another. "On the morrow you'll see me in a far truer light—as a woman with a mission that stops for nothing, or no one."

The determination in her voice amused him. "You're a woman after my own heart," he assured her lightly. Then he bowed, displaying courtly manners she had not expected.

The small whitewashed chamber at the head of the stairs glowed with firelight. Most prominent among the room's sparse furnishings was a huge tester bed on which were heaped hand-woven blankets. So inviting was the prospect of lying on a soft mattress that Marged gazed with longing at the bed.

The young, dark-haired girl who stepped toward her was not uncomely, but her features were set in so surly an expression that she appeared ugly. It was all Glynis could do to answer civilly when she was spoken to as she sullenly assisted Marged in disrobing before helping her into the steaming tub in front of the hearth.

"The water feels heavenly. I've ridden so many miles, I ache all over." Marged sighed with contentment as she lifted her heavy black hair to keep it out of the bathwater. "There are hair brushes and a clean gown in my baggage."

"They're here," Glynis replied with a scowl. "You brought so much baggage—are you staying long?"

"No. As soon as we muster troops, I'll be leaving."

"Troops! Is Rhys going with you?"

"I expect he'll want to lead his men," Marged said, her eyes snapping open in surprise as Glynis cursed beneath her breath. The girl banged Marged's hairbrushes on the oak chest at the foot of the bed.

"Then 'twould have been best had you stayed where you belong." Angrily, Glynis thrust a brush in Marged's hand. "Rhys and I were to be wed at harvest."

That revealing remark accounted for Glynis's hostility—the Welshwoman sensed a rival. And, given Rhys's searching gaze and his unusually gallant speech, perhaps Glynis's fears were not without foundation. "Can you not be wed ere he departs?" she suggested.

Glynis scowled even harder, and shook her head. "He has eyes only for you."

"I'm a stranger, 'tis natural for him to look at me. You are his sweetheart..."

"Leave him alone!" Glynis spun about, her teeth gritting with the intensity of her emotion. "No doubt you come from court with your pretty ways, your fancy clothes, your blooded horse. You can have other men—Rhys is all I'll ever have. If you dare take him to your bed, I'll cut out your heart!"

Marged's green eyes flashed in anger as she snatched the towel from Glynis's hand. "I've no need to steal your sweetheart. I came here for an escort to accompany me to my father. Now get you gone from my sight, for neither have I need of your hostility."

Glynis spun about and charged weeping from the room, leaving Marged to prepare herself for bed.

Marged had scant contact with Glynis during the following days, as she accompanied Rhys to rally men to his banner. Come rain or shine, they rode into each village square, sometimes nothing more than a clearing in the middle of a primitive valley settlement. Rhys would dramatically retell the story of the Breton's treachery, asking for men to aid Sir Richard Bowen in repossessing his castle from the enemy. Recruits flocked eagerly to the brawny Welshman's side. Though they had not needed half, he commanded more than a hundred men, many of whom were skilled longbowmen. Marged swelled with pride as she pictured her father's delight at discovering she had brought an army of her own.

Marged's relationship with Rhys ran smoothly, but never again did he allow his admiration for her to show. At first she put his unusual curtness down to the strain of recruiting soldiers, until she noticed fresh bruises on Glynis's face. The lovers must have quarreled. Glynis's jealousy had forced Rhys to erect a polite barrier between his lovely kinswoman and himself.

"We'll set out tomorrow," Rhys announced one evening while they supped on rabbit stew before the hearth.

Marged gasped in surprise, having hardly expected to be able to put their plans in motion so soon.

"Are we ready? I'd thought we must surely wait until the end of the month."

"Nay, the summer's well advanced." Rhys paused, his brow furrowed. "Though I can see you're no simpering, foolish wench, are you sure you're prepared for the hardships of the journey? Coventry's a goodly distance. My soldiers are rough mountain men, not given to manners and social niceties."

Marged smiled reassuringly. "I'm used to rough soldiery. The Bowen men are hardly gentlemen. I'm prepared to find my father with or without your assistance—but I'd much prefer your company."

Rhys grinned and gripped her hand. "Then my company you shall have. You must dress like a lad. It's not wise to advertise a woman's presence among our ranks."

"It's a good idea, if I had clothing to suit."

"I know a lad from a valley farm who's about your height. If the clothes don't fit, the women can alter them."

Marged smiled, realizing that not for one moment had he doubted she would accompany him on the journey. "I'm handy with sword and bow. Why don't I pose as your nephew, no longer a page, nor yet a full-fledged squire."

"I've never had so comely an attendant." Rhys glanced up to find Glynis watching them from the doorway, her face set in a scowl. The discovery dampened his elation. He stood abruptly, brushing aside the crude map he had been studying. "We leave at dawn, wet or dry," he announced gruffly. "I'll be glad to be away from the valley—the mood here's turned bitter as gall."

Marged watched as he strode up to Glynis and wrenched her about before marching her up the narrow stair.

Toward herself Rhys had shown nothing but courtesy, yet Marged knew there was a darker, more primitive side to his nature, which he took great pains to hide. That unleashed brutality would cause Glynis much grief before the night was over.

Sun washed the Brecon valley in gold. Above the dark mountain peaks hovered mist, silver-tipped where light struck the thinning mass.

Marged was glad of her thick woolen cloak, which she wore against the morning chill. She waited astride her gelding in a boy's padded brown doublet, green hose, and rough leather boots. Without cumbersome skirts to entangle her legs, or confining bodices to stifle her breath, she felt amazingly free. Though it would have been wiser, Marged could not bear to trim her lustrous black hair. Instead she had plaited it tightly about her head, covering the sleek coronet with a faded felt hat over a green hood. The shadowing headgear also helped camouflage her strictly feminine face.

Impatient to be off, Rhys galloped back and forth beside the column, attending to last-minute details. He spared only a casual wave for Glynis, who stood sobbing in the doorway, before signaling his men to begin their journey.

Rhodri rode with them as far as the Bowenford turnoff, where Marged tearfully bid him goodbye. When his slender figure, riding the shaggy mountain pony, disappeared from view, she felt bereft. She had no reason to distrust her Welsh kinsman, but these rough men were still virtual strangers. And Marged admitted having a few qualms about her safety.

Happily, Marged's fears proved unfounded. Though Rhys found her highly attractive, he continued to treat her with respect due a noble kinswoman, and his men followed his example. Marged usually rode a pace behind him like the dutiful squire she was supposed to be, carrying his helmet and bearing his arms. At night she ached with fatigue.

Evan, Rhys's rightful squire, viewed her with the same smoldering hatred she had seen in Glynis's face. Had Marged not been strengthened by remembering that this hardship was necessary to restore Bowenford to its rightful lord, she would have found the journey to Coventry unbearable.

High summer waned as they traversed the remote Welsh valleys overshadowed by misted mountains. Long ago they had crossed the Wye. The rivers they forded now bore unfamiliar names: Lugg, Clun, Severn. Rhys stayed on the Welsh side of the border, where he had more hope of successfully begging rations for his troops from his own countrymen.

As they headed north, they heard conflicting stories about a decisive battle fought in early July at Northampton. Some accounts told of French Queen Margaret and the young Prince fleeing for their lives when King Harry was taken prisoner. Other reports said the Duke of York had accepted the King's promise of naming him heir to the throne; even now, the duke and his men took ship for France.

However disheartening the news, Rhys was convinced the defeated Lancastrian army would rally and deliver a death blow to the Yorkist rebels. They continued their journey undaunted.

In fact, so eager did Rhys appear for battle that Marged suspected he would travel to the ends of the earth if a fight was in the offing.

Though frequently lashed by rainstorms along the changeable borderland, the drenched Welsh troops did not halt, but plodded doggedly onward. Now Marged had to smile when she recalled her minor discomfort during her two-day ride to Brecon. She had not even known what it was like to be tired.

Though Rhys tried to ease her suffering, there was little he could do to cushion this long journey for a lady. When possible, he lodged Marged under a roof, but often their beds were deserted barns, hedgerows, or open fields. In fact, his undue concern for the comfort of his slender squire elicited many winks and muttered comments from local inhabitants. Only Rhys's fierce appearance and the strength of his army stilled the wagging peasant tongues.

One evening just before dusk, while they were scouting for shelter, they were startled by a disheveled lad who jumped from the hedgerow. He stood in the middle of the road, holding up his hands to halt the riders.

"What do you want?" Rhys demanded, urging his black mount closer to Marged's to protect her.

"Sir, I'm a poor lad leading my . . . my . . . lady . . . to her kinfolk. Our horses are lame. Can you spare us a mount?"

Rhys would have ridden on, had not Marged caught sight of a woman and a boy huddled behind a hedge for shelter against the harsh wind.

"See, she looks so tired. Can we not give them a ride to the nearest village?"

"We don't seek shelter in the village," the lad explained hastily. "If you're bound only a few miles, we'd be grateful for a ride."

"We're bound for England, lad. We've no time to waste on strangers." Rhys's manner was gruff. This strange party of travelers puzzled him. The woman's bedraggled gown was of silk, her cloak fur-edged. Yet so shabby did she appear as she crouched beneath the hawthorn hedge, she looked more like a beggar maid than a grand lady. The frail lad she held protectively against her side was pale as death.

"Come, lady, you can ride my mount," Marged offered generously as she slid from the saddle.

Instantly, Rhys was beside her, dark-browed, ready to condemn her foolhardy gesture. "Are you addled? What if they're decoys for a band of thieves?" he growled.

"With so much armed protection, we've little to fear from thieves," Marged called back over her shoulder as she leaned toward the noblewoman with outstretched hand. "Have you nowhere to lodge?" she asked the stranger.

"We're used to sleeping wherever we find ourselves. My son's very weak—he drank tainted water."

In the gathering twilight, Marged peered closely at the woman, who spoke with a heavy French accent. Where were her attendants? The single boy who accompanied her—a slender youth with a downy upper lip—offered poor protection. And there was something startlingly familiar about this woman's thin, haughty face. Even now, reduced as she was to so pitiful a state, her eyes flamed with arrogance.

"We'll carry you as far as yon barn," Rhys suggested. He had spotted a lopsided barn at the edge of the grainfield. "Have you money for food?"

The Frenchwoman lifted her head proudly, defiantly. "My servants robbed me, despicable cowards that they are. A helpless woman and a young boy are easy targets for the greedy."

Rhys shrugged, making a face over the woman's unbridled arrogance. After insisting that Marged remount her gelding, he led the woman to his own mount, then lifted the ailing boy to one of his soldiers' saddles. They set off in the gloom, plodding over the stubblefield. Marged took the noblewoman inside the barn. A mound of clean hay was set apart from the rest, and she pointed to it. "There, that'll make a sweet bed. My name's Marged," she added with a reassuring smile, hoping to set her at ease.

At first the noblewoman looked puzzled. "You're a woman!" she finally gasped in surprise. She glanced toward Rhys, who was posting sentries and deploying troops and horses about the barn. "So you go to war with your lover!" And the Frenchwoman, weary though she was, gave a tinkling laugh. "You're a brave wench. But then, women must be brave when our men fail us." A swift transformation to anger marred her high brow as she turned aside, her mouth set in a grim line.

Marged was about to disclaim Rhys as her lover, but decided against it. The Frenchwoman was taking pains over the boy's comfort. His lips were blue with cold. She spoke soothingly to him in French while she chafed his hands and smoothed back his lank hair. Though Marged had long ago been exposed to the language, she had mastered little. Two words, however, she could understand—*courage* and *king*.

"Now, lady, is there aught I can get you? I've a brush and a mirror in my saddlebag."

The Frenchwoman smiled somewhat derisively at Marged's offer. "Would you want to admire yourself if you looked like this?" she asked.

"Were I as lovely as you, madame, yes, I would seek to admire myself if I were covered in mud from head to toe!"

The compliment vastly pleased the Frenchwoman, who grasped Marged's fingers within her own cool white hand. "Would that I could have you with me always, Mistress Marged. You've a clever tongue for flattery. You do my heart good."

"Thank you, madame."

"Why do you call me that?"

"Because you're a French noblewoman. I know it sounds ridiculous, yet I'm convinced I know you from somewhere."

The other woman's expression turned guarded. "Know me? No—that's impossible. You can't know me. I've never traveled these parts before."

"What about Hereford, madame? I've often visited there with my father. Our castle lies nearby."

"Never," the Frenchwoman said sharply, turning away.

Even her mannerisms struck Marged as familiar. The way she fluttered her hands when upset, and that sharp, arrogant tilting of her head, as if she wore a crown—a crown! Marged fell back in awe. Suddenly, like a great tapestry unfolding, she saw again the grand procession to Hereford Cathedral. She had leaned from Master Henton's balcony to gaze upon King Harry Lancaster and his young French wife—

"Madame! Oh, madame! Forgive me for my ignorance,"

Marged gasped, falling to her knees in the straw. "You are the Queen!"

"No! Get up, you fool wench! I'm not the Queen . . ." The Frenchwoman's agitated voice faded as she observed the men listening from their posts around the small barn.

His face stricken, Rhys rushed inside and knelt on his knees before her; his soldiers, observing the moving scene, followed suit. "I too recognize you now, madame. I saw you in Chester Cathedral, dressed all in cloth of gold. Forgive me, but until now I knew you not."

Appalled, Queen Margaret shrank deeper into the shadows. These people appeared loyal, but without an armed entourage, she could not be too trusting. "You're Lancastrian supporters?" she asked, her eyes narrowed, her voice guarded.

"Yes. We're ever loyal to England's throne."

Queen Margaret hesitated. Then she smiled, inclining her head slightly toward the kneeling group, whose homage before a ragged woman with holes in her shoes appeared ludicrous. "I bless you for your loyalty. Carry England's heir to safety and you shall be rewarded."

"We need no reward beyond your blessing, madame," Rhys said reverently, taking the slender white hand she extended for his kiss. "My men will escort you without thought for their own danger."

Queen Margaret smiled again, woodenly. She indicated Marged. "Will you give me this wench to serve me?"

"Were she not a freewoman, I would insist on presenting her to you as a token of my devotion," Rhys said, standing when the Queen gestured for him to rise. "She will be delighted to wait on you."

Marged was not overjoyed by his statement. She forced a smile, going down on her knees before the Queen. "It will be my honor to serve you."

"We must make haste before our enemies learn our whereabouts. Those Yorkist traitors seek to kill my son. This brave lad is leading us to safety."

John, the bedraggled youth, smiled shyly as he stepped forward. "I'm taking the Queen to Harlech."

"We'll escort you part of the way," Marged offered quickly,

knowing those would be Rhys's wishes. When later he smiled at her, his hazel eyes warm, she knew she had pleased him with her suggestion.

Thus their journey to England in search of Sir Richard Bowen was delayed while they escorted King Harry's French consort through Wales' wildest country.

They finally parted from Queen Margaret one sunny morn beside Bala Lake, a great placid silver pool where herons skimmed the shining water, and fish leaped high to ruffle its silky surface. Supposedly, beneath this lake lay an enchanted palace, but Queen Margaret had neither the time, nor the interest to listen to the legend told by the vastly perturbed bard who was to escort her on the next leg of her journey.

Marged reined in beside Rhys on the barren hillside, to watch the white-robed bard leading Queen Margaret's horse into the green valley. Riding beside his mother was the young Lancastrian prince astride a milk-white pony. John Amesbury, the royal pair's youthful rescuer, brought up the rear.

"By God, am I glad to be shut of that arrogant bitch!"

Marged turned in the saddle, her jaw gaping with surprise at Rhys's unexpected statement. "You . . . you . . . she's the Queen!"

"That doesn't prevent her being an arrogant bitch. No wonder King Harry dallies not in her bed. One glare from those devilish eyes would castrate the staunchest man."

Laughing at the shocked expression on her lovely face, Rhys said, "Come, Cousin Marged, are we not eager for war? The year hastens on. And the nights grow cold. Today I heard that the King's army has rallied and heads north. Now race me to yon lake, my beauteous squire, for I'm weary of acting the servant, all mealy mouthed and proper. God damn all French queens and consign them to hell!" With that, Rhys set spur to his mount and careened down the slope toward the glistening lake.

Gasping with mingled surprise and delight, Marged urged her gelding to follow him. She rejoiced in the sharp wind slicing through her clothing and tugging at her hat, trying to snatch her coiled hair from its fastening. Rhys was right. She too was weary of attending Queen Margaret. The blood of the ancient princes of Powys waxed far too proud to enjoy servility!

{ *five* }

THE FROSTED GRASS sparkled beneath the rising sun as the horses labored uphill. Their breaths steamed and their hooves rang out hollowly on the frozen track before Rolfe paused to survey Bowenford, which in the distance looked somber against the pale sky. A series of questions surged through his mind. Would Marged welcome him with open arms? Had she, all these lonely months apart, ached for his kisses, his lovemaking? A smile played around his finely chiseled mouth as he pictured her dewy-eyed welcome, the touch of her shapely, clinging arms around his body. Impatiently he dismissed the dream; a fiery wench like Marged would never greet him softly and penitently. More likely she would try to scratch his eyes out for leaving her imprisoned in the castle so long.

His laughter pealed out as he urged his mount forward. What enjoyment subduing her would bring. And later, when he had won her over with sweet kisses and caresses—

Rolfe glanced up at the silent towers looming before him.

His throat went dry. It was unwise to re-create too vividly those hours pressed against her satin-smooth body, for the mere thought turned him as hot as the August sun.

Alys gaped in amazement at the small party of horsemen riding beneath the raised portcullis; their pennants, marked by the scarlet de Bretayne arms, flapped arrogantly in the gloom.

"Attire me suitably for company, you dolt," she cried impatiently, pushing Joan aside when she was handed a white linen gown and plain brown surcoat. "Bring the blue sarcenet with the velvet surcoat. Don't you know who just entered the castle?"

Mutely, Joan shook her head. It had not taken long for her to regret becoming Lady Alys's maid. Whatever she did was never to that lady's liking, and Lady Alys waxed more vindictive with each passing day.

"Sometimes I think you're naught but a peasant's get, so dense do you appear," Alys snapped as she squirmed inside the narrow, shimmering gown. "As my sister's barely removed from peasant stock herself, she'd not be difficult to deceive—not those—the velvet slippers, idiot!"

Joan ducked as a pair of kidskin shoes sailed over her head.

"Will you need me to attend you below, Lady Alys?" Joan asked, keeping her distance.

Alys peered at her reflection in the burnished metal disk she used as a mirror.

"Need you—of course I'll need you. Think you to lie abed till twelve of the clock while I wait upon myself?"

Alys impatiently thrust a wayward strand of hair beneath her gauze headdress. At last, when she was confident her appearance couldn't be improved, she thrust Joan before her down the chill stone stairs, and hastened toward the Great Hall.

Rolfe came indoors, glad of the welcoming warmth of this gloomy Hall. A tree trunk blazing on the stone hearth smoked the air with a resinous perfume. Servants curtsied and bowed to him, anxious not to appear lacking in courtesy. Though they had found numerous ways to outwit their temporary master, they didn't expect to be as successful with this Breton.

"Well, by God, the place appears as I left it," Rolfe remarked with surprise. "Chagall, why hang you back in the shadows? Come forward, lad, and give me an accounting of your time."

Chagall did as he was bid. His stomach pitched like a stormy sea over the prospect of having to reveal his glaring mishandling of their hostage. "Greetings, my lord, 'twas a surprise to see you riding through the gates."

Rolfe looked keenly at the slender, hesitant soldier, sensing something greatly amiss. "I've lingered these past months on the Marches in the service of the young Earl. As we didn't expect decisive action soon, he gave me leave to visit my new holding. How has the garrison fared in my absence?" He glanced about the shadowed Hall as he spoke. He was looking for Marged, but decided her pride would not allow her to come downstairs to greet him.

Chagall swallowed, and brushed back the hair from his moist brow. "All's gone well, my lord," he said, attempting to sound confident. "There've been few incidents. I tried to act in your stead as efficiently as if you, lord, had been issuing the orders."

He then made a great show of presenting a document on which he had laboriously listed each infringement of discipline, and each fine he had levied against the ranks as punishment. While his master scanned the pages, Chagall swallowed, preparing an answer for the inevitable question he knew was forthcoming. Had the nobleman not bedded the wench, his interest in her welfare might not be so great. A hostage was always valuable, but not necessarily a matter of life and death . . .

"Welcome to Bowenford," said Alys, stepping forward, a smile fixed on her wan face.

"Thank you, lady." Rolfe bowed slightly over her extended hand, touching her chill fingers to his lips. "I trust you've been treated with courtesy in my absence?"

"I've few complaints," she said sweetly.

Joan gulped at her mistress's unexpected statement. Complaints formed the warp and weft of Lady Alys's days!

Joan raised her eyes to meet the pale, steel-blue gaze of this Breton whose unexpected appearance had vastly sweetened her lady's disposition. His dark, handsome face momentarily robbed her of breath. She continued to stare, awestruck, until she felt her mistress's heel grind heavily upon her toes inside soft leather shoes.

Wincing, Joan obediently fell to her knees before their guest.

"This is my new maid, Lord Rolfe. An empty-headed chit she is, but then, we've little to choose from in this remote backwater."

He glanced casually at the bending golden head. The wench's comeliness had already caught his eye. But he had far more important matters before him than Alys's new maid. His jaw tightened impatiently over the time now being wasted on trivialities, when his sole purpose for being here burned his brain like molten steel.

"You've chosen well, lady. Now, must I stand here all day? My men are hungry. We will sup."

Alys turned aside and commanded the servants to bring forth platters of meat and bread.

Chagall, who had been most grateful for Lady Alys's timely interruption, made to follow that lady when Rolfe grabbed his sleeve and drew him aside.

"After we've supped, bring her down."

Chagall swallowed. "Who, Lord Rolfe?" he mumbled, stalling for time to prepare a brilliant defense of his misdeeds.

"I always knew you to be slow, lad, but not idiotic. Lady Marged, who else?"

"Oh, Lady Marged." Chagall looked down at his boots, where wisps from the rushes curled about the lacing. At last, growing uncomfortable beneath the piercing gaze of his superior, he realized there was nothing to do but confess the truth. He raised his eyes to meet those twin, steel-hard points, which bored through him like lances. "My lord, there's something I've not told you."

"Then tell me. I don't enjoy receiving news piecemeal. What misfortune has befallen Lady Marged?" Rolfe asked grimly.

By now a semicircle of curious soldiers and servants had drawn close. Rolfe waved them away impatiently. A great bustle of activity commenced, clattering plates and goblets, shrill commands and even sharper reprimands. Rolfe put his hand about the base of Chagall's slender neck and propelled him to the raised dais where the high table stood.

"Now tell me everything from the beginning," he ordered harshly, as he moved the reluctant soldier up the four shallow steps.

"Well, you see, my lord, it happened like this . . ." Chagall began, his face whiter than parchment.

The servants buzzed quietly in the background, and the men-at-arms glanced apprehensively around as Chagall haltingly divulged the story of Marged Bowen's escape.

Rolfe gnawed vigorously on a leg of spiced fowl, washing down the meat with glasses of rare wine tapped in honor of his homecoming. The more he heard, the angrier he grew until at last, unable to stand more, he rounded on Chagall in fury.

"So, like the fool you are, you allowed her to ride free of the castle?"

"Yes, my lord."

"God, what have you between your ears, lad—porridge? What did you expect her to do, once she had a swift horse beneath her?"

"You don't understand," he protested indignantly. "Though it anger you, lord, she—she—encouraged me to pay court to her."

Rolfe's gaze flicked over Chagall before returning to the half-filled goblet in front of him. "Encouraged? How mean you?"

"She pretended to be interested in me as a—nay, she *was* interested in me as—as a lover!"

Angry though he was, Rolfe's mouth curled in a derisive smile. "Now I've heard it all. What think you that a woman of such spirit would see in you, Chagall, simpering twit of a lad that you are?"

Indignantly, Chagall straightened his shoulders, his face crimson with embarrassment. "My lord, though I'm no champion in the lists, women have been known—"

"Spare me the details. Where is she now? Holed up in a neighbor's fortress? Well, by God, we'll drag her forth. They tell me no neighboring castle's as secure as Bowenford, and I stormed that easily enough."

Chagall glanced away. "I know not where she is."

"We'll soon find out," Rolfe growled, pushing back his chair.

At this point, Alys hastened forward and Chagall flashed her a look of deepest gratitude.

"May I have a word with you, my lord?"

"I've little time to waste in chat. You can assist me, however, by naming every stronghold within fifty miles of here."

Chagall stood to allow Alys his seat. When he dithered about uncomfortably in the background, Rolfe commanded him to fetch pen and paper.

"More wine?"

Rolfe nodded, allowing Alys to refill his goblet. Then, with the smooth liquid warmth trickling down his gullet, he turned expectantly toward her to hear what she had to say.

"There's little need for a list of neighboring castles. Marged won't be there."

"Then where is she?"

"Far from here."

"How far?"

"I know not."

"Then perhaps you'll tell me what you do know, before you try my ragged patience to the limit."

Alys smiled as she placed her slender hands on the table, where they could be seen to best advantage. "Once I was surly to you, my lord, for I resented being your prisoner. In recent months I've had much time to reconsider my attitude."

Inclining his head slightly, his mouth still grim, Rolfe acknowledged her apology.

"My stepsister's character is well known to me. And though 'tis true she did not reveal her exact destination, I know where she was bound. Nor did she flee the castle alone."

Rolfe's gasp of surprise was audible as he leaned closer. "What are you saying? Someone aided her escape? A man?"

She smiled again, pleased to have captured his complete attention with a few well-chosen words. It did her heart good to crush this conceited Breton's masculine pride with the same stroke by which she destroyed her stepsister's reputation.

"Hardly a man. A mere lad—but then, where males are concerned, Marged never was discriminating." The steely glint in his eyes boded no good, and she hastened on. "The nephew of the castle's huntsman was her accomplice. They fled to the Brecon hills. As far as I know, they are there still, for the lad's not been seen since."

"I don't believe it!"

"I know you must find it hard to accept that she chose a callow lad—"

"Her romantic choice has nothing to do with it," he snarled, draining his goblet. "Marged wouldn't do such a pointless thing. If she's fled to the mountains, it's for a purpose. Has she friends or relatives there?"

She frowned at his sharp question. "Her mother's family are Welsh. She probably has many kinsmen there—many lovers as well, considering her wanton nature."

The wine was already working its magic on his good sense, imparting a hot, liquid rage not easily cooled. Lurid pictures of Marged entwined in another's arms flitted through his mind. "I don't believe it," he uttered thickly.

"The servants have been questioned, and the huntsman and the falconer both agree with the story, my lord," said Chagall, pushing a roll of parchment, a quill, ink, and sand before his master. "I know I was a fool to trust her. And I'll gladly suffer whatever punishment you choose."

"Make no mistake about that," Rolfe snarled, turning about in his chair. "You were charged with the safekeeping of a hostage. A weak, puny wench. And you, with an armed garrison at your back, allowed her to escape. You defied my orders not to allow her beyond the walls, because she flattered your vanity. By the Christ, your sire did you an ill service the day he chose you for a soldier! Far better to have let you pule away your days beside a lute!" Rolfe paused, noting the mounting amusement in Alys's face.

Without a backward glance, Chagall fled his master's wrath on quaking legs. His lip curled in derision, Rolfe watched the yellow-haired figure collide with a serving wench in the doorway, spilling her platter of apples to the rushes. He shook his head in disbelief.

"He's the fool? 'Twas I who was the greater fool to have left him in charge. Yet of late he'd proved almost worthy of the name 'soldier.'"

"He really should not be blamed too harshly. Marged's quite clever at bending men to her will," Alys said, pleased to see a growing flush of anger creeping up his face.

Rolfe scowled. "Aye, she's a temptress all right." He half rose; then, thinking better of it, he sat down heavily in the carved master's chair. "I rode all night without sleep," he muttered, as a wave of wine-induced self-pity washed over him. God damn her for her treachery! All these months, while he had battled the desire to return to her, the little sorceress had been safely enfolded in another's arms. Not for one minute did he believe she had chosen a half-green lad as her lover; there were full-grown men aplenty who would welcome such women as she with open arms. God damn Marged for her treachery! God damn himself for his own stupidity!

"A chamber has been prepared for your rest, Lord Rolfe. I'll extend as much hospitality as I'm able in an effort to ease your disappointment."

Alys studied him with pleasure, realizing that the flight of her wanton stepsister had wounded him sorely. Men were such fools! How eager they were to consider themselves lovers without compare, waxing so confident after one swift plumbing that they never dreamed the object of their affections would ever have need of another's arms.

"Thank you, Lady Alys." He stood, planting his hands firmly on the hard edge of the table. "I'm pleased to find your manner changed for the better. I commend you on the transformation."

She smiled, her mouth tight. How dare he speak so condescendingly to her! But she was too wise to allow her anger to show.

"I'm no fool," she said as sweetly as she could manage. "When I'm bested by superior strength, I bend."

The answering smile he gave her was more like a snarl.

For three days Rolfe remained at Bowenford, his mood alternating between anger and pain. Chagall's punishment remained undecided.

Every morning, Rolfe hunted in the surrounding forests without success. The wild gallop through the lonely countryside relieved his heartache at being spurned by Marged. What had he expected? Misunderstanding and anger had already come between them before he left Bowenford. Until the last minute he had waited for Marged to relent and give him a handclasp, or at least a parting smile—he had not expected kisses. But she, overburdened with fierce Bowen pride, had remained unbending. Angered by her indifference, he rode forth to the Yorkist camp on that early summer morn in a towering rage, cursing the lovely creature who had destroyed his peace of mind. Yet, as he rode north during the weeks to come, his anger had gradually palled to discontent, then tolerance, and finally love. Aye, he had been fool enough to imagine himself deeply in love with that black-haired Welsh temptress. No more!

Rolfe reined in abruptly. Glowering, he sat with his hands clenched on the reins while branches whispered overhead, the leaves pattering like rain. Here he was, whining and moaning like a lovesick poet. God knows, there was no shortage of women. He had always known celibacy did not become him. Let Marged Bowen writhe in ecstasy within her lover's arms. The soft, pulsating warmth of a female body beneath his own would rapidly erase his painful memory of her.

His set jaw like steel, his hands clamped like vises on the leather, he wheeled about, startling the nearby members of his hunting party.

"Home!" he bellowed. "I've had enough of this fruitless pastime."

Then, leading the pack like a frenzied demon, he gave the stallion his head, careening over the mossy glades toward Bowenford.

"Why is it my punishment to have to endure such clumsiness?" Alys screeched, lashing out at Joan as she stooped to pick up the pieces of a shattered scent flagon.

"If you hadn't screamed at me so, perhaps my hands wouldn't have shaken," Joan retorted, her pretty face flushed.

"I can't believe my ears. Did you say what I thought you said? How dare you speak back to me, you—you penniless drab! How dare you raise your voice to me!"

Defiantly, Joan met her mistress's angry glare. She clutched the pieces of broken glass in the folds of her skirt. "I'm not some little village chit that you can speak to like dirt."

"How do I know you're not the get of a common laborer? A knight, indeed! How very romantic. More than likely your mother had no idea who fathered her brat."

Joan's hand trembled with anger, yet she was too wise to strike her mistress; Lady Alys had beaten her several times, for far less serious crimes. "My father was a knight. I told you true."

"Get out of my sight, you clumsy, arrogant creature. 'Tis a pity my sister didn't take you with her. Perchance you'd have been humbled long before now amidst those hill savages. No, I'm to blame, poor, soft-hearted fool that I am, for having allowed you special privileges. You've had more than enough chances to prove your worth."

Joan flung the shattered glass on the ash in the hearth. Blood was trickling from cuts on her fingers. "May I dress my wounds, Lady Alys?" she asked.

"Aye, go, before you bleed all over my new surcoat."

Long after Joan's departure, Alys pondered over a suitable method of humbling the arrogant little chit.

"A born whore if ever I saw one!" she muttered fiercely, and swished to the window. And to think she must be grateful for the doubtful privilege of having Joan Vaughn to serve her. A woman of her noble birth should be attended by a retinue instead of by one clumsy, base-born wench from a village. Being dependent for sustenance upon the master of Bowenford was a constant thorn in her side.

Across the meadows Alys could see riders returning from the hunt, their garments bright splashes against the changing landscape. Autumn already touched the trees with gold. Too soon it would be winter. She winced at the thought of spending another bleak winter at Bowenford, especially with only these dullards for company.

The familiar broad-shouldered figure of the Breton drew closer to the castle walls, his outsized horse covering the ground at a furious pace. As Alys watched, an idea surged to her brain—an idea so fitting, she gasped with delight. Tonight the handsome Breton would have a woman to soothe his temper and defuse the anger in his soul. Arrogant Joan would play the whore. Oh, why had she not thought of that solution before? She had seen the little fool gazing at him with admiration. After tonight, Joan would view the Breton in a far different light. When she came to him as a faceless whore, she'd learn soon enough about the dark lust in the male soul—that callous, despicable legacy devoid of even the pretense of affection. Aye, Joan would come to know the torment Alys had endured at the hands of her cruel husband. An evil smile suffused Alys's features as she dwelled on such sweet revenge. Wet with his sweat, debased by his coarse utterings, the wench's arrogance would soon flee.

Alys turned from the window, her high, fair brow puckering at a sudden distressing thought. What if the Breton treated Joan with respect? What if he actually gave the wretch pleasure instead of pain? Though she herself had never even approached pleasure in Hubert's loathsome embrace, she knew some women sought their paramours with delight. Perchance all men were not such bestial creatures.

Alys paused, her hand on the door. She had no intention of giving Joan pleasure. The Breton should have wine aplenty to release his basest carnal appetite, mixed with a draft of *Maman's* black powder. The recipe was in her ancient herbal, which she treasured with almost the same devotion as her pearl-inlaid psalter.

The exciting plan brought color to Alys's cheeks, and she hummed with pleasure as she descended the narrow stairs. With a single stroke she would debase haughty Joan and expose the shallowness of the Breton's supposed devotion to Marged. And, if perchance her stepsister's avowed hatred of the handsome Breton proved untrue, as Alys suspected, dearest Marged would be beside herself in anguish to discover how easily consoled he had been in her absence. All in all, this was the most satisfying scheme she had ever devised.

Rolfe lounged at the high table, a goblet of heavy wine in his hand, while he listened to a minstrel sing of brave deeds and stirring battles. The meal he had just finished had been far more enjoyable than he had expected. There had been a haunch of roast venison, platters of stuffed crane, fruit flummeries, and sugared confections. Lady Alys had dined him admirably. She had even provided entertainment, which, though hardly of the caliber of the French minstrels, was superb for so backward a region. In fact, had Lady Alys not gone to such obvious pains to please him, Rolfe would already have been on the road to the camp recently set up in the Marches for supporters of Edward, the Duke of York. So disappointed had she appeared when he announced his intention to depart, that he relented. One further day's delay mattered little.

"Will you take more wine, my lord?" Alys inquired sweetly, holding the jug poised above his goblet.

He glanced at her thin face with misting vision. Perhaps, on their previous meeting, he had misjudged this woman, for now she appeared suitably chastened, even anxious to please. "Thank you, Lady Alys, your hospitality knows no bounds," he replied thickly as he accepted the refilled goblet.

Alys smiled charmingly, her glance flicking toward the men-at-arms sprawled around the lower tables. A young lad was turning cartwheels about the Hall, while his sister played a tambour. All appeared most satisfactory.

"Please excuse me a moment, Lord Rolfe, I'm needed in the kitchens."

Rolfe nodded his assent, twisting in his chair to watch the children spin gay wheels of color about the Great Hall, to the drunken applause of his soldiers. He knew he should chastise the men for their rowdiness, but he decided not to spoil their sport.

Alys hastened through the chill stone corridors to her chamber, where Joan was waiting. Earlier in the evening she had craftily voiced her displeasure over an imagined fault, exiling the girl from the warmth and laughter of the Great Hall.

At her entrance, Joan leaped from the bed where she had been dozing.

"How dare you lie on my bed, you lazy creature! Have you no tasks to occupy your idle hands? It's still light enough for stitching," Alys railed, her tone not as sharp as usual, for her heart was not really in the scolding. "I declare, you're so lazy, I've a good mind to send you packing."

Joan's brown eyes widened, and her heart began a frightened beat. "Oh, lady, please, have pity on me," she said, trying to keep her voice steady. "I've nowhere else to go." And though it took much effort, she swallowed her pride and fell to her knees. "Please. I'll try harder to please you."

Alys looked contemptuously at her bent fair head and swished her skirts free of the young woman's clinging hand. "It's hopeless. You're not from gentle stock, as I was led to believe. Your every action proves that."

"I did not lie to you. My father was a knight."

"Your mother was nothing but a whore. 'Tis written all over your face. The artful way you smile at men, the way you sidle up to them, fluttering your eyelashes—a true daughter of a knight would never act so sluttish."

Appalled by the harsh, condemning words, Joan angrily rocked back on her heels, and glared up at her tall, unyielding mistress who, in her gown, looked like a column of sea-green silk that began to blur. "My mother was no whore!"

"Well, you can't stay here, and that's final," Alys snapped as she stopped pacing and looked at the prostrate girl.

"Oh, please, lady, force me not onto the highways," Joan pleaded, tears spilling down her pink cheeks. "I'll do anything for you. I'll even work in the kitchens. Only please, please, don't turn me out."

Alys listened to the wench's tearful pleas, vastly enjoying the sight of Joan, now humbled on her knees. "Anything?" she asked at last. "You say you're prepared to do anything if I allow you to stay at Bowenford?"

"Aye, lady, anything," Joan whispered, alerted by the sharp change in her mistress's voice. "What would you have me do?"

Snaking closer, Alys seized handfuls of Joan's golden hair and pulled the kneeling girl to her feet, ignoring Joan's gasps of pain. "You've repeatedly angered me with your airs, with references to your noble birth. We both know your mother chose the likeliest sire in the stable as your father. A knight, indeed! Your mother was naught but a whore, turned out by her family . . ." She stopped, for Joan winced, showing that Alys had struck truth. "Repeat after me: I am the nameless get of a common whore." Her eyes glittered menacingly as she twisted Joan's hair tightly about her hands. "Say it," she exhorted, foam flecking her thin lips. "Kneel and say it, or you'll be out on the roads this very night."

Tears stung Joan's eyes, but only when Alys bent her head back cruelly, repeating the sentence like a sacred litany, did her pride dissolve.

Joan's lips, gone dry, moved in a croaking confession. "I am the nameless get of a common whore."

"And don't you ever forget it!" Alys finally released the sobbing girl and stepped back to gloat. "From now on, there'll be no more mention of your knighted sire. You're nothing but a serving wench. I'll continue to house you out of Christian charity." Alys smiled as Joan gasped in relief. "But first, my dear, pretty Joan, you must perpetuate your accursed birth."

Joan looked at her mistress with loathing, at the same time feeling relief at not being cast out from these protective walls. "What else must I say?" she whispered, her pride, her dignity, sacrificed to appease this vindictive noblewoman.

"Because, by your own admission you're the true daughter of a whore, you are to pleasure our conquering lord. Men despise sluts and use them with contempt. So, as a final purging of your sinful pride, you are to be shown how men treat a paid woman. 'Tis a valuable lesson which should last you the rest of your days."

"Oh, please, lady, please. I'm chaste. Don't force me to this indignity."

"Ha! Chaste!" Alys struck her sharply across the mouth. "Don't lie to me! You're just like your mother. I can see it in your face. You aren't chaste. No doubt you're known to every knave this side of Pontrilas."

Joan wanted to refuse—the very words were on her lips—but the prospect of tramping the country lanes with winter coming on, of being raped by wandering bands of lawless men, stilled her tongue. Hanging her head in shame, she whispered, "Whatever is your will, Lady Alys."

"And don't think because he's handsome there'll be any joy to it," Alys screeched, dragging Joan to her feet. "Men are vile creatures. A woman's body is naught but a vessel for their amusement. You'll soon discover there's little sweetness in a man's bed. Oh, don't think I haven't seen you simpering at him, fluttering your eyelashes, trying to gain favors."

The room was already growing dim, and Alys hastily checked her tongue. Twilight was virtually spent. Had she already tarried too long? The potion she had mixed in the Breton's wine should have stirred him well enough by now, yet if he consumed too much, he may already have succumbed to sleep.

Gritting her teeth until her jaw ached, Alys grabbed Joan by the hair and dragged her toward the door. If she was too late, she would flog the vain, silly creature senseless.

"Go now," she screamed. "You know which is Lord Rolfe's room. Don't speak to him, he has no desire for discourse with a whore."

Once Joan was safely inside the Breton's chamber, Alys sped toward the Great Hall. She was dismayed to find the soldiers sprawling half off their benches; some were already snoring in the rushes. There were others, however, who could not be satisfied with sleep. Quickly she averted her eyes from the close-locked couples murmuring in the shadows. Those foolish kitchen sluts would discover soon enough there was but fleeting delight in a man's attentions. That was a lesson she had learned well from her debauched husband, God rot his soul!

Alys glanced toward the high table. To her relief, she found the Breton still in possession of his faculties, though he lolled indolently in his carved chair. He laughed while he diced with another soldier. Alys was cheered to discover him still capable of treating haughty Joan as she justly deserved.

"My lord, will you not retire? The hour grows late and you're to depart at dawn," Alys said, stepping behind him, trying to mask the excitement in her voice.

He turned around in surprise. "Why, Lady Alys, I thought you'd retired."

"I've been making further arrangements for your comfort," Alys said meaningfully, knowing he understood from the swift expression of surprise that crossed his handsome face.

"Then I shan't prove ungrateful by dallying below," he uttered thickly. When he stood, the murky, smoke-hazed Hall swam before his eyes. "I'll bid you good night," he mumbled to his companion.

Anxiously, Alys watched his broad-shouldered figure unsteadily crossing the Hall. Had she been too heavy-handed with the potion? An aphrodisiac was always difficult to administer.

By rights he should have requested a woman hours ago, yet perhaps the large quantity of wine rendered the formula less potent. Next time she would experiment with a different mixture.

"Go after your lord. Instruct him to pay the woman first."

The soldier with whom Rolfe had been gaming nodded and sprinted away, registering no surprise over the lady's suggestion. Women were as regularly provided for his master's amusement as were food and drink.

When Rolfe pushed open the door to his chamber, he was surprised to find the room in darkness; the shutters were already secured. A dying fire in the hearth provided the only source of light, and its red embers glowed faintly in a far corner, casting the rest of the chamber into deep shadow. It was so dark he could not see the woman who awaited him. Perhaps that was intentional—there might not have been a beauty available at such short notice. Lady Alys's thoughtfulness had surprised him greatly. Hostesses were frequently called upon to provide bodily comforts for their male guests. And not all hostesses had offered him paid women.

"Am I not to see your face?" he asked the unseen presence rustling under the bedcovers.

"Nay . . . I . . . I'm ashamed."

He shrugged indifferently over her tearful confession and secured the door. Normally fastidious about such liaisons, he wondered why he did not care to see the nameless creature who would soon dispel his gnawing ache. The strange wine must share the blame, he decided. Such a fine, heavy elixir it had been, he would take some back for young Edward of March, he thought, letting his mind wander along unrelated paths.

"Here's your silver," he mumbled, becoming aware of the leather purse clutched in his hand. "I was told you required payment first."

Rolfe struggled to remove his clothing, his hands unsteady, his legs virtually refusing to do as they were bid.

Loud sobs erupted from the bed. Christ, what a misery Lady Alys had procured for him! He paused, steadying himself against the bedpost. He had half a mind to forego this doubtful pleasure, yet as his eyes grew accustomed to the dark, he could dimly perceive the girl's soft body, the glint of her pale hair spread on the pillow. No longer hesitant, he threw off his clothing, knowing if he did not soon claim his prize, he would be physically unable to enjoy Lady Alys's generosity. It was strange that such a dried-up stick of a woman should be considerate of a man's baser needs. She was a widow; perchance she was used to providing women for her husband's guests.

When the bed dipped beneath his weight, Joan stiffened, steeling herself neither to weep nor shrink under his searching hands. Oh, how ashamed she was! This man, upon whom she had gazed with admiration, considered her naught but a common whore, a woman purchased to satisfy a need, much as a flagon of ale slaked his thirst, or a hunk of pork his hunger.

"What's your name?" he mumbled as he explored the silky contours of her soft breasts.

"Joan." She had intended to lie, but thought better of it. If she gave a false name and her lady learned of the deception, she would be beaten for lying.

"Joan, you're the comeliest wench I've known for several months," he said thickly, his mouth hot against her neck. "Come, be not so modest. You lie there stiff as a convent virgin."

Making a great effort to stay her tears, Joan allowed him to draw her close, to explore the secrets of her body, which she had guarded so virtuously for her future husband. Now it no longer mattered. There would be no husband—Lady Alys had seen to that. When first she laid eyes on Lord Rolfe, she had entertained romantic fantasies about his kisses, his embraces; she had even speculated modestly about his lovemaking, never realizing she was soon to be in his bed. But all the sweet delight she had imagined, the pleasure, the tenderness of his words, did not come. To him she was nothing. He knew not who she was, nor did he care. Her shame complete, Joan gritted her teeth to quiet her sobs.

Rolfe's concentration was hard won, though desire was a pounding furnace in his blood. He pulled the wench against him, fitting her to his body; when she tried to withdraw, he exerted even more force, wondering at this strange game.

"Look, Joan—or whatever your name is—tonight I'm not interested in games. You need not act the injured virgin. I'm far too drunk to care. Just lie still and be a good girl," he muttered, pinning her beneath him when she tried to squirm free. His mouth clamped as hard as steel over hers, devouring her lips, his teeth bruising her soft flesh.

"Oh, my lord, I'm—" she protested no more as he mounted her and the pain, which should have been sweet pleasure, robbed her of speech. Time stretched endlessly. Eventually, Joan returned from the blackness of pain to feel his hands against her face, his thick voice in her ear, unsteady, penitent—

"By the Christ! You weren't acting—you were virgin!"

She did not speak, but merely turned aside as tears coursed a river down her cheeks.

"Listen . . . I'm sorry . . . too much wine . . . I didn't mean to hurt you."

Joan nodded and bit her lip, moved by his obvious sincerity. "I know," she croaked. She lay silent, listening to rain dripping from the battlements.

Forcing himself from under a smothering blanket of weariness, Rolfe touched her arm when she moved to the far side of the bed. "Stay, if you wish. I'll not touch you again. God knows, I'm so weary, you're safe as . . ."

Joan was waiting for him to complete the sentence when she realized he had fallen asleep. Grief throbbed through her body in humiliating waves. She was afraid the shuddering bed would disturb him, but he slept like one dead. After tonight she would never feel the same worshiping admiration for a handsome man. What a romantic fool she had been! The wonderful act of love about which she had dreamed had nothing to do with tenderness and pleasure. Yet it was not his fault; he had not been unkind to her.

As her tears subsided, Joan slid from beneath the covers and crossed the room to the now sputtering fire to light the candle that had been on the chest beside the bed. How peacefully he slept! In fact, so deep was his slumber, it was unnatural. Fear flickered in her stomach as she reached out and laid her hand upon his chest, finding his matted black hair strange to the touch; she had never touched a man's naked body before. To her relief, she found that his heart beat low and steady.

Lady Alys must have given him a potion to induce sleep, for Joan had seen her stir a powder into the wine flagon. Though she was sure it had not been her mistress's intent, the dark room had salved a little of her pride. Tomorrow, when she faced Lord Rolfe, she knew he would not know it was she who had warmed his bed.

Cleaning herself as best she could, Joan replaced her shift and gown, and listened to the rain pattering against the stone. She felt surprisingly reluctant to leave this room, and the thought of Lady Alys eagerly awaiting a report of the encounter made her even more hesitant.

In the candlelight her gaze roamed over the sleeping man's broad shoulders, over his smooth back to his unblemished buttocks and lean, muscular thighs. As she gazed at him, a strange emotion stirred deep inside her belly, revealing that her romantic dreams were not wholly destroyed. Perhaps, given different circumstances, Lord Rolfe might have been tender toward her, for he did not appear to be a cruel man.

He lay on his stomach, his face turned from her. Tentatively she touched his black hair, lying like pitch upon the pillow; it felt springy beneath her fingers. Asleep, in the dim light, he appeared younger and more vulnerable, far less the masterful foreign conqueror. A fleeting memory of his pale blue eyes, which at first meeting had briefly regarded her with admiration, flashed before her. Tonight, had he known who she was, Lord Rolfe might even have treated her affectionately.

He had come back to Bowenford to woo Lady Marged. Now that she was lost to him, he would need another woman. Why couldn't she be that woman?

Joan clasped her hands, thrilled by the idea. That way she would leave Bowenford in glory. And best of all, Lord Rolfe would protect her from her mistress's vengeance! When he discovered she was no common wench, likely he would treat her as a lady—but he was to depart on the morrow!

Joan paced the room, shivering in the chill atmosphere. Naked as he was, he too must feel the cold. Tenderly she drew the covers over his shoulders, tucking the blanket around his powerful neck as if she covered a child. Sometimes men took women with them to battle, for her father had told her stirring tales of lovely ladies who followed their knights. Why could she not travel with Lord Rolfe? Though she doubted he would take her willingly to England. What if she hid inside a supply wagon until they were far away? Surely he wouldn't return her to Bowenford.

Joan ran across the deserted bailey in the pattering rain, heading for the black-shadowed supply wagons awaiting tomorrow's departure. Warily she glanced about, afraid one of the sentries had spotted her; satisfied she had not been seen, she turned back the waterproof covering on one of the wagons and scrambled inside where she secured the canvas as best she could before burrowing among the blankets.

In the dismal rainy dawn, Rolfe dragged himself into the saddle. He felt as if he had been felled like a tree trunk. His head pounded and his limbs ached so much, he could barely move. Sweet and potent Lady Alys's fine wine might have been, but it would never tempt him again.

"Godspeed, my lord," Alys said, impulsively reaching for his hand.

"Thank you, Lady Alys," he replied gruffly. A wry smile crossed his face as he leaned toward her to ask, "By the Christ, from whence did you buy such potent wine? I've never felt this close to death before."

Alys smiled, her cheeks dimpling. "Oh, 'tis on account of a secret potion I use to enhance the flavor. A recipe from my dear *maman's* family."

"Can I tempt you to part with a bottle to present to my commander?"

"Of course. You may take with you a goodly supply. In fact, I've already instructed your men to pack twelve bottles in the wagons."

"You're truly a generous lady," Rolfe said, lifting Alys's hand to his mouth.

The caressing warmth of his lips against her skin made Alys shudder. Stricken by her unexpected response, she gazed up at him, desperate to discard this unsettling emotion. His dark face was shadowed in the gloom, his luminous eyes appeared startlingly pale as he regarded her solemnly.

"My lord, we've found a wench . . ."

Alys jumped back, pulling away her hand as Rolfe shifted his attention to a soldier who pointed to the supply wagons. It was ridiculous to have been disarmed by his touch! This despised Breton was unworthy of even her smallest attention, and yet—

"A wench has been found hiding in a wagon, Lady Alys. Mayhap a dissatisfied kitchen maid athirst for adventure," Rolfe said, half turning in the saddle as a cloak-swathed figure was dragged from the wagon. "You'd best discipline the wench, but be not too harsh. No doubt she had a heart full of dreams."

Hardly comprehending his words, Alys stared up at him, seeing, as if for the first time, his beautiful, sensual mouth, and imagining the pressure of his lips against hers. Jealousy, hot and painful, washed over her body. To think she had knowingly thrust Joan in his bed, had given that insolent slut the privilege of his caresses, when she herself might have tasted at long last that mystical thing called *love!*

With a curt wave, Rolfe headed for the gate. He thought Lady Alys must also be suffering the aftereffects of the wine, for she stared at him like one crazed. He could spare no more valuable time for her. Rain dripped miserably inside his collar and he hunched down, trying to stay dry. All in all, he regretted not leaving yesterday as he had intended. Though at the time it had seemed enjoyable, this morning he cursed himself for drinking so much. Then suddenly he remembered the mystery wench! Christ, he had almost forgotten that private gift for which he should have thanked his hostess! The woman was already gone when he woke. In fact, he had not given her more than a passing thought, occupied as he was with the tasks of walking and dressing, which this morning seemed monumental, absorbing his entire attention.

As his head pounded with renewed fervor, he carefully adjusted his helmet to relieve the pressure. A scowl on his face, he motioned impatiently to the straggling troops, urging them forward. The prospect of two days' hard ride turned him as sour as quince jelly.

Standing frozen like a statue, Alys watched the riders canter over the drawbridge. She was so stunned by her unexpected passion, she was hardly aware when a soldier dragged a sobbing woman before her.

"Here, Lady Alys, isn't this your maid?"

The words shocked Alys back to the present. She blanched as she saw Joan dressed for traveling, squirming in the iron grip of the burly soldier. "So you're the wench who seeks to follow the soldiers!" Color burned fiery spots on Alys's cheeks.

"Will you deal with her, lady?"

"Aye, I'll deal with her, you can be sure of that," she said grimly, seizing Joan's arm and dragging her away.

The gray, rainy morning still hovered low over the castle as Joan huddled on the floor, her back bruised by the beating. Long ago her sobs had subsided, and now she was numb with sorrow for plans gone awry. Why, oh, why had Lady Alys decided to present Lord Rolfe with those bottles, exposing her hiding place?

"One taste of your true calling and you lose your wits," Alys snarled, dragging Joan upright. "I could rip every hair from your head, you wanton creature. Far from humbling you, I gave you a grand prize."

Joan looked at her angry mistress through pain-dazed eyes. "Think you playing the whore is a prize?"

"Don't you dare question me! So fine a man did I give you, I must have been out of my mind. You should have been sport for his men. After a dozen or so had used you, mayhap you'd have decided in favor of waiting on me. An overabundance of common soldier's lust would soon have sharpened your resolve to try harder to please."

Panting with suppressed rage, she threw Joan aside, and was beside herself with passion. What had she done? The Breton's bed had proved so delightful, the wanton creature had tried to follow him to war. Her method of humbling the arrogant little wretch had failed miserably. Alys longed to ask for details of the encounter, but her pride forbade the indulgence.

"Listen to me, you little whore! Never will I let you forget the day you tried to follow Lord Rolfe. You'll pay for it a hundredfold. Why think you he'd want to lay eyes on you again? To him you're nothing but a whore—a woman who sells herself for bread. Put aside your foolish ideas of love. He wouldn't even spit on you, were he not in desperate need. Never mention him again. Do you hear?"

Mutely, Joan nodded, though a new idea was already surging through her brain. If she did not get away from Bowenford, she knew she would eventually strike Lady Alys. It was growing harder to ignore her hateful taunts, her cruel ways. One wagon remained in the bailey. Even now, men hammered a repaired wheel in place. When the soldiers came indoors to sup, they wouldn't see her slip beneath the covering.

"I promise to abide by all your wishes, Lady Alys," she said, her eyes downcast. "May I have permission to go to the chapel to pray? Perhaps there, if I repent in true humility, I shall be granted absolution for my sins."

Alys stepped back, surprised by the girl's request. "Whores are denied the succor of heaven, don't you know that?" she snarled. Then, suddenly anxious to be rid of the reminder of her own foolishness, Alys thrust Joan away. "Aye, go, wear out your knees before the altar. But remember, there are not prayers enough to rid you of the stain of sin. Don't come down to sup. Prayer can be your sustenance for the rest of the day."

With that, Lady Alys marched to the door and, without a backward glance, stamped out.

For a few minutes Joan did not move, stunned by the unexpected granting of her request. Only when she realized the hammering had ceased, did she come alive. A glance through the window at the lowering sky assured her it still rained. The soldiers were no fools; they would enjoy their meal and the warm, dry Hall as long as they could, for it could be many a day before they indulged in such luxury again.

Before noon the rain stopped. Alys watched the repaired wagon lumbering beneath the raised portcullis, and her heart fluttered unexpectedly as she dwelled upon its destination. Rolfe might use supplies from the wagon; he might even ride beside it. With an ecstatic sigh, she clasped her palpitating heart, wondering at the strange anguish she had known all day. How she longed to follow that wagon! Yet a lady of noble birth did not act like an irresponsible kitchen wench. She must woo Rolfe with charm. Until now he had seen her only as temporary mistress of Bowenford; she must make him see her as a woman. When next they met, she would be finely arrayed. She would charm him. She would put even stronger love potions in his food, she decided, since the thought crossed her mind that he might remain unmoved by her seductive maneuvers. But most important of all, she would keep Joan out of his sight. Alys was far too clever to pit her charms against those of a woman ten years her junior.

Alys walked across the squelching bailey, her mind flitting between the delightfully stirring vision of Rolfe's handsome face and the nauseating reminder of naked Joan enfolded in his arms.

{ six }

SNOWFLAKES WHIRLED IN the north wind. Marged hunched low in the saddle and pulled her dark wool cloak tighter about her neck.

"A wild-goose chase," Rhys grumbled at her elbow, his dark face set in an ugly scowl. "To Yorkshire and back we go, obedient as little lambs. Though my sense tells me nay, I'd swear Sir Richard deliberately avoids us."

"You talk like a fool!"

"No woman speaks to me like that!"

"Let go of me."

Marged wrenched her bridle from his grasp. By spurring her gelding's flanks, she maintained a good distance between them, choosing to ride alone rather than suffer his churlish company.

During this long journey, possessiveness had gradually overtaken Rhys's chivalry. If she did not want to arouse his ire, she dared not stray far from his sight. Despite the growing tension between them, Rhys had remained tireless in his pursuit of her father's men. Yet, however diligent they were throughout the long, dark winter, they had stayed one step behind Sir Richard's force.

On a boulder-strewn hillock, Marged reined in her mount to survey the bleak landscape stretching to the horizon before her. They had ridden to the West Riding of Yorkshire in bitter weather, only to learn that at Sandal Magna, outside Wakefield, the Lancastrians had defeated the Duke of York beneath the walls of his mighty castle. After the battle, the Duke had been beheaded. His head, covered by a paper crown, was set atop the gates of York, and the grisly relic was flanked by the heads of York's young son, the Earl of Rutland, and his kinsman by marriage, the Earl of Salisbury.

"Come back here, you headstrong woman."

Marged wheeled around, ignoring Rhys's command. Long ago he had wanted to abandon their search, for he itched to join the Welsh chieftains flocking to the banner of Jasper Tudor, Earl of Pembroke. He had even argued reasonably that they might find Sir Richard riding with the Welsh earl. Marged had been sorely tempted to abandon their futile search, until she heard from a wounded Lancastrian that her father had fought at Wakefield. The victorious Lancastrian army had headed for London, pillaging the countryside on the way. Unburdened as the Brecon men were by loot and baggage, they felt it was just a matter of time before they met the main force.

"I lead the men and I give the orders," Rhys growled when he finally spurred to her side. "No more futility. We head for Wales. My men are chafing for action. 'Tis unfair to expect them to sit docilely by while their countrymen gird for battle."

"Then go! Give me a handful of men for protection, and I'll follow the Lancastrian army without you. If my father's not with them, we can meet on Welsh soil."

"No, Marged. I won't have it on my conscience."

And so, reluctant as ever, the Brecon men toiled along country lanes through mud and melting snow. Buffeted by the winter wind, they pressed southward. As a concession to Rhys, Marged agreed to ride the border in hope of meeting the main Welsh force bound for England.

On the edge of Clun Forest they pitched camp. The soldiers lit fires to warm their dampened spirits. Skilled hunters, the

Brecon men soon had the cooking pots boiling with rabbit stew.

A lump came to Marged's throat when she realized that within the week they would be in familiar territory. Poignant memories of Bowenford tugged at her heart. How long it seemed since that summer's day when she had fled her captors, fired with excitement over her quest. Now, more than six months later, she had come almost full circle without learning any more about her father's whereabouts than she had known the day she fled.

Marged relaxed in the fire's warmth, staring into the leaping flames and breathing the dank air, rich with woodsmoke. She was possessed by a wave of melancholy as thoughts of dear and familiar sights crowded her mind. Had Rolfe returned to Bowenford? Or did he now roam the north country with the defeated Yorkist troops? Though she had made discreet inquiries about him, no one remembered a Breton knight bearing his standard. Had Rolfe been slain at Wakefield? Reportedly, Yorkist casualties had been heavy. Her heart sickened, before she managed to dismiss the chilling thought.

"Here. My men confiscated wine to warm your belly."

Marged smiled her thanks as she accepted the cup of mulled wine. She did not ask Rhys what poor soul had been relieved of his bounty; miles of wandering had taught her that certain crimes became necessities when an army was on the march. "Thank you, it's very good," she added when he appeared to wait for praise.

"Why are you sad? Take heart. If we don't find your father soon, I'll take you either to Brecon, or back home—"

"No—I'll never give up! Not until I meet him face to face, or until I know he's dead, will I return!"

Rhys shrugged and turned aside, his face troubled. Determination ran like blood through lovely Marged's veins. On this bleak afternoon he did not choose to take issue with her. Of late, her very presence had become unsettling, for he was hard pressed to control his mounting romantic interest in her. Never had she given him cause to think his suit would be welcome, yet neither had she repulsed his friendship. Had he not been so taken with her beauty, long months ago he would have abandoned their search for Sir Richard, who, were the truth known, probably moldered under some unmarked sod. Intense desire to please Marged, to achieve glory that he would lay in homage at her feet, kept him traveling doggedly the length and breadth of the land while his men's discontent increased with each passing day.

Marged dozed and woke, and dozed again. Vivid dreams of Rolfe rocked her with bittersweet memory. She bolted awake sweating, pain gnawing her vitals. He had been lying beside her, the dream so vivid that she could still see his smile and feel his touch. Though nothing untoward had occurred during those moments of bliss, the promise of love shone in his eyes, making her deliriously happy.

She wrapped her cloak tight against the cold. No one tried to stop her as she stumbled away from the campfire. She was too anguished by poignant memories to face the circle of noisy men gathered about the blaze. Though Marged hated what he represented, she was not hypocrite enough to blame Rolfe for her seduction. Despite all previous efforts to vanquish those treacherous emotions, on this cold, foggy January afternoon she finally faced the truth: she loved him passionately. Even if she never saw him again, she knew no other man could supplant his memory.

Blindly, Marged reached for a nearby horse, who stood snorting great frosty clouds into the cold air. A laggard soldier had failed to unsaddle the beast. Almost without thought she was in the saddle, desperate for the solitude of the black, skeletal forest.

How long she rode, Marged did not know. Twilight was merely an extension of the gray afternoon. High above the towering trees, the full moon appeared and shone like a great silver ball, before low-scudding clouds obscured the light. A few moments later the moon reappeared to shine a ghostly path across the forest glade.

She sniffed the air. Woodsmoke hung in the dampness, revealing the presence of nearby campfires. Rhys would be furious when he discovered she had left the camp. In fact, she had long expected to hear the thump of pursuing hooves as he came in search of her. Her mount whickered and grew restless, disturbed by the scent of other beasts. This must be the far edge of the Brecon camp. So deep in thought had she been, she had ridden in circles.

A dark shape loomed out of the trees; by the bulky outline, Marged knew it was an armored man.

"Identify yourself," she cried as her horse plunged through the bracken.

"Nay, lad, *you* identify yourself," growled a deep voice.

A group of men suddenly emerged from the trees, and Marged found herself surrounded by soldiers. Though it was too dark to identify their livery, she knew they were not Rhys's Welshmen. Panicking, she swung her mount about, catching several soldiers off guard and felling them. But her desperate efforts to escape proved in vain. A dozen men ran forward and dragged on the horse's bridle until the animal reared, neighing in fright. Marged fell backward, hitting the ground with a sickening jolt. Rough hands grabbed her and dragged her to a campfire glowing orange through the trees.

"Who are you, lad?" demanded their commander, his rough, bearded face in the leaping firelight.

Marged said nothing. She glared at her captors while her mind raced, seeking a solution to her dilemma. Why had their scouts not reported the presence of soldiers? The Brecon camp could not be more than five miles in either direction. She was tempted to ask which faction these men supported, but fear that they were Yorkist troops stilled her tongue. In this territory, Lancastrian supporters would be few and far between.

"Maybe he's Welsh." Turning to a nearby soldier, the bearded leader told him to fetch one of the Welsh archers who rode with them.

The Welshman spoke to Marged at length in several dialects, but she remained mute.

"We should geld the idiot," someone suggested in the background.

"Aye, I'm of like thought. Perchance he has valuable knowledge. Let's take him back to Wigmore. Edward of March will soon loosen his tongue."

Edward of March! That familiar name sliced like a sword through Marged's consciousness. It was the young Earl of March whom Rolfe had chosen to support. Dare she hope he was in the Earl's camp?

The soldiers were taking no chances with their prisoner. Marged was trussed and slung across the captain's saddlebow.

The jarring night ride seemed to last an eternity. Blood pounded in her ears, drowning the men's voices; the hoofbeats created their own screaming world of pain. Somewhere along the way she lapsed into unconsciousness.

When daylight entered the narrow confines of her prison, the murky winter light revealed somber stone walls. Sometime in the night, Marged had been brought inside a castle and dumped in this cell, which, though cold, was not foul. She gave thanks for her good fortune.

Her jailor brought her a bowl of gruel and a crust of rye bread. She washed them down with a cup of mulled ale, which spread welcome warmth through her icy limbs.

"Come on, you surly bastard, let's see what you've got to say for yourself this morning. We've plenty of ways to loosen stubborn tongues." The hulking jailor chuckled as he dwelled on thoughts of her impending torture.

Marged was not afraid; long before she reached the rack, she intended to divulge her sex. Though Edward of March commanded the enemy, she had no reason to expect any less chivalrous treatment from him than she had received from Bowenford's conquerors.

Clumsy in her shackles, she stumbled down the chill stone corridors leading to the Great Hall, where she was to be brought before the Earl of March.

A monstrous fire burnished the vast hammer-beamed room with leaping orange light. So many people were in this lofty, banner-hung Hall, she could scarcely take in the spectacle before she was flung at the feet of a group of finely dressed men.

"Here's the spy, Your Grace."

Marged recognized the bearded captain's grating voice as he dragged her upright.

"Why do you think the lad's a spy?" asked a man standing apart from the others who warmed themselves at the blaze.

Marged looked up at the stranger, bold and unafraid—commanders were less wont to punish brave men than cowards. He was a tall, golden-haired man, splendidly attired in crimson velvet. A jeweled chain glittered at his neck. Though a full-pleated gown fell loosely about his knees, Marged was immediately aware of his strong, virile body.

"Rise and tell me your name," commanded the man.

Marged remained mute, though she boldly met his cornflower blue eyes. Could this be the young Earl? She had heard that Edward of March was comely and much adored by women. And this golden-haired nobleman's appearance was certainly pleasing, though his full mouth and soft chin suggested a tendency to indolence and love of pleasure.

"Shall I have him tortured?" asked her jailor eagerly.

The fair man waved him aside.

"Perchance the lad speaks Welsh."

"Nay, Your Grace, a Welsh archer got no further with him than the rest."

Freshly angered by Marged's stubborn refusal to speak, the bearded captain smashed her on the shoulder, sending her sprawling into the rushes. Tears filled her eyes and she could not prevent them spilling down her cheeks as she huddled there, trying to master her pain.

"The lad cries like a wench," scoffed her jailor, spitting in contempt. When he was about to drag her upright, he caught a sharp glance from the nobleman and shuffled away.

"Would you see the lad closer, Your Grace?"

Not waiting for his lord's answer, the captain yanked Marged to her feet and in the next second snatched the hood from her head. Though she raised her hands feebly in defense, it was too late. Heavy black plaits thumped against her back.

"By the Rood! This is no lad!" gasped the nobleman, stepping closer, the better to view his captive.

"A wench! But—Your Grace—we—we had no idea," stammered the bearded one, his face paling.

The golden-haired man pulled loose Marged's plaits, releasing a shimmering black cloud about her shoulders. A gasp of admiration echoed from the men grouped about the hearth.

"Why do you ape a lad with your dress? Explain yourself, wench."

Marged glared at the bearded soldier, not deigning to answer him. The admiration on his commander's face had not gone unnoticed by her, so she addressed her appeal to him. "I'm but a poor wench, my lord. Don't allow your men to treat me ill."

"Fetch a light," commanded the nobleman before he turned back to her. "Do you know who I am?" he asked, his resonant voice pleasant to her ears.

"You command this garrison."

He smiled, his hand straying to her glossy hair. "Aye, that I do. My name is Edward. What's yours?"

"Marged."

"A Welsh name. I'm familiar with the Welsh, for the Mortimers have kept the Marches many years."

"Are you the Earl of March?"

"Nay, I'm Edward, future King of England."

Marged swallowed, not choosing to dispute his statement. Now that the Duke of York was dead, his eldest son must consider himself heir to the throne.

"You do not bow the knee," Edward of March rebuked sharply, temper darkening his handsome face.

"My father supports Lancaster."

"I see." Edward scowled, but he stayed his supporters when they would have knocked her to her knees. "Why does a wench ride alone by night, dressed in lad's clothing?"

"I'm searching for my father."

"Who is he?"

"Sir Richard Bowen."

Edward shook his head. "I know him not. Yet, in truth, I'm acquainted with few of my enemies. Could your sire be amongst the fallen?"

"It's possible. If he lives, I intend to find him." Marged shuddered at her own statement. Instead of saying her father lived, she had begun to say "if he lives." The discovery was unsettling.

"Are you not afraid to travel alone?" Edward asked her, a tinge of admiration in his voice.

"No." Marged had already decided not to disclose Rhys's presence. This Yorkist force was far superior in size, and though recently Rhys's possessive attitude had angered her, he had always been loyal to their search. She had no wish to bring about his death.

"Take the wench away and attire her suitably," Edward commanded, before turning back to the high table where his meal grew cold.

Later that afternoon, when Marged was forced into the presence of Edward of March, she wore a saffron damask gown over a silver-embroidered kirtle. Her hair had been washed, brushed, and polished, and it floated about her shoulders in a fluttering midnight cloud.

"Ah, as I thought—you're a great beauty," Edward breathed, aroused and pleased by the seductive appearance of his prize. "Come, sup with me, Marged. I'm lonely for female companionship."

Marged dipped her knee as she knew she was expected to do, considering it wise not to antagonize her jailor. Perhaps, if she were careful, she could twist this man about her finger as she had Chagall. Yet her searching gaze told her Edward Plantagenet would be a far tougher challenge.

For one so large-limbed, Edward moved with surprising grace. His strong, well-turned calves were displayed to advantage in scarlet hose embroidered with silver. He intentionally revealed his splendid physique by wearing his red velvet gown unbuttoned.

Edward raised Marged from her knees.

He was so tall, she stared up at him in awe. It was not difficult to see why the Yorkists had rallied behind this splendid, golden-haired young man. He contrasted favorably with dour King Henry, whose reason was known to flee him periodically; this young Yorkist appeared relentlessly shrewd.

"Come, sup with me, sweet," Edward suggested huskily, his hand lingering on hers. "We've fat roast goose and plum puddings for your delight."

He led her to a low table set before the hearth. When Marged glanced about in curiosity at the wool rugs and ornately carved furniture, she belatedly discovered this room to be his bedchamber. And though she greatly admired the gold-embroidered hangings on the vast bed, set atop a stepped platform, she felt deeply uneasy.

She discovered that Edward was far younger than she had supposed. While he filled her trencher with fragrant slices of roast goose, she noted the bloom of youth upon his face—his full lips, long eyelashes, and soft skin as yet unhardened by long exposure to the elements. Even the faint stubble of beard above his upper lip suggested that Edward had not been shaving long.

Marged ate sparingly and drank even less, determined to maintain her senses. It might be Edward of March's intention that when the meal was done they would retire to that down-filled island inside the gold-embroidered hanging, but it was definitely not hers.

"The meal was very fine, Your Grace," Marged said at last, conscious of the uncomfortable silence stretching between them.

"Here, sweet, have some marchpane fruits—scarlet cherries to match your lips."

While she nibbled the sweet confection, she became aware of Edward inching closer. At last she sprang to her feet, anxious to escape his overwhelming physical presence.

"What is it?"

"The heat from the fire is too great," she protested lamely, staring through the narrow windows at the gray, misty fields beyond. "Where are we?" she asked, wondering how far from Bowenford this castle lay.

"Wigmore. 'Tis my family's stronghold, not far from Ludlow. We keep winter court here whilst awaiting the enemy," Edward replied amiably as he stood beside her.

Marged counted the hedgerows, the lanes, trying to visualize the way she had come. So intent was she upon her task, she was surprised to find the weight of his arm settling about her waist. When she would have pulled free, Edward held her fast.

"Nay, be not so hasty. You're a fascinating creature, Marged, the like of which I've never laid eyes on before. That face, that hair—come, will you not unbend to me? We are alone. And you are so very lovely."

Marged smiled, turning her face away as his breath wafted hot against her ear. Oh, Edward of March, I'm not nearly as innocent as you suppose, she thought. Aloud she said, "You are most kind, Your Grace."

"Edward," he urged huskily. "Call me by my Christian name."

"Edward—I must leave soon to resume my search. I can't dally the days away."

His arm tightened. "So tiny, so delicate," he murmured, not listening as he slipped his large hand about the back of her waist, measuring its narrow width. "I can easily span you with my hands, and yet . . ." Now his fingers stole upward, hovering below the deep curve of her breasts, pushed high by the gown's embroidered girdle.

Still smiling, Marged twisted from his grasp and went back to the hearth. "Your Grace, you overwhelm me with flattery. I'm but a poor wench."

Edward smiled too, not wholly deceived by her feigned naïveté. "You're very beautiful. I've always appreciated beautiful women. In fact, I'm prepared to make their lives very easy, if they please me."

"I don't understand," Marged whispered, playing for time.

"Oh, I think you understand me well enough."

Their eyes met and she saw lust blazing in the cornflower blue, the emotion aging Edward's face and robbing him of youthful vulnerability. The Earl of March was young, but he was not inexperienced.

"You're my captive. A man can do as he pleases with a captive woman."

"You're so chivalrous a knight, I trust you to treat me with respect." Marged gazed up into his face, outwardly trusting, though in truth her stomach pitched uneasily.

Edward's face clouded."You are my captive," he repeated.

"I raised not one finger in hostility against you. Why must I be your captive?"

"You are one of the enemy. Lancastrian spies are always taken captive."

"I'm no spy. I told you I'm searching for my father."

"Who *is* my enemy." Edward's mouth twitched into a smile. "Though your speech be pretty, Marged, you've little hope of talking yourself to freedom."

"Doesn't Edward of March treat enemy captives chivalrously?"

"Indeed . . . most chivalrously," he breathed, gently brushing her cheek and neck with his hand. "You're so beautiful, Marged, quite the most beautiful woman I've seen since I began my travels. Oh, come, play not cat-and-mouse with me," he dismissed impatiently as he pulled her into his arms. "There are far more satisfying games."

Marged turned aside to avoid his burning lips as he crushed her against his hard body. "I thank you for your praise."

When she struggled to free herself, Edward tightened his grip. "Say no more. Come, kiss me back. Hold me . . . oh, Marged, I'm most desirous of you."

"No . . . no!"

He lifted his burning face from her sleek hair, scowling in displeasure at her protests. "No? What do you mean—no?"

"I have no wish to bed you," Marged stated bluntly.

Edward blinked in surprise. "Why not?"

Marged hesitated. Should she tell him she loved another? Somehow she did not think Edward Plantagenet would care how many men she loved. He desired her body, not her heart. Eyes downcast, she said softly, "I don't know you well enough yet. Would not lovemaking be far sweeter if we knew each other first?"

The sternness melted from his face. "Aye, that it would, but we've no time for long acquaintance. Already my blood boils for you. Come then, let us sit and become better acquainted."

Besides their supper cushions, the only other seating was the canopied bed. Every delay, she hoped, would give her another chance to escape.

Edward lounged against the heaped pillows, his red velvet gown draping open to reveal his broad chest, slender waist, and muscular thighs. Conscious of her gaze on his body, he smiled, convinced that it would only be a matter of moments before she lay acquiescent in his arms. It was not his habit to wait overlong to mount a woman, yet this woman was so fascinatingly different, he did not begrudge the delay.

They spoke of their families, their homes, Edward giving scant attention to the conversation. While they talked, his hand strayed to Marged's soft neck, then slid to her shoulders. When his fingers strayed even lower, she pulled away.

Her unexpected resistance roused his temper.

"I will take you!" he declared angrily, grasping her wrist. "By force, if necessary. If you think I can't subdue you, you're a fool. There are many here who'd come to my assistance."

"To possess me willingly would give far greater pleasure than rape," Marged reminded him quietly as she met his gaze. Temper darkened his blue eyes, and his full mouth turned pettish. Like a spoiled boy, Edward was not used to having his desires thwarted.

"Then give yourself to me willingly," he suggested as he pushed her back on the satin coverlet.

Trapped beneath his weight, Marged ceased to struggle. Slyly she suggested, "First you must woo me like a lover."

He drew back, shaking his head in bewilderment as he gazed down at this dark-haired tormentress. "Do you not want me yet?" he asked in surprise. "I am to be your king."

"If I take you as a lover, it will be as Edward the man, not Edward the King," Marged responded softly. "Women are readily sacrificed to kings. There's little challenge in that."

Now Edward was even more bewildered. "No woman has ever played me like this before. By God, though, it does not set ill with me. The prospect of conquering you man-to-woman sets my blood athrob."

Marged allowed him to kiss her cheek, to stroke her hair, yet when his hand molded impatiently about her full breast, she thrust him away. "Not yet!"

"When?" he demanded with a scowl. "This game is proving not nearly as amusing as I expected."

Without awaiting her answer, Edward crushed Marged deep into the bed, imprisoning her there, the arousal of his loins pressing painfully against her thighs. When she struggled to be free of the threatened impalement, he smiled triumphantly.

"Will you not discover what delight I offer?" he invited huskily, his tongue tracing a passage down her cheek. "And in turn allow me to admire your body?"

"You've not yet wooed me sufficiently to arouse my lust, Edward of March. Have you no patience?"

Edward was panting and his hand shook as he cupped the underside of her right breast, moving no further when she stayed his hand. "I want you now," he said peevishly. "Yield to me—you must yield to me."

Marged shook her head. Twining her fingers in his abundant gold hair, she whispered, "First you must truly woo me. Think of the pleasure in knowing you have aroused me to lust."

"Is this not arousal enough?" he demanded, seizing her hand and imprisoning it against the throbbing torment that raised his hose. When Marged declined to mold her slender fingers about the burning brand, he thrust her aside with a sob of frustration.

Marged's stomach churned uneasily. How much further could she try him? A strong man such as he could already have taken her a dozen times, yet by his hard-won restraint, he revealed that rape was not his pleasure. Perhaps, in the past, his exalted station had always been sufficient to arouse women. She was different. She must pray that Edward of March had sufficient conceit to accept the challenge of wooing her to lust.

"I won't wait!"

"Then take me if you've a mind," Marged declared, stiffening on the gold coverlet, arms set tightly at her sides.

"No," Edward groaned, reeling from her. "Not like that!"

Marged watched him pace the room like a caged beast. Tonight she had managed to control him; tomorrow would be a different matter.

When at last Edward came back to her, he pressed her hand against his soft lips. "If I'm patient, will you come to me in mutual passion? Will you delight in my body?"

"When I'm fully aroused, I swear you'll have no cause for complaint," Marged promised warily.

"But how much longer must I wait?" he demanded in anguish. "How long will you torment me? My hands shake at the mere thought of touching your breasts. My mouth burns . . . how much longer?"

"Love never runs to the hourglass, surely you know that."

"Aye, I know it well enough." He looked down at her, his expression surly. "Tomorrow we're to have a grand banquet. I'll ply you with rich wines, with sweetmeats. There'll be mummers and jugglers, a masque for your delight—will you yield to me tomorrow?"

"Perhaps."

His eyes narrowed as he gazed at her; a niggling doubt about her sincerity destroyed his pleasure. The sight of her full breasts rising with each breath made him long to uncover her beauty, to bury his face against her smooth flesh, to kiss every inch of her body. "Think you I'm not virile enough to suit?" he asked suspiciously. "Anyone will tell you Edward of March is skilled at pleasing women."

"Oh, Edward," Marged reproached, taking his bejeweled

hand. "You need not seek to convince me of your virility. 'Tis not because I think you unworthy that I refuse your bed. You're a handsome, highly arousing man. Any woman would be proud to call you lover."

"Then why won't you call me so?" he cried eagerly, pulling her against him and showering her face with soft kisses. "Will you come to me tomorrow?"

"Let me seek you in my own time."

"I'll not wait overlong for you," he said, thrusting his hands at his sides. He could barely keep from forcing her, so much did she excite him. Never before had he docilely permitted a woman to withhold that which was his right to take.

"I'll not ask you to wait forever," Marged promised. She allowed him to kiss her mouth, but she stopped short of allowing the invasion of his tongue when he waxed bolder.

"I'm no buffoon to be trifled with—I *will* have you!"

Warily she drew away from him. Edward did not stop her when she walked toward the door. "You are truly as chivalrous as I've heard—nay, even more so, Your Grace, for never did they tell me of your patience with a woman."

"Perchance it was because I've never needed to exercise it before." Temper was again clouding his face, and Marged stepped quickly to the door. "When my patience runs its course, I'll take you, willing or nay," he reminded her gruffly.

"Have I your leave to depart Wigmore?"

"After you've yielded to me."

Marged drew in her breath. Edward was not going to be as easily manipulated as she had hoped. "And how long am I to be allowed?"

"A week should be time enough to ignite any woman's fire."

As she backed away, Marged remembered to drop a hasty curtsy.

Edward lounged against the bed, his handsome face surly. Even while he watched her backing away, he cursed himself anew for not taking her by force. Passion raged within his blood when he relived the delight of her body imprisoned beneath his. They had been alone in this room and he had let her go! Why had he turned so soft with her?

He leaped toward the door, anxious to remedy matters. When he looked down the winding corridor, she was nowhere to be seen. The clank of the guard's armaments echoed in the distance as the captive was taken to a room especially prepared for her in the south tower.

Reeling drunkenly, he smote the door with his doubled fist. A squeak surprised him, making him spin about to discover a young maid bearing a ewer of water and folded towels.

His vision blurred as he looked at her body, his lust inflamed to the boiling point. The wench was young and comely enough, thank God.

"Come here," he said.

Obediently the maid put down her burden and went to him. Gazing up at his blond magnificence, she could barely hear herself speak above the pounding of her heart. "Your Grace," she whispered in awe, "how may I serve you?"

"Like this," he uttered thickly.

He pressed her against the wall, and she gasped in surprise when he raised her skirts to her thighs. She shuddered as he impatiently ripped open his own garments; never once did she attempt to thwart him. With an anguished groan he hoisted her high and, pinioning her against the bruising stonework, welded her to his body. In blazing fury his passion was soon spent. He pulled free of the wench, allowing her to slide to the floor.

"Oh, Your Grace," she whispered in awe, hardly able to believe what had just taken place. She gazed up at him adoringly, her tear-stained face soft with wonder.

"You're an obliging wench. Now get you gone," Edward dismissed impatiently, having no further need of her.

"But . . . but . . ." she began, struggling to her feet. "Now that we've—"

"I said begone. Now is no different from before," he replied harshly. "Perhaps, at some future time, you may please me again."

The girl smiled in delight as she stooped to gather her towels, her head in a whirl as she dwelled on her lover's exalted station.

When the wench continued to stare at him, Edward waved her away. He had no desire to look upon the simpering creature. True, she had satisfied a desperate bodily need, but inwardly he still raged at her for not being the woman he wanted. At the final moment of release he had breathed *her* name—Marged! That appalling slip angered him more than all other aspects of this disappointing afternoon combined.

A scowl darkened his smooth face as he entered his chamber. Let the Welsh chit beware. If she played him too long at her foolish game, he would take her as swiftly as he had taken that nameless maid. And with about as much tenderness.

Marged sat at the high table in the smoky Great Hall of Wigmore Castle, surveying the noisy, brightly dressed throng. Garlands decked with scarlet ribbons decorated the harsh stone walls, while multi-hued satin banners and pennants hung from the rafters. A group of simpering females, hoping to catch the eye of young Edward of March himself, wore silks and sparkling jewelry, but none in the company was garbed more finely than she.

This morning a serving wench had delivered a sumptuous gown to her chamber. Edward's gift, designed to capture her favor, was of shimmering violet damask over a gold kirtle. The matching surcoat was edged with marten around the low neck. On her head she wore a heart-shaped hennin draped with violet gauze.

To complement her lavish gown, Edward wore an embroidered silk shirt, a purple doublet, and a knee-length gown trimmed with ermine, which he unfastened to draw attention to the virile body of which he was proud. Edward's strong white hands shone with rings, and his eyes shone with lust.

"Will you take more wine?" he inquired with solicitude as he gazed ravenously at his lovely captive.

Marged smiled nervously as she allowed him to refill her cup. Since the beginning of the feast she had been searching for Rolfe, or his men, among the assembled knights. But the French spoken in Wigmore's Great Hall was the language of the court. No unschooled Breton dialect invaded the lofty, smoke-hazed room.

Beneath the red brocade tablecover, Edward gripped her fingers, his hand hot, demanding. He even waxed bold enough to stroke her thighs beneath her clinging gown. Marged almost expected him to plunge his rapacious hands inside her bodice, so fixedly did he stare at her swelling breasts mounded above the marten fur.

"You're a sorceress. How well you know the art of inflaming

a man's lust," Edward said huskily. "I can scarce wait to end this feast to claim you. Sweet Jesus, the more I look at you, the less able I am to take to the dance floor." Edward grinned as he pulled aside his velvet gown to reveal the throbbing swell beneath his clinging tights. "See what mischief you've caused with nary a touch."

Marged smiled, though her alarm increased greatly. Each reminder of Edward's unbridled passion dimmed her hope of resisting his sexual demands.

They supped on spiced venison and almond flummeries while Marged's desperate mind sought a way to escape the mounting desire of her royal jailor. How simple it would have been to slip away, had he not hung on her every word, his breath rasping as he mentally possessed her. Other men and women moved freely about the gaily decorated hall, pausing in the shadows to kiss. The guards displayed even less restraint than their noble masters. Yet Marged realized glumly that even if Edward left her side, in her spectacular gown she could not leave without detection.

Her dilemma was partially solved when she found a dark cloak flung carelessly across a corner chest. The garment could readily disguise her identity.

Neighbors from Croft and other nearby castles were attending this winter revel. The sheer size of Edward's garrison allowed scant room for hospitality, so Marged expected that many of the guests would depart before dawn. The guests' horses were tethered in the bailey, for the stables were filled to capacity. If she were fortunate, she could attach herself to a departing group of guests and ride over the drawbridge to freedom.

At that moment a troupe of colorfully clad tumblers burst inside the room amid laughter and applause. So nimble were their cavortings as they formed human pyramids before collapsing into cartwheels and somersaults, they made Marged's head spin. She wished Edward were not at her elbow, laughing uproariously at the entertainment, for while the other guests were engrossed in the tumblers' antics, they would have given her a perfect chance to slip away.

For the third time Marged refilled Edward's gold wine cup, which he quickly drained. His face flushed red with drink and lust, he turned toward Marged and buried his hot mouth in her neck. "Stay here, sweet, for we must lead the next dance. I'm eager to show you to my guests. But you've plied me so generously with wine, I'm like to burst. Come, a kiss to speed me on my way."

Dutifully, Marged touched her lips to his, her mind elsewhere. "I'll await your return," she promised huskily, as her throat constricted. The closest garderobe was in an alcove off the Great Hall. There would be just enough time to slip away before he returned.

Edward rose, steadying himself against the edge of the table. His feet tangled in the dangling gold fringe of the tablecloth. Cursing beneath his breath, he let Marged free his pearl shoe clasp from the fabric, then wove through the throng of noisy revelers. He was suddenly halted when a youth dressed in cloth of silver began to sing in so pure and beautiful a voice that a hush descended over the noisy room. Marged gritted her teeth in aggravation. This unexpected development made Edward postpone his urgent visit to the garderobe. At last, after giving the minstrel a few minutes of his rapt attention, Edward finally strode from the Hall.

Almost before his purple velvet gown was lost to view, Marged leaped to her feet. The guests were still so enthralled by the singer that no one noticed as she pulled the voluminous brown cloak over her gown. Though it might seem strange for a fashionable lady not to wear a headdress, Marged pitched hers in a corner, lest it give her away. She edged around the wall where it was dark and smoke-hazed, but when the lad soared to his final note, she froze. A momentary silence had gripped the listeners. Only when they erupted into a gale of applause did she release her breath and speed out of the Hall, choosing the opposite direction from the garderobe. This narrow passage led to the kitchens. If Wigmore was built along similar lines to Bowenford, the kitchen entrance would give ready access to the bailey.

No one questioned her, or even seemed to notice as she hastened inside the huge, vaulted kitchen, which blazed like Hades. Its baking ovens were filled with bread and its open pits were roasting whole animal carcasses on spits. Two doors were set in the wall nearby. Marged had no time for error; she made her selection by the chill of the iron door ring.

Like a slap in the face, the icy January wind took her breath away. Shuddering, she pulled her cloak tight, drawing down the hood to hide her face. It was pitch black and she stumbled on the uneven ground before she finally accustomed herself to the dark. The acrid smell of animals drew her northward and she was soon rewarded by the sound of jingling metal trappings and snorting horses.

"Which mount, lady?" asked a muffled groom, leaping to his feet at her approach.

His unexpected appearance startled her, and Marged pretended not to hear. When the man repeated his question, she pointed to the closest beast. The big animal was grandly caparisoned, and at first she thought she had chosen poorly, for the man paused.

"My lord's been gone this hour past," he muttered as he unlooped the reins and led forth her selection. "You'd best hasten, lady, if you don't want to feel his wrath."

The groom's suggestive leer aided Marged in grasping the probable situation. The horse, standing alone, must belong to a lady whose angry husband had ridden ahead. She was probably one of those laughing women who flirted with knights in the shadows.

"Aye, I'll hasten. The birch makes a surly friend." Marged smiled at the groom in thanks for his warning.

"My lord said I wasn't to give you the beast, but then, my hearing was never sharp."

Marged allowed the groom to help her into the saddle, not taking offense when his hand strayed to her ankle, or when he steadied her overlong so that he might probe her soft thigh. Such liberties were small payment for freedom.

Waving to the obliging groom, Marged wheeled the unresponsive horse around and regretted her selection as they moved slowly toward the drawbridge. The soldier at the gate recognized the horse's trappings, and waved Marged on.

As they crossed the moat, Marged prayed the animal's mistress would stay occupied with her paramour until she was safely away from Wigmore. Not until the castle was out of sight did Marged kick the chestnut's flanks, urging him sharply to the left. The animal must have been used to traveling in the opposite direction, for he snorted his displeasure and skidded to a halt, stubbornly refusing to move. In desperation she lashed at him, cursing soundly over his willfulness. There was no time to lose. When Edward first found her missing, he might assume that she too was answering a call of nature, but when she failed to return, his suspicions would mount. When his latest prize could not be found within the castle, he would set up a hue and cry to shake Wigmore's mighty walls.

Sleet stung her face as the chestnut finally hit stride. This was an ill night for riding abroad, yet prisoners rarely had a choice as to the time or manner of their escape.

Marged followed what she assumed to be the road south. Alert for sounds of pursuit, she could not believe her good fortune as they traversed the sunken lanes unchallenged. Heath and dark hedgerows sped past as the horse grew eager to gallop in the rolling countryside. Despite the cold wind, her lack of money, or even knowledge of her surroundings, Marged offered fervent thanks for her deliverance. She was a free woman again.

{ seven }

For two days Marged meandered about the wintry Herefordshire countryside. Being unfamiliar with the wooded region and having to avoid the highway in case she encountered a search party from Wigmore, she found her progress further hampered by thick mist. On the third day she was appalled to see familiar landmarks looming out of the morning gloom. She had traveled in a circle!

So hungry and dispirited did she feel, she risked capture by begging shelter from a peasant woman who lived in a roadside copse. Though it pricked her conscience to do so, Marged told the woman a tragic tale of flight from a brutal husband who served Edward of March. The woman readily accepted this satisfying explanation of her torn gown and bedraggled appearance.

Early next morning the peasant woman woke Marged, all adither with excitement over a troop of soldiers she had seen heading this way.

Heart pounding with fear, Marged went to investigate the

troops for herself. In all probability they were Edward of March's men, come in search of her.

"Mayhap they can guide you home, lady," the woman suggested eagerly as the first armored horsemen clattered up the lane.

To Marged's surprise, the troops were not carrying Yorkist banners. Curious to learn whose men they were, she hid behind a bramble thicket to watch them. Though their numbers were large and well equipped, the soldiers straggled in an undisciplined fashion across the neighboring farmland. When Marged realized the men were speaking Welsh, she emerged boldly from her hiding place to address a passing lad whose banner bore the scarlet Welsh dragon on a field of green and white.

"Where are you bound?"

"To join the King's army."

"Which lord do you support?"

"My master rides with Pembroke."

Joy suffused Marged's features. "Jasper Tudor—my father's his man! Oh, do you know aught of Sir Richard Bowen?" But to her great disappointment, the lad shook his head. "Where's your master now? I want to question him."

Already tiring of her cross-examination, the lad shrugged, saying, "Up ahead, I suppose," before he galloped after his companions.

Marged thanked the peasant woman for her generosity. She gave her a strip of marten from her hem to pay for her bed and board. Then, seething with excitement and convinced she was nearing the end of her search, she saddled her horse and followed the straggling Welsh army.

An icy wind from the mountains raked the open fields, but Marged felt so exhilarated, she bravely squared her shoulders and rode into the teeth of the wind.

Soldiers straggled in all directions. As she rode past, the men mistook her for a camp follower, and their bawdy suggestions made her so uneasy that she quickened her horse's gait in case they tried to drag her from the saddle. Though her uncharitable attitude disgruntled them, she found to her relief that they made no effort to detain her.

In late afternoon, after the army pitched camp, Marged rode tirelessly from group to group, inquiring about her father. The only promising news she heard was from a blacksmith who had reshod Sir Richard's mount last month. The smith thought the Bowen men rode with Pembroke's father, Owen Tudor, who had married the widow of the English King.

Wrapped in her heavy cloak, Marged dozed beside a crackling campfire, on a choice bed that the kindly wife of a Welsh chieftain had allowed her. As the misty afternoon became the numb chill of night, she grew increasingly grateful for the woman's generosity.

Just before dark, a party of soldiers galloped into camp to warn of the presence of a large body of Yorkist troops across the River Lugg. Within minutes the camp was in an uproar, as plans for the morrow were swiftly changed. Messengers carried the revised orders to outlying camps. Whether Edward of March held the bridge or not, the Lancastrian commander intended to cross the Lugg.

The threat of this impending clash dashed Marged's hopes of catching up to the main body of troops the next day. The only comforting assurance she knew, as she huddled in her cloak beside the campfire, was that last month her father had been alive.

On Candlemas Day, February 2, 1461, the opposing armies of Lancaster and York faced each other across the River Lugg.

Edward of March felt uneasy about his troop's morale, for the men considered it sacrilege to fight on a holy day. And his force, though larger, was not as well equipped as the combined armies of the Earls of Pembroke and Wiltshire. Edward possessed one advantage, though: Sir Richard Croft, of nearby Croft Castle, had given him invaluable information about the surrounding terrain. Subsequently, archers were strategically placed to rain deadly crossfire on the Lancastrians as they attempted to ford the river. Wig Marsh was selected as the battleground, the boggy land making the Lancastrian advance hazardous. Edward would allow them to attack first.

As he emerged from his blue-striped tent, Edward's breath formed clouds in the frosty air. The sun had not yet risen, and the men looked like faceless shadows. To his right lay the camp of the Breton knight whose force he had so eagerly awaited. Rolfe de Bretayne had arrived yesterday from Shrewsbury, bringing a well-honed fighting force for the coming fray.

Edward raised his mailed hand in greeting as the dark-haired Breton loomed out of the shadows. "Are your men prepared to give their utmost? This being a holy day, many are reluctant to be engaged."

"My men know no distinction between holy days and the others," Rolfe replied as he pulled on his gauntlets. His squire held out his battle helm.

"I wish I could say the same for mine," Edward remarked glumly, falling into stride beside his trusted comrade. "If the battle goes ill, you know to what they'll attribute our defeat."

"Fear not. Today I feel lucky."

"Then, by God, I'll ride with you. I'm in sore need of luck," Edward decided grimly.

Edward had command of the center, which was to defend the bridge across the Lugg. The remaining troops were already deployed in Wig Marsh, awaiting the Lancastrians.

As the sun struggled into view, a collective groan of dismay issued from the ranks. Fearful men gazed heavenward, gaping at the unusual phenomenon of three suns brightly rayed against the sky. The awestruck Yorkist soldiers were consumed by fear. Was this a heavenly rebuke for daring to do battle on a holy day?

Edward, too, stared in awe, momentarily nonplussed by the appearance of this triple sun, as if representing Father, Son, and Holy Ghost. The Blessed Trinity!

Fired by a sudden idea, Edward fell to his knees, proclaiming loudly, "'Tis a heavenly omen. See, the sign of the Trinity to bless our cause."

Immediately the wails changed to gasps of reverent delight as, one by one, soldiers fell to their knees to offer prayers of thanks. Edward's nimble mind, ever working to his advantage, had reversed what might indeed have proved an ill omen. Now, instead of fear of holy retribution, his men basked in heavenly approval.

Rolfe knelt beside the young Earl, marveling at the swiftness of the armies' changing mood. Then, as they raised their heads, their prayers over, Rolfe pointed to the east: like a river in full spate, the Lancastrian horde thundered forth.

All day the holy-omened battle raged. Long before dark, young Edward of March, buoyed by the tide of his own swift-changing fortune, became the undisputed victor. The Lancastrian center, hampered by the river crossing and boggy ground, was raked by deadly crossfire from Edward's well-deployed archers. When the Lancastrian wings returned, fired by their own apparent victory, they found to their horror that their main force had been routed.

Yelling frenzied battle cries, the triumphant Yorkists swarmed over the field as Edward ordered his men to finish off the weakened enemy; giving no quarter, they delivered death blows in payment for the bloodbath on Wakefield Green. This new generation of antagonists dispensed with the former bonds of chivalry.

When darkness fell on that bleak winter afternoon, thousands lay dead or dying on Wig Marsh. The River Lugg, twenty feet across at this time of year, was swollen with bodies.

All day the women in the Lancastrian camp beyond the wooded hill had anxiously waited for word, scouring pots, packing supplies, listening for sounds of fighting blowing on the brisk wind; Marged was among them.

"Flee! All is lost!" a party of battered warriors shouted as they rode into the camp. The exhausted men fell from their saddles amid their wailing womenfolk, who tried in vain to staunch their gaping wounds.

"What of my father?" Marged asked of a youth whose head she cradled on her lap while she wiped blood from his eyes. "Did you see Sir Richard Bowen?"

"Aye, I fought beside his men," the lad gasped, his eyes already glazing in the gathering dark. "He's bad wounded—his army scattered."

Fear gripped Marged's heart. "Where is he? I must go to him."

"Chased to Hereford . . . water . . . water . . ."

Marged held a cup to the lad's lips. Her stomach lurched in fear for her father's safety. It was ironic that after traveling all these miles, she had missed finding him by one day.

"Which way to Hereford?" she demanded of a weary man slumped beside the campfire. The man gestured vaguely toward a road stretching southward, far into the black night.

The lad in her arms was already still. Marged laid him on the grass and asked one of the Welshmen's wives if she would take charge of the body. Then she climbed into the saddle and spurred her horse south.

Straggling parties of fleeing troops choked the Hereford road. The shrouding darkness was fraught with a multitude of cries and groans. Though Marged felt compassion for the wounded soldiers, she had no time to offer succor. All her energy was directed toward finding her father and staying ahead of the triumphant Yorkist army, who even now overran the scattered Lancastrian camps, putting all to the sword.

When she finally reached Hereford, sixteen miles to the south, the city was in turmoil. The gates stood wide to admit straggling soldiers. Every inn, every churchyard, every byway, was choked with wounded. Exhausted from hunger and lack of sleep, she found that the driving need to find her father gave her strength. She asked at makeshift hospitals, or of squires ministering to their masters' wounds, if any knew of Sir Richard Bowen's fate.

Dawn was already lightening the winter sky when Marged leaned weakly against the door of the Black Boar Tavern. She longed to abandon her search. Her body cried out for sleep. Yet without money she could not purchase lodgings, and there were too many undisciplined troops roaming the streets to contemplate sleeping outdoors.

Out of habit, yet without much hope of learning anything, Marged accosted a squire who hastened over the yard carrying a bowl of water and wads of linen.

"I'm looking for my father, Sir Richard Bowen," Marged began, her voice weak with fatigue. "Do you know him?"

The squire was reluctant to stop. "No. With whom did he fight?"

"Owen Tudor, the Earl's father."

The lad glanced sharply at her. "Owen Tudor's taken. Ask Tom over there. He should know."

Marged crossed the yard, repeatedly turning her ankles on the uneven cobbles. She saw wounded men near a horse shed, lying side by side like logs, while shadowed figures cleaned and bandaged wounds, or offered water and murmured prayers.

"Which of you is Tom?"

"I am." A gawky lad with corn-yellow hair glanced up from the injured man he was tending, surprised to see a dirty wench in so fine a gown. "What do you want with me?"

"I was told you know Sir Richard Bowen—one of Owen Tudor's men."

"Why do you seek him?" Tom asked suspiciously as he rocked back on his heels, peering up at her from under a thatch of hair.

"I'm his daughter."

The lad's face softened. "Upstairs." He jerked his thumb toward the rickety stairs leading to the upper story.

For a moment Marged stood without comprehending, watching the lad trying to pack his lord's massive wound. "Upstairs," she repeated at last, knowing, even if Tom did not, that his task was hopeless. "Did you say upstairs?"

"Aye, Sir Richard was brought in earlier."

Marged grasped the splintered bannister and dragged her unwilling legs up the shallow treads. As she approached the upper rooms she could hear a chorus of groans interspersed with cries of pain. Near at hand came the monotonous tones of a priest administering Extreme Unction.

Marged beat on the scarred panel of the first door. A weary, white-faced man opened to her. "Is Sir Richard Bowen within?" she asked. The man shook his head and turned away.

At the third door she found her father. A squire, his head swathed in a bloody bandage, ushered her inside the room, where four wounded men lay on a bed of straw. The acrid smell of the stables directly below mingled with the stench of blood and death.

Marged fell to her knees as she tried to identify her father by the feeble gleam of a rushlight stuffed in a crevice in the wall. He was lying in the corner, and unlike the others, who tossed and moaned, Sir Richard lay still. When Marged felt for his hand, she found it resting in a dark, sticky puddle.

"Father," she whispered, her voice breaking with emotion. "It's me—Marged."

At first he did not stir; then, hearing the familiar voice, Sir

Richard lifted his swollen eyelids and saw the blurred figure leaning over him. "Is it really you?" he croaked through parched, cracked lips.

"Come, let me take you from this place. Let me take you home."

"I'm close to home already. A man has only so much blood—mine's all but spent. Nay, fret not," he whispered, when Marged shrilly demanded that the ministering squires attend him. "They're urgently needed elsewhere."

"Why are you alone? Where are our men?"

"Most are dead. Through Sir Joce's treachery we bore the brunt of the river fight . . ." Sir Richard gripped Marged's hand and glanced nervously toward the door. "The enemy pursue me. Go while you're still able."

"These men are your friends," Marged insisted.

Even as she spoke, a cry of alarm came from the innyard; the grinding clash of steel followed. The men ministering to the wounded exclaimed in concern for their own safety.

"Lady, you'd best flee while you have the chance," one of the squires suggested as he shouldered his bleeding master. Stubbornly, Marged shook her head.

Several other men appeared in the doorway to help carry the wounded. "Shall we take your father also?" asked one of the men.

"I cannot pay you."

"We're taking them to the church. No money's needed. We'll come back for him."

Marged nodded her thanks. As she leaned closer to her father, she could hear the breath rattling in his throat; his face was clammy and cold. In his head and chest were four massive wounds, indicating that a goodly portion of the stain on these floorboards was Bowen blood. She marveled at his stamina in riding the sixteen miles to Hereford. The sickening truth was painful to accept: Sir Richard would never leave this room alive. She had found him too late.

"Marged—are you still here?"

"Yes."

"Nay, don't weep for me, you foolish wench," Sir Richard admonished, as her tears splashed against his grizzled cheek.

"What do you in Hereford?"

Here within this sordid room, the burning purpose that had driven her to Yorkshire and back was dying. Far better that he never know Bowenford was taken, Marged decided grimly. "I came in search of you," she said, biting back her grief.

Sir Richard's mouth twitched in a faint smile. "Take me home then, love," he whispered. "Lay me to rest beneath the trees."

A great choking lump constricted her throat; she struggled to contain her tears for his sake. The growing clash of swords and angry voices filled the room, but Marged leaned back against the splintered wall, still clutching her father's hand, and let a wave of weariness wash over her. He murmured some last instruction, but when she leaned closer, she could not understand his feeble words.

The door smashed open, the clang of armor shattering the quiet.

Like a she-cat, Marged leaped up, ready to defend her father. She identified Yorkist livery on the foremost soldier's chest. "Get back! You shall not take him," she cried.

"Is it Sir Richard Bowen?" a voice demanded from the rear of the jostling men.

Marged gripped her father's dagger.

A tall, helmeted man in a bloodied surcoat detached himself from the soldiers thronging the narrow gallery. His armorial device of raised portcullis on a crimson ground was barely recognizable, held together as it was by shreds of linen.

"Don't you know me, Marged?" echoed a dear, familiar voice.

Rolfe reached down to disarm her, but the dagger slipped from her trembling hands. She fell forward in exhaustion.

"Leave me," she gasped. "Oh, leave me."

Effortlessly, Rolfe swept her up in his arms, pressing a fleeting kiss against her glossy hair. "Be gentle with him," he commanded the men who came forward to lift Sir Richard.

"'Tis too late for gentle handling, my lord—he's dead."

"Then carry his body below. Here, take this silver to pay the transportation home."

In a dark nightmare of noise, Marged was carried down the

stairs and across the cobbled yard. Men fought around her; the din of clashing arms and shrieks of pain screamed through her mind until, unable to resist any longer, she rested her aching head against the strong shoulder of him who carried her, then gave herself up to sleep.

Winter sunlight spread its feeble fingers across the dingy plaster wall. Marged lay abed, staring at this unfamiliar room with its shabby furnishings. Disturbed by the mounting roar of voices from the street, she dragged herself slowly, heavily from the bed, surprised to find herself still fully clothed, and creaked open the aged latticed pane. Leaning out, she recoiled in horror from the sight below. A headsman's block was surrounded by a roaring crowd, and blood flowed like a river over the stone steps, into the cobbled marketplace.

The memory of her father bleeding to death at the Black Boar Tavern returned in a wave of anguish. How much kinder it had been when she enjoyed the oblivion of sleep. She leaned weakly against the window frame, not needing to identify the banners to know who conducted this hasty execution: the Yorkists were executing Lancastrian traitors. Conquering armies all followed a similar pattern. Being the closest important city to the battle site, Hereford was the perfect location for the spectacle. At least her father had been spared the public shame of a traitor's death. Lurid tales were told of corpses being dragged to the block and beheaded out of vengeance, but Rolfe would not allow that—Rolfe!

Marged reeled from the window. She was still so weary, it was difficult to order events of the past few days. Throbbing pain mounted in her temples as she recalled it was he who had carried her from that tawdry room. Even now his compassionate orders that her father's body be handled with care echoed through her brain—

"You're awake."

Marged raised her eyes to find him standing there. Today, though he still wore armor, Rolfe was clean-shaven, the blood washed from his hands and face. "How did you find me?" she whispered, her body a swirling tumult of emotions.

"I was told a beautiful woman searched for Sir Richard Bowen. I knew it had to be you. I scoured Hereford in search of you, and had all but given up hope when we finally reached the Black Boar."

"And now you've found me, will you return me to Bowenford as your prisoner?"

He shut the door and regarded her solemnly. The sudden roar of the crowd filled the room, and she stepped aside as he strode to the window.

"Owen Tudor will soon be made to pay for his royal lust," Rolfe announced grimly.

Marged watched the red-velvet-clad Welshman—Owen Tudor—mount the steps below. He appeared relaxed and almost lighthearted. Still relying on his well-known charm to carry him through even this calamity, the lover of Queen Katherine of Valois smiled as he faced his executioner.

"Why does he smile in the face of death?"

"Probably because he doesn't believe death awaits him. Forever has he swayed people by charm. He has no reason to think today will be any different."

"But he is to die?"

"Aye, he's to die—see, he waves to the crowd."

Marged watched with morbid fascination as the aged charmer exhibited no fear, convinced, even in the shadow of the block, that he would be granted clemency. Not until they ripped away the collar of his doublet did he blanch. Owen Tudor turned to address the crowd, but the wind blew away his soft, musical speech, and Marged could not hear what he was saying. Just before the gleaming axe descended on his bared neck, she turned aside, unable to witness the death stroke.

When a cry went up from the spectators, Marged knew the deed was done.

Rolfe was intently watching some activity below, and when Marged looked down, she shuddered to see Owen Tudor's severed head reposing on the highest step of the market cross. The crowd jeered as a woman washed the blood from its face and combed its hair before surrounding the head with blazing candles for the salvation of his soul.

Rolfe closed the window, turning his back on the morbid spectacle.

"Are you hungry?" he asked at length, his expression guarded. Though he wished not to recall it, Rolfe could not forget the gloating pleasure in Alys's face when she had told him about her stepsister's infidelity. He wondered where her Welsh lover was now.

"Yes. It's a long time since I've eaten."

"I've already ordered food, but likely the servants have been too busy watching the executions to bring it."

Their pride hobbled their tongues. The minutes ticked by like hours as they regarded each other, harboring both resentment and longing for forbidden things.

"I've made arrangements for your father's body to be treated with dignity."

"Thank you," she whispered, absurdly close to tears. Angered by her own weakness, she squared her shoulders and raised her head. "I have no money to pay you now. Someday soon, my lord, I intend to settle the debt."

He nodded, accepting her proud vow. The longer he looked at her, the more his nerves jangled. Unable to endure the silence any longer, he growled, "Perchance your Welsh lover can provide the money—if he's still in Hereford."

The blood drained from Marged's face. "Lover? Which lover is that?"

"Have you more than one?"

"I've not even one."

He smiled grimly. "That's not what I was told."

"Then you must question the truthfulness of your source," she snapped back. She felt desperate to escape his disturbing presence. Too many memories were aroused by the sight of him, memories best left undisturbed. "I've decided I'm not hungry after all. If you'll release my mount, I'll accompany my father's body home."

"And where will you go after that?"

"It matters not."

"It matters immensely! I risked my skin to find you—at least I'm owed some explanation."

"Explanation of what? Oh, of how I fled Bowenford, I suppose. You can obtain that explanation from your trusted lieutenant, Chagall. You don't need it from me."

"I've already heard several versions of your escape."

"Good, then you have no need of mine," Marged snapped.

A knock on the door interrupted them, and Rolfe marched to the door. "'Tis water for washing."

"Thank you, but as I'm leaving, I've no time for such niceties."

"You'll make use of it because its already paid for," he declared stubbornly. "Wash, lady, enjoy—the service is free." And with that he stalked from the room.

While Marged bathed, she smarted over Rolfe's churlish attitude. So much for her pathetic daydreams of the dark-haired Breton's undying love! Not once had he proved tender, or even kind. True, he had arranged for her father's body to be taken home. And she had thanked him for his thoughtfulness. Their debt was clear.

When she was washed and dressed in the clean homespun gown he provided, she stepped back to the window to stare at the gray sky stretching interminably before her. How lonely and bereft, how totally disheartened she was to discover that the one magical relationship she had allowed herself to cherish had come to naught. Lust, desire—those had been the words Rolfe de Bretayne had used to describe their coming together. She was the one who had been fool enough to read something more into his emotions. In admitting the truth, she could not prevent a shuddering half-sob, half-sigh from escaping her lips. She set her jaw grimly. She was a Bowen! Cowardice was not a family trait. She was alive—and, at this moment, still free.

Marged's stormy emotions were calmer when Rolfe returned. He had removed his armor and changed his battle-stained doublet. Despite his fresh clothing, he still had the same turbulent expression on his face.

"Your horse is fed and curried. I've given orders that you may leave whenever you wish. You're my prisoner no longer."

"Thank you, my lord," Marged said stiffly. "The meal arrived some time ago. It's likely cold by now. Here, I saved some for you—"

"I've already supped. The food was intended for you."

Marged looked at his set face and, seeing the steely glint in his eyes, remembered how lambent with sweet passion his blue eyes could be. All those foolish dreams of love she had known in Clun Forest appeared to have had no foundation in reality. It was far too hard to equate this hard, battle-weary stranger with the ardent lover who had kissed her so sweetly.

"What is it?" Rolfe demanded gruffly, his black brows drawn together, puzzled by the changing emotions witnessed in her face.

"Nothing," Marged whispered, looking away.

"Will you return to him?" he demanded at last, unable to keep the burning question to himself.

"I don't understand."

"The Welshman you sought in the mountains."

"Rhys?"

"Aye, if that be his name," Rolfe growled, his fists clenched. "At least we make progress. You're no longer denying it. Though perhaps I've not much, I feel I've some right to know who—or what—he is."

"Rhys is my kinsman. That's all! He's not my lover, nor has he ever been. Unlike you, my lord, I don't seek bed partners wherever I lodge."

Rolfe's hand shot out and seized her arm, his fingers gouging her soft flesh. "I was told the lad who led you to the mountains was your lover also."

"Then you were played for a fool!"

"Your own sister told me."

"Alys! Oh, I respected your intelligence more than that! Surely you don't think she's a credible witness?"

"Tell me true," he began, his voice cracking as he gazed deeply into her face, silvered by the dying winter light. "Tell me true—have you another lover besides—"

Mentally, Marged supplied the missing part of his speech. "I've *no* lover, my lord," she corrected him, shaking free of his grasp.

Rolfe stared at her, his face grim. "I believe you."

Though they no longer touched, the sheer force of his masculinity spanned the shabby room, firing her with longing for what might have been. So weak did she feel, Marged was convinced her legs would buckle. The fire sputtered and a log splintered in the hearth, making them both start in alarm.

"Last autumn I came to Bowenford to see you, riding without sleep from Shrewsbury."

"Oh—I—I didn't know," Marged stammered uncomfortably, wounded by the knowledge. "I'm not responsible for the lies they told you. Or for what Chagall might have boasted . . ." She glanced away from his piercing blue gaze, yet surely it mattered not what this conquering Breton thought about her morals?

"You led him on for a purpose. Even I know you'd find small comfort in a weakling like Chagall."

Marged's head snapped up as she heard a glimmer of humor in his voice. "You sound damnably sure of yourself."

"Aye, well, at least that part of me's not changed."

Rolfe crossed to the hearthstone where he lit a candle, trimmed it, and set it in a brass holder on the table. "Do you know why I galloped to Bowenford that day, all aquake as an untried boy?"

"No. But I'm sure you're going to enlighten me," Marged replied stiffly.

"I rode all night long, aflame with an emotion I identified as . . . love!"

His unexpected statement hung in the quiet room. Though she tried to steel herself not to react, Marged failed. Tears she had thought long since spent, trickled down her cheeks. "You loved me?" she whispered in disbelief.

"No. I *love* you," Rolfe corrected her sternly as he stepped toward her. "There's a vast difference between the two." He forced himself to keep his distance, though his arms ached to pull her against him. "What do you propose to do about it?"

"Do?"

A smile tugged at the corners of his mouth as he gazed at her, so achingly beautiful in her homespun gown.

"Aye, do—I've a multitude of tasks awaiting your decision."

Marged's brittle nerves snapped. "Then go! Don't let me keep you from important tasks."

"I've paid for this lodging," he reminded, still not permitting himself to do what his body ached to accomplish.

"Then perhaps *I* should go."

Through a blur of tears, she watched his face soften as he took a step toward her.

"I've a far better suggestion. Let's neither of us go. The room is warm, the bed soft."

"No! I thank you for your help—without you I should have fared ill—but you paid for nothing besides this room."

She stepped backward as he advanced. Panic raced through her body. She felt weak, her usual tenacity chipped away by the traumatic events of recent weeks.

"You are mine!"

"No!"

He ignored her protests, and deftly followed her dodging movements until, tiring of the game at last, he stepped on her skirts, imprisoning her.

"Enough!" he growled. His arms about her, he demanded gruffly, "Will you fight the night away?"

Marged panicked against his iron-hard chest and his imprisoning arms. She was not sure whether this was a dream or a nightmare come true. His face lay in shadow, but she was sure he did not smile.

"Well, if you've added rape to your crimes, Rolfe de Bretayne, take me then, because I shan't come to you willingly," she declared bravely, feeling as helpless as a trapped moth before his overwhelming strength. As he pressed her close, the treacherous firing of her blood rekindled memories of that other time when he had consumed her with passionate fire. Against her will, Marged's thighs strained toward him.

"Hypocrite," he scoffed, all too aware of the betraying surge in her blood.

She tried to free her wrists to strike him. He held her fast. The blows she delivered with her soft-shod feet only amused him.

"I want you as I've never wanted you before," he revealed huskily. "Come to me, not in anger but in love."

Her face stony, Marged exerted all her willpower in a last desperate effort to free herself. But his warm arms, which she had long ached to lie in, felt like steel bands. "Love me, Marged. Nothing else matters," he breathed into her hair.

Like a great dam bursting, her love overcame her pride; she sighed, deep and shuddering, and her lips trembled as she gave herself up to the strength of his body. Rolfe's exclamation of sheer delight was music in her ears. "Stay with me," she whispered, so weak with longing for him that her legs buckled.

He swept her quickly into his arms, showering her face with

kisses, and as if in a dream, he carried her to the bed. He was desperate to hold her against him, to feel again the delight of their bodies closely wrapped in the bittersweet anguish of desire.

"Oh, darling, I thought maybe you were dead," Marged murmured, her face pressed in the comforting hollow of his neck. "It doesn't matter if you must leave tomorrow, just so long as you love me tonight."

"Oh, Marged, my love, my love," he breathed hoarsely, fighting the constriction in his throat.

Their mouths met and were consumed by fire. Never before had Marged experienced such painful pleasure. The heavy-limbed aching of her body as he caressed her, as he kissed her with the well-remembered sweetness of long ago, was agony to endure.

He shuddered as he pulled apart the lacing of her bodice. Eagerly he cupped the full beauty of her breasts, soft as silk, pliant, throbbing. When he traced his thumbs over her raised nipples, Marged moaned in delight. She strained toward him, seeking the imprisonment of his lean hands, terribly aroused by his caresses.

Whispering love-words, she traced his lean cheeks, his high-bridged nose, his fiery lips. Lightly he kissed her fingers, forcing himself to hold back to extend their pleasure. In grim silence he assisted her with his clothing, aching to feel the fiery caress of her sensitive hands awakening him to such splendor that he could hardly breathe.

In the flickering yellow fireglow, they gazed rapturously at each other's body. Unlike the last time, the safety of this locked door added a sense of security to their lovemaking. Like a magnificent god, he stretched beside her on the curtained bed, firelight bronzing his powerful shoulders and muscular arms. Marged was awestruck by his beauty. Her admiring gaze swept from his wide, smooth shoulders to his taut belly. A scar jagged toward his navel, another puckered the skin on his inner arm, both proclaiming his profession without marring his beauty. The dark mat of hair on his chest formed an elongated triangle, drawing her gaze down to the embodiment of his passion.

"I never dreamed a man could look so beautiful," she whispered as she gently caressed his throbbing, burning flesh, darkly engorged with desire. Marged bent her head and kissed the velvet-smooth tip of his manhood, arousing him to exquisite pleasure.

He groaned, sinking his hands in her hair, imprisoning her head against him while he trembled beneath the terrible delight of her darting tongue. Too close to release was she bringing him, until he was forced to wrench away her mouth.

Bringing her head up, he welded his lips to hers in a searing kiss. No longer were their caresses gentle. His demanding tongue ravaged hers as they threshed, limbs entwined, on the down-filled mattress. His ears roared like a crashing sea, and he pinned Marged beneath him. The magnificent sensation of her silken limbs, the marvelous resiliency of her full, upthrusting breasts and firm thighs burning against his flesh, drove him nearly insane with need.

Marged was drowning in a sea of ecstasy, made delirious by his hands, by his kisses, by the terrible demands of the swollen pressure against her thighs. When Rolfe finally positioned her against the mounded pillows, when he parted her legs, she sobbed in anguish for him to complete what he had begun. Eagerly she strained upward, desperate to receive his burning flesh, writhing blindly until she encountered that throbbing impalement. Unable to endure a moment longer, Rolfe plunged inside her in a blazing thrust. And Marged strained to take him deep within her body.

His hungering mouth bruised hers, and their breaths mingled as Rolfe moved slowly, rhythmically, careful not to end their pleasure too soon. Twice he drew back. She sobbed in delight, clutching his broad, smooth back. Carried higher and higher as her ecstasy mounted, she finally raked her nails across his flesh, but he didn't notice the pain.

Rolfe moved even faster as he swept her to that vast blackness where their mutual passion exploded in a blaze of fire. Down, down Marged plunged, wracked by pleasure, until the silent room was filled with her cries. Tonight she relinquished the last vestige of herself, sacrificing all to him whom she had been born to love.

{ *eight* }

LAYERS OF CLOUD hung low in the gray morning sky. A cold wind, blowing off the mountains, swept Hereford's narrow streets and swirled smoke above the chimneypots.

Marged shivered as she stood in the shadow of the timbered inn, waiting for Rolfe's departure. A dozen times last night as she lay in his arms, as she listened to the beat of his heart and smelled the fragrance of his body, she had prayed that day would never break. Once again they had shared their deepest passion on the eve of departure. This morning he was to join the Yorkist army on its march to rendezvous with Richard Neville, Earl of Warwick, Edward of March's powerful cousin.

"The time is nigh, sweet," Rolfe said huskily. How he longed to be free of his sworn obligation, so he could take her far from Hereford. "I like it not, your riding alone. Are you sure you won't take men to guard you?"

"No. You need all your troops. The roads along the border will be clear. Bowenford's little more than a day's ride."

They stood silently in the cobbled innyard, longing to say

tender things, but the jostling troops maneuvering into riding order intruded on their privacy.

"I'll come back for you, I swear." He took her hand and pressed it to his lips. "My written orders ensure your safety at Bowenford. Now that Chagall's bound for Brittany with a flea in his ear, they've a new commander who knows you not."

Marged smiled at him, trying to fix his handsome face in her memory, every detail so dear, so beloved. Impulsively she touched his cheek and he seized her hand, pressing it to his mouth, his blue eyes soft with love. She shuddered with emotion. Her eyes were glazed with tears as she whispered, "God keep you well."

"And you."

Rolfe's mounted men stood ready, their impatient mounts snorting and pawing the ground. With a sigh he reluctantly took his horse's reins from the groom, and was debating whether to embrace her before his men when Marged forced his decision. Gripping his armored shoulders, she stood on tiptoe and pressed her soft mouth eagerly to his. "Return safe to me," she whispered, trying to swallow the ache in her throat.

Turning to his embarrassed squire, who was flushing to the roots of his flaxen hair, he took his red-plumed helmet.

Marged stepped back, forcing a smile, though her heart ached at the prospect of losing him only hours after their reunion.

Rolfe swung into the saddle and raised his hand in farewell. Then he was gone, riding to the head of the column, steeling himself against the temptation to look back.

The vast procession of armored men and wagons slowly rattled out of the Black Boar's yard. A handful of women were riding behind the baggage wagons, muffled to their eyes against the winter cold. Common soldiers' wives often followed their men into battle to cook their meals and minister to their wounds. For the first time in her life, Marged wished to be a lowly kitchen maid, free to follow wherever her beloved led.

When the last wagon passed, Marged found something startlingly familiar about the wench bringing up the rear of the cavalcade. Not until she rode through Hereford's winding streets, keeping to the center kennel to avoid the jostling crowd, did enlightenment dawn. The soldier's wench reminded her of

Joan Vaughn, the orphan who had sought her charity. It was an unpleasant reminder of a life that would never be the same, now that her father was dead.

Marged realized in surprise that her stepbrother Martin was master of Bowenford. When she reached home she would send a messenger to Sir Humphrey Lloyd, telling him of their bereavement and asking him to break the news gently to her brothers.

As Marged rode through the wooded border valley, the rising wind delivered intermittent showers of sleet. The darkening sky revealed a building winter storm. She passed a signpost pointing the way to Aconbury Priory, and though it lay in the opposite direction from Bowenford, she decided to seek shelter there until the storm passed. Already, Merback Hill, Sugar Loaf, and the Skirrid were nothing but blurs in the distance.

When she left the main road to follow the narrow lane to the priory, her vision was obscured by the high hawthorn hedge atop crumbling banks wildly tangled with russeted ferns and dead grass. To her horror, when she rounded a bend, Marged found the road blocked by a party of Yorkist soldiers.

Thinking only of flight, she wheeled her mount about and plunged through the first break in the bank. Even as she galloped across a stubblefield made drab by winter, the soldiers' shouts of glee signaled that they intended to pursue her. Desperate to escape, she increased her horse's pace. Not usually a slow animal, this morning he appeared sluggish. She had barely reached a straggling wood when the soldiers burst into view and scattered across the field.

Though Marged had no actual reason to fear these men, her instinct drove her deeper into the woodland. Among the common soldiery, rape was hardly deemed a crime. Triumphant after the bloodlust of their recent battle, these Yorkists probably considered her fair game. As Marged plunged through tangled thickets of gorse and beech saplings, another thought pounded icy fear through her veins. When they had finished with her, perhaps the men would return her to Edward of March! How she wished she had not been so foolishly confident about her safety when Rolfe offered protection.

Cold air seared her lungs. Marged gasped as the icy wind

whipped her hood from her head, sending her black hair streaming like a banner behind her. The horse was almost blown, and though he still galloped, Marged knew she must soon rest him. Sounds of pursuit still echoed loud in the winter quiet, forcing her on. She had hoped that once she disappeared in this rough terrain, the soldiers would fall back, but losing sight of their quarry seemed only to have spurred them on.

Marged raced across a clearing, ducking to avoid a tangle of branches as she reentered the trees. A limb cracked loudly in the frosty air as it smashed her across the chest. Unprepared for the force of the blow, Marged toppled from the saddle with a scream of fright. Her heedless mount galloped on.

For a few minutes she lay stunned on the mossy ground. Myriad lights flashed before her eyes and a strange, burning taste filled her mouth. At last Marged tentatively moved her legs and lifted her arms. Though each movement was filled with excruciating pain, she was relieved to find she was not badly hurt.

"Lie still, wench," a man commanded.

Marged gasped in shock, fear prickling through her veins. She must have been too stunned to hear the soldier's approaching hoofbeats.

"Here, let me see if aught is broken."

A dark figure loomed out of the misty blur. The man knelt beside her, his knowledgeable hands searching her limbs for broken bones.

Momentarily defeated, Marged lay submissively beneath his examination, her dark hair obscuring her vision. A fine blue velvet doublet and gold rings glinting on his hands were all she saw of her captor.

The man finally scooped her hair from her face, chuckling as he said, "You're all but blinded by your tresses. Soft and black as night they—"

Their eyes met. And Marged sucked in her breath in horror. She was gazing into the softly handsome face of Edward of March.

"You!" He rocked back on his heels. "By all that's holy! Never again did I expect to set eyes on you."

"Let me alone! I'm no longer your prisoner!" Marged cried. When she struggled to sit up, her head swam and a wave of nausea flooded to her throat. With a moan, she fell back.

A delirious rush of excitement filled Edward's veins as he gazed upon his wayward prize. He had seethed with anger when she gave him the slip, yet he had to admit a certain admiration for her audacity. This past week he had reconsidered his behavior, and come to the conclusion that if ever he saw the wench again, he would pursue her in a far gentler manner. In fact, so much had she intrigued him, he had lit a sea of candles in Wigmore chapel, petitioning the saints to allow him one more chance to win the raven-haired beauty.

Edward was more than a little awestruck by the swift granting of his prayer, especially since that blessing came hot on the heels of his overwhelming victory at Mortimer's Cross. This fresh reminder that his life was touched by divine destiny sent a chill down his spine.

"Lie still," he urged huskily when Marged struggled to get up. "Here, sweet, you're freezing." Edward stripped off his fine fur-lined doublet and draped the garment, still warm from his body, about her shoulders. Cradling her in his arms, he eased Marged gently to a sitting position against a nearby tree. Though she knew she must escape, every time she moved, a hideous giddy sensation took hold of her.

"I've a flask of wine on my saddle. I'll bring it to you."

Marged was freshly surprised by his changed attitude. Without his doublet, clad only in white shirt and hose, royal Edward could easily have been taken for a yeoman's son. "Thank you for your kindness," she mumbled.

He flashed her an engaging smile before he sprinted through the trees, reappearing a few minutes later leading a fine black horse. From the saddlebow he took a wine flask. Gently cradling her head against his knee, he put the flask to her lips. She coughed and spluttered over the unexpected richness of Malmsey.

Presently the soldiers appeared through the trees, surprised and relieved to have found both their master and quarry.

"The wench is injured. We'll carry her to the priory," Edward said when several men came forward to lift her.

The soldiers had intended to suggest that this comely wench would provide good sport, but something in their commander's face stilled their bawdy tongues.

It was Edward himself who lifted Marged, holding her tenderly against his broad chest. He walked with measured tread, and she was aware of the steady beat of his heart. A soldier took her until Edward was in the saddle, then he handed Marged up to his lord, as carefully as if she were made of fine crystal.

The procession set off slowly, following the forest path to Aconbury Priory.

With every movement, Marged was overcome by fresh waves of sickness. Edward whispered soothing words to her as he tried to lessen the motion of his cantering horse. Several times Marged dozed, forcing herself awake when she realized it was not Rolfe, but Edward Plantagenet who nuzzled her face and pressed his lips against her brow.

A welcoming fire blazed in the solar of the priory guesthouse, where a pallet was prepared for Marged. She was covered with wool blankets. A novice brought her a bitter herbal brew to relieve her pain.

Minutes later, lulled by the warm fire and the soothing concoction, she sank deeper and deeper into the soft pallet, as if suspended on a cloud.

When Marged awoke, she could hear voices close at hand, and her blurred vision gradually cleared to reveal two figures standing beside a leaded window overlooking the barren garden. They were Edward of March and a middle-aged woman. Because of his high rank, the woman was treating him with deference, listening most patiently to his speech.

"So you see, Reverend Mother, I've little choice," Edward concluded gravely.

The prioress of this Augustinian priory nodded in understanding. "Yes, I do see your position, Your Grace. Could the lady stay here? She'll be well cared for."

"No." Edward's voice trembled with suppressed anger at her suggestion, and the prioress fell silent. "It's my duty to take her where she can live according to her station. A royal ward cannot be sloughed off like a peasant. Besides, she'll need a dowry and suitable marriage prospects, when the time comes," Edward added as an afterthought, his very tone suggesting he had given scant consideration to those matters.

Marged tried to sit up, but her heavy limbs seemed to be tied to the pallet; even her head refused to move.

Edward paced the floor in agitation. "I can tarry no longer. Even now, 'twill be a hard ride to catch up to the main body of troops. Aye, it was ill-occasioned of me to decide on a morning's hunt. Likely heaven will punish me for straying from my duty." He glanced piously toward the rafters as he spoke.

The prioress hid a smile. "Your Grace, if I cannot persuade you otherwise, we'll ready the lady for travel."

"Thank you, Reverend Mother, you're most understanding." Edward knelt reverently to kiss the prioress's ring. When she gazed into his face, his cornflower-blue eyes wide and guileless, even that worthy lady was not impervious to young Edward's charms. "Your ward will be ready before noon," she said.

After they had left the room, Marged puzzled over the fragmented conversation. Surely it was she they discussed, yet their words made little sense. She was no one's ward. Unless Edward, mindful of the prioress's sensibilities, had fabricated the story to explain his unusual interest in a strange young woman whom he had just rescued from the forest.

Marged's thoughts soon became hopelessly jumbled as she dozed before the hearth. From out of a comforting gray blanket appeared the novice who had ministered to her before, bearing a second herbal remedy.

"Drink this tonic, lady. You'll soon be revived."

Marged did as she was bid, finding that the sickly sweet brew masked the taste of an herb she could not identify. True to the novice's promise, the room gradually came into focus. Above her head, Marged could see mighty stone arches and wooden crossbeams. The solar's stone walls were draped with wine-velvet hangings and tapestries of brilliant hues. As she lay there contentedly looking about the room, she slowly felt herself enough restored to sit.

"There, didn't I say you'd feel better?" asked the novice gleefully. "Aconbury's famed for its herbal remedies."

Though chilly and austere, Aconbury Priory was not nearly as comfortless as she would have expected. In almost no time, she had been washed, her hair rinsed in rose water, and her underlinen replaced by lavender-scented garments. The novice apologized for the simple gown of ruby velvet she proffered, it being the only suitable raiment available at such short notice.

Marged smoothed the crumpled skirts, noting that although it was exceedingly plain and old-fashioned, the gown was of the finest silk velvet and had likely been left by a former priory guest.

When Marged was ready, the novice escorted her to the solar, where Edward of March was waiting impatiently.

"Ah, you're feeling much better," he observed, his eyes lit with pleasure as he watched her walk without pain.

"I'd never have forgiven myself if any harm had befallen you," he said, and turned to the novice who hovered in the background, saying, "You may leave us."

As she had been instructed by the prioress to remain as chaperon, the novice continued to stand on the threshold. Edward finally thundered, "Go!" before she fled in fright from this overwhelming royal presence.

"It does my heart good to find you well again."

"Thank you for taking care of me," Marged said guardedly, wary of this new Edward.

He moved closer until his doublet brushed her arm. "I care for you immensely, in a far different manner . . ."

"Your Grace, I'm a free woman on my way home," Marged reminded him sharply.

"Home? And where is that?"

"The castle of Bowenford."

"On the Wye?"

Marged nodded, turned uneasy by his unexpectedly knowledgeable question.

Edward casually withdrew a parchment from his sleeve. "Here is a list of properties forfeit to the Crown," he said as he unrolled the parchment and thrust it beneath her nose. "Look close, Lady Marged, and tell me what you see."

Nausea gripped her as Marged stared at the blurred words above his polished fingernail. "'Bowenford Castle, held by Sir Richard Bowen, traitor to the house of York, enemy of—' No! it can't be!"

Edward smiled, his face suddenly crafty, devoid of charm. "I assure you it's true. Many properties are now forfeit. Enemy holdings will be reapportioned as I see fit. My trusted lieutenant has already taken charge of your castle."

"De Bretayne?" Marged rasped, a spark of hope kindling in her breast.

"Nay, he was only temporary landlord. Another man, hand-picked by me. De Bretayne's worthy of a much finer prize." Something in Marged's changing expression halted Edward's speech.

"What think you of the Breton?" he asked sharply. An unexpected pang of jealousy speared his heart when he recalled that the dark-haired Breton was a handsome devil, with a sizable reputation with women; surely to God, he hadn't—

"Need you even ask what I think of him," Marged snapped, highly aware of the tension-charged moment, "after he seized my home by treachery?"

Edward's eyes narrowed over her swift declaration. He stared at her a moment; then, satisfied with her answer, he patted her shoulder. "Former enemies will soon become your friends—even the Earl of March."

Marged allowed her indrawn breath to escape now that the danger was past. Edward was far too possessive for her to arm him with the knowledge of her love for Rolfe. While he had given her little reason to suspect him capable of such crimes, headstrong Edward, her instincts warned her, might have no qualms about engineering a rival's death.

"Now I have no home. I'm dispossessed."

"Nay, you'll always have a home with me."

"Though you honor me with the invitation, you know I cannot stay with you."

"You've not the choice," Edward cried, his tone belligerent. He gripped her wrist. "You're a ward of the Crown."

"No!"

"Yes! And, by God, it's a position of honor for which you should be thankful," Edward cried as her eyes flashed with anger and she tried to pull free.

"No. I'm a free woman and I want to go home."

Edward yanked her against him. His nostrils flared in anger as he snarled. "Home? Remember, you have no home, you ungrateful chit! Would that I'd taken you when I had the chance—" He stopped, horrified by his unguarded speech. What of this second chance miraculously granted by the saints?

Hastily swallowing his anger, Edward forced a pleasanter tone. "It's considered an honor, not a punishment, to become a royal ward. Fret not. I'll take you to London. You can live in Baynard's Castle, my mother's home. In her youth she was a beauty—the Rose of Raby, they called her. People have only lately nicknamed her 'Proud Cis.' She'll like you well."

"If you bear any affection for me, please don't take me to London. I know nothing beyond the Marches. 'Tis where my soul's at ease," Marged pleaded, tears stinging her eyes.

"It's an honor," Edward repeated stubbornly, his voice grating. "Especially for the daughter of a knight killed on the enemy side. Indeed, had your father been a staunch Lancastrian, I doubt I could have publicly accepted you."

"What do you mean? My father *was* a staunch Lancastrian."

Humor lightened his eyes. "Aye, of a surety—if we promised him the right to keep his land, he pledged readily enough for York."

"You lie!"

Edward's face hardened. "Your loyalty's misplaced. I've no more time to bandy words. You travel either as a prisoner or as a free woman, it's your choice—but travel to London you will!"

Edward spun on his heel and strode to the door, his fur-lined doublet as bright as a kingfisher's feathers beneath the lighted sconce.

Stunned, Marged stared after him, gradually becoming aware of her trembling legs and of her heart thundering beneath her borrowed velvet gown. Edward of March had given her a lean choice.

Cold wind and driving rain hampered the army's movement through the Cotswolds. The rolling meadows, tree-crowned knolls, and mellow ironstone manor houses of the region's prosperous wool merchants blended into a sodden tapestry. Winter heliotrope and celandine provided tantalizing glimpses of the spring to come. As the travelers plodded southward beneath darkened skies, their mounts often sank belly-deep in watery ruts. Concerned for her health, Edward provided Marged with a litter. And though she sometimes used the vehicle at his insistence, she far preferred to travel on horseback.

At Chipping Norton, Edward made arrangements for Marged to be lodged in a comfortable limestone manor house belonging to the town's leading merchant.

Through the mullioned windows, Marged watched clouds scudding like foam across the sky. Far from cheering her, the wan spring sunshine turned her melancholy. At great risk of discovery she had tried to find out if they were to rendezvous with the de Bretayne troops. She learned nothing. Likely Edward was fully aware of Rolfe's movements, yet she was far too wise to ask what he knew. Several times of late when Rolfe's name was mentioned, Edward watched her with narrowed eyes. The discovery that he was even mildly suspicious deeply alarmed her. At eighteen years of age, the shrewd Edward was fast gaining a sense of his own destiny and would suffer no love slight gently.

"Ah, there you are, anxiously awaiting me." Edward's resonant voice preceded his entrance. He strode inside the room, dressed for riding in a plum-colored doublet and matching kid boots.

Marged turned to greet him, a fixed smile on her face. "I was watching the clouds, Your Grace. Had you told me when to expect your return, I'd have watched for you also."

Edward smiled, delighted by her pretty speech. When he looked at this woman, not only did his loins burn, but his heart quickened and his stomach pitched. Many were the nights he had lain awake contemplating the taking of her, yet he was no nearer that goal than he had been the day he rescued her in the forest.

"I've a gift for you."

Only then did Marged notice he held his hand behind his back. "Another gift! Surely you've already given me plenty. No more."

"There's one gift I'd bestow right willingly if only you'd let me," he murmured ardently. "You're a cruel wench to keep me waiting so long."

"I've told you, my heart's already sworn to another," Marged parried gaily. With a tinkling laugh she twisted away when he would have clasped her in his arms. Though she tried to appear lighthearted, her mounting unease made her role more difficult to play.

"Naught but a chivalrous game," Edward dismissed scornfully. Still smiling, he labored to keep his hot temper in check as he mentally reviewed her breathless confession of falling under the spell of a foreign knight at a tournament. "All wenches take champions to worship from afar. A nameless knight at a list—what possible comfort can you gain from love like that? I offer you so much more."

Edward slit his eyes as he watched her standing before the windows in the pale afternoon light, aching to possess her. His greatest pleasure lay not in forcing her to his bed, but from her loving submission. "Here," he said impatiently, producing the secret from behind his back.

He thrust a jewel-bright heap of fabric into Marged's hands. This latest gift was a shimmering purple cloak lined with marten.

"Oh, it's so beautiful! Surely you honor me too much," she protested as she unrolled the garment, letting the heavy fabric spill to the rushes.

"No protests. Wear it as a reminder of me. The color matches your palfrey's trappings."

She swallowed uneasily. Three days ago Edward had presented her with a handsome white palfrey caparisoned in royal purple velvet dagged with gold; strings of jangling gold bells hung from the Spanish leather harness. If Edward of March had his way, by the time they reached London she would be outfitted to be a princess.

In the beginning she had declined his lavish gifts, relenting only when her refusals aroused his towering Plantagenet rage.

"Thank you for your generosity," Marged said softly, her green eyes troubled.

Edward gazed rapturously upon her as he drew the heavy cloak about her shoulders. His heart raced with love. "For all these days I've treated you with honor. Never once have I tried to force you to come to me."

"You're been most chivalrous."

"My patience wears thin," he reminded her hoarsely. "Come, allow me one small kiss for my pains." Without waiting for her assent, Edward eagerly swept her against him.

Enfolded in his huge arms, pressed tight against his broad chest, Marged felt smothered. She resisted the impulse to shudder as she mentally compared his kiss to Rolfe's. If only she were free to say, "I cannot love you, Edward of March. I belong to Rolfe de Bretayne." But such devastating honesty would sound the death knell for the Breton knight to whom she had given her heart.

"I *will* make you my mistress," he warned grimly before he turned and strode away, his ominous threat echoing in the quiet room.

At long last, mighty Warwick arrived. Not as a conquering hero, but more like a whipped cur, his tail between his legs. He had been roundly defeated at the second battle of St. Albans. Feeble King Henry, whom Warwick had manipulated like a puppet, had been recaptured by his militant wife, ending forever any hope of a treaty with the Lancastrians.

Marching through rain, through mud, he had led the remnants of his battered force by back roads to avoid their victorious enemy. London he left to fend for itself. His final hope for glory lay in his young cousin Edward of March, the Rose of Rouen, the handsome, golden prince who wanted to found a new dynasty.

"Where is the King?" Edward demanded testily when he had heard out his cousin's tale of woe and liked it not.

"*You* are the King," said Warwick, bending his knee.

As Warwick spoke, a heavenly shaft of sunlight speared the heavy clouds to strike this tall, fair young man on whose broad shoulders rested the fortunes of the House of York. A slow smile formed on Edward's soft mouth, broadening until his blue eyes shone as bright as lapis against his suntanned face. The King! Now he was truly the fourth Edward, the first of the House of York!

Edward turned to his cousin and raised him from the floor. "Come, let us delay no further. We march on London. We may yet be in time to claim the throne."

When she received the news that London had not yet fallen to Queen Margaret, Marged was walking in the walled garden of her merchant host. Edward had excitedly disclosed that if they made haste they would secure the nation's capital for York.

This startling news made his attachment for her of far greater significance. No longer was Edward merely the Earl of March, but possibly the next King of England. "Am I to accompany you to the palace?" Marged asked uneasily.

"Of a surety, my love, your King commands it." Edward laughed at her shocked expression. A bundle of nervous energy, he restlessly paced the gravel walkway. He cut an impressive figure in his russet gown edged with ermine, splendid enough for a sovereign. "Now you must reach a decision," he said at last.

She froze at his words. Her tremulous hand seized a nearby branch for strength. "Decision?" she asked hoarsely, knowing he meant but one thing.

"Aye. There must be no untidy ends when we ride triumphant into London."

Growing impatient over her silence, he waited no longer. He seized Marged's shoulder and swung her about. She was standing on the raised flagged walkway of the rosebeds, he on the grass below. The difference in their statures compensated for, Edward eagerly molded her body against his, ignoring her struggles to free herself.

"No," Marged cried in warning as his manhood flared against her, hot, throbbing, leaving her in no doubt about his desire to claim her.

"Yes," Edward growled, his even white teeth gritted, his expression grim. "You can no longer refuse your King."

"You are not yet crowned . . ."

He shook her in anger. "Taunt me not with petty details. Yield to me tonight, Marged—ah, God, torment me no longer! I'm out of my wits with longing for you. Have I not given you gifts aplenty?"

"They were given without bonds—or so you led me to believe," she reminded him, struggling, yet knowing she was no match for his strength. The rising wind fanned her blazing cheeks and stole uncomfortably inside the collar of her gown.

"I want you now! Be not so heartless! Can you not feel—I've a mind to take you here. Why must I wait until tonight?"

She started to protest, but his mouth clamped down on hers in a suffocating kiss that he fully expected would vanquish her will. But she remained aloof, steeling her thighs against the forcing heat of his desire.

Muttering an oath, he thrust her from him, his eyes dark with rage. "You Welsh bitch!" he spat, his chivalry forgotten. "How dare you resist? You know who I am, yet still you hold out against my will. I won't stand for it!"

Marged cast one terrified glance at his livid face before she turned and fled. Her soft-soled shoes of velvet made her slip twice on the loamy ground, and on the last fall she grazed her hand against the rough stone wall; yet she ran on, seeking to escape her would-be lover, who had swiftly changed from lamb to lion once the crown of England was dangled before him.

He captured her beside the vine-hung archway that gave access to the lawn. Wrenching her about, he dragged her into a secluded corner where gnarled branches of espaliered apple trees terraced the Cotswold stone, and forced her against the wall.

"No," she gasped, her green eyes blazing with anger. "I don't love you. I don't want to lie with you."

He cursed roundly at her honesty, panting as he wrestled with her. "When will you want me?" he demanded, banging her against the wall.

"Perhaps I'll never want you!"

Again he bellowed in rage, wanting to hurt her in payment for wounding his vanity to the core. "You bitch!" he spat, rattling her until her hair tumbled about her shoulders. "Yield to me you will! I demand it!"

Tears glazed her vision. With all her strength she prayed that Rolfe would come to her rescue, yet she knew her fate rested solely on her own wits. "Please, Edward," she began, appealing to the softness in his soul.

But today, swelled with power, Edward was not prepared to be soft. "Please, Edward," he mimicked, scoffing at her words. He glared hostilely at her, longing to crush her beneath him on the damp ground, longing to make her his own. "You will yield," he ground out, beside himself with rage. He reached to his belt, and from its embossed leather scabbard he drew a jeweled dagger.

Terror flooded Marged's face as she stared in morbid fascination at the deadly weapon clutched in his ring-bedecked hand, glinting in the murky light. "Would you kill me in order to lie with me?"

"Nay, I want you not lifeless and cold, but lie with me you will," he growled menacingly.

Horror filled her when Edward, gritting his teeth, laid the trembling blade against her throat. She tried not to quiver as she felt the blade caress her chin.

"Yield to me!"

"No!"

They glared into each other's eyes; his pupils were dilated with passion, and Marged's glittered with fresh determination. For what seemed an eternity they battled wills in the walled garden of Choatesworth Manor; doves cooed from the stone dovecoat, and in the distant yard a dog barked shrilly, the sound echoing in the damp air.

Just when Marged thought she must surrender—she could no longer hold her head above the razor-sharp blade—Edward moved his hand.

"God, you try me sore," he groaned, his mouth petulant. "Yet, for all your cruelty, I cannot maim you. It's not in my soul to destroy such beauty."

Tears of relief and fright spilled down her flushed cheeks.

Edward stared at the crystalline droplets quivering on the tips of her thick black lashes. Never before had she appeared so bewitching; like one possessed, he reached out his trembling hand, gasping as he encountered the warm life of her.

"Love me then in your own time," he said gruffly, his voice shaking with emotion. "Though I want you so sorely my body's consumed with fire, I'll try to be patient. You've won this day, Marged Bowen. I'll pursue you no longer."

Hardly able to believe his words, she watched him turn away, his head drooping dejectedly as he sheathed his jeweled dagger. Today, as never before, his actions betrayed his extreme youth. Alternately fiery and meek, he had capitulated his desires rather than injure her. A warm surge of emotion flickered briefly through Marged's veins. Here, in this winter-bare garden, she had come closest to feeling affection for young Edward of March.

{ nine }

On Friday, February 27, 1461, the Earl of March made a triumphant entry into London. Richard Neville, Earl of Warwick, rode beside him, anxious to ingratiate himself with the populace and sharply urging his cousin Ned to do likewise.

At the sight of this brave Plantagenet sapling and his powerful cousin, the citizenry went wild. They lined the roads to cheer, bang drums, and blow trumpets for this savior who had delivered them from Queen Margaret's lawless army, rumored to leave towns pillaged and women raped in its wake. Londoners had shivered in their beds for days, and many homes and businesses were still shuttered in anticipation of the advancing horde. But now, with Edward's victorious entry, the danger was miraculously lifted. By popular assent Edward of March was loudly acclaimed England's king.

True to his word, Edward housed Marged in Baynard's Castle, his family's home, while he waited for events to peak. Situated where Fleet Ditch ran into the Thames, the castle rose out of the water like a Venetian palace, its facade ornamented by a row of turrets. Despite his assurance she was not his prisoner, Marged was not allowed to leave her guarded lodgings. She had not yet met Edward's mother. In fact, so evasive had he become about her proposed wardship, Marged doubted he intended even to reveal her presence to Proud Cis. She suspected Edward's sole aim was to make her his mistress.

On a gray Wednesday, March 4, Warwick had arranged an open-air gathering at Paul's Cross, which stood at the corner of the churchyard and had become a popular rallying point for political speeches. So eager was London's citizenry for a glimpse of their handsome young King, the narrow streets leading from Ludgate Hill were choked with a waving, cheering multitude.

Long months of winter cold, trapped within St. Paul's vaulted stone walls, made the church frigid as a tomb. During the brief *Te Deum* which followed the speechmaking, Marged shivered so miserably inside her marten cloak that she could scarcely make the responses.

Daily she had scanned the swelling number of Yorkist supporters and their retainers converging on London, hoping to find Rolfe among them. Warwick had issued summonses for loyal lords to assemble in the capital. As each cavalcade of strangers clattered down the cobbled streets, her anxiety increased. Would he never come? Was she to remain forever at the mercy of this headstrong Plantagenet prince?

This morning, dressed in lustrous blue velvet, the plumes in his blue cap adding inches to his already great height, Edward Plantagenet cut an impressive figure as he stood in the blustery wind to address his subjects. When his parting speech was done and Warwick too had said his piece, Edward and his retinue traveled to the palace of Westminster. Parliament was not then sitting but he was not going to allow that fact to stand in his way. Thrones had fallen through similar delays, and Edward had no intention of allowing his hard-won prize to slip through his fingers.

Inside the gloomy, torchlit Hall, beneath the ancient smoke-blackened rafters, he ascended the marble chair called "the King's bench." Looking magnificent in royal robes, England's scepter in his hand, he pronounced himself King Edward the

Fourth. The assembled noblemen who, at Warwick's bidding, had come to pay homage, cheered lustily as Edward smiled on them from his marble throne. Today's simple ceremony would suffice to hold the throne; his formal coronation could take place later.

During the lavish banquet that followed in late afternoon, Marged merely picked at her food. Glazed boars' heads, gilded peacocks, sizzling haunches of venison, and choice suckling pigs failed to tempt her appetite. The other richly dressed guests guzzled vast quantities of wine and stuffed themselves greedily with food, taking advantage of their new King's generosity.

She felt ill at ease among these courtiers. Gladly would she have exchanged the miasma of spiced food, wine, human sweat, and the acrid smoke from flaring torches, for the sweet fresh smell of the Marches after rain.

Tearfully pleading a headache, she beseeched Edward to allow her to retire. To her disappointment, she found him most reluctant to dismiss the brightest jewel in his diadem.

"Retire? The night's still young, my love. Today's our day of triumph. Such splendor may never again be ours," he protested, imprisoning her hand in an iron clasp.

"My head's bursting with the noise. If I eat another morsel, I know I shall vomit."

"Then go vomit—but return in time for the next dance," he said sharply, thrusting inside the sugared almond he had been about to pop into her mouth.

Marged's stomach reeled a few minutes later when, despite her protests, Edward grabbed her hand and pulled her to the center of the room. The guests gaily formed a circle about them, joining hands to chant a bawdy peasant round. Accompanied by many drunken jests and laughter, Edward was quickly proclaimed lover without compare, and Marged his captured prize. Always delighted to be the center of attention, Edward swept Marged into his arms and kissed her soundly on the mouth.

"Oh, Edward," Marged gasped as she clutched his arm and half fell against him dizzily. The drunken, laughing dancers hooted in delight, considering her swoon to be sexual ecstasy.

Edward frowned. "Go, then," he growled in an undertone.

"Must I satisfy myself with another wench?"

"If you must," she whispered, her voice sounding muffled over the pounding in her head.

The gay peasant round at an end, the guests' attention shifted to a party of gaudy mummers who bounded inside the Hall.

Edward handed Marged to a nearby page, whom he charged with her safekeeping. Abruptly he swung about and singled out a lustrous redhead for the honor of his attention. But if he had thought to pain Marged by his indifference, he was sorely disappointed; she left the noisy Hall without a backward glance.

The searing air robbed Marged of breath as she stepped into the dark, walled garden. Though the wind carried the stench of London's streets, its icy embrace was welcome after the overheated Hall.

"Am I to escort you to your chamber, lady?" inquired the page as he huddled in an alcove to shelter from the wind. He propped the flaring torch in the corner, where it began to blacken the stone.

"Aye, if you will. First I must clear my head."

The lad nodded, preparing to await the lady's pleasure.

A loud rustling in the shrubbery startled Marged. A couple emerged from the bushes and sped across the winter-brown grass, the woman breaking into hysterical giggles as the man grabbed the streamers on her headdress and yanked the contraption from her head. With a squeal she reached to her head, too late to prevent a cascade of golden hair from falling about her shoulders. Though she protested loudly, once she came within a narrow beam of light spilling through the oriel windows, she halted, awaiting her swain.

Marged glanced casually at the wench's flushed face. Her own smile froze. Joan Vaughn, her half-sister's maid, stood in the flickering torchlight. This time there was no mistaking her identity.

"She-devil!" cried the young gallant in silver brocade as he leaped a narrow marble bench in pursuit of his quarry. "Mistress Joan the Tormentress should be thy name."

Eager for him to resume his pursuit, Joan again let loose a high-pitched laugh that jarred Marged's brittle nerves. They soon disappeared around a bend, their footsteps echoing down the stone corridor.

"What do you know about that woman?" Marged demanded of the page, who stood smiling after the departing couple.

"She entered London in the train of a foreign knight. From the look of things, she doesn't intend to leave with him."

"A foreign knight?"

"Aye, a handsome devil, much loved by the ladies. Breton, I think."

The breath choked in Marged's throat. Forcing back the pain, she croaked, "Is his name de Bretayne?"

"It could be. But then, lady, most foreign names sound alike."

To the page's delight, Marged walked swiftly toward the building. "Will you return to your chamber now?" he asked expectantly. The sooner he could dispose of this unexpected duty, the sooner he could pursue his own pleasure.

Marged nodded, not trusting herself with speech.

"My master's set his cap at her, though he has little hope of winning her attention. They say pretty Joan comes from Hereford way—"

"I've no wish to discuss her," Marged snapped, wanting to slap the lad for his idle gossip.

"As you will, lady. My apologies," the lad mumbled, bewildered by so sharp an address. When they reached Marged's chamber, the page thrust his flaring torch into an iron wall sconce, then knocked before unlatching the heavy door. A maid emerged from the shadows; curtsying, she held aloft a candle to light Marged's way.

Curtly she dismissed the page, who skipped eagerly away.

As she walked toward the hearth, tension stiffened her spine, making her movements awkward. Joan Vaughn and Rolfe—no, it could not be! Besides, pages gossiped like alewives. In numb misery she extended her slender hand to the blaze. It was no use making feeble excuses in an effort to lessen the pain. With her own eyes she had seen Joan Vaughn ride forth from the Black Boar. Like a fool, she had marveled over the resemblance of a nameless soldier's woman to Joan. Even now, Marged sought to comfort herself with the thought that perhaps Joan had not belonged to Rolfe in Hereford. The long journey across England had surely changed that fact. While she had been parrying Edward's unwelcome advances, traveling to

London a virtual prisoner, Joan had stolen her lover.

"Aren't you going to speak to me?"

Marged spun about, catching her breath in shock at the unexpected voice. Pain, liquid and hot, swirled through her body as Rolfe stepped away from the shadowed window, his skin appearing dark as a Moor's in this uncertain light.

"You!"

His mouth twitched to a faint smile. "Well, I've been welcomed with considerably more joy."

"Why did you admit him?" Marged demanded, rounding on the little maid who trembled beside the hearth.

"But lady, I thought... he said—"

"Don't blame the wench," he growled. "Go fetch wine and supper for us, there's a good girl," he said, his tone softening.

The frightened maid backed toward the door.

"I've supped already," Marged snapped, her emotions in a turmoil.

"I have not."

In all this time she had dreamed of the day Rolfe would deliver her out of Edward's unwelcome embrace; never once had she thought to quarrel with him. Even in her wildest nightmares she had not anticipated that jealousy over his relationship with another woman would curdle her stomach.

"When did you arrive?" she asked stiffly, avoiding the painful subject uppermost in her mind.

"Yesterday."

"You were at the ceremony at Westminster, then?"

"Yes, beloved, I was at Westminster. With my own eyes I saw our glorious leader proclaimed Edward the Fourth. Yet not in a hundred years was I prepared for what else I witnessed this day."

Marged's head snapped up as she heard the barely suppressed rage in his voice. Misery flooded over her in a sickening wave. He had seen her at Edward's side and wrongly concluded that she was the King's mistress! In all those romantic imaginings of deliverence, she had not foreseen his anger over her relationship with Edward, assuming he would never question her faithfulness.

"Think you I'm here because I want to be?" Anger surged through Marged's veins at the injustice of his insinuation. She wanted to scream at him, to push him away when she vividly pictured Joan's pretty, simpering face pressed against his. "Edward captured me and brought me here against my will!"

Rolfe smiled grimly as he looked down at her, pain at her betrayal stabbing like a knife in his heart. "'Tis a pretty tale, yet being privy to certain court gossip, I find it hard to believe. Apparently your relationship with our handsome monarch is not of such recent standing—they say he sported with you at Wigmore. Is that true?"

Numbly, Marged shook her head.

"Speak, for Christ's sake! Have you lost your tongue?" he growled, his knuckles white against his emerald velvet doublet. "Did you stay with him at Wigmore?"

"Edward first captured me there—yes," Marged admitted reluctantly.

"And you told me not! At Hereford you played the faithful lover, and all the while you were his!"

"No! I've never been his! Not once has Edward been to my bed."

"You must think me a fool to tell me such lies."

"They're not lies!"

"You swore you loved me true."

"I do love you true."

He swung about and marched to the hearth. In the fireglow, his blue eyes glinted like metal. "You, lady, are a liar. They tell me Edward's showered gifts on you. And that he lay with you each night."

"It's not true! He gave me gifts merely to persuade me to his bed."

"And what did you give him in return?"

"Nothing!"

"With my own eyes I watched him kiss you; the exchange was far from brotherly," Rolfe snarled. Suddenly coming more alive, he seized Marged's arm and pulled her against him. "I'm not so big a fool as to believe that young Edward, great lover of women, would be satisfied with nothing. A mere kiss is such a paltry reward—"

"You have my word. Despite the gossip, he's never taken me."

Their eyes met, raw emotion flickering between them. In

the charged atmosphere. Marged began to tremble uncontrollably.

"Would that I could believe you," he ground out.

At his words, the trembling that had beset her turned to blazing anger. "How dare you call me liar! How dare you accuse me of giving myself to another!"

"Surely, of all men, I have the right," he growled, gripping her shoulders until they ached. "We loved, lady, or have you forgotten, now that you've become the King's whore!"

Eyes blazing, Marged struck him hard across the cheek.

Rolfe stepped back, taken by surprise. Anger burned deep red across his dusky skin. "I'll not forget that."

"Neither shall I. Nor shall I forget your latest whore—empty-headed Joan!" Marged waited for him to hotly deny her charge. The betraying expression that crossed his lean face tore her heart to shreds. "Oh, God," she moaned, fighting tears, "you don't even deny it."

"Unlike you, lady, lying is not one of my failings. Though it was not my intention—"

"Enough! I don't want the details."

Rolfe seized her and shook her till her teeth rattled.

"You will listen! After your flight, I used the wench to relieve the pain of your betrayal. She was a nameless body. She meant no more to me than that."

White-lipped, Marged glared at him. "Nay, I'll not swallow that excuse. She's here in London. And she traveled with you from Hereford."

"Not at my invitation. She ran away from Bowenford."

"To be with you?"

"Yes."

A sob escaped Marged's compressed lips. Though she struggled to be free, he held her tightly until her peach satin gown ripped and the seed pearls sewn onto it bounced like grain to the rushes.

"You oaf, you're ruining my gown!"

"Edward will replace it with another, for he's ever generous."

Marged longed to dispute his remark, yet honesty forbade a denial. His eyes blazed. He grabbed the neck of her pearl-embroidered bodice and, ignoring her shrieks of alarm and attempts to stay his hand, brutally ripped the garment from neck to hem. He stared at the vision before him: her black hair was disheveled, her luscious breasts spilled like ripe fruit. Moving as in a dream, with an involuntary grunt, he captured the prizes so temptingly displayed before him.

At his touch, pain, fear, and excitement swirled through Marged's veins. She fought like a vixen against his caresses, gasping as he crushed her breasts, imprisoning her painfully. "Take your hands off me! I'll summon the guards," she cried, shaking her tangled mane out of her eyes, blinded by tears of pain.

"You're mine! Whether Edward stakes his claim or nay, you will yield to me . . ."

"Never! I'd sooner die than lie beneath you. Get you back to Brittany. And take Joan with you. For going to so much trouble to be with you, she surely deserves some reward."

Her mockery speared Rolfe like steel. Lamely his hands dropped from her ripe flesh, leaving fingerprints.

Weeping, she struggled to hold the edges of her gown together to hide her nakedness. Jaw tight, she raised her head, summoning the last vestiges of her dignity. "Get out! Never again do I want to lay eyes on you, you Breton cur!"

Rolfe blanched. Pain momentarily doused the fire of angry desire and spread through his veins, chill as the winter sea.

"Of a certainty, Lady Marged. Never again shall I approach you. Edward is welcome to your favors. You always were a treacherous bitch. Mayhap I'll take Joan home with me to Brittany. Unlike you, she's ever obliging."

Momentarily stunned, she finally let Rolfe's bitter words penetrate the pounding blood in her ears, and creep icy-cold down her spine. But when she would have cried, "Nay, come back, I did not mean it," pride clamped her lips shut.

Rolfe spun around, his emerald-green doublet dark in the gloom. A moment later he reached the door, not deigning to even turn for a final glimpse of Marged, breathtakingly arousing in her ruined gown, where flesh poked seductively through the shredded satin.

Maid and mistress stared at each other in shock. She had entered just as he stalked out. It was the maid who first regained her senses. "Oh, lady, what's happened to you?" the girl shrieked in dismay, racing to her disheveled mistress. The tray of food lay forgotten on the floor.

Grief stabbed Marged's heart. She wanted to resist the maid's comfort, to stand on her pride, but she found herself helpless in the face of sympathy. She allowed the girl to rock her like a baby as she sobbed against the linen-clad shoulder. Rolfe had gone. Never more would he come to her, afire with need, his mouth sweet and hot, his body throbbing with desire. Their love was over!

Once her devastating pain had lessened sufficiently, she wrapped her cloak about her ruined gown and paced the long corridor outside her door, furiously vacillating between love and hate. No man who loved her so dearly as he professed would treat her so cruelly. For Rolfe to have accused her brazenly of lying was insult enough, but to have viciously destroyed her gown, exposing her body like that of a common harlot—

"Have you come to make amends?" inquired a deep voice from the curtained alcove.

Gasping in alarm, Marged spun about, clutching her cloak about her body in defense. "Don't come near me," she warned him menacingly.

"Why, will you call forth the guard to defend your virtue?" Rolfe stepped toward her.

"You've not even the decency to apologize."

"I came to ask if you forgive me sufficiently to let me wear your colors in tomorrow's joust?"

"No! Perchance dear Joan will give you her garter to flaunt before the crowd."

His voice rasped as he said, "It's as I thought—Edward's to wear your favor."

"If he asks for it, you know I can't deny him."

He gave a derisive laugh. "Of a certainty, lady, one must never deny the King any favor he asks. Forgive me for my ignorance."

He made a mocking bow, and Marged clenched her fists in torment, longing to strike him—to caress him.

Unable to endure more, she turned and fled, her cheeks crimson with humiliation. Never again, she vowed, would she speak to him. He had dared to wait for her in the darkened corridor after his anger cooled, arrogantly convinced she would melt into his arms. Teeth gritting she half-turned at the door, secretly hoping he would be standing there. Perhaps, if he held out his arms to her, she would bend. Pride, after all, was too bitter a taskmaster. But when she turned the alcove was deserted—Rolfe had gone.

Rooks cawed loudly in the wind-wracked elms that formed the boundary of Eltham's tiltyard. When the uncertain spring sunshine finally speared the clouds with gold, a resounding cheer echoed through the stands at the welcome harbinger of warmer weather. Edward had devised this hastily arranged tournament as an expression of his gratitude for the noblemen who gave their support in his hour of triumph.

Billowing, colorful tents housed the competing knights, while around them milled an army of squires bearing armaments and grooms leading mighty destriers who neighed in eagerness for the coming sport.

The contests lasted through the day, as heavily armed contenders thundered through the lists to ram their opponents with blunted lances and unseat them. Royal Edward himself took part in the early jousts, wearing Marged's purple kerchief on his red-plumed helm.

By midafternoon, Marged's eyes burned and her head ached. For most of the night before, she had lain awake rehearsing speeches of forgiveness, then in the next breath angrily dismissing the effort. Today the pain of betrayal held her in its thrall. Vivid pictures of Rolfe embracing Joan flitted before her burning gaze. And to add salt to her raw wounds, Joan Vaughn, attired as brightly as a Flemish whore in carmine silk, gold veils fluttering from her horned headdress, was sitting in the stands to Marged's right. A swarm of courtiers buzzed around her, lavishing compliments to turn her vain head. Every time Joan's tinkling laughter pealed out, carrying far in the clear air, Marged gritted her teeth.

As afternoon shadows lengthened and the east wind sharpened, the assembly began to fidget in their seats. A banquet was to be followed by a masque and grand ball, and Edward's courtiers were eager for the next round of entertainment. The final joust of the day was being prepared below. A knight in black armor, sitting astride a great black destrier, paced beyond the tents, weighing his lance in his hand to get the feel of the weapon before he entered the lists.

"Come, Marged sweet, why so long a face? Have you still a headache?" Edward asked solicitously, turning about in his gold-draped seat.

"Yes. It must be the excitement," she replied lamely, her gaze stealing to Joan, who was fluttering a long carmine scarf over the heads of those seated below.

"Well, we'll soon sup. Good food and drink will surely revive you," Edward assured her confidently, turning his attention back to the tourney.

Warwick, who was now popularly nicknamed the Kingmaker, was seated beside his cousin. He glanced back at Marged, his expression thoughtful. Undeniably handsome, powerful, and popular, Richard Neville nevertheless always made her uneasy. Though outwardly affable, he struck her as possessing great guile.

The cloak she clutched about her body was heavy, yet the rising wind chilled her to the bone. To her surprise, Rolfe had taken no part in today's tourney. As each new combatant galloped forth, she had looked in vain for his standard. Perhaps he had already left London. That Joan had stayed behind, brazenly flaunting herself before the assembly, seemed small comfort.

A strident fanfare of trumpets announced the contenders for the final event. A flutter of interest circled the stands as heads craned forward to identify the two riders. The knight in black armor bore no insignia, causing the assembled courtiers to speculate about his identity.

"They say he's a foreign knight," said someone behind them.

Edward, overhearing the comment, smiled smugly, his attitude betraying his knowledge of the mystery knight's identity. Warwick too appeared pleased by the revived interest in this flagging event.

The black knight's opponent wore a blue surcoat depicting a gold wheatsheaf; he thundered before the royal box, doffing his plumed helm to receive Edward's indulgence. Smiling, Edward threw him a gold chain bearing the new device he had adopted since his victory at Mortimer's Cross: a gold sun in splendor recalling the parhelion that had shone to turn the tide of his last, victorious battle.

The knight clad in black cantered forth, maintaining the suspense of his unknown identity by not doffing his helm. Bowing solemnly from the saddle, he saluted his sovereign with his gleaming lance, and halted before Joan Vaughn; her voice, shrill with excitement, had been calling out to him. "Here, Sir Knight, honor me by wearing my favor."

He nodded, the funereal plumes atop his closed helm bobbing, and held out his mailed hand to receive the favor before galloping away.

"Are you excited, Lady Marged?" asked Edward meaningfully. "Was not your dream lover a mystery knight such as he? Black-clad and oh, so fascinating?"

Marged blanched, not wishing to have her lie paraded forth in public.

"Yes, Your Grace, he was a great champion."

"If the black knight wins, I'll insist on his taking off his helm, just for you, my sweet. You shall award his prize."

A hush descended over the stands as the knights rode to their places. The signal to advance was given, and the thundering hoofbeats of the rushing destriers echoed to the spectators, who gave such a great shout that it drowned out the clash of lances as the galloping contestants met. Neither rider was unhorsed.

Both knights returned to their starting places.

Whether it was the one knight's mysterious identity, or some other intangible emotion, the spectators were enthralled. Twice more the knights charged without decisive gain. Having completed the number of lance thrusts in the rules, the contestants switched to hand-to-hand combat. Each round involving the different weapons was to be limited to three blows in honor of the Holy Trinity, the number chosen by Edward in an uncharacteristic burst of piety.

On foot like giant turtles, the knights circled each other. Marged shut her eyes and covered her ears, her nerves jangling at the battering assault of crashing swords. In the last round, the knights switched to mace and axe, and as they swung, a shout of excitement was followed by groans of dismay, which forced Marged's eyes open. The black night was leaning over his sprawling opponent, who was too exhausted to continue. A great cheer went up as the blue knight's squires came forth to carry their fallen lord to his tent.

Jumping to his feet, Edward joined in the cheering for the victor; Warwick also stood to applaud, the courtiers following suit. Marged alone stayed seated, holding her aching head.

"Sir Knight, you fought well. Come forth to receive your prize."

Recalling that she was the one who must present the award, she hastily straightened her gown and forced a smile to her mouth.

The black knight had remounted his huge destrier and was slowly circling the roaring tilt field. He stopped at the royal box, which was draped in blue and gold satin, lavishly embroidered with the arms of York.

"We salute thee, Sir Knight. Come, show your face. Everyone's eager to learn your identity," Edward proclaimed, his resonant voice carried on the wind.

The black knight did not speak, nor did he raise his visor. Marged found him strangely inhuman in his steel armor, his closed black helm adding to his sinister appearance. She shuddered, wishing to have an end to this masquerade. The knight was inching forward, nudging his mount until the animal stood snorting less than a foot from Edward's makeshift throne. Then the mystery knight slowly removed his gauntlets, deliberately building suspense to enhance the crowd's excitement.

"Here, my love, present this to the champion." Edward pressed a gold helmet ornament into Marged's palm; the sharp metal sunburst grazed her skin.

"This too, my lady." Warwick handed Marged a heavy leather purse containing the reward for this final, spectacular combat.

Marged stood, swallowing her nervousness. Applause rippled through the stands at the sight of one so beautiful chosen to honor today's champion.

The black knight raised his mailed arms to his helm and uncoupled the fastenings. The buzz of excitement heightened. Inching up his helm, he removed it with a flourish. The breath was stifled in Marged's throat. Exposed was a handsome face she both loved and hated—Rolfe de Bretayne!

Edward smiled, extending his hand before turning to Marged and nudging her to present the prize. Rolfe remained unsmiling as their eyes met. All day the advantage had been his, for Marged had sat in plain sight behind the royal household. He had also seen her colors worn by England's monarch, the discovery bearing out his assumptions.

Marged swallowed, summoning courage despite the ache in her heart. A treacherous burning sensation began behind her eyes as she said, "For your valor, Sir Knight, you are awarded this purse of silver."

Rolfe accepted the silver. "Thank you, my lady."

"And also the personal device of our most gracious sovereign..." Marged's voice cracked. Clearing her throat, she hastened on, "the sun in splendor."

The glittering device was likewise politely received. He fastened the gold ornament to his black helm where later it would be permanently mounted. Following the presentation, he held aloft his plumed helm for all to see his esteemed award. A great cheer resounded from the stands.

"Do us the honor of attending tonight's ball, de Bretayne, accompanied by the lady of your choice. See, we've a goodly selection. Come, indulge us by revealing to whom the honor of today's combat shall be awarded." Warwick's voice, smoothly ingratiating, nevertheless bore a jagged edge. Even Edward looked askance at his popular cousin, wondering at the unusual request.

Marged swayed where she stood. She had been expecting a secret communication from him, some sign to show she still possessed his heart. Politely formal, he had maintained his silence, his blue eyes steely and remote.

"Yes, by all means select a lady, Champion," Edward joined, his gaze roaming with practiced eye over the assembled women.

Rolfe glanced about the gathering as if deliberating on a choice. Marged clenched her fists in a turmoil of expectancy.

"Have you made your selection, de Bretayne?"

"I have, Your Grace."

Eyes misted, Marged waited, disregarding all danger of discovery. Her heart raced when she realized the revelation would trigger Edward's jealousy, yet recklessly she dwelled only upon the delight of being reunited with her beloved.

"And who is she to be?" Edward prompted, chuckling as he feasted his eyes again on the delectable array of pretty faces and swelling bosoms.

"The lady whose colors I wear—Mistress Joan Vaughn."

The ensuing cheer drowned out Marged's strangled gasp of surprise. Swaying, she gripped the wooden rail as pain thundered a tempest in her ears.

"A right goodly choice. We commend your taste," Edward was saying as he half turned toward her.

Stricken, she watched white-faced as Rolfe unwound the carmine scarf from his helm and rode to the next section, standing in the stirrups to hold out the fluttering fabric. Joan half fell from her seat, exclaiming in joy. She leaned over the wooden barrier, her carmine bodice gaping to provide a stirring sight for the assembly. Rolfe looped the scarf about her shoulders, gently drawing her toward him in symbolic capture, and kissing his willing prize. Marged almost fainted.

Edward slipped his hand beneath her elbow and inclined her toward the steps. "All in all, it was a most entertaining afternoon, was it not, sweet?"

She could only nod agreement to Edward's affable remark as she stumbled blindly down the wooden steps, the pain of Rolfe's rejection crueler than any knife thrust.

{ ten }

ELTHAM PALACE BLAZED with light. This Thames valley palace was not as luxurious as Edward would have liked, yet it had seemed foolish to move so large an assembly back to London merely to feast. In time he would renovate Eltham to his own taste; plans already seethed in his brain.

The old-fashioned minstrels' gallery afforded a sweeping view of the festivities in the Great Hall. Edward smiled in contentment as he looked down on the brightly arrayed courtiers who milled below, thoroughly enjoying his hospitality. Tonight would be a night to remember, if only for the lavish round of entertainments to honor his ascension to the throne. The laughter and gaiety of his court, influenced by his own person, would soon sweep the cobwebs from the royal palaces. Edward knew he made a startling and welcome change from shabby, mad Henry, who had shuffled through the palace corridors like a mendicant friar. However, his full enjoyment of the moment was flawed by Marged's strange, almost martyred mood. For all his patience, he was no nearer to tasting the delights of her body. Why was she proving so stubborn? Surely she was not fool enough to be waiting for him to offer her the Crown!

Edward's jaw dropped and he gripped the carved monk's

head on the fretted screen before him. Was that it? Could the tormenting Welsh chit have set her sights so high? Sweat broke out on his brow as he reviewed the startling possibility. Much as he might want to wed her—and in truth, he was not certain he did—he could not marry the daughter of an insignificant Lancastrian. And his council would never stomach the added insult of her family fighting for Lancaster.

He craned forward, annoyed by the familiar surge in his loins as Marged entered the crowded Hall. Gowned in lustrous scarlet brocade, trimmed with dazzling gold, she appeared as delicate as the stained-glass maidens in the chapel window.

The faint gold tint that gave her complexion the bloom of a ripe peach would surely flourish inside the darkest dungeon. And what of her body? Was it not too the softest golden peach ever offered to man? Involuntarily, Edward licked his lips as excitement spiraled through his veins. His hands clenched as he pictured those full globes of her ripe breasts crushed within his grasp. He must have her soon!

Brooding, he left the minstrels' gallery, his crimson velvet robe swirling about his legs as he strode purposely to the stairs and paused there, struck by a most brilliant solution. He would return Bowenford to her! After so generous a gift, she would surely be eager to come to his bed.

Music and laughter swirled around Marged in a numbing blanket. Several cups of wine had temporarily dulled her anguish over Rolfe's rejection. What use was love, if it became a turmoil of pain? Love should bring joy, happiness—

"My sweet, come, I've a gift for you."

Marged blinked in surprise as Edward's deep voice whispered huskily in her ear. Forcing a smile, she turned to her King and hastily dropped a curtsy. Before she touched the rushes, he seized her hand and drew her upright.

"To the high table, where I'll present it."

"You've already been far too generous," Marged protested.

Tonight she did not decline Edward's supportive arm as they threaded their way through the weaving dancers. Not one to stand on ceremony when he was in a good mood, he waved the courtiers back to their dancing when they would have bowed before him.

Behind the table sat a cleric, his gray hair ruffled, his lantern jaw unshaved, looking as if he had been lately roused from sleep. When they approached the dais, the man shuffled backward and bowed stiffly.

"Here, put the paper down," Edward instructed impatiently, moving aside a silver bowl of grapes to make a place for the cleric to unroll his parchment.

The wine was truly working wonders on her disposition. Marged smiled up at Edward, finding him unusually handsome tonight in scarlet velvet lined with cloth of silver. She plucked a small bunch of grapes and gaily popped a swollen purple fruit in his mouth, laughing when Edward kissed her hand, when he then imprisoned her fingers and nibbled their tips, highly aroused by her unexpected flirtation.

"Here, my love, 'tis a gift dear to your heart," he declared eagerly, his voice cracking as he slid his arm about her small waist. When Marged allowed him to place his hand tantalizingly close to her breast, Edward could scarcely contain himself. He yearned to be hidden from view so he might pursue his advantage. Suddenly realizing the music had stopped, he glanced about to discover the courtiers watching him expectantly. Damn the loose-tongued wretch who'd whispered there was important business afoot!

Marged too became aware of the lull in the festivities, but wine-besotted as she was, she had no objection to being stared at. The man she loved had forsaken her for another. Why should she not enjoy the favor of the King? Beyond partnering her in tonight's opening dance, Rolfe had not sought Joan's company, yet the terrible humiliation of being passed over in favor of that giggling nobody was proof enough of his rejection.

"What great gift are you to give me? A palace, Your Grace?" Marged asked throatily as she stepped closer to Edward where he stood before the high table.

"That too would I gladly give you," Edward began; then, realizing he could be overheard, he self-consciously cleared his throat and moved away from her intoxicating body. In a clear, ringing voice he announced, "Insomuch as you have pleased us greatly, Lady Marged Bowen, we hereby remove all restriction upon your property. We restore all titles and lands pertaining to the demesne of Bowenford in the Welsh March. We also restore your civil rights and remove all stain of attainder."

The joyful news was slow to register on Marged's senses. Great tears welled in her eyes and spilled down her flushed cheeks when she finally grasped the content of this special gift. Bowenford was hers! She was free to return home! No longer need she dally at this court, trying to elude Edward's panting attention, torn with anguish over Rolfe's indifference.

"I thank you, Your Grace, from the bottom of my heart. No greater gift could you have granted me than this," she whispered, her voice trembling. Marged went down on her knees on the carpeted step.

Edward's large, beringed hand shook as he grasped her shoulder. There was one further gift not yet received, but that would come. "Inasmuch as Bowenford can be returned to its original state, I will strive most diligently so to do."

Discreet applause echoed about the Hall before the guests turned to each other, tongues wagging merrily about Edward's transparent generosity.

As Marged stepped from the dais, she uttered a cry of distress. She had almost fallen into Rolfe's arms. Tonight he was achingly handsome in an emerald doublet and tights with red-laced kid boots reaching to his muscular thighs. It was almost more than she could bear when, with a mocking smile, he said, "Congratulations, lady. Such generosity is often hard won."

Marged could not prevent tears forming afresh at his scornful comment. His mouth quirked to a smile, yet his eyes remained as hard as steel. Miserably she watched him stride away, her pain mounting when he headed for giggling Joan in her gaudy carmine gown. Though he had not stated it, his eyes showed that he believed Edward's generosity was in payment for her body. Ironically, this most cherished reward—Bowenford—had destroyed all chance of her regaining Rolfe's love. There was no way to convince him now that she was not Edward's mistress.

The parchment clenched in her fists, she turned and walked blindly through the Hall.

The musicians struck up a gay dance, and laughing couples

were taking their places in the center of the torchlit Hall. Edward glanced about, seeking Marged as his partner. He beckoned to her, but she failed to respond.

Head high, tears shimmering on her lashes, Marged was blind to all save the agonizing sight of giggling Joan in Rolfe's strong arms, the swift blending of black hair and gold tresses as they kissed.

Snow fluttered past Edward's leaded window as he sat before the hearth. He had summoned Rolfe de Bretayne to his chamber for a private audience, and he was waiting for the Breton's arrival. Not one to sit still for long, Edward the Fourth crossed to the window and looked down on the street, where the March wind gusted great clouds of smoke to the tall gables.

"You sent for me, Your Grace?"

Edward turned his dazzling smile on his friend. "By the Christ, Breton, have you forgotten my name's Edward?"

"No, nor have I forgotten our friendship in times past."

"You speak as if that friendship were over." Puzzled, Edward raised his cornflower-blue gaze to the unsmiling man before him. "Surely you're not bound for Brittany already? We still have nine tenths of a kingdom to win."

"I'm prepared to take up arms today, if that be your wish."

"Good." Though Edward smiled, unexplained tension remained between them. "Come, sit down, stand not on ceremony. Malmsey?"

"Aye, Malmsey will suit well enough."

He filled a goblet almost to the brim and handed it to him. "Warwick goes ahead to gather forces," he said between gulps. "Fauconberg follows within days, with the foot soldiers. I too intend to head north after we learn which way the wind blows."

"In what force are the Lancastrians?"

"Strong, but not invincible." Edward lounged in his chair, studying the man before him. Perhaps it was unwise to entrust this precious mission to one so handsome, he mused, his eyes narrowing. Aye, he could well see what women found attractive about this dark Breton. In such total contrast was this man's coloring to his own, they were a perfect representation of light and dark. Yet what was there to fear? After the tourney, de Bretayne had cast aside his chance to claim Marged as prize, choosing instead that flirtatious little blond dumpling. So much for Warwick's insinuations. At times his cousin could be a trial. Jealousy was likely the reason for his slanderous gossip; he was ever wary of men singled out for honors. It was as well Warwick would soon be about the business he did best, for Edward found himself increasingly reluctant to drop so treasured a friendship merely because his cousin did not approve.

"Tell me, de Bretayne, would you be willing to perform a personal favor for me?"

"Anything. Be not afraid to ask."

"I want you to escort a noble lady to her home. No doubt there are others who could manage the task as well—in fact, some have already put themselves forward—it's you I choose. As you're now my official champion, who could be more fitting to escort a fair damsel back to her web-shrouded turret?"

Rolfe's mouth twitched over the young king's poetic description. "Whatever you wish. My sword's as ready to defend a damsel as an army."

"This damsel is most precious to me."

When he beheld the insistence in Edward's grave face, a pulse in Rolfe's throat began to throb erratically. Surely it could not be she! To travel beside her for as long as it would take to reach the Welsh March would be damned nigh impossible to endure! "Are you not to reveal her identity?" Rolfe asked gruffly.

"In good time." Edward laughed, his mood brightening as he leaned across the table. "I needn't remind you that suspense is a very useful device to keep interest alive. You used the ruse most admirably yesterday. At times I even wondered myself if it was really you inside that black armor."

Rolfe waited, tense, anxious to have this particular mystery at an end. "When am I to leave on this mission?"

"Tomorrow at dawn, provided this weather doesn't prove hampering," Edward replied, glancing at the sky. To his immense satisfaction, the snow had ceased.

"I'll ready my men for departure," he said, standing. "Is there anything else I need know?"

"No, my friend. And you are a true friend, not one of those self-serving, perfumed jackanapes who cluster around me like flies about dung." Edward chuckled as he stood, his immense height bringing him a good four inches above the Breton. "Lady Marged will be surprised to find it's you who are to escort her home. A word of warning, de Bretayne—try not to antagonize her. You must get along. It's time to bury our differences. In fact, it's my devout wish that you and she be friends. Two people so dear to my heart must not be at odds."

Rolfe was on the verge of withdrawing his offer. Any feeble excuse would suffice to free him from this unwanted obligation. As Edward had said, any of a dozen others could perform the task as well. But short of revealing the truth about his past relationship with Marged, he could think of nothing to say in his defense. Grimly he walked to the door, only remembering to bow to his sovereign at the last minute.

"Look not so grim," Edward admonished with a laugh. "This journey will not be without compensation. A fat reward shall be yours once the task's complete. And you may take pretty Joan with you, my friend. I'll warrant the nights will not seem near as cold."

Rolfe fashioned a grin at Edward's humorous suggestion, his features stiffly unresponsive. "Thank you . . . Edward, you are ever generous."

With gritted teeth, Rolfe reviewed his meek reply as he crossed the bleak, windswept courtyard to the east wing of the palace. What a fool he had been! There were a multitude of ways he could have declined this honor without revealing the truth of their relationship. Now his course was set. He must obey his sovereign, but there would be little joy to the errand.

Perhaps it was as well he had given his word. By their close proximity in the ensuing weeks, he could prove to himself once and for all that his passion for Marged was dead.

Clouds gamboled like spring lambs across the rain-washed sky, as Marged bid a tearful goodbye to the handful of friends she had made in London. Maud, the young maid who had waited on her during her stay, was to accompany her back to Bowenford.

Though she had expected him to be present, Edward had been called away to an urgent meeting of the war council. Instead of his presence, he conveyed his regard in typical fashion—an exquisite gold chain, at the end of which hung enameled white roses. The accompanying note was suitably tormented.

Marged frowned as she thrust the love note into the velvet purse hanging from her chatelaine. Edward's promise to visit her before the month was out made her uneasy. Safe within Bowenford's strong walls she might be, yet England's king had ready access to all manors and castles. In return for his splendid gift, he would surely demand the ultimate payment. Marged winced at the bleak reminder of the months she'd spent spurning the King's advances.

Grim-mouthed, she looked out for one last time on the clustered gables of London town. Smoky, sooty, and noxious in sound and smell, it would be no hardship to leave. The thought that within the week she would be back among the forested hills of the Marches lifted her spirits.

The cavalcade clopped slowly beneath the stone stable arch, and into the narrow, cobbled street beyond. Edward had promised an armed escort for her journey. The soldiers must have intended to join them en route, for only four menservants, Maud, and Marged herself rode out of the palace precincts. Two loaded sumpters carried Edward's gifts, luxuries both for her body and her household. She felt a pang of guilt over her lack of affection. Perhaps it was the ulterior motive behind his generosity that robbed the gifts of their luster. Or was it more because her heart ached for that cruel knave who had trampled her tenderest emotions beneath his mailed foot?

Marged clenched her hands on the reins and defiantly raised her head, keeping her back ramrod-stiff, her chin uptilted in pride. She was a Bowen, and not given to whimpering and feebleness. Let him have his flighty Joan. Perchance a wench of such simple mentality flattered his ego, for she supposed giggling Joan was far more malleable than she.

As they approached the West Gate, Marged saw a body of mounted soldiers, which she supposed was the promised escort.

"Oh, lady, I'm sore afraid of such a long journey," Maud confided, her thin lips trembling in fear as she looked about the teeming city streets. "I hear tell they're savages on the Marches."

Marged laughed, her spirits rising as they drew closer to the gateway and freedom. "Nay, who told you such nonsense? My mother was Welsh, and I'm no savage. We live in a grand castle, not a pigsty."

The girl smiled gratefully as Marged squeezed her bony little hand, anxious to impart courage before they were jostled apart.

The captain of the troop of soldiers clattered over the cobbles toward her. "Are you Lady Marged Bowen?" he asked.

"Yes. Are you the escort provided by the King?"

"Yes, lady. Our commander will join us presently. In fact, that's his party arriving now. Come, move the sumpters closer."

The menservants were not skilled with pack animals, and Marged wished she had brought grooms instead. Here in the shadows of the city wall, the air was cold. She huddled inside her purple cloak, anxious to be on the high road. The commander's party contained several women; she could see their cloaks fluttering in the strong March wind that swept keenly about the buildings.

The troops maneuvered into riding order, and the four menservants formed a shield around Marged and her maid, as they had been instructed by their royal master, to protect their precious charge from the common soldiers. Not wishing to invite robbers, this royal guard did not display the King's arms, but traveled steel-jacketed and anonymous.

Marged leaned across her horse's head to rest her back, which ached from her ramrod-straight carriage. All helmeted soldiers looked very much alike, she thought absently. Many of these soldiers bore a striking resemblance to Rolfe's men.

"Am I not to speak to your commander?" she asked the soldier who had greeted her at her approach.

"He did not say. Do you wish to speak to him, lady?"

"Certainly. I'm entitled to know under whose protection I travel."

The man disappeared to the rear of the rank. She watched him single out a man and speak to him. The stranger shook his head. What arrogance! Their commander must deem her unworthy of his attention.

Smarting under the insult, she kept close to the eaves of the nearby buildings, allowing most of the troop to clatter past her through the gate. The four menservants waited beside her, not questioning her actions. At last, when the street was clear, she urged her purple-caparisoned mount forward, heading for the tall commander, who stood quaffing bread and ale beside his lady's saddlebow.

Twin spots of angry color flared on her cheeks as she jostled her mount out of the way of a lumbering goods wagon, momentarily losing sight of the soldier whose back was toward her. When the wagon finally creaked out of the way, the commander was already mounted, his helmet in place, the visor down. His lady and her maids had ridden through the city gate.

"Do you consider yourself too noble to speak to me?" she demanded, urging her mount alongside his. "I'm insulted that you didn't even care to introduce yourself. The King would think ill of your manners, sir."

Amid the press of people traveling back and forth through the West Gate, the two riders held their ground, swaying aboard their mounts like vessels at sea. The commander finally grabbed her horse's bridle, steadying Marged alongside. With his free hand he reached to his helmet and smashed back his visor.

"We've been introduced long months ago, lady," Rolfe snarled. "As this was no journey of my choosing, the less we see of each other the better."

She stared in disbelief, pain hitting her so hard that she felt as if she had been dealt a physical blow. What macabre jest was this? Surely the Breton was not to escort her to Bowenford! It could not be true!

"I shan't go with you."

"That's an interesting statement, but a pointless one."

"How could Edward do such a cruel thing? He surely does not realize—"

"Dear Edward chose me himself. Have sense, you fool woman. Edward knows nothing about us, thank God—unless you breathed the truth to him while disarmed with passion!"

"Damn you!" she wrenched her horse's bridle free. "You haven't changed one bit."

"Neither have you, lady." With that angry retort, he maneuvered his mount about and, as fast as he was able, rode through the gate and onto the highway.

Torn between anger and pain, her mouth set in a grim line, Marged followed his example. Never in all her wildest fancies had she anticipated that he would be her escort home. She secretly longed for him still—in her dreams, Joan Vaughn was not riding beside him. Perhaps, had she been the same foolish little wench who had fled Bowenford, she might have schemed to win him back, eagerly competing with Joan for his affections. But that foolish wench was long since dead. Never again would she sacrifice her pride for Rolfe de Bretayne.

Two days out from London, they broke a wheel on the supply wagon. The delay cost them half a day, forcing them to sleep under the stars instead of safely inside a local manor. Though heaped blankets and down pillows from the wagon made a passable bed, Marged chafed at the inconvenience.

They pitched camp in a grove of birches. The trees' papery silver bark gleamed ghostly in the light of the rising moon. Overhead, clusters of purple blossoms lingered amid knots of ripening leaves. The gusting night wind blew cold, fluttering the branches until they sighed and moaned.

The mournful wind increased Marged's loneliness. She resolutely thrust aside weakening thoughts of Rolfe. All those bittersweet memories belonged to the past. If she must picture him, it should be as he was tonight, sitting with Joan and his men while they supped on rabbit stew and drank French wine generously provided by their grateful monarch.

An eerie scream, close at hand, startled her. Her scalp prickled. It was only a curious wood owl, perched on a nearby branch. She smiled in relief as her heart ceased its frenzied pace. When she slowly raised herself up, the better to see the brownish owl, she heard it give a great cry of tu whit, tu whoo, accompanied by a tremendous flapping of wings, before it soared above the treetops. For an instant the bird hung motionless, black-shadowed against the moon, before disappearing from sight. Marged was glad Maud was asleep. Had the faint-hearted maid heard the owl's eerie call, she would have sworn they were beset by witches.

A long shadow fell across the path as someone came silently upon her.

"Are you comfortable?" Rolfe asked gruffly. "I apologize for stranding you in the woods."

Tension screamed through Marged's limbs at the sound of

his voice. Mastering her emotions, she replied stiffly, "It could not be helped." And she drew her cloak tighter about her body in a primitive gesture of defense.

He smiled grimly at her action.

"Did you see the owl?" Marged asked at length, when he continued to stand there watching her.

"Yes. At this time of year they hunt food for their young. Need makes them bold . . ." he ended in a somewhat strangled voice.

She swallowed, not sure he still spoke about owls. His face was obscured, his elongated shadow black upon the moon-splashed glade. For one terrible moment that seemed to stretch into eternity, they stared at each other. It was far too dark to read his expression, yet Marged could feel the burning intensity of his gaze. Her heart lurched, then began to flutter uncontrollably as warmth flooded her veins. Despite all she had vowed, she waited, deliciously anticipating—

"Rolfe, love, come, 'tis cold alone."

That peevish, easily recognized demand shattered Marged's growing sense of well-being. "Go, 'Rolfe, love,' your sweetheart calls," she spat.

Without saying another word, Rolfe spun about and crunched back through the undergrowth. He left her only the whining March wind for comfort.

Spring settled warm and gentle on the land. Wood anemones covered the ground like patches of melting snow; primroses dusted the wayside banks; the low-lying meadows where the Thames and Windrush rivers met were carpeted with lilac lady's smock, and golden marsh marigold.

They had ridden over the rolling chalk downs into the beech-clad Chilterns, drawing ever closer to the Welsh border. No longer could Marged muster the thrill of excitement she had expected from this homeward journey. Even the spring flowers and mild, sunny days served to increase her depression. Rolfe's tormenting presence had robbed the journey of pleasure.

"Here, Lady Marged, won't you accept these violets? They're so sweet-smelling. My feet got soaked whilst I was gathering them."

Marged stiffened as she recognized the light voice. It cost

her much effort to turn about and face Joan Vaughn.

"No, thank you, Mistress Vaughn. You went to so much trouble, the flowers should be yours."

Joan had expected no more. "Why do you hate me?" she asked suddenly, blurting out the question that had clouded her days since they first left London.

"I barely know you."

"That's no excuse. You still hate me."

Marged fought for polite, casual words to hide the pain that tore her heart to shreds whenever she beheld this golden-haired wench with the pansy-soft eyes. On that stormy day when she had first met Joan Vaughn, she never thought the wench would cause her grief. Marged glanced desperately toward the rippling waters of the Windrush, seeking escape.

"Why do you hate me?" Joan repeated, her fair face guileless. "What have I done to offend you?"

"You ran away from Bowenford after we took you in out of charity. I do not repay ungratefulness with deep friendship," Marged remarked curtly before turning about.

Picking up the wicker basket of flowers she had plucked, she squelched across the meadow, moving as fast as she could, desperate to leave Joan Vaughn before she sacrificed her pride by revealing the truth.

Today they were lodged at an inn in the ancient town of Burford, close by the parish church of St. John. Marged found the homeward journey through steep, narrow streets a thousand miles long. At last, greatly out of breath, she finally reached the sanctuary of her room, where Maud awaited her.

"Please go below and see if my meal's prepared," she said, anxious to be alone in order to regain her composure.

When Maud had gone, Marged went to the window, where she stared at the blossoming garden set against a blue, cloud-wisped sky. The grass edged with nodding daffodils, the clusters of crocus nestled around the gnarled roots of a budding apple tree, were made ugly by the pain gnawing at her heart. To have lost Rolfe's love was punishment enough; she did not need the constant reminder of Joan hovering in the background, anxious to win her friendship. She must speak to him tonight and insist he control his woman.

Rocked by a sudden wave of grief, she threw herself across

the bed. She buried her face in the down pillows and wept long and hard.

A bitter smile played around her mouth as she finally calmed. Though her father was dead and her lover belonged to another, she still had Bowenford for comfort, that enduring pile of stone for which she had fought so well. She had put much effort into regaining her inheritance. Days and nights of holding Edward at bay, of allowing him to steal a kiss, a squeeze, protesting that she needed far more time to be sure. By such clever tactics she had finally regained her family home; by the same skill she had lost Rolfe's love.

The door handle clicked, and Marged tried to swallow the lump in her throat. "Put the tray over there," she croaked, her voice overburdened with tears.

The door closed and she assumed Maud had slipped outside. She was a good wench, ever mindful of her mistress's changing moods.

For a few minutes longer she lay there. Her sobs erupted anew, sending shivers coursing through her limbs. At last, her grief spent, she huddled in a ball of misery, trying to dispel the chill that crept over her body. Perhaps the warm meal would cheer her.

She thrust her tangled hair away from her flushed face. What a fool she was to lie here weeping about something she could not change. All these months away from Bowenford had made her more craven than she liked to admit.

The food was on the oak chest at the foot of the bed. Marged scrambled over the mattress to reach it. Just as her hand touched the covered bowl, an unexpected movement came out of the shadows. Everything happened so fast, she scarcely had time to cry out before her wrist was captured by a strong, sun-bronzed hand.

Rolfe stood unsmiling in the shadowed room, gazing down at her, his mouth grim. "Never did I think to hear you weep so hard," he said.

Her eyes were great dark pools as she raised them to his face. "My tears were not for your sight."

"No. And that fact moves me all the deeper."

"What do you do here, spying on me? Did you bribe the girl to let you bring my supper?"

"Yes—only I thought you would be pleased."

"Pleased! Pleased! God in heaven, why should I be pleased?"

He released her wrist and turned away. From beside the latticed window he said gruffly, "I was wrong. The other night I—I thought perhaps . . ."

Never before had she heard him at a loss for words. Pride, hurt, and love warred within Marged's heart until she thought she would go mad for the torment of it.

"I said naught to make you think I'd welcome you."

His uncertainty gone, he turned from the window. His jaw was tight, his eyes hard. "No, lady, you are right, you gave me no word of encouragement. I apologize for the mistake."

Regret surged in her veins before Marged gathered her wits sufficiently to say, "'Tis as well you're here, because I've a request to make before you leave. I am asking you to better control your whore. I'm not eager to befriend her."

His breath hissed like steam in the silent room.

"What did you say?" he demanded, taking a step toward her.

"I asked you to tell Joan to stay away from me!" Marged cried, her composure snapping. "Think you I'm a saint that I'd welcome the little bitch with open arms? You and she are a fitting couple. I've no wish for further intimacy with either of you."

Marged shuddered in fear as she looked at him. Anger blazed a trail over his lean cheeks, setting his features and stealing the softness from his eyes.

"You have no wish for intimacy," he repeated.

"That's what I said."

"Have you become so exalted within Edward's bed that we lowly peasants aren't fit to mingle with you?"

"Get out!"

"Answer me."

"I'll not lower myself to reply."

"You'll do as you are told."

As one mesmerized, Marged watched him come toward her, menacingly dark in his leather jack, his face as one with his curling black hair. The only betraying humanity to his features was the gleam in his eyes.

A gasp was torn from her lips as he wrenched her from the bed. Marged tried to escape, but he brought her up short, swinging her about, bruising her against his metal-studded chest. Only then did she realize he had locked the door, for she saw the key gleaming in his hand.

"See this," he growled, pushing the key in her face. "In payment for this, I want the truth."

"Don't you dare lay a hand on me! Leave me alone!" Marged struggled futilely in his grasp.

"Do you belong to Edward?"

"I've already answered that question."

"I want the truth."

"You've had it already," she exploded, kicking at him, struggling until her hair fell over her face. "How often must I tell you?"

"Say it one more time. Give me your word Edward of March has never taken you," Rolfe ground out, his hands enmeshed in her hair as he pulled her head back.

"You're hurting me! Let me go, you bastard!"

"Not until you've sworn."

"I owe you nothing! You're Joan's lover now—what does it matter whose bed I share?" Marged heard him grunt as if she had delivered a physical blow. "'Tis not pleasant to be spurned in public by one who professes to love me true."

"Nor did I enjoy watching you dally with *him*."

"Had you loved me as dear as you swore, you'd never have doubted my word."

Fury surged through him, and he shook her. "I came here not to argue the point."

"Why *did* you come?" Marged demanded, all caution cast aside.

His breath rasped as he looked down at her, barely able to distinguish anything beyond the blurred curves of her body, her perfumed tresses streaming over his arms. All reason flown, he tightened his grasp, pulling her stubborn body against his. "For this," he growled. And he kissed her.

She struggled beneath his brutal kiss, knowing she was dangerously close to revealing her true emotion. Fighting against his superior strength, she finally wrenched her mouth from his, tormented by the taste and pressure of his lips.

"Now you've taken what you want, get out."

"What makes you think I've taken what I want? That was just the beginning."

Seizing her, Rolfe lifted her from the ground, bruising her fragile flesh against his unyielding, steel-banded jack, refusing to release the pressure even when she gasped in pain. Turned temporarily insane with longing and desire, he forced her back against the foot of the bed.

"No! No!" Marged cried, threshing from side to side in desperation to free herself, lest she yield too readily to his passion. "Would you rape the King's mistress?" she screamed in thoughtless defense, seeking to extricate herself from this trap by any available means.

Above the surging fire of passion, the hateful words echoed until he groaned aloud in pain, sorely wounded by her defense. He had been struggling to unlace his hose as he prepared to claim her, but now his hand dropped uselessly at his side.

"So, at last we have the truth! You were ever a consummate liar, my love."

Though Marged cried out in dismay, though she sacrificed her pride and clung to his arm, he flung her away from him, his desire switched now to blazing anger. Throbbing with pain, she tried to pierce the gloom as he marched to the door and fitted the key to the lock.

"Don't go," she whispered.

But he did not hear as he threw open the door to reveal Maud hovering on the threshold, weeping softly over her lady's distress.

"Get you inside, wench, the King's mistress is in need of attention," he growled cruelly as he strode from the room.

Marged crumpled slowly at the foot of the bed. She listened in mute misery to his heavy steps thudding along the corridor, ringing like the knell of doom long after the sounds had ceased.

"Are you hurt, lady?" whispered Maud, tentatively reaching out to comfort her weeping mistress.

"Hurt beyond imagining—but only my heart is shattered," Marged replied, grateful for the warm hand of comfort. "Never allow our commander inside my room again."

"Nay, I promise. Even if he beats me," the girl vowed earnestly. "Come, sweet lady, your supper grows cold."

Hysteria shot through her frame at Maud's matter-of-fact statement. Perchance a cold supper would match her cold heart, she thought with grim humor, resisting the insane desire to laugh.

As they skirted Clun Forest, a light rain began to fall.

Marged's stomach pitched as memories of the beginning of her royal nightmare flooded back, memories of the night she wandered from Rhys's camp and was captured by Edward's men. She wondered, as she had often done before, about Rhys's reaction when he discovered she was taken. From time to time she had dwelled on the subject, alternately picturing his rage, his grief. It comforted her to think at least one soul missed her sufficiently to mourn. Since that night, she had had no further contact with her Welsh kinsman. It was likely Rhys had long since abandoned his search for her and joined the Welsh supporters of King Harry Lancaster. Whatever Rhys had felt, or done, mattered little now. Today nothing mattered. Her spirits were as low as the darkening sky.

Rolfe rode alongside her, his stallion snorting in high spirits. Since that tempestuous evening in Burford, he had kept his distance. Joan had been greatly offended when he insisted she was not to approach Lady Marged again, but, afraid of his anger, she had wisely abided by his wishes. His King would be pleased with the efficiency with which he had performed this task, he thought grimly, gritting his teeth against the nerve-jangling ordeal of speaking to her again.

"We'll seek temporary shelter beyond the bend in the road. There's a good hostelry less than five miles from here."

Marged nodded, her lips frozen shut.

"Are you dry enough, lady? I wouldn't want Edward's light o' love to take a chill."

She glared at him, eyes blazing in painful hostility, though she did not break her silence.

Without another word, Rolfe spurred his mount and returned to the head of the column, relieved to be free of her disturbing presence.

The wind increased, drenching them with showers blown from the sodden branches overhanging the path. Hunching lower in the saddle, Marged stared ahead into the gray blanket beyond her horse's ears. Not much longer to endure, she told herself in an effort at cheer, but the joyful truth did little to rouse her leaden spirits.

"My lord! My lord!"

Heads whipped about as cries of distress, followed by the clang of arms, came from the rear guard.

Uttering an oath of rage as he saw his men quickly engage with a robber band who had materialized out of the rain-soaked forest, Rolfe yelled for the men to protect Marged, before he raced to aid his beleaguered troops.

"There she is! That's March's whore! Take her captive!"

The eager shouts blew in the wind, making her heart thud in fear. She was the target of the attack! Oh, how she longed for weapons to defend herself! Rolfe's men, swords drawn, formed a grim circle about her. Somehow she did not feel as secure as she would have wished. Beside her, Maud was screaming hysterically, and though she hated to do so, Marged delivered the wench a resounding blow.

"Be quiet! Weeping helps no one."

Chastened, Maud hung her head, tears still streaming down her face.

"Come, lady, ride into the open," shouted one of Rolfe's soldiers. He seized her bridle and drew her mount away from the tree-darkened path.

Long before they reached safety, Marged's mount plunged in sudden fright, uttering a shrill scream of pain. A man, creeping stealthily from the foliage, had plunged a dagger into the animal's soft underbelly, ripping him open. Rearing, threshing, the frenzied horse bucked desperately to deposit his burden.

With a squeal of fright, she was unseated. Like that other terrible time when she had been thrown, she slid over the animal's hindquarters and bounced on the ground.

Lightning-swift, the knife-wielding peasant seized her and pressed his blade against her throat. Rolfe's men stepped back, not anxious to endanger her life.

"You're a traitor to the cause, Marged Bowen. Your father played us false," declared the man, his blunt, pockmarked face dark with rage.

She struggled to master her fear, for she had recognized him. "Sion, you were ever loyal to the Bowens," she gasped, as she remembered his name. "My father led you to battle in good faith."

Sion spat on the ground. He brought the wide-bladed knife closer to her windpipe. "Your father betrayed us. A hand in each pocket had Sir Richard, ready to move whichever way the wind blew. And you're no better than a whore, jumping in the usurper's bed, eager as a penny drab."

Color blazed in Marged's face, and she turned a look of sheer hatred on him. "How dare you speak so to me! I'm still your lord's daughter, you ungrateful wretch. Haven't we done well by you and yours these years past?"

"Aye, that you have. 'Tis other debts I'm repaying today," he growled, dragging her toward the shrubbery.

Helpless, the de Bretayne men stood by, debating whether to jump the peasant would risk their lady's life.

Maneuvering with surprising speed when he beheld their predicament, Rolfe galloped toward them, holding his bloodied sword aloft. The very ground quaked before his passage, and the men parted to let him by.

Sion blanched at the sight of this furious knight bearing down on him. He glanced about for his fellows, knowing he needed aid to stand him off. It had not been his plan to kill the Bowen woman, merely to capture her. Where were the soldiers who were supposed to come to his aid? They had assured him the Breton would already be dead!

Reining in less than a foot from them, Rolfe sent up a shower of mud. He leaped from the saddle, his sword at the ready; it gleamed crimson to the hilt.

"Let Lady Marged go," he demanded, holding the peasant's gaze while a couple of men slipped behind him.

"Nay, I've not power to release her to you," Sion mumbled, his glance wavering momentarily toward the trees, seeking friendly assistance that was not forthcoming. "She's to be held hostage for Lancaster."

"Are you willing to die for Lancaster?"

Hardly expecting the blunt question, Sion swallowed nervously, but did not slacken his grasp.

Marged had heard the men step behind her, and she understood Rolfe's plan. She prayed for them to hurry before Sion slashed her throat out of fear, for his hand already trembled alarmingly close to her windpipe.

Suddenly, Rolfe moved. Sion blinked in surprise, hardly expecting such speed from an armored man. Those of Rolfe's men who had crept behind the pair now sprang forward, taking advantage of the lull to whisk Marged from the peasant's grasp and drag her backwards through the dirt. When they finally set her back on her feet, cold mud squelching inside her boots, they apologized profusely for their rough treatment.

Sion sprawled lifeless in the mud.

"Are you all right?" Rolfe asked anxiously.

"Yes. Thank you for your bravery." Marged replied coldly. It was not what she wanted to say to him, nor did she want to stand here, stiff with pride, keeping a respectable distance between them.

They looked at each other, unsmiling. He had taken a step forward, preparing to speak, when Joan raced up to him.

"Rolfe, oh, Rolfe, are you hurt?" she cried, weeping copiously. She leaped to hug him, her arms tight about his shoulders, pulling his face down to hers to smother his grim mouth with kisses.

"I'm not hurt," Rolfe said gruffly as he forcibly set her aside. "Do you know this man?" he asked, turning back to Marged and attempting to ignore the emotion blazing in her eyes.

"He's from a farmstead within my father's demesne. Sion is his name."

"Have you any idea why he would turn hostile?"

"He says my father betrayed them."

His eyes narrowed. "You had naught to do with that."

She could not meet his eyes as she said, "He also hated me because of . . . of . . ."

"Edward," he supplied grimly, tightening his grip on his sword hilt. "I'll wager there's far more to this than meets the eye."

Not understanding, Marged looked askance at him. "More?"

"Aye." Turning aside, he told his men to drag forth one of the slain. "Strip him."

Obediently the soldiers ripped aside the leather jerkin, the homespun peasant shirt. A ripple of surprise came from them as scarlet fabric was revealed.

Rolfe rolled the corpse over with his foot. Stooping, he slashed away the ragged shirt sleeve to reveal a well-known insignia.

A wave of nausea gripped Marged as she recognized Warwick's crest showing a bear and ragged staff. "They're Neville men!" she cried in dismay.

"I suspected as much when I sliced a bastard earlier and his livery was exposed. That's a distinctive color. What worries me most is why Warwick set his men upon us."

"Perhaps there's someone he prefers for Edward," she offered reluctantly as Rolfe led her back to the supply wagon for a reviving cup of wine. "He doesn't always approve of Edward's choice of . . . of friends."

He smiled bitterly. "It wasn't you they wanted."

"But you heard . . . you saw . . ." she protested before he interrupted her.

"Had you been the prize, do you think they'd have abandoned you in a blockheaded yokel's charge? The traitor Sion was merely a decoy. No, I was their real target. And that worries me most of all."

"You! What quarrel has Warwick with you?"

He shook his head in bewilderment. "None that I know. But such men as he do not always voice their grievances aloud." He held out the wine flask to her.

She started in surprise as their hands brushed. She hoped he had not noticed her unguarded reaction. When she returned the flask to him, she was careful not to touch him.

"I'll get you another horse," he said, glancing to where the dying animal kicked, his entrails spilling in the mud. A compassionate soldier slit the palfrey's throat. "I hope you're not too distraught at having Edward's fine gift killed from under you?" he asked sarcastically.

Would she never get over that painful reaction to his every thrust? Holding her head high, Marged forced a sweet smile. "Being ever generous, as you so often point out, Edward will be only too pleased, I'm sure, to replace the animal when he visits me next month." Then, lifting her skirts, she turned and walked stiffly to the assembled men, moving more by sense than by sight, for her eyes were glazed with tears.

{ eleven }

FROM HER VANTAGE point atop the greening hill, Marged looked down on the lush valley of the Wye. Her heart rocked with emotion at the longed-for sight. There it lay—the rolling land of home. Before nightfall they would reach Bowenford. Yet because of the infuriating manner in which Rolfe had delayed this final stretch of the way, pausing to attend to the horses, to secure the vehicles, using almost any excuse to prolong their journey, Marged doubted she would sleep in her own bed tonight.

"Will you still ignore me at Bowenford, Lady Marged? Or can we be friends there?" Joan asked wistfully.

Marged drew in her breath. She spun about, her voice shrill with emotion as she demanded, "Must you always slip up on me like a cat? You're Alys's maid. She's the one to whom you must answer."

Joan's face clouded. "Lady Alys will beat me." Then, suddenly remembering a joyful fact, she blurted in surprise, "She'll have no power over me now! Rolfe won't let her hurt me. He's so kind—yet sometimes I think I please him not."

Grim-faced with pain, Marged turned away. She would not endure these confidences.

"Lady Marged," Joan cried shrilly, starting after her.

When the cloaked noblewoman failed to heed her cries, Joan stopped, a scowl darkening her face. By being *his* woman, she had gained innumerable privileges. She had even been to court, where she was flattered by jeweled nobles. Yet for all that, the most important favor of all eluded her. She yearned with all her heart to be accepted as an equal inside Bowenford castle. That humiliating scene wherein she had admitted to being base-born, the words gouged deep in her soul by Alys's lash, had left indelible memories. Had she been able to secure Lady Marged's friendship, her way to acceptance would have been assured.

She wheeled about, holding her head high in imitation of Marged's proud carriage. The haughty wretch! Well, she did not need Marged Bowen's crumbs of tolerance. She had Rolfe to protect her now! Rolfe loved her. He must love her, because he had not exchanged her for another, though many court ladies had boldly invited his favors. He does love me, he does, Joan vowed desperately, though the bitter truth stung tears to her eyes.

Seething with anger, Marged walked her mount away from the others. The men lay sprawled on the ground after their noon meal, dozing or gaming. Rolfe was nowhere in sight. No doubt he sought Joan to amuse him for a half hour before they resumed their journey. The idea stabbed painfully as Marged mounted the horse he had given her to ride.

No one prevented her from riding along the narrow trail down the hillside. The knowledge made Marged bold. Why must she await his pleasure? There were many passable back roads, and she could reach Bowenford by nightfall. The electrifying idea surged through her brain and she rode faster and faster, the freshening wind whipping color to her cheeks.

Growing even bolder, she galloped down the grassy hillock into the shallow valley, drawing closer to the meandering river hidden by the trees. Birch and oak rapidly gave way to goat willow as she neared, the river's scent, and the cries of birds sent a thrill through her body. She was almost home! Almost home! The thudding hooves took up the surging cry . . .

"Hold! God damn you, woman, hold!"

Marged's heart pitched; her stomach sank like lead. Rolfe was galloping flat-out over the sloping land toward her. Wasting little time in watching his approach, Marged wheeled her mount about and set off, desperately searching for a secret byway of which she had heard tell. The wild chase soon became a challenge that fired her blood. Let him gallop after her, for whatever good it would do him. This land was hers, and she knew it well.

Rapidly changing direction, she plunged her horse amid saplings coming to leaf, and thrust toward the depth of the forest. She shuddered at the impact of trapped winter cold. To her alarm, she could hear the thud of hooves behind her as he gained ground on her, the sounds echoing a hundredfold within the silent wood. And though her mount struggled valiantly, she could not urge the horse to greater speed.

"Hold!"

Again she ignored Rolfe's command as she led the animal into a copse where the ground squelched underfoot with spring damp. Her horse floundered in the mire. They reached high ground in time to see Rolfe, crouched low in the saddle, flying beneath the trees. A moment later he was at her side, his face dark with anger.

"God damn you, are you turned deaf!" he bellowed, grabbing her reins when she tried to outrun him.

Marged screamed in alarm, thinking she would be unseated when he pulled her mount up short and made the animal plunge and whinny with fright.

He seized her and wrestled her from the saddle. Fighting against capture, she kicked until his stallion shied and broke his grasp.

Exultation surged through her veins as she ducked under low-hanging branches and ran into the twilit forest. But Marged knew she was doomed when she heard his heavy footfalls closing the gap between them. Valiantly, she ran on until he grasped her shoulder.

Rolfe rasped a string of Breton curses as he pulled her about. "Where think you to go, little deer?" he demanded, surly, almost winded after his desperate pursuit.

"Home. 'Tis where I'm bound anyway, so surely you cannot object."

"You're bound there with me in attendance. No other way. I promised Edward I'd safely deliver his whore, and that's what I intend to do."

Marged's emotions were too ragged to bear his insults in silence. Her temper erupting, she slapped him hard across the cheek. "You've called me whore once too often."

Rolfe grabbed her, imprisoning her hands in his own; his gauntlets were cold and rough against her skin. "You're coming back with me."

"No. I'll go nowhere with you of my own free will."

"Then you'll go without it, but go you will. Can you not wait one more day to be shut of me?"

Marged heard a betraying catch in his gruff voice. Her head snapped up, and she met his iridescent blue eyes. He was wearing the purple doublet he had worn on the morning of the hunt. She blinked, momentarily disarmed by the reminder. That day she had fought hard against her emotions, but the overwhelming strength of his virility, the lure of his passion, had quickly vanquished her resistance. Even now, though his handsome face was set with anger, that other time seemed not so far distant. A ragged sigh escaped her lips, betraying to him that she was not nearly as unmoved by his closeness as she pretended.

"Marged, what happened?"

"Happened? I don't understand."

"Why did you trade my love for his?"

How she longed to say laughingly, "Because he's the King, you fool." He expected no less. Yet her lips would not form the glib lie. She raised her eyes to his, wounded afresh by a searing bolt of emotion as their gazes locked. All the sweetness that had once been between them flooded back with sickening clarity. When he made love to her, she had been transported through time and space, her raw nerves always shattered by the exquisite torment of his passion.

Rolfe shifted his feet, his boots sucking in the mud. "You've not answered me," he reminded her sternly.

Though Marged knew she should again take flight, she seemed rooted to the spot. Now she allowed herself the painful luxury of looking close into his face, of seeing those well-loved features and remembering all she had lost.

"I just want leave to go home," she whispered tearfully.

"'Tis where I'm taking you."

"I want to go alone."

"No. I'm charged with your safety."

His reminder of duty pained her. So close they had been, and now, with each elapsing minute, they drew further apart. "Need you bring *her* along to add to the insult?" she rapped.

He blinked, not expecting her explosive question. "It was your Edward's wish that she accompany me."

"He's not *my* Edward!"

A grim smile twitched the corners of his mouth. "Forgive me, lady, I was laboring under that delusion."

"You've labored under many delusions these months past."

"So you've taken pains to tell me. I wonder why I'm still not convinced."

Green eyes flashing, Marged made to turn about, desperate to be free of him. She had not the strength to endure another round of heated discourse.

"Marged!" Harsh, pained, his voice rang out, almost as a command.

She paused, her foot slipping on the sodden earth. "Yes?"

"Enough—Christ Jesus, enough!"

His rasping plea shredded her self-control. When Rolfe stepped toward her, she stood her ground, determined not to yield, defiant to the last.

"Bitch! Are you never to give me peace?" Roughly he grasped her arm. Sunlight filtered through the sparse branches, clearly revealing her quivering lower lip and tear-glazed eyes.

"Damn you, woman, don't you know I want you still?"

She gasped, trying to douse the leaping flames in her blood. Yet when she would have answered, her voice was buried beneath layers of pain.

"Is hate and bitterness all there is between us?" he went on. "Are you never to come to me again of your own accord? I will have you—willing or not."

She raised her head to meet his angry challenge, yearning suddenly to be done with all this pointless bickering, the lies, the deception.

"Joan's your woman now. What use have you for me?"

"Are you blind? Think you she could ever take your place?" he demanded harshly, forcing her against him, though she resisted his demand.

"Then why do you still take her to your bed?"

"Because she's available to me. She professed love while you profess only hate," he ground out, paining her with the truth.

Swallowing the building sobs in her throat, finding it nigh impossible to speak above the grinding pain, she whispered, "Ah, well now, at least we have the truth of it."

"Aye, you've got the truth, which is more than I ever had from you."

"I told you the truth long months ago, but you wouldn't believe me."

"Edward's no fool. He gives not jewels and castles without just cause."

"He's young and vain. He seeks to woo me to his bed."

His face granite-hard, Rolfe stared down at her, longing to believe, yet afraid of being hurt again. Had Marged yielded herself in his arms, his task would have been halved. But she never made tasks easier. "And what of me?" he ground out, trying to keep his voice emotionless.

"What of you? You seem to have found ready compensation for the loss of our earth-shattering love."

"Mock me not!"

He seized the back of her neck, twisting her face to his. He forced her to offer up her mouth when she would have turned aside, his angry kiss brutal with passion.

When at last he pulled away, Marged stared up at him, no longer able to fight the softening, burning ache that spread through her body. "Do you love me still?" she whispered though bruised lips.

"I'll love you forever."

"What of Joan?"

"Only say you'll be mine. I need no other."

She had vowed never again to sacrifice her pride to this

arrogant man, never again to place herself in a position where he could hurt her. But pressed close against his throbbing, arousing body, Marged could think of nothing beyond the screaming message leaping from his veins to hers.

"Oh, damn you, Rolfe de Bretayne, for your deceiving . . . I love you dear. I never really stopped loving you, even when you called me another's whore. And when you wounded me sore, I still loved you too much to arm Edward with the truth. He knows nothing of our love."

Their gazes locked. Marged shuddered at the message in his eyes; the blue grew limpid as he yearned for her with the same intensity against which she had fought all these months.

"Come to me later—nay, love me now. I cannot wait for night."

His husky words thrilled her beyond measure. Marged clung to him, aching to join him in passion as his manhood flared against her like molten steel. He showered her with passionate kisses, ravaging her mouth until it hurt.

They stepped to a moss-covered knoll crowned by weeping willows, where the chill wind swept through the cascading limbs, swollen with leaf buds.

"Will you let me love you beneath the willows like a peasant maid?"

"I care not where, as long as you love me. Oh, Rolfe, love me, take away the pain."

Tears mingled with their kisses. He held her against his warm body, shielding her from the brisk spring breeze, shuddering as she pressed ever closer. He was almost afraid to touch her ripe breasts, swelling within her blue velvet bodice, scant inches from his hands. When at last he made that contact, it seemed years between thought and deed.

"Oh, God, how much I love you," he groaned. "You don't know what agony it's been, picturing you with him."

"I needed not as much imagination to picture you with her," she reminded him bitterly, unable to keep from barbing him with her terrible pain.

"Sweet, I'm sorry," he murmured penitently. "Let's have an end of accusations, of bitterness and pain. Please forgive me. Say we'll love as before."

She smiled, moved by the sincerity of his husky voice; the

cobwebs of doubt were swept from her mind. How achingly handsome he was, how virile. No other woman, no other man, came between them now, alone on this island of passion beneath the budding willows, serenaded by the lapping Wye.

"Aye, I love you well. You've ruined me for all others, you Breton cur. My desire's aroused only by you. My body tingles only for you. My heart—"

Rolfe could endure her throaty, teasing words no longer. With an agonized gasp, he welded his mouth on hers, drowning her voice. Rolling her to her back, he shuddered in ecstasy as he pressed on her. How many nights he had ached to renew this bliss. He slowly unfastened her habit to reveal her full breasts, dark-tipped, upthrusting. His hands shook as he molded her pliant flesh, quickly rekindling the fierce passion he had thought buried forever.

Moving beneath his fiery caresses, Marged slid her hands over his neck and into his curling black hair. How she had longed to repeat this sweet intimacy, sobbing into her pillow because he no longer belonged to her. Now he was in her arms once more, his mouth hot with passion, his strong, muscular body throbbing against hers.

"Oh, Rolfe, I love you, I love you," she sobbed. Her tears splashed on his face as they rolled to their sides.

He swept her skirts above her thighs, stroking the silk-smooth flesh, advancing until he possessed the dark triangle between her legs. Marged writhed beneath the delight of his hand, uttering moans of ecstasy as he pressed his mouth upon the burning core of her passion. So much had she desired him, she was almost afraid of the delight of touching his swollen flesh. How smoothly, how perfectly he was formed. Scarcely able to breathe for the stifling ache of desire as she caressed his throbbing, heated flesh, she opened to him, desperate to become one with her beloved.

Rolfe covered her mouth with his when she cried out in delight at the longed-for sensation of that passion-hot invasion. She came close to bursting with the sheer pressure of his body. Never before had it been quite like this; never before had passion been so urgent, so tormented. He began to move, slowly, deliberately, torturing her with that hard, pulsing fire-brand. But soon he abandoned the practiced delaying art, for desire englulfed him in a black, abandoned wave, sweeping away all barriers.

Marged fought desperately to maintain control as he thrust again and again, battering down her willpower, releasing such a flood of passion that she screamed in agony. The floodgates flung wide open, she matched him stroke for stroke, soaring, building, until she was nearly insane with the pleasure of it. Her teeth penetrated his shoulder and she tasted salty blood.

In that time of fierce delight, which seemed to last indefinitely, they rebound their hearts, which had been severed by pain. Marged slowly came back to the chill forest, feeling the sharp wind against her exposed breasts. She shivered and he drew her into his arms, shielding her from the cold.

"Oh, sweetheart, you've made me whole again," she breathed. "It was so wonderful, I thought I was dying."

He smiled tenderly at her confession. "Me too," he whispered, tracing her tear-washed cheek with his tongue. "We were born for each other. What fools we were to spoil these past months. We must never again deceive each other."

She smiled and nodded, stroking his lean face, fingering his upper lip, where black stubble prickled his swarthy skin. "I promise. Oh, Rolfe, darling, you're all my life."

He swept her against him, shuddering with passion. Never before had he felt such tenderness for a woman.

Neither of them heard the steady clopping of approaching hooves. It was only when the animal paused, snorting as it scented other beasts, that they were alerted to intruders. Rolfe leaped up, rapidly concealing his nakedness. Marged's hands trembled in agitation as she thrust her skirts in place and fumbled with her bodice fastening. Simultaneously they beheld Joan Vaughn advancing up the incline.

"Now I understand the reason you hate me," Joan shrilled at Marged, her eyes brimming with jealous tears.

"Get back to camp," he snarled as he relaced his doublet.

"No! And you need take no pains to hide what you were doing on my account," Joan cried, fighting tears. "All this time she's wanted you. No wonder she could scarcely bring herself to be civil to me. I don't blame you. No man can resist—"

"That's enough!" He wrenched the horse's bridle about. "Get back to camp as you were ordered."

"Come with me."

"No. Lady Marged and I have much unfinished business. This is no casual bedding. So, if you know what's good for you, Mistress Vaughn, you'll keep your mouth shut!"

"Mistress Vaughn! Mistress Vaughn! How dare you address me so after—"

Breaking off a willow switch, he slashed the horse's hindquarters, sending the animal forward at a gallop. Joan shrieked in fright and threw herself against the horse's neck, desperately clutching his mane to keep from being unhorsed.

As the sound of thudding hooves receded, so did Marged's feeling of well-being. She felt again the cold wind, and damp ground, and hastily scrambled to her feet. An unexpected wave of dizziness assailed her and she leaned back against the tree, trying to maintain her balance. Rolfe stood his ground, hard, unyielding, making certain that Joan's mount continued its homeward flight. A shudder rippled through her as, much against her will, Marged admitted that the woman who had virtually caught them making love had lain with him also.

When at last he turned around to behold the frozen, injured expression on Marged's pale face, Rolfe cursed beneath his breath.

"Damn you, it doesn't alter matters."

Marged swallowed the growing lump in her throat. "No, it merely serves as a painful reminder."

"Reminder? Of what?"

"That she too was loved by you."

"Never. She was a soft female body available when I needed her. Nothing more."

"I doubt she regarded your relationship in that exact manner," she said tightly.

Moving from the tree, she walked past him in stony silence.

"What matter how she thought of it? Don't tell me you've gone soft over Mistress Vaughn's feelings."

Marged refused to argue. She unlooped her horse's reins and pulled herself into the saddle. Casting him one last bleak glance, she trotted back through the trees.

Had he shouted after her, had he leaped to the saddle and ridden her down, she would have capitulated her tormenting jealousy in tears. But he stood his ground, dark-faced, remote, as if carved from stone.

When they reached Bowenford, the night wind was wailing among the trees, lonely as a lost soul. Marged had exchanged not a word with Rolfe since their parting in the forest. All necessary discourse between them had been conducted by a third party. To add to her pain, during the final stretch of road, Joan Vaughn had ridden beside him, her golden hair fluttering loose about her shoulders.

When Joan had jostled for position at the front of the column and Rolfe had not sent her away, she cast Marged a triumphant smile. But neither did he speak to her, though Joan was not unduly alarmed by this lack of attention. Rolfe was ever a moody, volatile man, and she knew she had angered him greatly when she caught him dallying with Lady Marged in the forest. With the passing hours she had grown increasingly confident that she could soothe his angry mood. And though at first she had wept copiously over the memory, she had gradually regained her wits. Rolfe was not to be blamed. When he had arrived at Bowenford he had been seeking Lady Marged. And considering the haughty wretch likely threw herself at him, he would have been hard pressed to resist the invitation. That's all it had been—an opportunity to sample the noblewoman's enticing body.

Great gouts of flame from the smoking torches leaped like demons against the somber stone walls as the riders rode beneath Bowenford's raised portcullis. Seeming more like a funeral procession than a joyful homecoming, the tired riders slowly filed inside the outer bailey.

Marged constantly fought tears, annoyed by her own weakness. Oh, her impulse had been right when she vowed never to yield to him again, for that blissful forest reunion had dealt her less than joy. He had reawakened what she had striven so hard to forget. And though they had whispered that all was forgiven, she knew by her outraged reaction to Joan's loathsome presence that those vows had been naught but sweet lies. No doubt Rolfe too, though he would likely deny it, still resented Edward. She was sure, in his heart of hearts, he remained convinced she had yielded to the King.

"Oh, my lord, my lord, welcome. Such a pleasant surprise, I . . ." Alys's shrill voice died away as she beheld Marged. Sheer amazement flickered over her thin face, turned ghostly by the wavering torchlight. "You!"

"Are you not to welcome me home, sister?" Marged asked harshly, allowing the hurrying grooms to assist her in dismounting. *He* still sat astride his great horse, watching her, his expression stony.

"You were not expected."

"Neither were the others, but over *their* arrival your joy appears boundless."

Alys swallowed uneasily, wary of this woman whom she had thought gone forever from her life. "I believed you still dallied in the Welsh hills. It's what we were told. 'Twas even whispered you'd caught young York's fancy, but even we didn't believe so preposterous a tale."

Out of the corner of her eye, Marged saw Joan sidle her horse closer to Rolfe's in the gloom. He did not order her away. When Joan leaned forward to make some laughing comment, he smiled at her. Blood rushed to Marged's face, and her hands trembled.

"Then, sister dear, you should have been more trusting. Your spies told you true. I'm very well beloved of our gracious King. In fact, because of the love he bears me, he has removed the attainder against this land. I am come home, Alys. And here I intend to stay."

It was too dark to see Rolfe's reaction, but she knew he had heard her shrill statement, for she had purposely raised her voice for his benefit. Head high, she quickly crossed the bailey, anxious to be indoors. Her small greyhound bitch yapped excitedly at her heels.

Edward's men garrisoned the castle, living side by side with the native Welsh and the few Lancastrian survivors, who barely tolerated them. When Marged presented the King's charter to the soldier's captain, he knelt before her, swearing to abide by her commands. She was highly aware of Rolfe watching her from the shadowed doorway, yet she deliberately avoided him by walking in the opposite direction.

Ordering her chamber prepared, she claimed weariness and did not sup with the others in the Hall. To her relief, she discovered that Bron had returned home to nurse her ailing father, so at least she would be spared the Welshwoman's jealousy over Maud's presence.

Marged spent a miserable night in her isolated tower room, with only the dog for company. Though the fire blazed heartily and the bed was warm with heaped coverlets, she lay stiff as a board while she envisioned hateful scenes. Rolfe, Joan, and Alys probably supped before the hearth.

This afternoon she had foolishly thought Rolfe was hers again—until she saw him smile at Joan. In all likelihood the little whore would cajole him into sleeping with her tonight! Marged thumped about beneath the heavy covers. Cajole him! What a fool she was! Rolfe had always done as he wished. If he took Joan to his bed, it would be because he desired her, not from any sly trickery on the wench's part. Hot, anguished tears throbbed to her eyes over the awful truth of her observation. She buried her face in the pillow and sobbed herself to sleep.

In the cold gray dawn, she rose and dressed. Over her blue velvet gown she pulled a fur-lined cloak. Maud was sleeping on a hastily made pallet beside the bed. The maid must have come in last night after supper and lain down to sleep without disturbing her lady's rest. With similar consideration, Marged tiptoed over the creaking floorboards and left the room.

Few were stirring within the castle at this early hour. The fires were already stoked, and the kitchen ovens glowed. She pushed open the door to the bailey and stepped outside.

Marged was bound for her father's grave. When he had requested burial beneath the trees, she had known he meant his favorite spot beyond the castle walls, where low-hanging branches slapped the water, and the ground was carpeted with flowers.

The gray morning sky was lightening as a wan sun struggled through the clouds. Outside the tall, forbidding castle walls, she paused, taking deep breaths of sharp clean air. Never again would she go to London. All she wanted in life was here. Tears stung her eyes as she looked about her beloved land, budding afresh with the promise of the new season. Bowenford was rightfully hers again. God knows she had earned it, she thought grimly.

Underfoot, the springy turf was starred with primroses, while beneath the trees, bluebells spread a lilac mist. A pair of startled yellowhammers fled the gorse bushes when she approached the clearing where a mound and plain stone cross marked Sir Richard's grave. Flanked by gorse, surrounded by bluebells, and watched over by towering trees, the site was a fitting resting place.

Overwhelming grief welled to the surface and she fell to her knees on the spongy ground. Burying her face in her hands, she rocked back and forth, recalling the anguish of his final hours in that stinking Hereford inn. News had later reached her that both Arthur and Martin had succumbed to the sweating sickness while held prisoner by Lord Sag. She alone remained of the Bowen line. This land, this castle—birthright of the Bowens—was hers to preserve for future generations. Today, in this peaceful glade, she felt woefully inept.

Rolfe came upon Marged kneeling on the earth, her lustrous black hair tumbled wildly about her shoulders. A lump rose in his throat as he saw her wholly abandoned to grief. When he stepped forward and gently placed his hand on her shoulder to offer comfort, she stiffened beneath his touch.

"You shouldn't be out here alone. Come back indoors."

Mustering what dignity she could manage with her earth-stained gown and flyaway hair, she stood slowly. Her tear-ravaged face was set, her manner proud, when she turned to face him.

"I came to pay my last respects."

"I know. But come indoors now and sup. A storm's brewing."

Marged had not noticed the lowering sky, nor felt the damp wind, nor seen the distant mountains capped in black. The heavy branches overhead tossed restlessly, awaiting the tempest. "I'll return when I'm ready."

"You don't choose to come back with me?"

"No."

His mouth was set in a grim line as he spun about. Beneath the trees stood his horse, whose approaching hoofbeats must have been masked by her sobs. Numbly she watched him swing into the saddle and glower at her, charging the woodland with his brooding presence.

Now that she was no longer alone with her grief, Marged found little comfort in these wild surroundings. Refusing to look at him, she set off along the woodland path. At first she thought he was not going to follow, but then she heard the steady clopping of hooves as he slowly traveled the beaten track. When she finally entered the castle precincts, he still maintained a respectable distance between them, allowing her the solitude of grief.

Short of a few servants who hastily bowed, Marged walked unnoticed through the Great Hall. From the high table she took a hunk of fresh bread and spread it with butter, while a servant hastened forward to offer ale and thick honey. There was no sign of Joan. No doubt the slut still lay abed, exhausted after last night's pleasures; at times, Rolfe possessed an insatiable appetite for lovemaking.

The bread turned to sawdust in her mouth. Hastily washing down the unappetizing breakfast, Marged headed for her room. As she ascended the tower stairs, she could hear Alys shrilly berating a servant somewhere nearby.

Several hours later, when her chamber door creaked open, Marged was surprised to see Rolfe framed in the doorway, a crumpled parchment in his hand.

"Word from the King," he announced, coming straight to the point.

She gulped, not welcoming the news. "Is he coming here?" she asked, carefully folding her embroidery.

He smiled sarcastically at her question before he strode across the room to light two candles from the slow-burning logs on the hearth. So gloomy was the day becoming, even this extra light seemed scarcely enough. Beyond the open window, thunder rolled menacingly close and lightning cut a jagged flash through the dark sky.

"Grow you lonely for his attentions already?"

"He promised to visit me."

"Well, my love, that promise must await more important events. Warwick and Fauconberg head north. Edward left London two days ago. I'm commanded to join him on the way.

So, I'm afraid you'll have to tend to your own affairs here on the March. My men already prepare for departure."

A gasp escaped her lips, though Marged fought hard against the telltale slip. "Leaving?" she managed, biting her tongue in a futile effort to hold back that self-betrayal.

"Aye, leaving. What, my love, don't tell me it causes you grief? You've been like a haughty stranger to me these hours past."

"You don't appear to have suffered for it," Marged snapped, wanting to hurt him in payment for her own pain. "Poor Mistress Joan is long in recovering from your tender ministrations. She still lies abed."

With a snarled oath, he grabbed her wrist. "Stop it! We vowed to end this bickering. What more must I do to prove it's you alone I want?"

Wide-eyed, she stared at him. "You mean you didn't . . . Joan didn't . . ."

"Joan lay abed unmolested by me."

"But I thought you and she . . . when we rode inside the castle . . ." Marged stammered, at a loss for words. In truth, all her facts had been naught but wild imagination. Not once had she seen him with Joan.

"And what of your proud reminder about Edward's panting interest?" he demanded, shaking her, his patience almost spent. "I'm not mistaken in assuming those words were meant for my ears too."

"They were merely to wound because . . . because I thought . . . oh, why must you always set my wits ajangle?" she cried, thrusting him away.

He teetered a moment, taken by surprise. Then his face darkened as he stepped toward her. "You're mine! I intend to stake my claim one more time before I leave."

"No! I won't be used like a paid harlot, then discarded while you go storming about the country to answer Edward's every whim!"

"Is that so?"

"Yes, it's so. Now get out! Perhaps when you return you'll be more civil. By then, I hope detestable Joan Vaughn will be many miles from here. Then and only then will I consider your suit. Until you send her away, I'll not believe your fervent vows."

She gripped the bedpost, alarmed by the temper flaring in his face. Steel-hard were his eyes, grim his mouth. Now, as he looked at her and saw her quivering mouth, his lip curled to reveal even, dazzlingly white teeth against his dark face. He moved suddenly, making the candle flames jump and throw sinister shadows across his features.

"No woman dictates what I do and when," he declared harshly. "My duty is plain. When I'm summoned, I respond. 'Tis a vow I'm sworn to uphold. But we won't wait for my return to settle this dispute, lady. Today, within the hour, I intend to have your answer. And it shall be settled for all time. No longer will I beg or plead—"

"Ha! When did you ever beg or plead?" she demanded in anger.

He made no reply; instead he pulled her into his embrace, locking his arms tightly about her.

"Now, you little hellcat, be still! For once, leash your tongue and hear me out."

She struggled against his strength, panicking as she felt that old familiar tension mounting in her thighs, even now curling to her belly in a building wave as his hot hands pressed firmly against her buttocks. "Are you planning to rape me?"

"If 'tis the only way I can have you—yes, the thought had crossed my mind. Now give me your answer true and without venom. Do you love me enough to wait—"

With a great wrench, she broke free. "There'll be no more vows made by me until you send that harlot packing. How can I believe your sincerity when she's forever fawning over you, smiling, trying to win—"

He gave her only a glancing blow, but with sufficient strength to silence her words. "So—you've given your answer. It's as I thought!"

He turned about and slammed the door, drawing the bolt so the metal grated harshly. When again he faced her, his lean, handsome face made Marged shudder with fear and excitement. She could read the unmistakable message recognized by women the world over, unvoiced, yet nevertheless clear . . .

"How dare you! By your actions today, you've proved you're naught but a Breton mercenary, no better, despite Edward's loyal support, his gifts and awards."

Rolfe tilted his head, his lip curled in scorn. "Well said, lady. I could also say the same for you. Despite Edward's loyal support, his gifts, his awards, you remain naught but a tormenting, tantalizing little bitch. And those insults delivered, where does that leave us, Marged Bowen?"

Panting, she watched him begin to unfasten his clothing, his movements unhurried, determined, relentless. "What are you doing?" she cried, stepping back defensively toward the bed. "You wouldn't dare!"

His unbuckled jack clanked on the floor beside his sword and daggers. He unlaced his purple doublet; he unlaced his linen shirt. Mesmerized, she stared at the parting fabric, dazzlingly white against his dark chest. A sharp wave of excitement speared her stomach, speeding gooseflesh to her arms and legs as he took two steps toward her. When he reached for her, she scrambled to the bed, where she crouched, wary and alert.

"Aren't you going to scream?" he mocked, watching her, awaiting her next move.

"That would please you, wouldn't it?"

He shrugged as he reached to his waist and untied the points of his hose.

They both leaped in alarm as a shattering crash of thunder reverberated through the stone walls, echoing and re-echoing off the battlements. A sudden swoosh of rain flooding the stonework followed. Marged, her attention momentarily distracted, gasped when his strong hands closed over her upper arms and swiftly yanked her toward him, holding her above the bed, his arms trembling with exertion.

"Do you want me to hurt you?"

She shook her head defiantly, swishing her long black hair until it stung his face, which heightened his anger. He pulled her to the floor. Feet jarring, Marged landed hard on the rushes, scraping her spine against the barley-twist posts at the foot of the bed. The bed curtains jangled on their brass rings; the gold fringe bobbed about her feet.

When she opened her mouth to protest, he welded his mouth

over hers, taking her breath. Then he bent her backward across the feather bolster until the pain became so intense that she was forced to relax her spine and let him pin her against the covers.

"Love me, damn you!" he growled, his eyes boring into hers.

Marged shut her lids tight, only snapping them open when he ripped her blue bodice so that her enticingly full breasts swung free. He shuddered violently at the arousing sight, thrusting aside her defending hands.

"Why do you always insist on ripping my clothing!" she demanded angrily through gritted teeth.

"Why, is this another of dear Edward's offerings?"

"It matters not where it came from."

He was not listening as he imprisoned her wrists above her head. With his free hand he fondled her breasts, exerting just enough pressure to make pleasure almost pain.

Mustering her utmost willpower, Marged sought to resist his tantalizing caresses, and had all but mastered her treacherous emotions when he bent his dark head and slowly traced his tongue about her hardening nipples. Then he bounced her back on the bed, pressing her deep into the feather mattress. For a few minutes they fought, rolling from the foot of the bed to the head and back again, until, tiring of the game, he pinned her beneath him, his weight temporarily crushing the breath from her body.

She shuddered, neither resisting nor acquiescing. Time hung suspended as she stared at him, aching to be taken, yet fighting against the despicable weakness . . .

"Do you still doubt I can take you against your will?"

"No."

"Would you have me take you by force?"

"If that's your wish. You, my lord, are solely in charge of today's sport. I assume this to be another of your jousts," she said cuttingly, her green eyes flashing.

His eyes were clouded as he looked down at her. "Is that your final word?"

She nodded, her lips compressed against the stirring emotions besetting her body. In vain she tried to deny the heated softening between her legs, fought hard to keep from straining to meet the bruising pressure of his arousal.

"Then, my sweet Welsh bitch, today I'll make true that lie which first I told our people."

He pulled her hands above her head and, inserting his knee between her thighs, hoisted her skirts above her hips. She struggled to keep her legs together, but he relentlessly pried them apart. Grim-faced, he reached to his hose to withdraw that which she longed to possess, a weapon of such delight that even now she shuddered in delicious anticipation. She kept her eyes tightly closed, stubbornly refusing to look at his nakedness. The hot, tormenting prickle of his black hair against her breasts made her draw in her breath, holding it until, out of sheer pain, she must release the long-held sigh.

Still keeping one of her hands imprisoned, Rolfe forced the other down. In one nerve-jangling movement she found her fingers cupped about his throbbing manhood, thickly engorged by passion.

"Touch me, you treacherous little bitch," he whispered huskily, his hot tongue tracing her nose, her cheek, straying to her ear and neck.

Her pride told her to remain stone cold and remote, but for once in her life she ignored the command. Of their own accord, her eager fingers felt that sweet, pulsating brand, set alight by the raging fire in his blood. She shuddered anew as his fingers gently parted her, probing the passion-sweet chamber she had tried to defend. Her lips curved as she heard him chuckle at the discovery.

"You lying bitch! You're hot and wet," he breathed, his mouth demanding against her neck.

"Wretch! Would you really have raped me?" she asked huskily against his ear, her indignation receding as her pleasure increased. "You would, wouldn't you?"

"Aye, if I had to. But I doubt you could long remain unmoved. You're the hottest little bitch on these Marches, my love, we both know that."

She wound her fingers in his hair, twisting the strands, wanting to hurt him. He only laughed as he spread her legs, matching her shudders as he entered her in a burst of heat. Her attention shifted from his hair to his nipples, which she squeezed hard.

"Come, give in. You've lost the battle, sweetheart. Love me. Love me, make it count for all the months we must be apart," he urged breathlessly, his mouth a tormenting wave of heated kisses.

She finally capitulated with an anguished moan as her arms went about his broad, smooth back. Again and again, her mouth found his. She kissed his eyelids, his nose, his brow; she could not kiss him enough, nor could she hold him close enough, nor take him deeply enough inside her. Desperately she clung to him, willing them to be always joined in agonizing, searing passion.

He moved slowly, deliberately, bringing her the utmost pleasure until, not content, she urged him to greater speed. So desperate was she to have his ultimate expression of love, she writhed like a tormented soul, bruising, devouring, until their passion exploded in mutual ecstasy.

Later, Rolfe asked her accusingly, "Why did you make me hasten so? Never will I fully understand you." He eased to his side, withdrawing from her.

"Nay, sweet lover without compare, you're not done yet. Such a paltry performance will not satisfy me more than half an hour," she whispered throatily.

Gently she fondled his manhood, discovering he was on fire and far from soft.

He smiled in sheer pleasure, his eyes clear, bright blue in the golden candleglow. Outside, the rain beat steadily against the stonework, and a chill breeze swept through the open casement. "First let me close the window," he suggested, getting out of bed.

She retreated inside the covers, uttering a deep sigh of contentment. While Rolfe latched the casement, she watched him. His muscular back faced her, the skin golden, smooth, and hot. His broad shoulders tapered to a narrow waist, perfectly formed buttocks, and lean, strong flanks. Even the recollection of his arousing touch beset her with shudders. When he turned about, freshly aroused, her shudders were not merely from memory.

An eternity passed before he crossed the rush-strewn floor to her eagerly outstretched arms. A welcoming smile lit her face. "Ah, come, love me again, sweetheart. You've many unsettled debts—a multitude of sleepless nights and gallons of tears, for which you have to pay."

He grinned as he slid beside her. "Why think you I incurred so monstrous an account," he whispered wickedly as he took her in his arms, "if not for the pleasure of settling the score?"

Marged laughed throatily at his words. She buried her face in his neck, kissing him, her teeth snagging his flesh. "You're all that matters to me," she whispered. Tears filled her eyes, so deep was the emotion behind that vow.

"I've waited a lifetime to hear you say that. Nothing else you can ever say will I cherish more."

"There's something else, love, which I warrant you'll value just as high."

When he had shut the casement, the gusting wind extinguished the candles. Now the room lay in semidarkness. He tried to pierce the gloom, anxious to see her lovely face as he asked, "And what is that?"

"Make love to me until I beg for mercy."

"'Tis the sweetest command I've ever received," he whispered. Then he fitted her against his magnificent body, matching their pulses, their passion, guiding her expertly until their souls were one.

{ twelve }

THE RISING SUN cut a gash above the distant mountains.

Marged nestled inside her fur-lined cloak, surfeited with Rolfe's lovemaking. Yet this morning when she saw his drawn face and dark-shadowed eyes, she had almost regretted being a party to his night-long revelry. Happiness flooded through her at the memory of those beautiful, bittersweet hours they had shared, passion shadowed by the knowledge they soon must part. Never again would she doubt his love.

"Where's your lord?" Marged presently asked the man who held Rolfe's saddled horse.

"He said he had one final task to perform, lady," the man replied, hiding a smile.

So she watched and waited, wondering at the importance of the chore that kept Rolfe away from his men at this final hour. A few minutes later she had her answer.

Ducking beneath the low archway over the postern gate, he emerged in the bailey, his arms full of rain-drenched bluebells.

"Here, sweetheart, 'tis the only gift I could find at so short a notice," he whispered as he held out the blooms, sweet with the pale fragrance of spring.

Marged beheld his handsome face through a crystalline veil of tears. "You've already gifted me better than any man alive," she whispered brokenly, fighting for speech through trembling lips.

Bluebells dropped about them on the grass as he clasped her in his arms. "I'll come back to you," he vowed when their lips parted. "There's nothing in heaven or hell to keep me from it."

Marged managed a smile, despite a sudden chill of foreboding that shot through her as she watched him mount his horse. Today, beneath his metal-banded jack, he wore the brown and orange striped doublet he had worn on the first morning he strode arrogantly inside her bedchamber. His lean face set, eyes slitted against the cold wind, Rolfe looked every inch the soldier. So rapidly did he change, she found it hard to reconcile his two selves.

Rolfe's helmet flamed in the rising sun as he placed it on his head. Leaving his visor up, he walked his horse to the front of the column, checking men and supplies as he went.

When he returned, Marged had mastered her fear. Since her premonition had been so strong, she felt compelled to warn him that danger lay ahead. As he bid her a final goodbye, Marged seized his hand, her eyes darkly intense as she pleaded, "Take care, love, please, take no risks. I've a feeling all will not go well."

Rolfe grinned and squeezed her hand. "Another of your Welsh traits, woman? Do you see into the future?"

Marged nodded. "Don't scoff. The skill is one of my mother's most valuable gifts."

"Nay, I don't scoff. To please you, I promise to keep a constant watch for danger. Knowing you await me will be my greatest incentive to survive." Rolfe leaned from the saddle, and grasping her shoulders, he lifted her up. It was difficult to exchange kisses through his open visor.

"God keep you well," she whispered, longing to cling to him, to beg him to stay, but she would not shame him before his men.

"And you. Remember, I'll always love you."

Marged's lips echoed his parting vow, her voice silenced

by tears. Rolfe stopped a few feet away to wave again, seeming reluctant to begin his journey. Then, resolutely, he turned his horse's head toward the gate and did not look back.

Anxious to watch him till the last, Marged sped to the east tower, her lightly shod feet flying over the worn stone treads. She leaned from the narrow, latticed window, calling to him and waving her kerchief to attract his attention.

Cries echoed from the nearby battlements, where Alys and Joan leaned over the wall, waving their kerchiefs in farewell.

After allowing one final, searching look at the east tower window, Rolfe abruptly wheeled his mount about and galloped after his men, who were already crossing the ford.

Marged stayed at the window to watch the column until they were no more than black dots amid the greening trees. When she finally came down from the tower, her lips tightened in aggravation as she beheld Joan, golden hair streaming, clothing disheveled, weeping as if her heart would break.

"Why are you in the solar?" Marged demanded icily.

Beseechingly, Joan gazed up at her through her tears. "He loves me too," she declared defiantly.

"That was not my question."

"The wench is here because she waits on me," Alys replied sharply.

Marged spun about. She had not noticed her stepsister huddled in the corner, pretending to sew. Alys's face was parchment-white, her mouth tight.

"Forgive me. I didn't see you."

Alys thrust her sewing aside. Then, drawing herself to her full height, she faced her stepsister. "Now that Bowenford belongs to you, what am I to do? Do you wish me to pack my belongings and take to the roads?"

"Don't be ridiculous. You can stay here as you've always done."

"Thank you, sister dear, for your boundless charity."

"Sarcasm becomes you ill," Marged snapped. "Need I remind you, I'm not bound to keep you. I do so out of the kindness of my heart. With father dead, the duty's ended."

Alys gasped, her thin lips forming a shocked circle. "How dare you!" she managed at last.

"I dare, Alys, because it's the truth."

For a long time after Marged had left the room, Alys and Joan remained in the solar. Alys's nerves were close to snapping under the steady onslaught of Joan's piteous wails. At last, unable to endure the torment a minute longer, she cried, "Have done with your weeping! Or I'll give you something to weep about."

Joan gulped convulsively, and her sobs gradually subsided. "You promised to treat me kindly," she reminded Alys, her full red lips pouting.

"More fool me," Alys snapped, viewing the distraught girl with disdain. "I should have flayed your back to ribbons for daring to run away. In fact, had he not pleaded so sweetly for you, 'twas exactly what I intended."

"He loves me dearly," Joan whispered, her mouth trembling afresh.

Alys snorted, not deigning to challenge the statement. She suspected that Marged was unaware of the private arrangement to which she had agreed. Rolfe had come upon her last night in the Great Hall while she sat dreaming beside the hearth. How handsome he had been, though his eyes had been darkly shadowed, his lean face drawn. Of course, *she'd* kept him busy in her room most of the day. Alys's mouth formed a network of unlovely lines around its corners at the reminder of what they did behind that locked door. Marged was an insatiable demon, sapping precious strength Rolfe needed for battle.

Swallowing uncomfortably, Alys crossed to the window. In all honesty, she could not say she herself would have refused his lovemaking, impending battle or nay. But, being a high-born lady, she would have used far more restraint than had that wild Welsh peasant who dared call herself a lady.

Alys leaned her flushed cheek against the ice-cold masonry. He had taken her hand and asked a favor, though when she discovered it concerned that sluttish Joan's future, she had turned somewhat peevish. But he soon dissolved her resistance with his charming smile. Reluctantly she had solemnly promised not to punish the wench for following the troops, and to reinstate her as her maid if that was the girl's wish. And though it angered her considerably, she had even promised she would not allow Joan to deliberately antagonize Marged.

Spinning about, Alys snapped, "Now, you wanton slut, get

you washed and brush your hair. I won't have a maid who looks like a dockside drab."

Aghast, Joan's brown eyes grew round. "Maid! I'm no longer your maid!"

"There you're wrong. When I promised Rolfe I'd not have you beaten, he also asked me to take you back as my maid." Alys thought it better not to add, "if it is your wish," for such generosity was vastly out of place. "Though your skin was to be spared a beating, your lazy, wanton body was not to be spared from work. I've a multitude of tasks awaiting you."

"He took me as his woman. I'm not supposed to wait on you," Joan declared haughtily, refusing to accept a truth she found too terrible to face.

With an exclamation of disgust, Alys seized Joan's wrist and yanked her to her feet. "Listen, you wretch, my stepsister is his *woman,* as you crudely put it. Not you. Was it *you* he spent his final hours with? Was it *you* he tenderly kissed farewell? Was it *you* he—"

"Stop! Oh, stop, be not so cruel," Joan moaned, sinking to the rushes.

A triumphant smile crossed Alys's thin face. "If you know, why continue to delude yourself?" she demanded shortly.

"I love him so—he's the only man I'll ever want."

"You fool girl, you'll soon learn people don't often get what they want in life," Alys snapped, dragging the weeping girl upright. "Put him from your mind. You were, for a brief time, his whore—now you're nothing to him. You're merely my maid Joan."

Joan looked at her mistress through a wavering veil of tears, hating her so much in that instant, she wanted to rip out her throat.

"It's naught but the truth. Think you you're the first serving wench he's bedded and forgotten? Only a noblewoman could hope to satisfy him for more than a few nights." When Joan's mouth opened to protest that she *was* a noblewoman, Alys fixed her with such a malicious glare that the proud words died before escaping her lips.

"If Lady Marged were gone, he'd want me again, I know he would," she declared stubbornly as she tossed back her tangled hair. "Lady, you bear your stepsister no love."

"Aye, that's true."

"Would you help me regain Rolfe's favor? He did love me, I swear, whether you choose to believe me or nay. Together we were . . ."

"I've no desire to hear your witless reminiscences," Alys snapped, spinning about. She must fight an unexpected flood of nausea which rushed to her throat.

"Help me win him back."

"There's no way."

"If Lady Marged were to leave again—if she were to disappear . . ."

Alys paused in mid-flight. Something about the silly wench's suggestion intrigued her. True, if Marged were gone, Rolfe would need another woman. Flighty Joan would be only too eager to help bring about Marged's downfall, never suspecting for one moment that she was about to seal her own fate. Forcing a smile, Alys turned about.

"You know what you're suggesting is outrageous?"

"You'll not help me, then?"

"I didn't say that." Alys smiled grimly as hope rekindled on Joan's tear-stained face. "What fate do you propose for our mutual enemy?"

"I'd thought perhaps you, being so learned and far cleverer than I, would be the one to suggest," Joan said, trying to manipulate Alys with flattery. She fluttered her damp eyelashes, her large brown eyes beseeching. "Tell me only what I must do to help."

Perhaps Joan was not such a witless creature after all, thought Alys with surprise, warming slightly to the maid. "I'll give the subject some thought," she allowed. "First you must swear never to divulge what we have discussed today."

"Oh, yes, lady, I promise."

Alys smiled. The wench thought her not as clever as she professed.

"Are you prepared to swear on the sacred relics? If you're not, then I wash my hands of the whole affair. I'm not fool enough to chance having a loose-tongued little bitch chatting to all and sundry—"

"Nay, Lady Alys, be not angry. I'll swear a sacred oath."

Alys sighed in relief, and her mouth creased into a smile. "Very well. Come, then."

"Where?" Joan asked, gathering her skirts and hastening after her mistress.

"To the chapel, you fool, where else?"

Marged dismounted and handed her horse's reins to a waiting groom.

"They've been seeking you these hours past, Lady Marged," the man said.

"Seeking me? What for?"

"'Tis a grave matter concerning the maid you brought home—Maud."

Her stomach churning with apprehension, Marged wondered if this was the forerunner of the danger she had foreseen? All day, as Marged rode through the sparsely leaved woods, she had been afraid that apprehensive feeling meant Rolfe faced death in battle. Now she was not sure.

The Great Hall was dark after the bright sunlight. Marged stood in the doorway, blinking as she accustomed herself to the gloom.

"There you are!" Alys bustled from where she had been sitting beside the hearth. "You were away so long, I thought you'd left us again."

"What's happened to Maud?"

"The fool maid's likely broken her back," Alys stated shrilly.

"What!" Shock rocked Marged. Now she noticed a straw pallet before the hearth, where a blanket-swathed figure lay. Ignoring Alys, she ran to the fireside. "Oh, Maud, Maud, love, what's happened to you?" she whispered, tears springing to her eyes.

Maud's thin blue lips twisted to a grimace and she squeezed Marged's hand feebly.

"I . . . fell, lady."

"Fell! From where?"

The maid only shook her head, tears brimming, and turned aside.

"She lost her footing on the stair," proffered a nearby soldier.

"I suspect there's far more to this than you're admitting."

"Nay, Lady, it's as I say," the man defended gruffly, though his dark eyes shifted, refusing to meet her gaze.

"Tell me the rest of it or, Edward's man or not, I'll have you flogged," Marged declared in anger as she rounded on the soldier who stood nearby. Alys gasped in dismay at her stepsister's recklessness. "How did she fall? Was she pushed?" Marged demanded sternly, gratified by the man's obvious discomfort.

"Nay, no one pushed her, lady. It was an unfortunate accident, that's all."

"Explain yourself!"

The man looked down at the rushes, a flush spreading over his coarse face. "One of my men had his way with her," he mumbled uncomfortably.

Marged steeled herself not to react. "And then?" she prompted grimly.

"The wench ran from him. She lost her footing on the tower stairs."

At the terrible reminder of the crime, Maud moaned in shame.

"Have you sent for a physician?"

"I've given her potions to ease the pain," Alys said as she came to Marged's side.

"Thank you for your concern. 'Tis likely the only reason she's not out of her head," Marged said, drawing Alys away from the injured girl. "There's a physician near Pontrilas. We'll send for him."

"Joan's already gone for more potions," Alys revealed, her eyes sharp on Marged's face.

"We need more than old wives' simples," Marged dismissed scornfully.

Alys flinched at the reprimand. It was a pity the accident victim had not been her hated stepsister instead of the foolish maid. "Don't underestimate the power of potions, sister dear. Many have lived to . . ." Her words faded, for Marged was already haughtily marching toward the group of sullen soldiers.

"Where's the man responsible for this?" Marged demanded angrily. "Deliver him to me at once!"

"I . . . I don't know where he is, lady."

"Don't know! How can you not know? Has he left the castle?"

"Nay."

"Then bring him to me."

"I'll try to find him, lady." The confused soldier backed away.

For over an hour, Marged waited impatiently while the soldiers searched the castle without success. Mat Runyon was the man's name, and she repeated it to herself in scorn as she soothed Maud's fever with cool cloths. The maid was delirious, her pulse jumping erratically. Were Alys's strong potions doing more harm than good? Marged wondered as she knelt to sponge Maud's thin white face. Though she knew she was not directly to blame for this mishap, she shared a degree of guilt for bringing Maud to Bowenford.

"Marged."

She glanced up to find Alys at her side, her sharp face lit with a curiously malevolent light. "Have they found him?" Marged cried.

"The men say he's fled down the haunted passage to the old wing."

"Then send them after him."

"They're afraid."

Uttering a curse beneath her breath, Marged got up from her knees. "I'll fetch him," she declared. Her jaw was set with determination, her eyes hard. "He must be made to look upon the damage he has caused. He must be punished."

Alys smiled, fluttering her sparse eyelashes in mock admiration. "Ah, you've such courage."

The unexpected praise checked Marged's speech. Again she felt a swirl of unease. "You're being uncommonly kind to me today," she remarked accusingly, looking closely into Alys's peevish face, but learning nothing.

"'Tis only that I know you bear great affection for the wench," Alys murmured sweetly.

"Come with me," Marged suggested suddenly, surprising herself by the request.

"I . . . well, I . . ."

"You've always scorned the ghost stories as being believed only by the ignorant Welsh," Marged reminded her cleverly. "You said a true-born lady would never believe such foolishness."

Alys blanched. "Aye, I do recall saying something of that nature," she mumbled vaguely.

"Then come with me. 'Tis as well not to enter that wing alone.

I've little fear of the supernatural, or of Mat Runyon's anger, but the old stones are slimy and uneven. If I slipped—"

"It would be days before you were found," Alys completed in a strange, high-pitched tone. "Quite right, dear Marged, you shouldn't go alone. I'll come with you."

Marged spun about to face the soldiers who were grumbling among themselves as they stood sheepishly before the hearth. "You cowards! Two helpless women have more courage between them than a troop of the King's men."

"We're trained to kill flesh-and-blood foes, lady," snarled the captain, angered by her statement. Never, in a thousand years, would he have described either of these women as helpless. "I'll accompany you to the old wing," he said, loath to make even that concession.

Marged began to say he would not be needed, but thought better of it. "Thank you, Captain, that's very generous of you."

Into the bowels of the castle they went, their footsteps echoing like those of an army along the narrow corridors. Carrying a flaring torch aloft, the captain led them through dank passages at the bottom of which lay a cavern filled by the rising Wye. This aged part of the castle was reputed to be haunted by the slaughtered defenders of an ancient Welsh fort who bled to keep this land free years before the Normans came. Neither the castle's Welsh servants nor Edward's soldiers, who had listened gullibly to these hair-raising tales, would venture beyond the west-wing door.

"We're nearly there," the captain said, his throat going dry as he glanced fearfully behind him.

"We're still with you, Captain. Or are you seeking some less substantial companion?"

The soldier turned about and glowered at Marged, not appreciating her humor. Before a thick door at the end of the corridor, he halted. Tormented by his appalling show of cowardice, he nevertheless could not overcome his fear. "For my mind, lady, 'twould be better if Runyon were left to rot down here," he growled. "There's little point in finding him. He can't mend the wench."

"You're right, Captain, but when I'm done with him, he'll wish he could," Marged declared grimly. "Give me the torch. You've my permission to go."

"Should I wait?"

"There's no need."

Marged listened to his heavy footsteps pounding desperately away along the corridor. At the next bend he would have the benefit of a blazing torch, no doubt imparting a dose of courage.

"Coward!" Alys sniffed disdainfully, glancing about at the thick fungus covering the wall. "I'll ruin my gown," she protested, pulling her trailing skirts away from the wet stonework.

"If you're wise, you'll loop your skirts about your waist. 'Tis an unlikely place for fluttering silks."

"You must be mad! I'll not expose my legs to public view!"

"No one beside Runyon and the ghostly inhabitants will see," Marged reminded her, stifling a grin. "As for me, I've often seen your legs, and a skinnier pair of—"

"I didn't come to be insulted."

"No, you're right, you did not," Marged agreed penitently as she relented. "I'm deeply grateful for your aid. The little wench is special to me. Come, let's get this unpleasant task over."

Because she did not admit to fear did not mean Marged was unafraid of the dangers within this abandoned wing. Her stomach churned apprehensively as she creaked open the door. A wave of noxious air hit her in the face.

Alys gasped, retreating a pace before the onslaught. Having recovered a few minutes later, and taking Marged's advice to loop her skirts about her waist, she followed her stepsister. They gripped each other's arms when the footing grew slippery.

"Runyon, you wretch, come out. There's no use hiding. We know you're to blame," Marged shouted. Her voice echoed eerily along the deserted corridors to the cavern pool. They waited for an answer. None came.

"See, isn't that daylight?" Alys hissed, leaning over Marged's shoulder.

"Perhaps it's filtering from the cavern," Marged whispered back, having no idea why she was whispering. She could hear Alys's teeth chattering as they drew closer to the murky beam piercing the darkness. They both shrieked in unison when something soft and furry ran across their feet.

"It's only a rat," Marged said, while Alys clutched her racing heart.

The path grew much steeper, and Marged had trouble keeping her footing. Under her hand, Marged felt an iron ring.

"There's a door here in the wall."

"Leave it. He won't be in there. Likely he's crouching in the corridor, frightened out of his wits," Alys said, urging Marged forward along the corridor.

"Here, you hold the torch." Ignoring her stepsister's protest, Marged twisted the iron handle. Creaks and groans filled the tunnel, but the door would not open. She threw her weight against the thick wood. Something was blocking the way.

"Let's turn back." The torchlight wavered frantically over the walls and ceiling as Alys's hands shook from cold and fright. "Perchance he's already swum to freedom."

"Aye, and perchance he hasn't."

One final time, Marged tried the door. Suddenly it yielded and she fell inside a cavernous room. The flickering torch revealed a clutter of boxes and barrels, all festooned with cobwebs. A dark shape that had been slumped against the door, preventing their entering, was lying in a heap on the floor next to the threshold. They had found Mat Runyon.

"Bring the light," she commanded, crossing to the soldier's inert body. Suddenly the door creaked shut, and the room was plunged into darkness. Fear pounded through her limbs as Marged heard Alys's frantic steps receding down the corridor.

"Alys, come back. Come back!"

Her throat ached, her neck went stiff as she repeatedly bellowed the unheeded command. Marged stood in the pitch-dark room, almost afraid to move because of the broken flooring. Alys had left her alone in this uncharted maze, without even a light. Marged's heart raced frantically and she clenched her fists, shuddering repeatedly until she mastered her fright.

The passage down which they had come was not too crooked, so, even without a light, it might be possible to retrace her steps. Her confidence flooded back by leaps and bounds. Before she opened the door, Marged crouched beside the still form of Edward's foolish young soldier. Curiously, she felt no further desire for vengeance. He must be very young, she thought, touching his smooth, beardless face. The man was not dead, for a weak pulse still thumped in his neck. But when she shook him and called his name, he did not respond.

If an English soldier had found his way this far without a light, surely she could find her way back. The walls were slippery beneath her groping hands. After what seemed hours, she reached a spot where faint light penetrated the gloom; it shone through a shaft ahead of her. In the distance, the distinctive cry of a gull persuaded her to follow the light. Marged ventured a few feet; already the air was fresher and heavily tanged with the smell of the river.

Growing confident, she quickened her pace, but found her progress suddenly stopped short. A rockfall partially blocked the narrowing path. She climbed over the great chunks of rock, finding the air freshening by the minute.

The slide left far behind her, she drew closer to the light and heard the sound of water lapping against stone. Feeling excited, Marged took a few steps forward and suddenly encountered a black void. Screaming, she slithered and bounced until the breath was knocked out of her. Coming to rest on a floor slimy with vegetation and serrated with jagged barnacles, she slumped against a loose boulder that teetered precariously.

When she determined that she was not dying, or even badly hurt, she looked about the rock walls for a means of escape. To her horror, she could see water gleaming black below her. She had fallen onto a ledge above a pit. Had the boulder been dislodged by her weight, she would have plunged to her death.

Burying her face in her hands, she succumbed to a hysterical fit of weeping. She might be trapped forever on this ledge above black waters, and below cliff walls too steep and slimy to climb. Her only hope of rescue was a dying man. Whether or not Alys could successfully explain events did not matter, since as Marged knew, the soldiers could not be persuaded to risk a search.

Having washed, brushed her hair, and put on her gray silk gown, Alys made a leisurely descent to the Great Hall. Joan awaited her, the packets of deadly herbs safely concealed in her skirts.

"What's happened?" Joan wanted to know, glancing from the agitated soldiers to the dying maid on the pallet.

"The girl's broken her back. There's little more I can do for her," Alys dismissed. "Did you get the potions?"

"Everything you asked for. Where's *she?"* Joan asked in a hoarse whisper.

A triumphant smile spread across Alys's haughty features. "Come, let's go into the solar and refresh ourselves."

Baffled, but obeying readily, Joan pulled off her cloak and followed her mistress. A fire had been lit in the solar, and a platter of honey cakes and wine stood on the ivory-inlaid table beside the hearth.

"Where is she?" Joan repeated, her mouth stuffed with cake, for she had not eaten since dawn. "Has she gone? Are the potions for naught?"

Alys smiled as she stretched like a cat before the hearth, holding her long narrow feet to the blaze. "My dear stepsister has met with an unfortunate accident."

"What!"

"Oh 'tis a long story, which no doubt you'll hear oft repeated by the others. It's sufficient to say she wandered down into the old part of the castle and disappeared."

"They'll search for her," Joan pointed out practically. "She's still mistress here."

The taunting reminder had not been delivered innocently, and Alys's smile withered. "No, they're terrified of ghosts. Besides, I told them a great creature dripping blood chased us with a battle-ax. Marged fell and I was too afraid to rescue her."

"And they believed that!"

Alys's eyes narrowed. "Of course they believed it. What makes you think it isn't true?"

Joan gulped a draft of sweet red wine and carefully considered her answer. "Naught—except our secret."

"No one else knows about 'our secret'—do they?"

"I've told no one."

"Good. Then we've no cause for concern. By the time Rolfe returns, it'll be too late to save her. We'll tell him the tragic tale. We'll weep with him, and then—"

"He'll be mine again!" Joan gasped, her eyes shining with delight.

"Quite. Yours again," Alys repeated, glancing away. She took the wine decanter and refilled her cup.

Alys's head still reeled from today's events. Had she

planned such a thing, she could not have arranged matters better. Fate had delivered a perfect plan into her hands. Unless one of the fools plucked up sufficient courage to go in search of her, Marged would never be found. If and when such a brave effort was proposed, however, Alys intended to retell her bloodcurdling yarn with such skill that no one would dare venture below.

"How did you lure her into the dungeons?" Joan asked at length, reluctant to break into her mistress's train of thought. She was bursting to learn the details of this earth-shattering event.

"We were seeking the maid's . . . violator," Alys said, hesitating over the term. "The silly creature fell and broke her back while trying to defend her virtue. Still, we couldn't have asked for a more fortunate set of circumstances. Will you have another cake, Joan dear?"

Joan gulped over the unexpected endearment, growing increasingly wary of this powerful woman. True, Lady Alys had helped her to an extent she'd never dreamed of, clearing the way for her to repossess the man she loved. And yet . . .

Joan's eyes narrowed as she studied Alys's narrow face in the fading daylight. Something about this changed woman warned her to beware.

A bemused smile played about Alys's thin mouth as she went to the window, where she leaned against the closed casement, gazing dreamily into space. "No!" she cried suddenly, jumping back and startling Joan. "I don't believe it! Surely he can't be returning!"

With a shriek of joy, Joan leaped toward the window. "Rolfe," she cried in delight. "It is he! It is!"

"Well, if it's he, you little fool, you'd best kiss him goodbye. He'll be down there in a flash to release his beloved Marged from her fate," Alys snarled in anger, thrusting Joan aside. She opened the casement and peered out, straining to identify the column of riders moving like a giant serpent over the rolling landscape.

Finally, as a standard became visible through the trees, Joan cried out in disappointment, "It's not he."

Alys spun about, her relief that the rider was not Rolfe giving way to anxiety. The lead rider's standard, emblazoned with the Welsh dragon, came clearly into view.

Men milled about the guardroom in panic, and Alys tried to issue them shrill commands, but no one paid her any heed.

"We'd best not challenge them, but wait to see if they come in peace," decided the captain at last, reluctant to engage his small garrison of unhoned troops in battle.

"Are you out of your wits as well as your courage?" Alys lashed out as she stalked about the battlements. Her eyes stung in the cold wind as she surveyed the billowing ranks moving over the rolling landscape. "Secure the gates! Draw in the bridge! I doubt they'll care to dally long in this godforsaken hole."

"I'll treat with them first," the captain declared stubbornly.

"And what good will that do? If you discover them to be foes, 'twill be too late to secure the castle," Alys screamed, trying to make herself heard over the hoofbeats and jangling harnesses of the approaching force.

"We'll treat with them," was all he said as he sped below.

Grimly, Alys stood her ground, shivering with cold as she watched the large body of men massing beyond the moat. A lone rider detached himself from the others and rode forward. A second man, carrying the Welsh standard and a white flag of truce, came from the ranks and fell in step behind his leader. So far, so good.

"Who are you that you come out of the night? Identify yourself!" bellowed Edward's captain, his bluff, hearty voice vastly belying his cowardice.

"We come in peace. I am Rhys ap Morgan, Lord of Dinas Cwm in the Brecon valley. I seek my kinswoman Marged, daughter of Eirlys the Fair."

Alys's heart plunged to her belly as she deciphered that proud declaration; she had some difficulty in understanding his heavily accented speech. So this was the Welshman to whom Marged had fled the day she escaped Bowenford! He had come looking for her with an army big enough to conquer the Marches!

The captain's helmeted head poked through the tower door. "He says—"

"I heard him. Admit them. They're too strong to fight."

"Yes, lady."

Making a supreme effort to compose herself, Alys descended the winding stairs. She was determined to brave this unpleasant twist of circumstances to the bitter end.

As Alys watched Rhys swaggering toward her in the Great Hall, she quailed inwardly. One glance at this dark-browed Welshman told her he would not easily be fobbed off with half-truths. But he was Welsh. And that was greatly to her advantage. Such firm believers in witchcraft and the supernatural were they, she should have no difficulty in frightening him sufficiently to keep him firmly on this side of the west door.

"Welcome, my lord. I've ordered a meal prepared for you," she said brightly, advancing toward him.

Rhys bowed over her outstretched hand. "Thank you, Lady . . . ?"

"Alys. I'm Marged's stepsister."

"It's my great pleasure to meet you, Lady Alys," he said smoothly. Alys was surprised by his courteous manners, for she had expected him to be barbaric. Somewhat disconcerted, she led Rhys to the table, which had been hastily set for a meal.

"Where's Marged?" he asked next, withdrawing a chair for Alys to be seated.

"Oh, had you not heard? She's gone from Bowenford some time past."

Rhys's dark-skinned face turned sly. "Nay, lady, the tale I heard was quite to the contrary."

"Oh?" said Alys in surprise, nervously clasping her hands beneath the fringed tablecover. "Then you must tell me what it is you've heard, Lord Rhys, for I'm in ignorance of it."

Rhys rocked back on his chair, immediately making himself at home. "Marged returned within the week to repossess her lands, having been presented with this castle by the Yorkist king—stop me if I'm wrong," he interjected lightly, enjoying the staunch disapproval he read in Alys's haughty face. Spreading his booted feet before the hearth, he sighed in feigned contentment as he glanced about the room. "'Tis a fine Hall—one I wouldn't mind owning, given half the chance."

"What you say is true," Alys allowed woodenly. "Marged did come here."

"And she didn't leave with her escort, for no woman was

amongst the mercenary's troops."

Alys swallowed. She had grossly underestimated Rhys ap Morgan. She cursed herself for the mistake. "Very well, I suppose I must reveal the truth. I grow faint at the thought of retelling so terrible a tale, yet such a tragedy—"

"Tragedy! What tragedy?" The smile vanished from Rhys's face, and his black brows drew together as he leaned forward, intent on her words.

Alys smiled, her confidence returning. Perhaps she had not underestimated him after all.

While they supped on roast venison in wine sauce, and drank fresh ale, Alys told her horrid tale. After drawing out the history of the cavern's haunting, pretending to have difficulty in even voicing the terrible events, she found to her horror that, far from having the required effect, her pitiful tale drove him into a towering rage.

"You bitch!" Rhys bellowed, pounding his fist on the table. "You spineless bitch! You left her down there alone!"

"I was out of my wits with terror!"

"God damn you for it!" Rhys leaped to his feet, upsetting a flagon of wine sauce so that it flowed in a scarlet river to the rushes. Calling to his men, whom he roused from their supper, he stood before Alys, threatening and hostile. "Now tell me—very carefully—where this place is and how we get there."

"But the spirits! Oh, surely you're not thinking of going down there! It's more than my life's worth to venture beyond that door," Alys wept, her tears not entirely false.

"You don't need to accompany us—though, by God, I ought to make you come below as punishment. Poor Marged. So bitter it is tonight with that wind—tell me, woman, where she is. Tell me all of it."

"But the evil spirits—oh, they're waiting . . . the spirits . . . the spirits," Alys wailed, giving a flawless performance.

Her acting ability was lost on Rhys. He grabbed her wrist, twisting it painfully. "Sod the spirits! Tell me how to reach her."

And so, amid many delaying tears and wails, Alys finally gave out the details of Marged's whereabouts. He barely heard her out before he dragged forth the Welsh servants, drilling them for facts about the subterranean passages.

* * *

Marged huddled in a ball, trying to keep warm. A numbing chill rose from the water, piercing her flesh with a thousand needles. There was a constant barrage of eerie sounds echoing through the abandoned tunnels: scampering rats, flurries of loosened rock, and drips from the slimy walls. All played on her mind until she expected at any moment to see a ghostly army of Welsh warriors battling her to defend their citadel.

At first she had taken much comfort from recalling the last glowing hours spent with Rolfe; she had even indulged in fantasies about his rescuing her from her prison. Fool! He would be on the other side of Hereford by now, and if he chose to journey at night, he was likely deeper into England than that. Eventually, as weariness overcame her, she dozed.

But before long, mysterious sounds disturbed her rest. Marged's teeth chattered as she thought of logical explanations for the echo of tramping feet, the distinctive splash of oars breaking the water below. Yet none came to mind. Edward's men were far too frightened to venture here, and the Welsh feared an eternal curse in punishment for disturbing the shades of their ancestors. Marged's scalp prickled as the footsteps drew nearer. Steeling herself for the appearance of those bloody apparitions, she waited.

"Marged. Marged. Marged. Marged."

Groaning, she clapped her hands over her ears to shut out the sound. From all sides the voices bombarded her. She gritted her teeth against them.

"Marged, *bach,* where are you?"

The question penetrated her consciousness. That voice was real. By his very use of the affectionate Welsh word meaning "little one," this man told her he was a friend.

"Here. In this shaft." Her voice echoed and re-echoed about the cavern.

"How far above the water?" shouted someone from below.

Tears of relief stung her eyes as Marged shouted, "Behind the boulder, halfway up."

In her excitement, she leaned against the precarious rock, trying to pierce the gloom. To her horror, she felt the rock shift. Powder showered into the water as a rockslide began.

Desperately she threw herself against the wall, clutching at slimy strands of vegetation. Now there was nothing between her and the black pit. A wave of hopelessness washed over her when she realized the boulder had probably swamped her brave rescuers. Tears trickled down her cheeks.

"*Cariad,* call to me again."

The familiar voice echoed again, raising Marged's hopes. "Here, just above the water. Here I am," she cried. She prayed the rescuers were not just part of her delirium. The man sounded like Rhys. Yet how could that be? Rhys had left these parts long months ago. When she disappeared in Clun Forest, he had likely given her up for dead.

"Again *cariad,* call again."

The voice was much closer. Marged shuddered in anticipation. She shouted again and again until her throat was raw. From directly above her came a muttered curse, followed by a shower of fine rock trickling down the shaft.

"Rhys, is it really you?"

"Aye, 'tis me. Oh, *bach,* how am I going to get you out? I'm too big to climb down the shaft." Emotion cracked his voice as Rhys leaned against the rock, puzzling over the dilemma. Finally mastering his wits, he straightened, the gruff assertion back in his voice as he shouted, "Idris! Ianto! Are you still there?"

The names echoed about the cavern. When the sound died away, answering shouts, followed by the splash of oars, came from the water below Marged.

"*Duw,* where's the lantern?"

"The water doused it."

Rhys cursed anew. He turned and yelled to his men.

Shortly afterward, bright tongues of flame lit the entrance to Marged's prison. She reached for him, but Rhys's shadowed form was too far away to touch.

"Ianto, see the light, boyo?"

An affirmative reply echoed from the water.

"Row toward it."

Oars splashed directly below, though she could see nothing in the solid blackness. Rhys lay on his side and thrust the torch through the shaft until the flames were only a couple of feet from her. The glare splashed her giant shadow across the rock.

"We can see her!" called Ianto in excitement.

"Can you reach her?" Rhys asked, his voice strained from his prone position.

"I think so."

Marged closed her eyes, overcome by a wave of dizziness. It seemed an eternity before the stocky Ianto appeared. His dark hair was tangled in slime, and his hands appeared raw and bleeding. When he stretched one of them out to her, she seized it thankfully, but when she moved she slithered precariously, and the vegetation proved too frail a handhold. She slid downward, a grassy clump still in her hand, and crashed into Ianto. They tumbled together into the icy water, making a tremendous splash.

Before long, someone was pulling her face out of the water, bearing her up into the boat. Water poured from her hair and skirts, and as she fell against the wooden seat, she pulled trailing vegetation from her face. Ianto's companion quickly threw a blanket over her. She coughed and spluttered as the men put their backs to the oars and slowly pulled toward the cavern entrance.

{ thirteen }

"HOW DARE YOU accuse me of abandoning you!" Alys demanded, her shrill weeping not entirely for effect. The surly, dark-browed Welshman filled her with fear. She could not even speak without his burning gaze devouring her composure.

"Because you slammed the door and took the light," Marged said evenly, trying to master her temper. She longed to strike Alys. It was only through the utmost willpower that she kept her emotions in check.

"But the apparition!" Alys protested as she clutched her heart. "I swear something dreadful was coming toward me. You know I've never been blessed with much courage."

That was true, Marged thought as she fixed Alys with a level gaze. "Very well. We'll have an end of it. You can leave us. 'Tis fortunate Rhys arrived in time, or I'd have died down there. Do you realize that?"

"Oh, yes! It's all so terrible! But I just couldn't face that hideous creature," Alys sobbed, wringing her hands.

"Get out of my sight, you puling wretch!" Rhys snarled,

his patience exhausted. "You don't deserve compassion. Thank God our Marged's none the worse for her ordeal."

Alys turned away, twin spots of color burning high on her cheeks. Her knees shook and she steeled herself against the fit of trembling that now overcame her. The Welshman was right, more's the pity—"our Marged" was none the worse for wear. The anguish she had endured since that dread visit inside the haunted wing, the hope, the fear, had all been for naught. "Our Marged" remained unharmed.

When Alys was out of earshot, Rhys turned to Marged, a smile on his hard face. "That one turns my stomach."

"Alys has always been a trial. There's never been any love lost between us—" Marged's brows drew together as she read fresh suspicion in Rhys's face. He was ever eager to avenge any injustice done her. "Let us have an end of it. As you say, I'm unharmed."

"If that's your wish," he agreed reluctantly, not anxious to put the disturbing subject to rest.

"Must you leave tomorrow?"

"We go to meet the enemy. I can't delay about that," Rhys declared with relish, his white teeth flashing against his swarthy skin. "We might even clash with the Yorkist dog who brought you home. He'll not be too far away."

"Likely you will," Marged murmured, getting to her feet. "As a hostess, I know I should not be so lacking in hospitality, but I'm weary for sleep. Thank you from the bottom of my heart for rescuing me. I can never thank you enough."

"Be not so hasty, *bach*. There's something of great importance I would ask."

Marged quailed before the intensity in his face. Though Rhys had not named the subject, she could almost guess what it was. "I doubt I'll make much sense, so weary am I," she parried hastily.

"Little sense is required for this. Merely a simple answer will do," Rhys assured her as he rose and prepared to accompany her upstairs.

"Very well. We can discuss it over a cup of wine before I retire."

"Why so formal, *cariad?*" Rhys asked, slipping his hand beneath her elbow as he guided her up the tower stairs. "Have you forgotten, we lived as intimately as brother and sister for many months?"

"I've not forgotten."

Rhys said no more, yet Marged sensed that her restraint greatly displeased him. He followed her inside the room, sadly empty now that Maud was dead, and closed the door. He could not sit. Bristling with tension, he paced before the hearth while Marged poured their wine. After quaffing the wine in one draft, he held out his cup for a refill. A crooked smile played about his mouth as he said, "Much courage is required for what I'm about to propose."

His statement assured Marged that her worst fears were founded. Rhys intended to make romantic overtures to her. "Courage," she repeated uneasily, her back toward him as she poured the wine. "You've never lacked that quality before. Oh, Rhys, I can't thank you enough for rescuing me. Had you not happened by, I'd surely have starved to death. You saved my—" Marged gasped in surprise as she turned to find him standing directly behind her.

"There's a more fitting way to thank me," Rhys suggested, his voice taut, his dark face grimly intense.

"I'll be in your debt for the rest of my life."

"Stop it! You know what I'm trying to say. Don't play me like a court strumpet," Rhys snarled unexpectedly as he snatched the glass of wine from her hand. "Before I go any further, answer me this—what is Edward of March to you?"

"A friend."

"They say he beds you."

"Gossip is full of untruths. 'Tis true Edward desires me," Marged corrected him calmly.

"I'll not fault him for that." His lips twitched in humor. "The York sprig has discerning taste, after all."

Marged smiled sweetly as she sidestepped him and went to the glowing hearth. "Rhys, I think I know what you're about to propose."

"Not to beg you to sleep with me, though that's a wish which haunts my dreams," he blurted honestly, the wine warming him.

"What then?"

"I want to marry you."

"Marry!" Marged blanched at the thought. "What about Glynis?"

"Bah, Glynis! There's no comparison. 'Tis like comparing diamonds to dross. I've vast holdings, Marged. Though not rich like yours, my land covers twin mountaintops and the valley between. More than a thousand men owe allegiance to me. In Brecon, I'm a veritable prince."

Marged smiled at his boasts. "What you say is true, yet it's not for more possessions I intend to marry."

It was Rhys's turn to smile. "Nay, I can see the luxury you keep here. This land is richly fertile. Your demesne must be very valuable."

"That's not what I meant."

"What did you mean?"

"We're not in love. Loving my future husband is most important to me."

"*You* may not be in love . . ." Rhys glanced away, his hazel eyes troubled. "These months past I've fought this feeling—so intense at times, I could scarcely draw breath when you were near. For all that time, and much against my men's wishes, I searched for your father out of love for you. I wanted you to be proud of me, to love me in return."

"Oh, Rhys, I'm deeply in your debt. For your selfless loyalty, I owe you much. Even before this, I was greatly beholden to you."

"Beholden! From you I want emotion—passion—I want love in return."

"I cannot give it. Please don't press me. I love you as a kinsman, as a dear, dear friend—"

"But not as a lover."

"No, not as a lover."

Rhys spun about in anger, smiting his fist in his open palm. "Then you lied to me. Edward of York does mean something to you."

"No. It's as I said—young Edward's naught but my friend."

"Then if it's not me, nor royal Edward, who do you want?"

"No one," Marged lied, her voice little more than a whisper. "I've chosen no man."

"Don't trifle with me, woman!" Rhys snarled, gripping her slender wrist. "I'm no fool. I can see the truth in your face.

Play me not false. I don't suffer treachery lightly. If you don't love Edward, then it must be someone at court, or here within the castle—a soldier—surely to God you don't whore with one of the ranks . . ."

"I whore with no one!" Marged cried, her temper rising. She wrenched free of him. "This entire conversation is pointless. You are my friend, but I cannot marry you. Now go, leave me. Tomorrow we'll both be more cool-headed."

"I'll leave when you've given me his name. Until I have it, here I stay."

"Then you'll have a long wait."

"That suits me, *cariad*." Rhys dropped on the bed. "Staying the night will serve my purpose. In order to protect your reputation, you'll have to take me as husband."

Seething with rage, Marged glared at him. She had much to thank Rhys for, yet she had no intention of repaying him with her body. No man was owed that much! "This is my room. I'm asking you to leave before I call the guards."

"What a pretty sight they'll find—you pinned beneath me, your gown torn. How will you explain my presence in the first place? Fine ladies don't entertain men in their bedchambers unless they intend wrongdoing."

"I only invited you here because I thought I could trust you. You pretended to be my friend."

"I am your friend—but I'd fain be your lover. Oh, Marged, Marged, you need a strong man, a husband to help you rule this land. You admit Edward desires you. He'll not be content to leave you in peace."

Rhys's argument made much sense. "That's something I must deal with when the time comes," Marged said stiffly.

"If you have a strong husband with an army of his own, Edward won't risk antagonizing him," Rhys pointed out shrewdly. He slid from the high bed and came toward her, his tone cajoling. "Are you afraid I'll not love you well? Some would not care, yet you have that look of slumbering passion. Fear not, Marged, I'll be gentle—oh, love, you'll not have cause for disappointment."

"That's not the reason I turned down your suit."

The softness gone, Rhys gripped her arms and pulled her toward him. "Tell me who he is!"

There was nothing for it but the truth. Taking a deep breath, Marged said, "He's someone I loved long before I met you." In a whisper, she added, "Rolfe de Bretayne."

"De Bretayne." Puzzled, Rhys repeated the unfamiliar name. Then his face darkened when he realized his rival's identity. "That Breton dog! The mercenary who supports York's jackals! Our enemy!"

Marged shrank from his rage. With each bellowed epithet, his anger mounted close to boiling. Desperately seeking something on which to vent his temper, Rhys grabbed the wine cups and hurled them against the hearth.

"I love him," she said simply.

"You bitch! Have you no more discretion than to tie yourself to the first dog you meet?"

Marged's face grew stony. "Get out! You've had my answer. Be satisfied. I'll marry no other while he lives."

Rhys stood immobile, hatred turning his craggy features ugly. "While he lives," he repeated almost to himself. "Well, lady fair, that may not be overlong." Having delivered that ominous threat, Rhys wrenched open the door and strode from the room.

Long after he had gone, the door still shuddered on its hinges. So much emotion had been discharged within this room, Marged's strength was sapped by it. She plunged inside her bed, burrowing deep beneath the covers in a desperate effort to overcome the numbing cold that beset her.

Warmth gradually seeped into her veins, and she began to relax. Men were often enraged when denied a desired object. Edward had even pulled his dagger on her, threatening to slit her throat when she would not yield to him. Rhys's violent anger over her rejection was not surprising. The most alarming aspect of tonight's events was that now Rhys knew her lover's identity. Such insane passion blazed within Rhys's soul, Marged was deathly afraid for Rolfe's safety. The only comfort she could take was that many miles separated them, and the combined armies of York and Lancaster made a formidable buffer in between.

Rain blew out of the howling March wind as Marged lay beneath her covers. The servants brought her a hot posset laced with brandy, followed by a platter of succulent roast capon stuffed with sage and onion.

To her relief, the evening progressed without Rhys coming back to plead his suit. Just in case anger overruled his better judgment, he would find a man-at-arms stationed outside her room. Tomorrow, given time to consider the situation, he might not be so furious over his discovery that she preferred their enemy to him.

The wind rattled the narrow casements and bent the candle flames in a frenzied dance. Raindrops splattered down the chimney. Lulled by the incessant music, she finally drifted asleep.

When she awoke sometime later, she could still hear the fierce wind howling about the tower; in fact, so strong were its drafts inside the room, the candles had blown out. The only light came from a votive candle flickering in a niche that sheltered a statue of Our Lady. An unusual sound made Marged cock her head to one side. Needing to reassure herself that the guard was still at his post, she slithered from her bed, shuddering with cold as she hurried to the door.

The door creaked open and a cold wind gusted down the corridor. A dark shadow moved against the wall.

"Guard, what hour is it?"

"Near dawn, lady," the man replied, his gruff voice muffled.

"Thank you. Good night."

The man gave no reply.

Marged closed the door. She dashed back to bed, where she slid beneath the covers, shivering deliciously as she plunged her ice-cold feet into the still-warm depths of the feather mattress.

"Near dawn, but not near enough to cause us concern."

Marged froze at the unexpected voice. The door stood open. Though it was difficult to identify him by the feeble votive light, Marged's stomach curdled in fear as she recognized Rhys. Her lips barely formed the words to challenge his entry before he slid home the bolt. She was trapped! Above the mournful shriek of the wind, Marged could hear her own pounding heart.

"Get out before I call the guard."

"He won't hear you."

Rhys advanced toward the bed. At the foot of the shallow

steps he stopped, legs straddled, a hand on his dagger. "I offered you my name, my honor, if you'd take me as husband."

"Please, Rhys, don't spoil our friendship. Can we not still be friends?" Marged pleaded, her agile mind racing for a solution. If she could only keep him talking until she reached the jeweled dagger in her girdle flung over the chest at the foot of the bed . . .

But Rhys was not to be distracted. In one bound he was up the steps. Too late, Marged leaped to the far side of the vast bed; he flung himself on top of her.

"Going somewhere?" he asked, his breath hot against her face.

Marged's protests were quickly drowned by his brutal mouth. He kissed her savagely, bruising her lips against her teeth.

When at last she regained the power of speech, she spat, "Think you to take me against my will? My men will be here in minutes. Go now, whilst we're still friends. I can't marry you because I love another. Even if I loved no one, 'twould not change my mind. You're like a brother to me. Nothing more."

His dark-shadowed face was grim above hers. "A brother, is it? Then we'll commit incest, for take you I will."

Marged struggled to be free of his weight. Her screams for help were drowned by the tearing wind over the battlements.

"Love me, damn you," he growled, his hands like vises. "Love me of your own accord, and I swear I won't hurt you. You've passion aplenty for a traitorous Breton dog—can't you muster a little for your own kinsman?" Rhys struggled to pin her flailing legs beneath his.

"If you take me at all, it'll be against my will."

"Then so be it, lady! You've laid down the rules," he spat in anger. Rhys rattled her almost senseless, enraged to think that she, who had gladly spread her legs for a foreign mercenary, denied him the same privilege. "I saved your life. Before that, I wasted months of my youth searching for your sire. Surely I'm owed something for that."

"I'll give you gold."

"Gold!" Rhys bellowed in rage at the insult. "The only payment I demand lies between your legs."

They struggled frantically amid the heaped covers. Cursing, Rhys flung the bedding aside, giving her time to make a bid for freedom.

Bellowing as he leaped from the bed, he grabbed her and swung her about, crashing her against the wall. Stunned, Marged fought for breath, denying the pain that racked her body. The blow made the votive light quiver recklessly on its stand before it toppled to the rushes.

Shock so slowed her reactions that even this diversion did not give Marged sufficient time to escape. She was struggling frantically with the iron bolt when Rhys seized her and swung her away from the door.

"Trying to smoke me out, are you? You must be mad! Fire the rushes and we may neither of us get out alive."

"The guards would soon come to investigate a fire."

"If you want more light, *cariad,* I can always oblige," Rhys snarled as he flung her across the bed. From the broken votive light he lit four candles in a brass holder. When he set the flickering candles on the carved oak chest at the foot of the bed, the winking light revealed the small dagger hanging from her girdle.

Rhys grinned as he confiscated the weapon. He cradled the silver-handled dagger in his hands for a moment before crossing to the window. Wrenching open the casement, he flung the dagger over the battlements.

Marged's breath rasped as she lay on the bed, desperate to escape, but unable to find a way. Firing the rushes would have been a good idea, if only she had thought of it first. Now Rhys would be doubly on guard against any move toward the candles.

He watched her as he pulled open his black doublet to expose his broad, heavily furred chest; a narrow silver crucifix glinted against the black hair. His mouth bitter, Rhys stepped toward her. "Now you," he commanded harshly, indicating her shift.

"No."

"Then I'll rip it off. That will be more pleasurable."

When he grasped her embroidered shift, Marged relented. The thin fabric was nearly transparent in the candlelight. Rhys's hungry gaze fastened on those twin peaks pushing out the supple fabric in quivering hillocks. As Marged pulled up her shift, his gaze followed the sweep of her shapely legs, soft thighs, and curving hips, tantalizingly exposed. Unconsciously he licked his thick lips, hardly able to endure further torment. When Marged reached for the bedcovers to hide her nakedness, he stayed her hand.

"Nay, what was good enough for a Breton cur should be good enough for a loyal Welshman," he mocked, grasping her wrists as he twisted her arms cruelly above her head.

"I hate you! I swear you'll regret ever coming to Bowenford."

Rhys ignored her threats as he feasted his eyes on her beautiful, arousing body. Those magnificent globes of translucent flesh captured his attention. With a half sob, he felt her breasts with his free hand, shuddering with delight as he finally possessed that of which he had dreamed. Then his mouth fastened over her breast, his lips brutally demanding. He swept the length of her body, his teeth coming into play as his caresses grew more frenzied.

Marged's futile efforts to defend her modesty only met with scornful laughter. She fought desperately against him, but Rhys easily subdued her. Her resistance seemed to heighten his arousal.

Rhys fumbled with his clothing, pulling the lacings loose. Swiftly he stripped off his hose and his tight linen drawers, unashamedly revealing his nakedness. When Rhys saw Marged's eyes close tightly, he shook her in fury.

"Open your eyes! Look upon a real man. Likely you'll discover a vast difference between dogs and men."

When she refused to obey, he struck her across the mouth, bringing tears to her eyes. Through a burning haze of tears, his cruel face came into focus, mouth snarling, eyes black with rage. This was the Rhys whom Glynis had known, this brutal man who pinned her helplessly beneath him was the legendary Rhys ap Morgan, who inspired terror in all who crossed him.

"Look at me," Rhys commanded. He pulled her up by her hair, forcing her to gaze on his nakedness.

Marged quailed at the sight of his turgid flesh, dark with blood and fully aroused. Instead of inspiring desire, Rhys's bursting flesh, shuddering in anticipation beneath her gaze, turned her ice cold. The thought of receiving his seed inside the secret places of her body, defiling the sanctuary she held in trust for the man she loved, repelled her.

Impatiently, Rhys seized Marged's hand, molding it about his thick, surging organ. When she gouged his flesh, intending to inflict pain, he shivered in fierce delight. As she continued to rake her nails along his tender skin, Rhys snarled an oath and smashed her back on the bed.

Slowly he forced her legs apart on the soft mattress, pinning her arms down. At the last, touched by momentary remorse, he drew back, his hard mouth softening slightly as he gazed down on her quivering resistance.

"You still have the option of being taken without force," he reminded her gruffly, steeling himself against the quickening delight of her naked flesh pressed against his. "You don't have to be hurt."

"Not hurt! What do you call this? Was it supposed to be pleasure?" she challenged, her green eyes flashing as she threshed about, desperate to dislodge his weight.

"You've had only a taste of the pain I can inflict." Uttering a string of Welsh curses, Rhys fell upon her, abandoning himself to lust. In an agony of gnashing teeth and bruising hands, he invaded her body again and again. At last, flagging in the fury of his assault, he slid from her.

"Bitch," he growled at last when he had regained his breath. "'Twas all your doing. I never intended to hurt you. I always dreamed it would be different."

"I hope to God it was different enough to satisfy you," Marged spat bitterly as she dragged the covers over her bruised body. She trembled with a mixture of cold, pain, and disgust.

Filled with anger and remorse, he looked down at her, lying spent and breathless against the pillow. How much he had loved and worshiped her! His dreams of her reciprocating his deep emotion were dead. In passionate rage he had defiled that beauty, had stolen by sheer force that which she had sought to keep from him. The act had slaked his lust, but it had not come close to satisfying his soul.

"I'll be back," Rhys promised grimly as he flung himself from the bed. Marged did not reply. As he fumbled with his clothing, he could hear her sobbing quietly. Why didn't she swear at him, rage at him like other women? "You'll welcome me yet," he growled as he buckled his belt and thrust a pair of gleaming daggers beneath the leather.

"Not if you were the last man on earth!" Marged declared defiantly.

"As far as you're concerned, you ungrateful bitch, that statement may prove true," he muttered darkly. He strode to the door, pausing in the deep black shadow beyond the flickering candles to gaze at her devastated beauty one final time. "I've laid claim to you. When the Breton's dead, you'll welcome me to your bed readily enough."

Marged's tears stopped before his footsteps faded away. She could summon the guards to arrest him, but he had already taken what he wanted. What she'd gladly given Rolfe. At the reminder of her beloved, a terrible chill of shame crept through Marged's bruised body. Oh, my love, she whispered in remorse. Tears pricked her eyes as she pictured his reaction to hearing of the cruel payment her Welsh kinsman had extracted. He would surely challenge Rhys to avenge her honor.

Clenching her fists against the horror of such calamity, she knew she must never reveal tonight's humiliation. No one must ever know about her shame. Rhys's character was such that she did not think he would boast about his conquest. What about the sentry? It was surely time to change the guard, for beyond the window the heavy sky was already tinged with light. How strange that no one had found his body.

Marged went to the door, reeling slightly from the exertion. She ached in every muscle. She leaned against the wall until her dizzy spell passed. When she opened the door, there was a swift rattle of armaments as someone came to attention. "Guard! Are you well?" she asked incredulously.

"Aye, lady, very well. And you?"

In the light of a sputtering sconce, she noted his sly grin. Now Marged understood what must have taken place. Rhys had pretended they were lovers, bribing the man to admit him. She could not blame the soldier. Given her already burgeoning reputation for dalliance, one more lover visiting in the night was hardly cause for concern. The two Bretons, the young Yorkist king, and now this Welshman—oh, she could imagine the laughter in the guardroom as the men discussed her unusual capacity for lovemaking.

"Yes, I'm . . . quite . . . well," she mumbled, stepping back into the shadowed room.

"Stormy nights can be most useful, eh, lady?" And the man chuckled suggestively.

With a shudder of horror, Marged hastily closed and leaned against the door, her stomach churning with nausea at the realization that her terrible secret would be poorly kept.

Rhys and his army left soon after dawn. Though she supposed it would elicit much comment, Marged stayed within her chamber until they had gone, unable to face her violator in the revealing light of day.

The Welsh soldiers rode hard, their leader driving them like one possessed. His face grim, his body tense, he made a solemn vow. When next York and Lancaster met, he would not abandon the field until the hated Breton was dead! And as he headed north, huddled against the bitter wind, the very hoofbeats seemed to echo that detested name . . . de Bretayne . . . de Bretayne . . . de Bretayne . . .

Edward's army had left London on March thirteenth, bound for York, where Queen Margaret's Lancastrian forces were headquartered. The army paused at intervals to recruit men who gladly flocked to what they thought would be the winning side. The vast Yorkist tide, composed of more than twenty-five thousand men, flowed northward.

Suffering numerous delays caused by inclement weather and lack of forage, Rolfe did not reach Edward's main force until dusk of March twenty-eighth. His tired men rode past the Yorkshire village of Saxton in the vanguard of Edward's straggling wagon train.

"By all that's holy! De Bretayne!" Edward greeted him heartily. He had spotted the Breton's distinctive red banners flapping in the fierce north wind as the late arrivals skirted the encampment in search of its commander. "God knows, I wouldn't have relished a fight without you."

"By God! Don't tell me you waited the battle for us again?" Rolfe cried, forcing himself to the comradely exchange. Despite Marged's assurances that nineteen-year-old Edward had not been her lover, each time Rolfe looked at the golden-haired giant, jealousy rose in his stomach like bile.

"Aye, that we did," Edward chuckled.

Rolfe, commanding his men to follow, fell in step behind Edward's charger as they rode to his red-striped field tent. There the young King offered Rolfe a cup of mulled wine and a dish of steaming camp stew.

"My belly has a hole in it the size of Yorkshire."

"Well, 'tis likely to grow bigger if we don't soon reach York," Edward commented gloomily, revealing for the first time that he was not as confident about their position as Rolfe had supposed. "The enemy's got a goodly force. Fauconberg's already drawn blood—Clifford and his men are dead. Our spies tell us Somerset commands more than fifty thousand."

Rolfe drained his cup and held it out for a refill. "So, when did the Lancastrians become invincible?"

"Norfolk's not yet come," said Edward, as he leaned forward, his blue eyes troubled. "We cannot hold out any longer, facing such a vast force. If he doesn't hurry, we must battle without him."

"There's a whole night yet to go. Perchance he'll appear before dawn."

"Will you stay close by?"

"Aye, but I'll sleep with my men."

"Who knows, our foes may even decline to fight until Norfolk arrives. Tomorrow's Palm Sunday."

Rolfe grinned. "We seem destined to do battle on holy days."

The answering grin that Edward flashed was decidedly weak.

When their camp was secure, Rolfe made a final round of his troops' position, encouraging his men and sympathizing with the sentries who kept watch in the teeth of a bitter wind. To his great unease, he had discovered that the enemy lay less than a half-mile north, beyond the village of Towton. He was taking no chances on a surprise night attack. The last of their food had already been distributed this morning, yet despite empty bellies, his men's morale remained high. An impending fight always bolstered the Breton soldiers' spirits.

The raw north wind howled across miles of open heath and moorland. Rolfe, trying to revive himself from the numbing effects of this Yorkshire spring, blew on his hands and stamped his feet. For the first time that day, he indulged in thoughts of Marged . . . her warm body within the downy coverlets . . . sweet kisses hotly exchanged . . .

He grunted, forcing such thoughts to the back of his mind. It was such a raw night, he doubted he would get much rest without the added hardship of bittersweet memory. The campfire, which had never been large, had already gone out for lack of fuel. Soldiers huddled together for warmth as the bitter wind, sharp with the scent of snow, howled like a demented soul across the exposed plateau, defying the proverbial description of March. In like a lion, out like a lamb. Growing drowsy, Rolfe decided that in this perverse northern county, the month must blow out with the fury of a lion. A few minutes later he was sound asleep.

When he woke in the cold dawn of Palm Sunday, 1461, he found that the men wore thin blankets of snow. The wind's wintery whine continued unabated.

Grim-faced, he fitted his steel helmet on his head and, with the help of his squire, buckled on his full plate armor. At least the steel would cut the wind, though in his opinion the added weight and lack of maneuverability far outweighed its advantages.

He had a fairly accurate picture of the surrounding terrain, which he had scouted last night in the gathering dusk. Their position did not fill him with joy. The army faced an open depression between two ridges called Towton Heath. It was here that the Lancastrians, under Somerset, had chosen to make their stand. To their immediate left the ground sloped away to the steep-banked River Cock, now swollen with melting snow. To their right lay marshland. To the north was York, headquarters of the enemy; to the south, the River Aire, its bridges destroyed.

Edward, in high spirits this bitter morning, seemed to be everywhere at once. He rode tirelessly about the field, inspiring the men through his own abiding confidence. Last night's trepidation had flown as he was swept up in the excitement of preparing for battle. The burning question on every tongue remained, where were Norfolk's troops?

By the time the ranks were drawn up in battle order, it had begun to snow heavily. A thick white curtain reduced visibility nearly to zero, isolating the soldiers in a world bounded by their immediate neighbors. The wind had gradually shifted southerly, and as the Yorkist troops advanced, the blinding snow blew directly in the enemies' faces.

Once the opening volleys of arrows were exchanged, the mass of troops engaged in hand-to-hand combat. Snow, blood, and slush formed a slippery quagmire underfoot as the deadly battle raged back and forth.

Throughout the morning, Rolfe's men were pushed relentlessly westward. Squelching through marshland, driven toward the steep banks of Cock Beck, they soon lost sight of Edward's men. Rolfe was too busy staving off the assorted blows of foes to spare much thought for the young King's position. In places the heath was so littered with the slain that men clambered over the fallen to fight. This meadow, afterward renamed Bloody Meadow, was the site of the heaviest casualties. The steep slopes of Cock Beck echoed with the cries of the wounded and with the deafening, unrelenting clash of men, who, frenzied with bloodlust, delivered blow after blow in payment for Wakefield, where perished the final flower of chivalry in this bitter civil war.

The Yorkist force had slowly given ground, for too few men remained to fill the widening gaps in the ranks. Toward noon, the battle reached a crisis. Then, out of the snowy gloom, appeared Norfolk's banners; the arrival of his badly needed reinforcements shifted the tide of battle. Relentlessly the fresh troops smashed into the battle's right flank, turning the conflict about, driving the massed fighting men toward Cock Burn's suicidal bank.

A charging knight unhorsed Rolfe, who barely managed to struggle to his feet before he was set upon by a heavily armed band of Lancastrians. By some strange quirk, the leader of this fierce Lancastrian band had singled him out for mortal combat.

"Come forth, you Breton dog. Give me the pleasure of spilling your brains," bellowed the man, his dark face demonic beneath his conical steel helmet.

Rolfe's field of vision was severly limited through the bars of his closed visor. He lurched about, slipping on the bloody slush, unable to recapture his horse, whinnying nearby. Like a whirlwind, his lightly armed enemy launched a vicious frontal attack, pounding his breastplate with a spiked flail. The blows rang as loud as a dozen church bells in his head, until Rolfe thought his eardrums would burst. His own flail and mace swung hopelessly out of reach on his saddle.

"Fight, you damned coward! I'll not be content to murder you!" bellowed his challenger.

Rolfe raised his bloody sword and lashed at his enemy's upraised arm, piercing his padded jambeson. Far from repelling his opponent, the strike seemed only to spur him to greater bravery. Turned nearly insane by bloodlust, the man leaped forward, seeming to rejoice in his own trickling blood as he drew his sword, eager for combat.

"Who are you?" Rolfe demanded, as they parried and thrust and slashed. The sheer frenzy of this man's attack suggested he had a far more personal score to settle than mere loyalty to the opposing faction.

"Listen well, Breton, for 'tis a name you'll carry to your grave," bellowed the dark-visaged man. "I'm Rhys ap Morgan. You stole the woman I love. For that you will die."

And Rolfe finally understood. Marged's Welsh kinsman, enraged beyond all reason, thirsted for his blood. Tightening his grip on his slippery sword, he lashed at his enemy with renewed fury. Battering back and forth, they hacked at each other with more force than skill. After delivering a mighty blow, Rolfe quailed when his sword shattered against the Welshman's breastplate. He clutched naught but a blunted dagger in his bloody fist.

Uttering a wild, triumphant screech, Rhys leaped forward for the kill. But the ground underfoot had become a shifting quagmire of bloody mud, and he floundered ankle-deep in the ooze. Lunging forward, Rolfe smashed his enemy in the side, bowling him over. They grappled for Rhys's sword in the icy slush. So strong was the Welshman's grip that Rolfe, exhausted from hours of combat, was hard pressed to break it. Rhys's supporters had stood aside, honoring his command to leave the Breton for him; now they closed in, anxious to protect their lord.

Though he fought hard against this fresh assault, Rolfe was forced backward. Suddenly, in the rapidly changing fortunes of war, his enemies became the besieged. A yelling mass of bloodthirsty Yorkists fell upon the Welshmen, slashing indiscriminately after seeing one of their comrades in danger.

Rolfe staggered to his feet like a giant turtle in his heavy steel armor. As he turned, the Welsh leader swooped down on him, screaming curses as he hacked viciously at Rolfe's battered armor. Rhys's face was swollen and bruised; blood trickled from a dozen wounds on his lightly protected body. Suddenly his sword shattered. Bellowing for vengeance, Rhys came at Rolfe with bare hands, his useless sword flung in the slush.

They grappled in the slush, rolling against bodies, and avoiding the trampling feet of men engaging the enemy. Rolfe finally pinned Rhys beneath him, trapping him there by the sheer weight of his armor. The Welshman's hands went like lightning for his throat, now exposed because his helm latch and leather straps had been broken, and the helmet ripped away. Gasping, almost blacking out, Rolfe managed to get his own hands around his opponent's sinewy throat. Desperately willing strength to his fingers, he found the death grip on his own throat slackened, then released, until the grasping hands slid free. Beneath him, Rhys ap Morgan lay still, his face contorted in a deathmask of hate.

Gagging, Rolfe lay fighting for breath, having barely enough presence of mind to roll over on his back, out of the suffocating mud. Awareness gradually drifted back in the form of a thundering noise in his ears. Then a spattering shower of slush enveloped him as a horseman galloped across the carpet of dead. The horse's flying rear hoof caught Rolfe on the temple, producing violent sparks in the unfathomable darkness of his mind. Nausea gripped him in a rocking wave, his last conscious memory. Then there was nothing.

The dark afternoon slid rapidly into dusk before Rolfe finally regained consciousness. Propping himself on his elbow, he painfully levered his way out from under a heap of mangled corpses. So overjoyed was he to discover that he still lived, he gave no thought to danger. Then, realizing he knew not whether this bloody marsh was Yorkist or Lancastrian, he dropped down, lying still among the slain. All seemed quiet.

The fighting appeared to have rushed over this land and moved on.

Rolfe staggered about the soggy terrain, greatly hampered by his battered armor. The assault of flail and mace had broken vulnerable spots in the plate, and he winced as the shattered metal cut into his flesh like knives. Blurred shapes moved about the field as fighting raged in isolated pockets, but the brunt of the battle seemed to have slid over the steep banks of Cock Beck. He retrieved a sword from one of the fallen, not knowing what trial would await him beyond the ridge.

He was totally unprepared for the appalling scene of slaughter revealed below. The land bordering the flooding beck was thick with bodies. Once men were pushed over the steep bank, they slid helplessly to their deaths. The swift, blood-engorged waters were choked with corpses, forming a gruesome bridge that aided their comrades' flight. As the Lancastrians retreated fully, they didn't pause to do battle with the horseless Rolfe. They were more anxious to save their own necks from the pursuing Yorkists, who were too crazed with bloodlust to spare Rolfe more than a cursory glance.

In a daze he wandered away from that chasm of death and destruction, seeking his own lines. Hundreds of the fallen were emblazoned with Yorkist emblems. He even began to wonder if fleeing Yorkists, not Lancastrians, dammed narrow Cock Beck.

He staggered about in the rapidly thickening dusk, vainly trying to catch a riderless horse. The animals, crazed by the smell of blood, refused to be captured. At last, too weary to continue and ever mindful of his own disorientation, Rolfe sank thankfully atop a mound of the slain. He held his head in his hands as he retched violently. Sweat trickled into the wounds made by his splintered plate, smarting like a thousand beestings.

"My lord—God be praised!" came a gruff voice out of the gloom.

Eager hands pulled him to his feet. Rolfe blinked owlishly, trying to focus on his savior. The soldier was his own, but in this befuddled state, he could not recall the man's name.

"Aye—thank God," Rolfe croaked. "You've saved my life."

"Nay, lord, 'tis you who saved mine."

The soldier led forth Rolfe's own charger, who whinnied with pleasure at the sight of his master. He could scarcely sit in the saddle. He slumped there, ears numb and face stinging in the merciless wind. As dusk slid into night, a terrible silence engulfed the field, broken only by flurries of snow and a mournfully howling wind. The great, decisive battle of Towton Heath was over. And Edward of York was the undisputed victor.

The victorious army rode triumphantly into York, with young Edward and his cousin Warwick leading it. Above the Micklegate Bar reposed the head of Edward's father, his uncle Salisbury, and Edmund of Rutland, his younger brother, forming a macabre trio to bid them welcome to the city. Queen Margaret had ordered these grisly, crow-pecked relics placed there after the battle of Wakefield.

Edward's first official act was to have the heads removed and interred with the noble remains at Pontefract. Then, following the custom of the times, he readily supplied noble Lancastrian heads to fill the empty space on Micklegate Bar.

"You've served me well," said Edward, smiling affectionately upon the dark head bowed before him.

"You are most generous, Your Grace." Rolfe deemed the formal title appropriate because of Warwick's presence. Since they had entered the city two days ago, Edward's thirty-two-year-old cousin had never left his side. It was as if Warwick doubted the young Earl's ability to act independently.

"Few others rallied their troops to greater valor," Edward praised, glancing through the window at the wind-whipped trees. "You were ever my loyal friend."

"You yourself provided a model of inspiration, Your Grace," Rolfe praised sincerely. Wherever the line had been weakest, Edward had plunged through the ranks, leading reinforcements to fill the gap, encouraging his men against seemingly overwhelming odds.

"As you say, as you say." Edward smiled, pleased by his praise. "A fitting reward shall be yours, you may be assured of that. Something magnificent and vastly appropriate."

"Can we not discuss rewards at a later date?" cut in Warwick, his face set in a scowl.

Rolfe rose to his feet, increasingly wary of Edward's powerful relative. When he would have spoken, Warwick interrupted, his tone urgent.

"The days are wasting. You must show yourself to be a worthy King."

"We are to ride forth and meet our people," Edward explained to Rolfe.

"You are to *pacify* them," Warwick reminded him impatiently. "You've much need to dispel memories of former loyalty. To the common man, royalty remains a breed apart. The name of the king matters little."

"To create goodwill has always been our purpose," Edward defended, his face puckered with distress at Warwick's ominous warning. "'Twas to that end we *purchased* supplies for our troops—the French bitch always took what she wanted."

Warwick smiled, placing his hand placatingly on Edward's arm. "So far you've done well. But the task's far from complete." Warwick glanced toward Rolfe, reluctant to continue in his presence.

Receiving the implied message, he excused himself. "By your leave, Your Grace, I must attend to my troops."

"Go not alone," Edward cautioned, taking Rolfe's hand. "You've not healed. The physician said you were to avoid strenuous activity for at least a week. Just to be on the safe side, take someone with you when you ride abroad. By the Christ, we've no wish to lose both a good friend and a good general in one fell swoop."

He laughed with Edward, uncomfortably aware that Warwick did not join them. In the back of his mind he still puzzled over that incident on the road to Bowenford. He had not forgotten the insignia of bear and ragged staff on the casualties' sleeves. Rolfe did not need to have it spelled out to understand Warwick bore him little love.

"Your Grace's concern is touching. I promise to take care." Rolfe looked straight at Warwick, and was rewarded by having the great man turn aside rather than meet his gaze.

"Go then, friend," Edward said, "but return in time to sup with us tonight."

Rolfe accepted Edward's invitation. Then he bowed and backed from the room, conscious of Warwick's piercing gaze following his every move.

Barely waiting for the door to close before he spoke, Warwick snapped, "Must you surround yourself with foreign mercenaries, Ned? It sets ill with the common people. They have too many bitter memories of the former king's French minions."

"You can hardly compare de Bretayne to Gaveston, cousin," Edward reminded him good-humoredly. "And I'll swear I've never slept with him."

Warwick managed a taut smile. "Will you be serious?"

"When necessary." Edward's smile tightened. Through the diamond-paned window he watched Rolfe striding across the windswept courtyard before he disappeared through a door leading to the street. "De Bretayne's a good, loyal friend. I like and trust him."

"Loyal . . . to the best of your knowledge."

"What do you mean?"

"Oh, certain rumors have reached my ears," Warwick allowed casually as he strode toward the blazing hearth. "You're too trusting by far, Ned."

"Rumors about de Bretayne? He fought for me like a Trojan. No one at Towton could have any doubts concerning his loyalty," Edward said in amazement. "Think you I'd have my personal physician minister to an enemy?"

"I think you're a green and very inexperienced king," Warwick stated bluntly.

Edward's face hardened. "If there are accusations to be made, then speak them, cousin, or hold your tongue."

"There's a paper in existence, signed by your loyal friend de Bretayne, wherein he swears allegiance to the Lancastrians."

"I don't believe it! Never has he wavered in his support."

Warwick's mouth tightened grimly. "Then, of course, there's the matter concerning the Lady Marged."

"Which bears not one whit of truth to it!" Edward exploded, forcing down the niggling seeds of doubt not entirely vanquished in his mind.

"What if I produce evidence?"

"Aye . . . yet I doubt any evidence exists."

"But if I produce it?"

"If and when you produce it, you have my word I'll take you seriously. Beyond that, cousin, I promise nothing."

Edward watched his cousin cross that same cobbled courtyard, unease swirling through his belly. Marged was his! True, he had not yet taken her, but he would, given time. Warwick's slanders were totally unfounded. They must be unfounded.

That evening, Edward's face grew gray as he unrolled the parchment containing the list of knights and gentlemen sworn to support King Henry. Ever eager, Warwick strained over his shoulder, impatient until Edward's gaze lighted on that name, signed large, bold and assured.

"De Bretayne!"

"Did I not tell you?"

"Wait . . . there must be others of that name."

"Rolfe de Bretayne can be no other," Warwick pointed out suavely, holding the parchment near the candle flame. Warwick withdrew slightly to allow Edward time to study the paper. It was fortunate he had the foresight to present this condemning document at night. The forgery might not have stood a daylight scrutiny. As it was, the gloom, the shadows, the near-perfect alteration by inserting the name Rolfe in place of Joce . . .

"I know not if this is his signature," Edward protested in a strained voice.

"Why, Ned, we'll call him in to ask. Perchance he'll give you a sample of his handwriting to compare," Warwick mocked. "Have done! We cannot put the man on his guard. He'll be across the Channel before dawn. Trust me, Ned. Have I not always had your best interests at heart?"

Edward nodded, fighting the burning emotion surging in his belly. He could not easily accept this evidence that de Bretayne was a traitor. He was his loyal friend—besides, he liked Rolfe far better than he liked his own cousin Dickon. Yet Warwick usually had England's interests at heart, and countless times he had laid his life on the line. Now that he was to be king, Edward knew that the destiny of the House of York had become the destiny of England.

"Is this the only evidence of his treachery?"

"There are numerous sworn statements."

"Statements are too easily bought," Edward declared stubbornly. "Leave me. Let me reconsider."

Warwick slid his arm comfortingly about Edward's great bowed shoulders, slipping a sheet of folded paper next to his arm on the table. "Afterward, if there's still doubt in your mind, perhaps this will help sway your conscience."

For a few minutes after Warwick had departed, Edward remained slumped in his chair, staring at the battered parchment. A forgery? Yes, he would not put that deception past Warwick. Many people had warned him about his powerful cousin's ambition, suggesting that Warwick sought to rule the land, with Edward as puppet king. Because of those warnings and his own distrust of his cousin, he had not allowed Warwick free rein. He had no intention of becoming merely a figurehead. Perhaps there was some conspiracy afoot. Did his cousin seek to remove Rolfe from favor because the Breton was his loyal friend?

The second paper fluttered to the rushes. Edward stooped to pick it up. But it had nothing to do with the conflict between the royal houses of York and Lancaster. As one already dead, Edward stared glassy-eyed at the unfolded parchment, fighting a multitude of emotions that sickened, stunned, and angered him at once. For months Warwick had insinuated—nay, outright accused—de Bretayne of having more than a passing interest in Marged. Warwick's accusations were unfounded no longer!

Nausea churned his stomach as he read: "*My dearest Marged, my heart aches to see you again. No loyalty ever bound me more securely than the fetters of your heart. At night I'm tormented by memories of your sweet kisses . . .*"

"No," Edward bellowed, leaping to his feet and flinging the offending missive across the room. "No," he groaned, his head in his hands. It could not be true. Not his lovely Marged, not she who had played him cleverly all these months, winsome, encouraging, yet at the last always withholding that which he desperately sought. Now it was clear why she had not wished to bed him—she had been the Breton's woman all along!

God, what a fool he had been to grant de Bretayne the honor of escorting her to Bowenford. How they both must have laughed at their sovereign's gullibility.

Spinning about, the damning letter trembling in his large hand, Edward strode to the door and wrenched it open, letting it crash on its hinge as he bellowed for the guard.

He had been a witless fool! He would be a fool no longer.

{ fourteen }

DAILY THE SEASON grew lustier. Blue speedwell, white stitchwort, buttercups, and dandelions sprinkled the meadows. The wooded hillsides were terraced with leaf-green haze. Beside the road the ebony blackthorn branches were stained white. Soon the stark apple orchards would be a foaming sea of pink and white blossoms, and the cuckoo's distinctive call would echo through the woods.

Marged paused in her daily ride about the demesne, her lovely face somber as she reined in on a slight knoll. When she reviewed Rhys's terrible anger over his discovery of her lover's identity, her stomach churned with fear. Had he gone in search of Rolfe? Had he wounded him? Or worse—killed him? Marged swallowed the mounting lump in her throat as she battled the surge of panic. Had she known where Rolfe was, she would have sent him a warning. As it was, she could only pray he was safe.

When Marged returned to Bowenford, she found a strange horse standing riderless in the bailey.

"'Tis a messenger for you, lady," answered the groom in reply to her agitated question.

Marged's sense of foreboding increased as she hastened indoors. Alys and Joan, who lately appeared to have overcome their animosity toward each other, glanced up in unison at her approach.

"Where's the messenger?" Marged asked.

"Supping in the the kitchens. I'll send for him."

"Don't bother, Alys. I'll speak to him there."

Marged swept from the Great Hall without sparing a greeting for Joan. Though she knew Rolfe no longer slept with her, Joan's mere presence was a constant source of irritation. She must give Alys her due. Usually her stepsister kept the wench occupied elsewhere, eliminating the need for confrontation.

The servants looked up in surprise, faces wreathed in smiles of welcome as Marged entered the vast, stone-arched kitchens. A surge of warmth from the huge ovens wafted around her, fragrant with the aroma of fresh-baked bread. The messenger was seated at a trestle with a mug of ale before him, a hunk of meat and bread in his fist.

"You have a message?" Marged asked, crossing to the table.

"Aye, from my master. 'Tis private," the man replied uncomfortably.

"Come, we'll talk outside," Marged suggested impatiently.

They moved from the black-shadowed wedge of the buildings into the sun-splashed center of the bailey. Marged sat on the painted wooden bench, looking expectantly at this strange young man who wore no distinguishing livery.

"Here, lady, he said to give it to no other."

With a trembling hand, Marged accepted the parchment. She broke the unfamiliar seal and unfolded the crackling message. She did not recognize the handwriting.

Lady Marged,

My master is taken prisoner. He bids me warn you the King is privy to your secret.

Your faithful servant,
Yves Destier,
freeman in the service of Rolfe de Bretayne.

Eyes dark with fear, Marged looked searchingly at the messenger.

"Where is Monsieur Destier?"

"In Hereford, lady."

"Will you take me to him?"

The man shuffled his feet uncomfortably. "He did not tell me—"

"He'll want to see me, I know he will. His lord is in grave danger."

The man nodded agreement reluctantly, and Marged flew back inside the castle to pack provisions for immediate departure, her heart pounding frantically as she reviewed the message. Destier must be one of Rolfe's lieutenants, though why he was here in Hereford and not at his master's side, she did not know.

"Oh, Marged, surely you aren't leaving," Alys wailed in distress when she heard the news. "I've prepared fish pasties especially for supper."

"I'll take them with me," Marged assured her stepsister as she thrust a change of clothes, a heavy cloak, and extra shoes inside her saddlebag.

Alys, somewhat mollified by her promise, watched with interest, even offering suggestions about what to take with her on the journey. She had been given no reason for Marged's urgent departure. Knowing her stepsister well, Alys assumed the message concerned either Rolfe or the young King. Nothing but a surprise rendezvous with a man would make Marged so disturbed. Stifling pangs of jealousy, Alys prayed the man in question was young Edward of York, yet even if Marged journeyed to meet Rolfe, it mattered little. In all likelihood, dearest Marged would never reach Hereford.

"Here, Lady Marged—your provisions." Joan smiled shyly as she handed Marged a covered wicker basket.

Marged forced a tight smile. The food would have carried easier in a saddlebag, but she took care not to mention it. To have either Joan or Alys concerned about her welfare was a minor miracle in itself.

"Thank you both for your help. I'll likely be back within a few days."

Alys smiled absently as she glanced toward the pale blue

sky, stretching into infinity beyond the stone-arched window. "Have a pleasant journey," she said sweetly.

When Marged glanced back, both Alys and Joan were waving to her from the battlements. Had she not been so preoccupied with worry about Rolfe's safety, she would have found their concern highly suspicious; as it was, she waved abstractedly before she cantered down the slope toward the Hereford road.

"Well, that's that," said Alys, turning from the window after her hated stepsister had disappeared from view.

"How long will it take?"

"Take? Whatever do you mean, wench?" Alys smiled thinly, scarcely able to keep from gloating in triumph over her secret knowledge.

"Will you send word to him soon?" Joan asked eagerly as Alys glided past. "Oh, you must, Lady Alys, I'm beside myself with impatience. It's nigh on three weeks since I've seen him."

"When I decide what to do, perhaps I'll reveal my plans to you," Alys allowed haughtily, her brows knitted in aggravation. It was all very well taking Joan into her confidence, but the scatterbrained little wretch had already caused her much unease. Fellow conspirators though they had become, she never felt secure in Joan's knowledge of those black schemes.

"Oh, lady, please . . ." Joan's voice faded as Alys swept from the solar.

So fond of tormenting her was Lady Alys, Joan consoled herself that her lady's changed attitude sprang from her desire to wound. Of late, a disturbing thought gnawed at her peace of mind. Joan told herself the notion was ridiculous, yet she could not help wondering if her mistress had a secret passion for Rolfe. Many small telltale signs heightened her suspicions. Surely, Lady Alys was as celibate as a nun! Never once had she betrayed any interest in men. But if her suspicions were founded, her own life was as much in danger as Lady Marged's. Always one to choose the pleasant, easy solution to a problem, however, Joan soon forced herself to laugh over the preposterous idea. What a fool she was being! She must be addled to even consider Lady Alys capable of lusting after a man. Many times her mistress had regaled her with tales of the torment she had endured at the hands of her detested husband. Worry over the outcome of today's events had turned her fanciful.

Joan leaned on the stone window frame, her eyes unfocused as she pictured Lady Marged pausing to sup along the highway. Such delectable fish pasties were bound to tempt her appetite. Their plan was so simple, she almost hugged herself with delight. Best of all, no one would ever suspect. It was doubtful that anyone would suspect poison had ended the noblewoman's life. Lady Marged would die miles from Bowenford, the victim of water from a tainted well, or of rotten fare from a wayside hostelry, or even exposure, unused to the bitter night wind as she was. There would be absolutely nothing to link her death with Lady Alys's chance preparation of saffron fish pasties.

The cold wind soon brought Marged's black hair tumbling about her shoulders, for she had not taken time to secure her abundant tresses beneath a headdress. The force of the wind, increased by her horse's pace, probed her cloak with icy fingers.

By late afternoon the sky had clouded ominously. When rain splattered about them, Marged decided to rest her mount. They could also break their fast, for though he had not complained, Marged suspected that the messenger was ravenously hungry.

"Come, 'tis a good excuse to sup," she called to the young man. They had barely exchanged a half-dozen words since they left Bowenford. The messenger appeared uneasy in her presence, though she had tried to make him relax. She wondered if he feared his master's wrath when they arrived together in Hereford.

"See, already the clouds are breaking to the east," Marged pointed out, weather-wise about the changeable Marcher climate. "Spring showers are soon done."

Marged handed the man some bread. There were slices of venison, chunks of buttered bread, salted beef strips, and Alys's fresh-baked fish pasties. The bottle of ale had soured, and Marged grimaced before she spat the offending liquid to the ground. The messenger, whose taste was not so discerning, accepted the remainder of the bottle with relish.

"Would you like these fish pasties? My stepsister made them. No doubt they're delicious," she added when the man appeared reluctant. "Alys rarely treats us to a sample of her baking, even though she's a fine cook. But I'm not overfond of fish pasties. Besides, my appetite's flown. I'll sup with far more pleasure inside your master's house."

"You're most generous, lady," the man said, eagerly accepting the flaky golden pasties.

The young man's name was Watkin, Marged discovered later when she resumed her efforts at conversation while they were awaiting the shower's end. To get Watkin to converse was like drawing blood from stone. Eventually she abandoned the effort and concentrated instead on a slice of bread and spiced venison. Watkin, thankful that her unnerving efforts at conversation were over, munched contentedly on his meal. In all, he consumed four fish pasties, the bottle of sour ale, and most of the salt beef and bread.

Though rain still splashed intermittently through the branches, patches of blue sky peered inquisitively between the gold-edged clouds. The April shower was over.

"For which part of Hereford are we bound?" Marged asked as she walked her horse into the open.

"My master lodges near Blackfriars."

"I'm not familiar with Blackfriars. Master Henton, the armorer, was a friend of my father's. He lives near the Cathedral's close."

Watkin glumly shook his head, not recognizing the name.

The stiff breeze sent showers cascading from the leafing trees as they rode toward Hereford. The peculiar blue haze for which this region was known had already settled over the hills. Roadside puddles flowed crimson, tainted by Herefordshire's vivid red earth. The messenger had frequently excused himself these past miles. An overabundance of rich food must be playing havoc with his digestion.

While she waited impatiently for Watkin to reappear, her attention was attracted to sprays of delicate almond blossoms hanging over an orchard wall.

"What ails you?" Marged demanded sharply as he staggered

around the corner, his arms clasped about his stomach.

"I'm too ill to go on."

Marged blanched at the unexpected news. "Here, come rest on the grass. I'll fetch you water from yon farm."

Watkin nodded his thanks, his sweating face waxy, his lips pale.

After tethering their mounts to a stone ring beside the farm gate, Marged ran up the narrow track to the shaded farmhouse. A pack of dogs swooped about the corner of the tumbledown dwelling, teeth bared, hair standing on end. Marged scrambled atop an iron gate, where she clung precariously until someone came outside to investigate the commotion.

A surly man with a gray-flecked beard quieted the dogs. "What do you want?"

"May I beg a cup of water from your well?"

"Aye, you're welcome to it," the man said, his lecherous gaze sweeping the soft contours beneath her gaping cloak. "Likely you'll stay to sup," he suggested, licking slack lips.

"No. The water's for my manservant who's been taken ill."

The news did not please the farmer, who considered an unaccompanied female fair game. However, he did not deny her the cup of water. "Happen I'll come with you, see what ails him," he grumbled, shooing away the growling dogs.

Long before they reached the roadside, they could hear Watkin's groans of agony. Marged knelt beside the messenger, offering water. His jaw was so tense he could not swallow.

Warily the farmer skirted the ailing man. "Be it plague?" he demanded suspiciously.

"Of course not. He drank soured ale. Likely that's the cause of his discomfort."

"There's been plague hereabouts. Always is, after battles and such."

"It's not plague!" Marged cried as she and the farmer glared at each other. "Will you help me carry him to shelter?"

The farmer shook his head. "Nay, get you gone. I don't want plague on my land."

"It's not plague, I tell you," Marged declared fiercely, gritting her teeth in anger. During the past half hour the sky had darkened ominously; raindrops began to splash against her face.

Watkin lay in the grass, retching helplessly, but expelling nothing. His face had assumed a strange greenish pallor, and his pulse was erratic. "If you won't help us, then I'll seek help elsewhere."

"No one about here'll give you the time of day. You'd best leave him. He won't last till dark," the farmer observed sagely. "I seen beasts aplenty in their final throes."

Ignoring the farmer's gloomy prediction, Marged untethered the horse, preparing to ride further afield to seek help. Watkin suddenly gave a strangled cry as his limbs contorted in a violent seizure. She watched in horrid fascination, nausea flooding to her throat as the alarming sight tugged her memory. Years ago, her pet hunting dog had died a terrible death; the tremors, the convulsions, the stiffening were the same.

"He be gone."

"No! He can't be!"

"See for yourself."

The farmer pushed Watkin with the toe of his boot. The young messenger's eyes had rolled back into his head, showing only the whites. Marged shuddered and turned away.

"Get him off my land, wench. We don't want plague here," the man growled menacingly.

Marged deliberated briefly, knowing she could not remove the dead man by herself. "If I give you gold, will you bury him for me?" she asked, wondering if a single gold piece would be sufficient to soothe the man's fear of plague.

After some hesitation, the farmer reluctantly accepted her offer.

Marged led the messenger's horse back onto the Hereford road. Fear of being isolated with the farmer had made her more callous than usual over the disposal of Watkin's body. She knew that without protection she would be fair game for the man's lust. She quickened her pace, finding it difficult to travel with the riderless horse tagging behind. The intermittent showers would bring an early dusk; she had to reach Hereford before the city gates were closed for the night.

Galloping recklessly, trying to hold her damp cloak about her, Marged clattered up to the city's massive stone walls just as the dying sun burnished the distant hills. It had stopped raining over an hour ago.

The guards at the gate allowed her to enter without question. Only when she asked for directions to Blackfriars did the men eye her curiously. "Sim be going home, wench. Likely he'll be only too glad to show you," suggested one of the men.

Marged had no desire for the man's company, nor did she like the suggestive winks the guards exchanged when a young blond soldier emerged from the stable leading a rawboned horse. Sim readily agreed to escort her, refusing her offer of payment for the service. His lack of interest in money was also disturbing. Marged wondered if he intended to extract his own price before they reached their destination.

Only the harsh reminder that Rolfe's life depended on her actions forced Marged to accompany the broad-shouldered young soldier down the dimly lit street. Soon the familiar landmarks of Hereford Castle looming above the streets and the old red sandstone cathedral made her feel more secure.

"Blackfriars be beyond the cattle market," the soldier said as he reigned in. His appreciative smile swept Marged from head to toe. They had stopped beneath a lantern swinging over a tavern door. Much noise came from the tavern's interior, where the patrons made merry. "What say you to sharing a jug of ale with me, my pretty?"

"No, though I thank you kindly. I've urgent business with Monsieur Destier. Could you inquire within for his lodging?"

The soldier hesitated a moment before disappearing inside the taproom to reappear a few minutes later. "The Bear and Billet. You never told me you'd come to meet your lover," he added accusingly.

"Nor did I."

"Go on, a pretty piece like you asking for some Frenchy—tell me another."

To Marged's alarm, the soldier grabbed her arm, yanked her from the saddle, and struggled to press her body against his. When she opened her mouth to scream for help, his hot lips clamped suffocatingly over hers. She struggled in his embrace, hitting him, pushing him, all to no avail. The man's hands stole impudently beneath her cloak, and he mumbled appreciatively as he kneaded her breast, provocatively outlined by her damp bodice.

"Go on, he'll never miss a piece. Such nice firm ones they

be. Come, pretty, let's 'ave a look at 'em."

Marged twisted and turned as he fumbled with her bodice fastening. The tavern door creaked open and a couple of men emerged, momentarily distracting the soldier. Seizing her opportunity, she squirmed frantically out of his imprisoning arms.

With a chuckle, the soldier grasped her cloak and yanked Marged back. By now the tavern's patrons were offering bawdy advice, to which the soldier jokingly replied. He swung Marged around to face him, sure of his conquest. Swiftly she drew up her knee and delivered a sharp blow to his genitals. The soldier bellowed as he doubled over, retching with pain and shock.

A tableau of astonished faces swept past her as Marged grasped the reins of the messenger's horse, and swung into the saddle, kicking her mount's flanks to urge him forward. In a clattering burst of sound she charged down the dark, winding street toward the cattle market, leaving the groaning soldier vomiting in the gutter. Though she had gained a slight advantage, Marged knew it was a brief respite. The enraged soldier would soon be on her trail, seeking vengeance. No soft wooing awaited her now! Brutal rape would be her reward, once he recovered sufficiently to perform.

There were few lanterns to light the street, and she could barely distinguish the signs creaking above the doorways as she clattered past. Already, fierce shouts came from the direction of the tavern.

Her flight made awkward by the riderless horse, which stumbled and hesitated, slowing her flight, Marged headed for a low stone building, which proved to be Blackfriars Monastery. Choosing a narrow street running at right angles from the monastery, she skidded around on the corner on treacherously slick cobbles. Her horse reared in protest, whinnying and threshing his forelegs; Marged kicked his flanks harshly, having no time to indulge the horse's delicacy.

While she rode, Marged prayed fervently that a winking lantern at the end of the street was the Bear and Billet. To her immense relief, through the gloom appeared a creaking board depicting a crude rendition of a shaggy bear clutching a staff. Marged clattered past the lighted front of the inn, seeking the entrance to the stable. Through a stone arch she plunged into inky darkness, shouting for the hostler to take her horse.

She sat shivering in the cold, becoming aware of the sounds of pursuit.

A hostler, carrying a lantern, finally emerged from the inn. He politely touched his forelock in greeting as Marged slid from the saddle.

She was safely in the passage outside Monsieur Destier's room when the noisy rabble finally entered the innyard. Amid much angry bellowing and shouting, the unruly group was turned away by the Bear and Billet's indignant landlord, who threatened to have them thrown in jail if they did not leave quietly.

Marged heaved a sigh of relief when the door opened.

"Madame." Yves Destier bowed to her. "Come inside, I've been expecting you. Where's my man?" he asked, glancing down the empty passage, searching for Watkin.

"I'm sorry to have to tell you—he's dead. Either tainted ale or an existing ailment killed him outside Hereford. I gave a local farmer a gold piece to bury him."

Yves Destier sighed, swiftly masking the distress that clouded his seamed features. "Thank you, my lady. You must allow me to reimburse you for the expense."

The stocky Fenchman lit at the fireplace a couple of candles stuck in wine bottles, and brought them to the rickety table, where Marged sat tense and expectant. "Where's Rolfe?" she demanded, unable to stand the suspense. "That's why I came—to set him free."

Destier grimaced at her blithe expectations. "Would that it be so simple. He's not here."

"Where, then?"

"York."

Marged gasped in surprise. She had been given no reason for the assumption, but all along she had thought him imprisoned nearby. "Why, oh, why? Edward was ever his friend."

"A woman can be a powerful antidote to friendship."

"So Edward knows about us."

"He has a letter written to you by my lord."

"How?"

"Warwick has as many spies as a dog has fleas."

Marged paled at his mention of that powerful name. Richard Neville had never been her friend, yet she wondered at his animosity toward Rolfe, who had ever been loyal to the Yorkist cause. "Edward arrested him on the strength of a letter he wrote to me?"

"Not for that alone. They also hold a condemning document. They say 'tis a loyalty oath signed by my master."

"To Edward?"

"Nay, lady. To Harry Lancaster."

Marged gasped audibly at the revelation. "It can't be true. Rolfe arrived in England long after such documents were signed and sealed."

"Then it's as I suspected—a forgery."

"Warwick?"

Destier shrugged. "He's the most likely culprit. All the young King's friends are suspect unless Warwick hand-selects them."

"Tell me more about the document."

"I know little about it beyond its mention in the warrant for his arrest. It links him with known Lancastrian traitors."

"That's impossible. I know Rolfe had no interest in the Lancastrian cause—if only because he felt it doomed to failure."

Destier grinned as he offered her a cup of wine. "So you can shed no light on the paper. I had hoped, considering your father's signature was there also—"

"My father! Sir Richard Bowen?" Marged gasped, her eyes growing round at the discovery.

"That is the name. I don't recall the other names. That alone stuck in my mind."

"The paper Edward holds must be a copy."

Destier shrugged.

"I say that because the original document is locked inside a brass-bound box in the cathedral. To my knowledge, Father signed only one loyalty oath, and that's housed there."

"You're sure?"

"Positive. Many people have suggested he later turned coats by pledging for York, but I was with him the day he gave his written oath. Rolfe's signature cannot be on that paper."

"How is it Edward would accept a forgery? I always thought

he considered my master his man."

Marged racked her brains to recall the men who had accompanied her father to the bishop's house on that snowy January day. Master Henton had led them, being closely related to the bishop . . .

"Sir Joce!" she gasped in dismay as the hawk-nosed visage of their former enemy flashed before her. "Sir Joce signed that oath. At the time I viewed it with suspicion, for he was ever a traitor." Marged swallowed, belatedly remembering to whom she spoke.

Destier smiled. "My lord's uncle was not beloved by me, either. We can go no further; Sir Joce fell at Mortimer's Cross."

"You don't understand. I don't seek to question Sir Joce, I'm merely telling you the de Bretayne name appears on that parchment, but the signer was Sir Joce, not Rolfe."

Leaning forward, Destier whistled in surprise. "And what simpler forgery could they perform than to substitute 'Rolfe' for 'Joce'?"

"We'll have the parchment tonight, if I have my way."

Marged persuaded Destier to escort her to the armorer's house.

Master Henton opened reluctantly to them, being vastly suspicious of callers so late in the night. Only because he had deep affection for Marged and her family did he consider her plan, though he doubted his ability to spirit away so valuable a paper.

"You must, otherwise an innocent man will die."

Master Henton cleared his throat, touched by Marged's lovely tear-filled eyes. "He wouldn't be the first," he commented gruffly as he slipped on his fur-lined cloak.

"But he's the first I've loved," she whispered, smiling at him through her tears. "We will accompany you."

"No," Master Henton said quickly. "The fewer men abroad, the better; I'm not that well received these days in ecclesiastical circles. Only because a few of the bishop's household owe me favors have I even a hope of being admitted. Wait here. And if I'm not back before dawn, you'd best head for the city gates."

Marged nodded, troubled by the armorer's lack of faith in his mission.

The windy night seemed to last an eternity. Huddled in a

blanket on the settle, Marged dozed before the hearth in Master Henton's paneled parlor; Destier slept before the fire, wrapped in his cloak.

Dawn was breaking when the armorer finally returned, his face florid with cold and fatigue.

"Here, by God, lady, though it's likely to cost me a pretty penny in the future," he grumbled, thrusting a rolled parchment in her hands.

"God be praised! You may have saved Rolfe's life."

Only then did the armorer's heavy face soften in a smile. Reaching for her ebony locks, Master Henton absently stroked the softness as he said, "To see you this happy makes the payment worthwhile. Had I a daughter, wench, I'd wish her to be like you."

Tears pricked Marged's eyes and she seized his hand and kissed it.

"God bless you, Master Henton," she whispered.

"And you, Lady Marged. Now, rouse yon snoring foreigner and be on your way. For Christ's sweet sake, treat the parchment with care. When you return, I must replace it in its hiding place."

"I promise to guard it with my life."

Days of frigid journeying, changing horses often for fresh mounts, eventually brought them to the appointed place, outside Pontefract.

It was as Marged feared: Edward had left for Durham three days before. Furthermore, getting wind of a rescue plot, he had requested that the Breton knight be taken to a secret location.

In the face of such apparent hopelessness, Marged bowed her head in grief. All was lost! Without an army at her back, she had no hope of rescuing her lover. It was likely that Rolfe was secreted in the depths of an invincible castle, safe from all help.

"Lady, grieve not," Destier said gruffly, his hand soothing on Marged's shoulder. "All's not lost. One of my men has a plan you might find intriguing, though I consider it far too dangerous for you to take a part in."

Her head snapped up. "Too dangerous, Monsieur Destier?

However slim the chance, however reckless the mission, I'll attempt the rescue."

"Then come. Gaston will tell you what he intends."

A burly giant of a man, Gaston appeared bashful in so fine a lady's presence. Despite the fact that Marged was disheveled and travel-weary, he fumbled and stuttered, overawed by her rank.

"Tell me your plan, for I've none better," she coaxed, eager to hear the man's suggestion.

"From loose gossip, I learned that the new prison is to be Middleham," Gaston revealed breathlessly. "If we make haste, we can intercept the party."

Marged's face lit with hope. "Do you know when he is to be moved?"

"Today, but they won't depart before noon, for they're ever a lazy lot and enjoy their beds. Besides, the afternoon's warmer for travel."

Breathlessly, Marged listened to the man's proposal. To illustrate his point, he drew a crude map in the mud, showing her how the road to Middleham lay through a heavily forested area.

"He proposes that we ambush them in the forest of Gautres," Destier revealed after an animated conversation with the soldier in their native tongue. "'Tis a dangerous proposal, but not impossible. We've a goodly force of men who'll fight to the death to release their lord."

"Then we must leave at once. Don't tell me it's too dangerous, Monsieur," Marged warned grimly, her mouth tight with determination. "I've come this far. It's far too late for me to turn back now."

Smiling, Destier made her a slight bow. "Madame, such a suggestion was furthest from my mind. Likely my lord will boil me in oil when he finds out, but . . ." He gave a typical Gallic shrug. "Come, we've little time to lose."

The ancient forest of Gautres stretched north of York. Here the trees were still in early leaf. As yet the fruit trees had not blossomed, and bullfinches were busy plucking the buds. The party of soldiers cantered along the highway, buffeted by the sharp wind sweeping the open fields and whining through the sparse trees at the forest's edge. Beside the road, cowslips poked yellow heads through the rank grasses, and tawny hares darted from their path. In the hazy distance an azure carpet of bluebells swayed in the breeze.

Here where the undergrowth was dense enough to hide horses, fifteen well-armed soldiers waited, fiercely determined to rescue their lord.

Marged listened tensely, alert for the sound of distant horses. After a long time she was rewarded by the thud of hooves and the muffled jingle of harnesses echoing through the trees. Imitating a birdcall, the lookout, who was posted in a tall, spreading chestnut, signaled the approach of the royal party. All around her, men loosened their scabbards and prepared to fight.

Edward's men were becoming visible through the trees. To Marged's relief the King's soldiers, apparently expecting no opposition, were few, only a handful more than their own. Destier had warned the lookout to sight their lord among the riders before he gave the final signal.

Tension mounted as the riders moved closer, laughter and voices rumbling in the still forest. Squawking birds, disturbed by the approaching riders, swooped overhead to shatter the quiet.

As the King's soldiers rounded the bend, thinning to two abreast on the narrow stretch of road, an arrow sang from the treetops. A wounded man's screams jolted the woodland stillness. Mass confusion erupted as the King's soldiers passed the alarm, trying to rally about their valuable charge, yet prevented from doing so by the narrow, steep-banked path.

From all directions, Rolfe's men galloped into the open, advance and rear guard engaging simultaneously. Marged, disguised as a page, galloped beside Destier. She spotted Rolfe immediately, astride a rawboned nag, his bound hands resting before him on the saddlebow.

At first Rolfe did not guess the attackers' identity, thinking perhaps they had been set upon by outlaws. However, the welcome diversion provided opportunity to escape. His horse was tethered to the mounts of the soldiers flanking him. When the first clash erupted, the two men moved closer, pressing against his mount, holding him captive in the saddle while they relied on their fellows to give battle.

Destier galloped toward his master. Not until the last minute did Rolfe recognize him. He shouted a greeting, the unexpected foreign phrase startling the captor on his right just long enough for his purpose. Raising his bound wrists, Rolfe brought them down hard on the man's exposed neck, stunning him so that he swayed precariously in the saddle. Kicking his captor's horse, he ground his spurred heel into the animal's flank, setting the horse plunging.

Riding close, Destier slashed the tethers, cutting Rolfe free of his captors. Overjoyed at the unexpected sight of his lieutenant, he held out his wrists, urging his man not to be afraid. Rolfe gritted his teeth as the shining blade severed his bonds. When he shook his wrists, his numb flesh tingled as agonizing life surged hotly through his veins. Destier thrust a sword into his hand.

The King's men had rallied and were bearing down on them, determined to recapture their prize. Marged grasped Rolfe's bridle, tugging, urging him to the right, where ferns shrouded an uphill track.

Clashing steel and the cries of wounded men rent the air. Terrified horses screamed amid the budding trees as they fell beneath their riders. The Breton troops cut a savage swath through the enemy ranks, freshly determined to rescue their lord.

Rolfe effectively wielded his sword as he slowly regained feeling in his hands. Four men bore down on him and he cleverly maneuvered his mount through the undergrowth to meet them head-on. Cutting his way through the enemy, he sought to rejoin his own men. A slender soldier whom he did not recognize was besieged as men swarmed about, threatening to unhorse him. The lad's swordplay left something to be desired, Rolfe observed wryly as he came to his rescue. Then a sudden, terrifying thought rocked his body. That was no lad! Even now as he studied the slender form, he could see there was far too much chest to the lad for those narrow shoulders, far too delicate hands—God in heaven, it was Marged!

Filled with fury he plowed through men and horses, hacking, cursing, kicking his mount to greater speed as he joined the melee. Several of his men rode to Marged's rescue, but Rolfe was the closest. Edward's soldiers had already seized her by the sword arm and wrenched away her weapon. She fought desperately to stay in the saddle, futilely biting and kicking, to evade capture.

The fury of the Bretons' charge scattered the King's men.

"Christ, woman, can you never stay home!" Rolfe bellowed, wrenching at Marged's reins with his free hand. "For the love of God, hold on!"

Tears of relief gushed from her eyes as, gripping the bridle of Marged's horse, he raced her alongside him, heading for the trees. Destier rode ahead, pointing the way with his sword. A few minutes more and they would be safe. Blood trickled down Marged's arm. As he rode, Rolfe swiftly assessed her wounds; she had a scratch on her arm where her shirtsleeve was rent, and blood oozed from a slash on her neck.

Suddenly, Marged shouted a warning, her eyes wide with fear. Rolfe attempted to maneuver about to face the danger, but he was woefully late. A stinging sword slash caught him on the shoulder, rending his padded jambeson. He wore no jack, and the sword sliced keenly through the wool-padded garment. Soon the padding, bursting through the rip, was crimson with blood.

As the soldier closed in for the kill, Rolfe thrust upward with all his might, lifting the man clear of his saddle, where he hung for a moment, spitted on the blade. Blood gushed a river from his deep wound as the man toppled to the ground.

"This way! Oh, God, Rolfe, hurry!" Marged screamed, unable to reach him because of the milling enemy troops trying to regroup. Men fought around her, both friend and enemy engaged in deadly combat.

Gritting his teeth against the throbbing pain and the mounting weakness, Rolfe put his head down, crouching in the saddle as he plunged through a narrow opening in the fight, careening crazily about in a half-circle before he righted his excited mount and galloped after a departing soldier up the hilly track. He clung to the saddle, lying forward on the animal's neck as he fought to maintain his senses. The loss of blood gradually robbed him of strength. For how long he rode, or to where, he did not know. All he knew was the driving desire for freedom thudding through his veins.

"Lay him down," Marged ordered when at last they stopped to rest. The King's men had pursued them for a short distance before abandoning the chase. The paths of this dense forest twisted and turned through thickets, up hills, and over streams. Edward's men had little advantage over the Bretons, for they too were foreigners to the region.

"Will he die?" she whispered, afraid of Destier's answer.

"Let us hope not," was all the Frenchman said.

"The wound is very near the heart," Marged said, her grim observation causing fresh concern among the soldiers. Eager hands helped her remove the damaged garments, carefully prying the shredded, bloody wool out of the open wound. Tearing strips from her shirttail, Marged tried to bind the gaping wound.

"We must carry him to shelter. Come, we cannot stay here. It will soon be dark."

Very carefully the men bore their wounded lord to his saddle, where he slumped, so weak he could barely stay upright. Men rode on either side to support him over the rough ground.

Cold twilight washed the bare fields as they emerged from the western fringe of the forest. In the window of a nearby farmstead, a light twinkled. It was to this dwelling that Marged rode, seeking shelter for the night. The kindly farmer and his wife agreed to let them shelter in their barn.

Marged did not sleep, but hovered anxiously over her wounded lover, afraid to leave him because of the severity of his condition. He was ashen, his face drawn and haggard; the blue-black smudge of beard covering his jaw only accentuated his pallor.

"Sleep. You can do no more for him. The salves, the posset, are the best we can do," Destier said, crouching beside her where she knelt at his wounded master's side. "Sleep, if only for a few hours."

Though she was reluctant to leave Rolfe, Marged knew Destier was right. She must rest, the better to nurse him. Tomorrow his condition could reach an even more crucial stage. Perchance he would die! The very thought set her teeth chattering.

She curled in the straw, staring out at the dark, star-sprinkled sky visible over the top half of the stable door. She had begged salves and potions from the good farm wife, giving her a gold locket in payment. The medicines were the only ones locally available. With a heavy heart she realized Rolfe's recovery lay more in the hands of his Maker than in the restorative powers of the old wife's remedies.

{ fifteen }

ROLFE OPENED HIS eyes to the pale golden dazzle of morning light filtering through the trees. He was weak, but for the first time in over a week, he felt alive. Stirring gingerly—for he had soon learned not to make sudden moves—he eased himself from his pallet. The movement did not begin the bleeding; the fresh bandages swathing his chest and midsection were unspotted.

"Have you an appetite this morning, my lord?"

Marged's question brought a lazy smile to his mouth. She was the dearest, loveliest woman on earth. In fact, her sweet voice had been his only tie with reality during those horrendous nightmares that filled his days and nights when wound fever raged in him.

Rolfe turned to find her watching him, the sunlight dappling her face with gold. "Aye, and before long 'twill not just be for food, you evil wench," he warned huskily.

Marged flew to his side, taking care not to press against his healing wound. With his good arm, Rolfe enfolded her against him. Resting his face against her smooth, perfumed hair, he fought shudders of emotion. It was too soon, he chided himself impatiently, but it could not be forbidden much longer . . .

"I've long been expecting one of your wicked invitations." Marged slid her hand up into his hair before she teasingly stroked the hot, smooth skin beneath his collar.

"Have I ever told you how much I love you?" he whispered as he crushed her against his side, careless of his wound. "You saved my life, you reckless wench."

Marged smiled as she strained up to kiss him, hiding her inner fear. Yesterday, when she had gone to the nearby village for supplies, she learned that Edward's soldiers had been questioning the villagers about Rolfe. A goodly sum had been set on his head. These villagers were too poor to allow the reward to go uncollected. Even now they formed patrols, hoping to catch the fugitive and claim the bounty.

"Rolfe," Marged ventured sometime later when they had finished their meal, "there's something of importance I must tell you."

He grinned. "And what's that?"

Her heart lurched as she saw the tenderness in his eyes. Would that she need recount merely love talk instead of the grave discovery she must reveal. "Your life's in danger."

The softness fled from his eyes, hardening and refining the blue. "Tell me everything."

"Edward's put a price on your head."

The alarming news turned him grim. There was but one thing left to do. "We'll take ship for Brittany," he decided gruffly. "Tomorrow, if possible."

"No! You only admit guilt by running. Your name has to be cleared or you'll ever be a fugitive. Edward must give you a full pardon."

"I agree, sweet, that would be preferable, but hardly likely. The age for miracles is past. My name's tainted by my love for you—there's no remedy for that."

Marged gulped, afraid he spoke the truth, yet desperately fighting the loathsome fact. "Edward considers you a traitor to York. We need only prove that the document he holds is false—"

"No. I've no more time to waste in futility. If Edward chooses to believe his cousin instead of me, what chance have I of ever proving my innocence?"

She had been on the verge of revealing her intention to present to Edward the original Lancastrian pledge. The words faded from her lips when she beheld Rolfe's white-lipped fury over Edward's betrayal of his loyalty.

Gaston raced toward them through the trees. "My lord, we must flee! A party of riders is coming this way."

The man had scarcely finished speaking before Rolfe was thrusting Marged before him, urging her toward the horses tethered beneath the trees.

They moved through the fringe of the wood, observing the mounted party, who proved to be no more than a prior and his followers on a pilgrimage to a nearby shrine. However, the diversion gave Marged time to reconsider her plans. Rolfe was too angry, too set against petitioning Edward for clemency; she must speak to the King herself.

Two days later, Marged found the perfect opportunity to put her plans in motion. Her heart thumped wildly as she bid Rolfe a tender farewell. So hard did she press against him, and so fervent were her parting kisses, she was afraid she had given herself away.

He mistook her anxiety for passion. Marged's heart lurched when he held her close to whisper, "Tonight I'll make love to you. God, how I ache to hold you as before. We've followed the doctor's orders close enough—'tis high time for a little 'strenuous activity.' God knows, most physicians are ancient bags of bones with naught but icewater in their veins. They never make allowances for a man's baser passions."

Tears stung her eyes at the thought of leaving him. Why did she not wait until tomorrow? One day's delay in following Edward's trail would surely not be important.

"Come, Lady Marged, dally not. The drovers are impatient to be away," urged the soldier who was to accompany her to a nearby town, where she intended to purchase salves for dressing Rolfe's wound. A passing party of drovers had offered to show them the way.

Marged smiled and nodded. However much she was tempted to delay, she knew there would be no better opportunity than this to slip away from camp. The knowledge of her planned deception churned her stomach as she gave Rolfe a parting kiss.

With leaden heart, Marged clopped along the spring-fresh lanes where the roadside grass was thick with lacy cow parsley. Thrushes and blackbirds sang sweetly in the trees, and butterflies hovered about the pink and white May blossom. Despite the lovely surroundings, Marged felt as if she rode to her doom. Just to reassure herself that the valuable evidence was safe, she touched the crackling parchment inside her bodice. Once Edward read this genuine roll of Lancastrian supporters, he would know the paper he possessed was a forgery. There would be no reason to hold Rolfe prisoner. It would not alter the fact that Rolfe was her lover, yet surely not even Edward Plantagenet would condemn a man out of jealousy.

At the crowded marketplace, Marged purchased the needed supplies. She entrusted the packets of herbs and bowls of salve to the young soldier, knowing he would carry them to his commander.

Nervously she awaited her opportunity to slip away. In an attempt to bore the man until he shunned her company, she feigned wide-eyed interest in a juggler and his ragged assistant. Next she haggled at length over purchases from ribbons to mutton pasties, desperate to drive the soldier to the limits of his endurance. Marged had to compliment him on his patience. It was only after an extremely tiresome session of examining lace cloths and embroidered gloves that the man finally excused himself to go in search of a flagon of ale.

Once the soldier had disappeared under the awning of the crowded ale-seller's booth, Marged raced to where the horses were tethered. She gave the lad minding the beasts a groat to watch the soldier's horse. Then, swinging into the saddle, she skirted the marketplace, alert for the soldier's reappearance.

Marged had heard from soldiers in town that Edward was headed for Preston, a goodly ride south. If the young King had not been so restless about his progress, he would have unknowingly allowed Marged a more leisurely journey. As it was, Edward spent each night in a different town. If she missed him at Preston, she would have to ride on until she found him. Convinced of his great charm and unchallenged right to the throne, Edward considered a day ample time in which to sway the townsfolk to his cause.

Preston was a mean, narrow-streeted town. Dilapidated timber houses huddled together, while the dingy streets overflowed with refuse. In the town square, Marged learned from townsfolk that the King was dining in a bow-fronted dwelling overlooking the square, at a banquet hosted by the city aldermen.

It was cold and cheerless as Marged waited for the banquet to end. Some time earlier it had begun to rain in earnest, the heavy shower rapidly emptying the square of people. The only shelter she could find was a drafty alehouse doorway, where she pressed against the splintered door, out of reach of the raking wind.

Eventually the jovial, corpulent aldermen departed, loudly singing the praises of their handsome young King. After the final guest had gone, Marged hastened across the cobbles to the King's lodging. What if Edward refused to see her, she thought belatedly, as she knocked on the oak door. Dismissing the alarming thought, Marged pulled her hood over her hair, where rain beaded the glossy strands, and waited.

"What do you want?" demanded the servant who finally came in answer to her knock.

"I come to petition King Edward."

"The King hasn't time for the likes of you. Begone," the man dismissed her gruffly.

"Please—you need only give him my message. I promise he'll want to see me."

The man stubbornly shook his head.

"Here, take this valuable ring in payment for your time," Marged urged, slipping the engraved gold band from her finger. "Please, good man, knock at the King's door. Tell him Marged waits without."

The servant hesitated, his eyes fixed greedily on the winking gold ring.

"He's kind. I promise he won't have you beaten. What have you to lose?"

What indeed? The man's eyes glowed as he took the ring before he closed the door and shuffled away, leaving her standing outside. Rain dripped dismally from the eaves, trickling in rivulets inside Marged's cloak. This was a foolhardy adventure, yet the urgency of Rolfe's plight precluded plans of great forethought.

At last, Marged heard steps in the flagged passage beyond

the door. Swallowing, she drew herself up to her full height while her knees shook with anticipation. The door creaked open to reveal the manservant.

"He says you can come in," whispered the servant conspiratorially. He had swiftly put his own construction on this wench's mission.

Marged stepped into the gloomy passage, with its mingled odors of roast meat, woodsmoke and beeswax. A movement at the head of the carved stairs drew her attention. She gasped with relief and apprehension as she saw Edward himself watching her from the shadows.

"Your Grace," she whispered, sinking into a deep curtsy.

"So it is you! I thought the old fool must be addled."

"I must speak with you alone. It's of the gravest concern."

Edward slowly descended the stairs, his dark, pleated gown gleaming with jewels. "Speak then, wench. Is that all you would do?" he inquired in amusement as he reached her side. Drawing Marged to her feet, Edward smiled down at her from his great height. "You've not changed a whit, my love."

"Nor you, Your Grace."

Edward glanced toward the manservant, who stood all agog in the doorway. "Bring refreshment. Then leave us alone."

Marged slowly ascended the stair at Edward's side. She was unsure what his reaction would be when she revealed the reason for her visit. By word and glance, it was obvious Edward was expecting a far more romantic purpose to today's meeting.

When at last Marged found courage to broach the subject, the King's anger proved far greater than she had anticipated.

"By all that's holy! You come here to plead for him!"

"You're a good and just King. You know Rolfe is innocent of the charges you level against him."

"He's your lover! That's a charge he can't escape. Or do you seek to lie as prettily as you were wont to do in the past?"

Marged stared at the rushes. "I'll not lie to you—he is the foreign knight who stole my heart."

"You let me believe he was unknown to you, some shadowy memory from your girlhood," Edward exploded, slamming down a jeweled goblet on the oak table. "Did you not? Answer me, you wretched wench."

"Yes, I let you think it was so," she confessed in a weak

voice. "I loved him long before I met you. It was an emotion I could not prevent."

Edward's mouth turned surly as he lounged in the carved, high-backed chair, listening to her defense. He wanted her still. God damn the woman for her arresting beauty. It would have been immensely satisfying to turn her away, his desire extinguished.

"He was my friend. I trusted him," Edward growled as he shifted in the great chair.

"He is still your friend."

"Friends don't sign oaths in support of my enemies."

"Rolfe never signed such a document."

"Don't lie. I have his signature bold and black. He signed, all right, as did your sire—also my loyal subject, I presume. Your lover is a traitor! My cousin warned me but, trusting fool that I am, I chose to believe what I wanted instead of the facts. You played me false. He played me false. Together you joined in iniquity."

"Please, Your Grace, hear me out." Marged went to her knees before him. "I bring proof to sway you. I was present when my father signed that loyalty oath. At that time, Rolfe was across the Channel."

Edward fought the desire to pull her head into his lap. "You'd say anything to save him."

"Perhaps, yet in this I speak the truth."

"Where is this proof?"

Marged rocked back, fighting tears. Here in this fire-splashed chamber, everything seemed unreal. It was hard to remember that this golden-haired giant who now glowered petulantly at her was the same man who once desired her so strongly, he had held her at knifepoint to make her yield.

"Your Grace, if I show you this paper, will you relent?"

Edward shrugged. "I cannot say. Show me the document first."

Marged unlooped her damp cloak, conscious of the searing passage of Edward's lecherous gaze, raking her ample bodice. She unlaced the silver ribbons, slackening the fabric, noting how he leaned forward with quickened breath, anxious to glimpse that which she had always kept hidden from him. Marged turned aside to withdraw the rolled parchment. When she turned around, Edward's scowl had deepened.

"I'll bring lights. You must study this well."

The King poured himself a cup of Malmsey while he waited for Marged to light a brass candlestick at the hearth. Bearing the branched sconce, she went to the oak table and unrolled the parchment.

Sighing in annoyance over the imposition, Edward reluctantly walked around the table.

"See, there's de Bretayne's name!" he cried in anger, stubbing his finger accusingly on the bold black signature. Then, as Edward peered closer, he discovered that the name read "Joce," not "Rolfe." The discovery nonplussed him. "What trickery do you practice here?"

"No trickery, Your Grace. This is the original document."

"How do I know *this* isn't the forgery?" he demanded.

"This roll has been safely kept inside Hereford Cathedral. A loyal friend allowed me to bring it to prove Rolfe's innocence to you. It was his uncle, Sir Joce, who signed in support of Lancaster. And even he you cannot wholly condemn as traitor, for he turned coats at Mortimer's Cross and cost my father his life."

Edward's color heightened. "You'd do anything to save his neck."

"Inquire of your many spies. They will surely back my words."

"You presume too much! This passion you foster for the Breton's made you careless," Edward growled. "I'm the King. It's not for you to give me orders."

Marged swallowed uneasily. How far could she push him? This was not the same hot-blooded young earl she had known. Sovereignty appeared to have aged and strengthened him. Yet Rolfe's life depended on her ability to handle this situation wisely. Taking her courage in both hands, Marged decided to gamble that beneath his new-found maturity there still lurked remnants of Edward's old headstrong character.

She stepped forward, tossing her head defiantly. "Then we'll question your beloved cousin Warwick, for surely he's but a stone's throw away. I'll call him for you, Your Grace, 'twill put you to little trouble."

"Warwick's not here," Edward snapped as Marged went to

the door, preparing to go in search of the Kingmaker. "He stays with Fauconberg to subdue the Scots."

She paused, her head reeling. If Warwick was not here, then Edward was solely in charge of his own affairs. Her back was to him as she said, "'Tis whispered you make no move without his approval." When she turned about, Marged was rewarded by signs of Edward's mounting anger. He abhorred the suggestion that he danced to Warwick's tune. If there was any move calculated to rob him of his sovereign dignity, this was it.

"They also whisper you're but a puppet dancing on Warwick's string... nay, I've never believed that tale," Marged added hastily as Edward came from his chair, his face stormy. "You were ever known as courageous and fair in your dealings—the same cannot be said for cousin Warwick."

"I am the King! The throne is mine alone!"

"Then, Your Grace, will you consent to compare documents? You can readily see a forgery has taken place. The copy of the loyalty oath you hold is false, altered by Rolfe's enemies to blacken his name."

"Did you ride alone from the Marches, eager to save his skin? Or does he lurk in the back room of some tavern, awaiting the outcome of this meeting?"

"I came without his permission or his knowledge. Yet by now I'm sure he knows I came in search of you. Here, this is the proof to set him free."

"If I accept this document as genuine—perhaps rescind my orders—how am I to be rewarded?"

There was no mistaking the meaning behind Edward's words. Marged swallowed and took a step backward. "Your reward will be the knowledge that you have seen justice served."

"Ha! What miserable payment is that for the loss of one I craved above all others? No. Take your bogus parchment back to Hereford."

Blood flushed Marged's face. When she spoke her voice cracked. "You're saying I've come all this way for naught?"

"Yes. Unless, of course, you have any suggestions for remedying matters."

Again, that barely veiled hint. Stung with anger, Marged

faced him. "Am I to exchange my body for his freedom? Is that what you propose?"

More assured now, Edward flashed her a lazy smile. "It's an admirable suggestion, Lady Marged. Surely the Breton's head is worth such a small sacrifice. Besides, most wenches consider it an honor to bed the King."

"As you probably know by now, I'm not 'most wenches.'"

"Aye, and it's not to your advantage," Edward spat, his mouth surly. "Take lodgings in the town. Let me ponder the subject."

"How long will you keep me dangling?"

He shrugged and stretched out his hand toward her, then thought better of it. "I travel first to Warrington, thence to Manchester. I promise, before we leave Manchester Castle, you shall have my decision."

"Thank you, Your Grace, you've been most kind," Marged said stiffly. She dipped a curtsy.

"Have you enough money to pay for lodging?"

"For a few nights."

Edward opened the door, allowing his arm to brush her shoulder, his leg to press against hers, before she moved away. "Good. You'll not find this progress boring. I'll even welcome you as a member of my household, if you wish."

"Thank you, Your Grace, but I prefer not to confuse the issue."

Edward's smile faded. Even before Marged had descended the stairs, his plans were laid. In coming here to petition him to spare her lover's life, she had presented him with the perfect weapon. His mouth slowly relaxed and he began to whistle under his breath. Marged Bowen would be forced to yield. And the proud, beautiful Welshwoman would be vastly humbled in the process.

Not at Warrington, nor at Manchester, did Edward reach a decision. From Manchester the royal party veered southwest into the county of Cheshire. Here at last, within the ancient walled city of Chester, he sent word that he wished a private audience with her.

She wore the only gown she had brought with her. The flowing dark blue silk trimmed with spangled red flowers made her appear slimmer than ever, the deep color accentuating the pallor of her face. This senseless waiting had tautened her nerves almost to breaking point.

The reflection that looked back at her from the dingy mirror was pale as death. Marged tweaked her cheeks, trying to bring healthy color to her face. She wore no jewelry, for her valuables had been traded in Yorkshire for medicines, and again at Preston to gain the King's audience. Given his past generosity, she had wondered if Edward would ply her with expensive gifts, the better to woo her to his will. This time the King had sent nothing to soften her resistance.

"Welcome, Lady Marged. The night's chill for spring." Edward nodded in dismissal to the servant. "We have mulled wine and almond cakes."

Marged smiled stiffly as she accepted the wine cup and a small almond cake. Edward was splendidly attired in a magenta velvet doublet and silver hose; his silver-lined gown lay across a nearby chair.

"I thought we'd reach London before you chose to give me your answer."

"My time's been spent trying to pacify the northerners," Edward said as he stirred the fire. "I've had little room for much else."

Marged swallowed her impatience. To reveal that she was aware his decision about Rolfe's future had been made before he left Preston would avail her nothing. "I hope, Your Grace, you've decided to examine the parchment."

"No. There's no need. I accept your word that it's the original."

The gasp of amazement that escaped her lips made him smile.

"You sound surprised."

"Surprised is hardly the emotion. Oh, Your Grace, you're most kind . . ."

"You misunderstand me, Lady Marged. Because I accept the document's validity does not mean I've granted a reprieve. My order still stands."

This time Marged's gasp was of dismay. "But you said . . . you . . ."

"I agree the document is the original, and I've no wish to examine it."

"Then you don't intend to pardon Rolfe?"

"At the moment I've not reached a final decision."

"How much longer must I wait?"

"That depends entirely on you."

Edward smiled at Marged, beckoning her closer to the fire. "Once I was nearly out of my mind with need of you, but you were callous towards my pain. At every turn you repulsed my affection. Think you I'd deal leniently with the man who caused me such torment? A man who, while professing to be my friend, took the one woman I craved above all others?"

Marged took pains to mask her astonishment. Had she not known otherwise, she would have sworn Edward had pined away these past months in strictest celibacy, spurning all others because he was denied the woman of his choice. In fact, so sincere did he sound, she wondered if he believed the preposterous notion himself.

"Never did I encourage you to woo me."

"No, you did not, yet you accepted gifts from me, gifts only a lover would give. By doing so, you allowed me to hope."

"When I tried to return your gifts, you became enraged," she reminded him bitterly.

Edward ignored her remark. "All that time I pined for you, sick with calf-love. Then, lady, I gradually learned to live without you."

While he spoke, Edward caressed her cheek, his soft, beringed hand glittering in the fireglow.

"I never intended to cause you pain, nor to deceive you about my affections."

"Until you came to plead your lover's cause, I'd put your tempting beauty from my mind..."

"Please, Your Grace, if you don't intend to pardon Rolfe, then allow me to leave. Let's have an end to this cruel game. Senselessly have I ridden from Preston in the royal train. I should have known you had no intention of granting my request."

Marged turned from him to hide her tears. Though she fought hard, so dejected, so angrily humiliated did she feel, she could not contain her grief.

"I will grant the boon you seek."

She stopped in the middle of the paneled room, hardly able to believe her ears. His voice, smooth and cozening, echoed through her head. "Am I hearing things? Did you say you intend to grant my boon?"

"That's right."

Trembling with joy, she spun about, seeing Edward as a broad pillar of color, blurred with tears. "Oh, Your Grace!" she whispered, overcome with emotion.

"De Bretayne can go free tomorrow, provided he set sail for Brittany on the next tide."

"He's prepared to return home."

"Not permanently, of course—oh, no, I don't intend to exile him. We merely want a cooling-off period. I'm told de Bretayne fought well in my defense at Towton. Apparently his loyalty was never seriously in doubt, though many Neville men are prepared to swear otherwise. What I choose to hear rests solely on you."

Marged blinked, her joy rapidly receding. The old craftiness appeared in Edward's handsome face. His mouth tightened and he lowered his lids, hiding the deviousness in his bright gaze. At last he had found a way to force her to his bed! A great wave of nausea overcame her as Marged realized Edward had planned this revenge from the first.

"Tell me clearly what you want me to do," she whispered. "Haven't we played cat-and-mouse long enough?"

"Either you're exceedingly dense, my love, or I'm failing to make myself clear. All right, if you want the terms spelled out—de Bretayne's pardon in exchange for your body."

"That's most generous of you."

"There's no cause for sarcasm. Your decision depends on the affection you bear the Breton. Only this morning I had a fresh report of his whereabouts. When I decide to move, it'll be but a matter of hours before he's under arrest. And this time he'll not escape. He'll be shackled to his jailors. That should stop his daring plans."

"Then?" Marged whispered, stunned by Edward's revelation.

"He'll be imprisoned and executed."

"You'd follow through with a lie out of revenge for not having me?"

"I wanted you, but he *took* you. That's reason enough for his death!"

Marged met his angry glare, finding Edward stripped of his kingly attributes. Before her stood a bitterly spurned man wielding the power of England's throne. Edward was determined to extract blood payment for his hurt.

"What stake has Warwick in this crime?"

"Warwick is my cousin and my friend."

The door handle trembled in Marged's hand. "How much time have I to decide?"

Edward smiled, his ill humor mastered. As if he were amused by some private joke, his smile deepened as he said, "Ah, I can see you expect me to be patient while you consider my proposal."

Marged's answer was a barely perceptible nod; she was afraid that if she opened her mouth, all her anger at being deceived would spill forth. Such devastating honesty could sound Rolfe's death knell.

"Have you heard of Eccleshall, Lady Marged?"

Again, she only nodded.

"'Tis the stop before I arrive at Cannock Chase, where I intend to hunt." Barely able to contain his humor, Edward advanced toward her. "I'll be exceedingly generous, my love. Ere we stop there for the night, I'll expect your answer. The accommodations should make a fitting setting for your sacrifice. Think you that's time enough for you to reach a decision?"

"Yes, it's time enough."

Not until morning, when Marged casually inquired of the household servants as to their intended destination, did she discover that Edward had again deceived her. The source of his humor was readily apparent—Eccleshall was tonight's resting place!

Seething with anger, she mounted her horse and followed the royal procession through the wooded countryside, careful to keep her distance from Edward lest temper overcome her prudence. The warm air was alive with birdsong; the towering trees were in fresh leaf. Beside the road, wildflowers spangled the grass colorfully, but the heavenly day and the idyllic surroundings were wasted on her. Marged kept seeing Rolfe's anguished look when he learned the price she had paid for his freedom.

A bitter smile uptilted the corners of her full mouth as she reached a decision. Speeding her horse's pace, she careened frantically along the rutted lane, trampling lacy flowerets of cow parsley beneath the flying hooves, scattering startled birds in the roadside orchard. Both men would be amply rewarded by her noble sacrifice: Rolfe would be granted his life, Edward the assuasion of his lust.

When they halted for the noon meal, Marged sent a servant with a message for the King.

Evening slid slowly into night. Sweet, cool air flooded through the open windows, stirring the velvet draperies, the French wall tapestries, as Marged strode purposely along the long gallery to the King's chamber.

This manor was luxurious, yet had it been a peasant's hovel, she could not have hated it more. She neither cared about who owned the home, nor that carefree summer lay around the corner, spilling scented color across the Staffordshire countryside. She thought only of the ordeal she was about to face. Never before had she purchased anything with her body. The feeling that she was made a whore by this unholy transaction haunted her as she resolutely turned the sharp angle of the corridor and entered the west wing.

At the end of the corridor, a servant was waiting. He bowed low and backed away, indicating that the door was unlatched.

Marged paused, summoning courage. Nervously she smoothed the slim skirts of her dark silk gown and patted her black hair in place. Then, drawing herself to her full height, shoulders back, fists clenched, she stepped toward that oaken door, which stood ajar, allowing a chink of light to wash her feet with gold.

"Come not like a lamb to the slaughter," Edward remarked easily as she walked inside the room.

At first, Marged did not see him in the gloomy room. A lone candle burned on a chest beside the door. A fire was sputtering in the grate, the burning fruitwood adding a pleasant sweetness to the released smoke. Marged tensed anew as she saw Edward lounging against the windowsill, where he watched the sun's demise.

"Your Grace." She sank to her knees, head bowed, ever the dutiful subject.

The floor quaked beneath his weight as Edward marched across the room and yanked her to her feet. "I summoned you hither for pleasure, not punishment. Ere you fulfill your part of the bargain, we'll have smiles," he snarled irritably.

"Forgive me, Your Grace. I'll try not to be surly."

Edward muttered beneath his breath as he went to light more candles. Holding a branched candelabrum aloft, he studied her closely, his face an unfathomable blur beyond the sea of light.

"Aren't you going to ask to see his signed pardon?"

"You're an honorable man. I trust you to keep your part of the bargain," Marged said, fighting down a building wave of nausea.

"Nevertheless, I'll show it to you."

Edward went to the bedside chest to withdraw a rolled parchment and light a second brace of candles from the lighted sconce beside the bed.

Marged glanced about at the well-appointed chamber. The coat of arms over the hooded hearth glittered; the floor rushes smelled sweetly of rosemary, dried chamomile flowers, and rose petals. Before the fireplace a curly-piled lamb's pelt had been spread, and the walls were covered in gold-fringed rose brocade panels and brightly woven tapestries. The sight of the great bed set her stomach rolling, reminding her of her sole purpose within this room.

Dully she watched Edward stride to the windows and pull the heavy draperies, shutting out the intrusion of night from their intimate trysting place.

"Come here," he beckoned her, his large hands glinting with precious stones.

She slowly walked to him, her feet feeling leaden. Fragrant rose petals and chamomile blossoms slipped inside her velvet shoes as her feet sank in the deep rush carpet. Eventually she stood before him, ill at ease to find Edward awesomely regal in his rose brocade gown; the great hanging sleeves were edged with vair; the fastenings glittered with gold.

"Here, my love, is your payment."

Marged glanced at the parchment he held out to her. Though she did not bother to read all the words, she satisfied herself as to the contents of Edward's pardon. Rolfe was to be allowed one weeks's grace to leave these shores. During that time no charges were to be pressed.

"Thank you, Your Grace."

Edward nodded and laid aside the parchment. "Think you he'll appreciate your sacrifice?"

Marged winced at his attempted humor. There was no answer she could give. Instead she looked at the closest tapestry, where a silver-horned unicorn sat inside a golden fence while beauteous ladies plucked scarlet blossoms growing around his hooves.

"Do you like it?" Edward asked softly, returning her to the present.

"It's very lovely."

"It's yours—nay, refuse me not. Surely, on this night of nights, I can indulge my pleasure in giving gifts. It will look well on the wall of your chamber."

"Yes. Thank you, Your Grace."

"Your formality offends me. You must call me Edward, as you were wont to do long months ago."

"I'm sorry . . . Edward."

He smiled, shaking his head in bewilderment. "Little did I expect to find you tamed."

"Would you wish to have me rave at you in anger? I think not. Besides, the pardon you so lightly regard is too valuable for me to risk such foolishness."

Her words did not please him, yet Edward chose not to take issue over them. This was the night about which he had dreamed since he first laid eyes on this beautiful woman. Long denial had fueled his desire to fever pitch. Had she dared deny him still, he doubted he could have let her go free. He would have imprisoned the Breton in the darkest dungeon, and this enchanting Welshwoman in his bedchamber.

"Nay, I've no wish to bed a ranting fishwife. But, sweet one, I would prefer a willing partner."

At Edward's gentle reminder, unease radiated through Marged's body. Though the expression was forced, she smiled prettily at him, revealing her pearly white teeth. By his swiftly changing expression, she could see he was pleased. Marged knew she would not be aroused to deep passion; such involvement must be feigned. Edward was not a man to be satisfied with passive lovemaking. If she displeased him, Rolfe's hard-earned pardon might be cast into the fire.

"You must have patience," she said sweetly, raising her large green eyes to his. "I'm turned shy maiden in your presence."

His mouth quirked. "You're not blushing—'tis merely the fire's warmth."

"Never before have we been so intimate, yet so far apart."

"That's true. Yet in those days I didn't know . . ." Edward stopped, finding this subject not to his liking. In fact, if he were not careful, the crafty Welsh chit would turn his humor sour. "In those days I thought your heart unclaimed. Now we're both far wiser," he concluded tersely. "Tonight I demand you love me not as your King, nor because you intend to purchase *his* freedom with your heat." Marged winced at his blunt words. Edward sought her black silky hair, marveling aloud at its delicate texture. "Tonight we will be sweethearts. Nothing less will satisfy me. Your purchase has a set price, lady, and you must be willing to pay it."

"I'm willing." Marged lowered her gaze from his probing eyes, focusing instead on the golden ornaments decorating his rose velvet slippers.

Edward swiftly pulled her hair from its coils, freeing the midnight cloud about her shoulders. He ached to weld their bodies together as one, yet he forced himself to patience; he had waited far too long and suffered far too much for love of this black-hearted wench to want it quickly over. Marged Bowen was no penny drab, no tavern harlot to swiftly douse lust's fires; Marged Bowen was a goddess among women. And since the day he had lit candles petitioning the saints to send her to his bed, Edward had hardly been free of her taunting memory.

"Are you a witch?" he demanded suddenly, his eyes narrowing over the disturbing thought.

Marged's head came up, her eyes wide with surprise. "A witch! Nay, Your Grace. Who speaks such slander?"

"No one. 'Tis merely when I review my agonizing need of you, undiminished after all this time, I wonder at its strength.

No other woman ever fired me with such longing, nor inspired me to near rcverence by her beauty. The power of your attraction seems not of this world."

"You flatter me greatly, Your—Edward."

"Come." His hands were gentle as he drew her toward him. "Come, love, kiss me of your own accord. Whisper my name and tell me that you love me dear."

Marged swallowed. Though his request would be easily granted, the deception behind the lies filled her with anguish. If Rolfe could see her now, he would be beside himself with rage and torment. She could not refuse Edward his fantasies; she did not even question them. Rolfe's life depended on her acting skill.

"Edward, be patient with me," she whispered, noting his cynical smile and not understanding its source.

"Don't become too involved in your role of sacrificial virgin," he reminded her sharply. "You forget, I know the Breton plumbed you well these months past. There's no need for such empty convent pleas."

To Marged's immense relief, a few moments later his building anger had slid from him like a cloak. She sat on his lap while he cuddled her, kissing her earlobes, her neck, stroking her hair and face. Sweet rose and musk mingled in a heady cloud about him. His kisses were soft, his hands gentle as he slowly began the game that promised such high reward. Marged gritted her teeth, freshly determined to please him.

Besides the fire sputtering in the hearth, the only sound was Edward's harsh breathing. No longer could he contain his hands. He whispered love words to her while he caressed her body. Eager as a schoolboy, he plundered her ripe breasts, shuddering at the arousing discovery of those firm white globes of flesh.

"To think all these months you kept them hid from me," he whispered hoarsely, molding her alabaster breasts in his large hands, exerting firm yet gentle pressure, as he explored his cherished new playthings. "I swear, they're the loveliest breasts in all Christendom."

While Edward nuzzled her breasts, teasing her nipples erect, Marged slid her hands through his thick golden hair. How she longed for a miracle to take place. If only this blond giant in her arms could be magically transformed into the man she loved.

At last, satisfied with his exploration, he unlaced her gown and slipped it down. Edward gently set Marged on her feet. The dark blue silk gown rested snugly on her hips, revealing her narrow waist, her full, tremulous breasts. The delicious sight made him shudder with delight.

"Christ Jesus, you look like a beautiful slave wench on the auction block," he breathed raggedly. With shaking hands, he caught fistfuls of her fluttering black hair and drew her toward him. His mouth was scalding as he kissed her deeply, thoroughly, insatiably, while he greedily fondled her exposed breasts.

"Do you want me to take it off?" Marged whispered when his hand became entangled in the confining fabric of her gown.

"Not yet. I want to admire you a little longer."

Breathless, he turned her around, fitting her shapely back against his body. His hands slid around to her breasts, which he thrust up and out while he devoured her neck and shoulders with his burning mouth, leaving trails of bruises in the wake of his passion. Edward trembled as he gazed down at that arousing, twin-hillocked beauty imprisoned in his hands, and his manhood surged eagerly against her.

"Tonight you're my slave. You'll do anything I ask."

She smiled agreeably at his hoarse suggestion. "Anything you wish, Edward," she assured, praying that his sexual tastes did not stretch to loathsome aberrations.

Taking a final deep, shuddering breath, Edward retreated a pace. If only he could have a portrait of her like this, naked to the waist, her black hair a silken cloak about her shoulders. She was the loveliest creature on earth, and at this moment he would gladly have given her his crown, his kingdom, so intense was his adoration. Yet Edward's was not spiritual passion. His worship of her beauty was wholly carnal. While he gazed at her perfection, agonizing spears of heat flashed through his limbs as he fought to master the desire that lifted the front of his heavy brocade gown.

On shaking legs he finally reached his makeshift throne

beside the flickering hearth. Desire had so disarmed him, he could scarcely stand. "Stay where you are so I can admire you," he ordered gruffly as he sank thankfully into the velvet cushions.

Marged stood as he requested, awaiting his next summons. The heat from the fire felt pleasant on her bare skin.

The firelight created the illusion of a glittering sculpture of metal—exquisite and unattainable.

Edward stared at her and licked his lips. With shaking hands he began to unfasten the gold clasps on his robe.

Marged was aware of his highly aroused state. Most women would have been flattered that their King so desired them that he was virtually beside himself with need. Perhaps, had she never met Rolfe, she too would have been glad of the King's favor. Edward Plantagenet, that golden monarch whose beauty turned women's heads, was hers to manipulate as she saw fit. Such fortune smiled on few, but Marged wanted it not. The shadowy memory of a dark-haired man invaded her mind, more poignant, more real than this rose-scented bower.

At last the elaborate clasps of goldsmith's work were undone. Slowly, seductively, Edward allowed the rich fabric to part. Beneath the gown he was naked. Marged's gaze was riveted on his greatly swollen manhood, unashamedly exposed to her eyes.

"There, I too have a secret to reveal," he whispered, his mouth twitching in delight as he intercepted her gaze. "Now, slave girl, come hither. Your master commands your presence."

Marged moved stiffly, knowing, almost before Edward issued the command, what was required of her.

"Kneel."

She did as she was bid, trembling as she sank into the soft lambswool rug. Edward positioned her head, pulling her mouth toward his engorged flesh. He quivered in anticipation of the promised delight. When he pressed her face against that scalding brand, Marged obediently took the swollen tip between her lips. Edward moaned in ecstasy as her soft lips encircled his manhood, her teeth raking provocatively. Such delight did he experience, he thought he would explode with need. It took his utmost control to prolong the moment.

"Do it now," he croaked urgently between gritted teeth.

Marged gagged as he thrust forward. Retreating somewhat from his eagerness, she managed to position his thick organ to cause herself the least discomfort. As her tongue swirled about Edward's smooth flesh, flicking, darting, the way Rolfe had taught her, anguished tears pricked her eyes. When she had marveled at this strange mode of lovemaking, pleased to give her lover such delight, little had she thought she would be practicing her skill on England's King . . .

"Stop—oh, God!" Edward cried out. He clamped his hands about her head, crushing her skull as she moved her searing tongue once too often. It was too late. Edward's shuddering passion exploded with such fury, he barely noiced when she struggled to withdraw her mouth.

His copious seed spurted forth, shooting to the rug. And Marged wanted to vomit. No longer could she delude herself that the end reward pardoned her actions. Tonight Edward had degraded her, stripping her pride, her dignity, making her no different from any wench in London's stews. His hand shook as he smoothed her hair, lifting the thick black curtain from her brow. By the time he tilted her face up to his, Marged had carefully composed her features until none of her revulsion showed.

Edward smiled down at her, the throes of his passion complete. "You tried me sore with your artful mouth," he confessed with a grin. "I never knew you possessed such skills to inflame a man."

Marged was grateful he did not ask from where she had gained her knowledge. Edward drew her to her feet. After eagerly embracing her and showering her with grateful kisses, he led her to the bed. He was eager to mount her, his manhood already roused as stiffly as before.

"Am I not a worthy man?" he asked, taking her hand and placing it around his erection. "You've not told me how pleased you are to discover so bountiful a weapon."

Marged smiled, but only with her mouth. "You are indeed virile, Your Grace."

"And ever hot to ride a beautiful woman. Would you have me pleasure you too?"

"If that is your wish."

"Come, stroke me, slave. Love me well with your eager little hands, but take care not to spill me too soon. This time I want to come inside your belly."

Edward's whispered directions echoed through her head as Marged lay beside him on the great bed. He exposed to her with pride his thickly veined manhood, eager for her praise, anxious to arouse her desire. His broad frame, thick with a golden pelt stretching from neck to groin, reminded her of a magnificent animal. This King was so attractive to women, it was said that all who saw him would gladly welcome him to their beds. Indeed, even she found no fault with his body. No, Edward was not to blame for the dead weight where her heart had been. In all honesty, though he had humbled her, he had dealt gently with her, causing her no physical discomfort.

Marged's gown still settled in silken folds about her hips, and he did not hasten to strip it from her. Slowly she caressed him, trailing her mouth over his belly, his thighs, following his directions as if she were on stage. This was the only manner in which she could force herself to make love to him, denying her sworn pledge to Rolfe, thrusting aside the treasured memories of their lovemaking. These empty caresses she plied with such skill were but a travesty of passion.

At last Edward stayed her hands, gently pushing her away. "Take off your gown. Let me see what other secrets you hide from me."

Marged slid from the bed and unfastened her gown's final lacings; loosening the garment, she allowed it to fall around her ankles. At the arousing sight of her nakedness, Edward's manhood leaped visibly, straining toward the ceiling in the eagerness of his desire. Impatiently he motioned for her to come back to bed.

"You're exquisite," he praised her, molding the silken sweep of her flesh against his. He stroked her firm, rounded hips and traced the sweeping curve of her buttocks. When he finally bent his head to nibble her flesh, Marged was alarmed to discover a flicker of remembered response; she steeled herself against the reaction as his hot tongue circled her navel.

"Open," Edward ordered impatiently as she exerted unconscious pressure to keep her thighs together.

Warned by the sudden terseness in his voice, Marged forced herself to relax against the soft down mattress.

Edward reached to the bedside chest to draw the candle closer, the better to admire her body. Murmuring in appreciation, kissing her, he stroked her thighs as he parted the dark barrier shielding her innermost core from his hot-eyed gaze. He echoed surprise at finding her skin darkly pigmented beyond the delicate rose as he thoroughly examined the most private parts of her body. His fingers continued exploring what was denied to his gaze.

His touch, though eager, was gentle. Marged had only to shift and sigh to satisfy his ego. His manhood was stretched taut, the veins darkly engorged, the skin threatening to split. Marged looked at him in curiosity, aroused in a mildly lustful way as her own primitive nature responded to his probing.

"We're a fitting pair, Lady Marged. Would that you could be my queen . . . ah, what beautiful babes we would make," he whispered.

His mouth came down on hers, clamping her lips bruisingly against her teeth. Then, shuddering, gasping, no longer able to endure, Edward parted the soft, yielding folds between her thighs. Marged gasped as he plunged inside her, burying himself to the hilt, sobbing in anguish as he spilled his seed in an agony of delight.

Four more assaults did Edward make upon his "slave" before he finally drifted into a deep, untroubled sleep, his arms wrapped possessively about her tired body.

Marged lay awake in the fire-splashed room. During the night it had begun to rain, and she listened to it tinkling against the windowpane. She glanced about the shadowed room, at the dim tapestries, at his magnificent rose gown discarded in a heap on the rushes, until her gaze finally alighted on the rolled parchment. Tears pricked her eyes. There was little use in crying now. Edward had already sated himself handsomely on her body. Though not as enthusiastic as he would have wished, her play-acting had satisfied. Now, weary in both mind and body, she must take what comfort she could from the knowledge that because she had played the whore, Rolfe was a free man.

* * *

They faced each other hostilely in the red parlor, the gray morning sky rising stormily beyond the windows.

"If you don't trust me, Lady Marged, you can hire a varlet from the village," Edward growled as he slammed the rolled parchment on the table. This morning he was no longer the ardent lover. His lust sated, he had again become England's King.

"Would you agree to that?" Marged asked guardedly, more wary of him when daylight revealed the crafty gleam in his blue eyes.

"Yes, damn it, hire a dozen couriers if you wish. My men will reveal his hiding place to them."

Taking Edward at his word, Marged hired three servants from the nobleman's household to deliver Rolfe's pardon. She reread the parchment one final time before she allowed Edward to seal it. He made a great trouble of the task, grumbling that she did not trust him as he pressed his signet in the melted wax.

"Here, you will also send him this letter."

Marged stared in horror at the sheet of paper Edward thrust into her hands. Rolfe would know she had not written this letter, but the facts would not reassure him that these were not her sentiments. "No, that was never part of our bargain."

"Don't you want to send your beloved these tender sentiments?" Edward sneered as he scanned the neatly written script. "'My dearly beloved lord: By the grace of our most glorious sovereign, Edward, you are granted freedom to leave this land unharmed. Leaning upon our sovereign's generous and—'"

"Stop it!" Marged's eyes flashed yellow as a cat's in the gloomy parlor.

"Now I especially like this part," Edward continued, heartily enjoying her discomfort. "'So, choosing instead the protection offered by our beloved monarch, I bid you adieu—'"

"You deceived me!"

Edward's face hardened. "You forget yourself."

"You deceived me," Marged repeated, fighting the grief that burned in her eyes. "How could you? That letter is a pack of lies."

"If you don't send it, his pardon goes into the fire!"

"But you gave your word."

"My word's still good. You fulfilled your part of the bargain. I found no fault with you. The pardon merely awaits delivery."

"Edward, please don't make me sign it. When he receives the pardon, he'll surely guess how I obtained it. Is that not pain enough?"

Her tears failed to move him. Young Edward of March would have taken her in his arms and soothed her hurt; Edward the King had little use for such tender sentiments. "Think you he'll want you now? The word will spread through the kingdom before the weeks's out. Such noble sacrifices make avid gossip. Or had you forgotten, lady?"

Appalled, Marged stared at him, her eyes huge dark pools in her pale face. "Never did I think it would be made public! I thought it would be our secret."

Recognizing the sheer devastation in her voice, Edward relented somewhat. "Perchance, had last night been all there was between us, it could have remained secret. Now everyone will see you riding beside us. The King has a new whore, they'll whisper, for our dear friends and courtiers are ever anxious to point out our lechery and intemperance. You're to come with us to London."

"No! Oh, no!"

"Sign it."

Edward gripped her wrist and clasped the pen in her trembling fingers. So stony was his expression, Marged shuddered in fear. There was no doubt in her mind that if she refused to sign this condemning missive, Rolfe would be arrested. Then her sacrifice of feigned passion would have been for naught.

Barely able to see for tears, Marged scrawled her signature. Satisfied, Edward sanded and sealed the letter.

"You won't regret your decision," he whispered as they stood at the window, watching the couriers ride down the wide drive. "I promise to treat you kindly and lovingly."

Through a blur of tears, Marged stared sightless at the diamond-paned window, conscious of Edward's mouth on her neck while he toyed with her breasts through her silk bodice. Today life had taken a new turn. Any doubt Rolfe had harbored over her reason for following Edward would be answered by that hateful letter. When he read those smooth words, those lying praises of this generous monarch, his love would turn bitter . . .

{ sixteen }

COLD RAIN TRICKLED inside Rolfe's collar. He shrugged his hauberk more tightly around him and noticed how the countryside spread gray and dismal before him, the rolling Marcher landscape obscured by mist.

"How much farther, my lord?" asked Destier, troubled by his lord's silence.

"A couple of hours," Rolfe grunted, barely able to get out the words.

Destier fell back a pace, sensing that his company was not welcome. There had been a royal pardon, that much he knew. Surely his lord should have been overjoyed to be granted his freedom. Yet, from the hour of the messengers' arrival, Destier had been dismayed by the alien emotions that beset his master; anger, grief, and now bitter determination made him a virtual stranger. It was whispered in the ranks that Lady Marged had purchased the pardon with her body, a rumor Destier quelled harshly before it reached his lord's ears. Perhaps there had been no need, Destier reviewed. Lord Rolfe's embittered mouth, his clamped jaw, his eyes pale as winter sky, were signs he was already privy to the scandalous tale.

Toward noon the dark outline of a castle appeared through the mist. Rolfe reined in; his men followed suit. That other time when he had ridden through the night to Bowenford, there had been joy in his heart; today there was only bitterness. Bile rose in his throat every time he saw that parchment he carried in his saddlebag and realized its price.

"Forward!" he bellowed harshly. As he turned into the brisk wind, Rolfe clamped his jaw so tightly that his teeth ached.

The letter that had accompanied the official pass was not written in her hand. Had Marged anything to do with the composition of its hateful contents? He had even convinced himself that once the week's grace was over, Marged would leave her royal lover, since she would suppose Rolfe safely across the Channel. But two weeks passed and still she did not return to camp. Then he began to hear sly gossip about young Edward's lovely new whore. "Ned's black mare," they christened her in those salacious stories spread by minstrels and peddlers. It drove him nearly insane with pain and fury when he learned she had entered London at Edward's side, dressed as fine as a princess . . .

Rolfe raised his eyes to the fortification looming ahead. If he could not have Marged, then, by God, he would at least have Bowenford! This was where she would eventually return, if only to relieve her garrison. True, Edward could send troops on her behalf, but by then they would be prepared for assault.

"Get you up to the gate, Rafe. You know what to do," he growled to the young soldier who came to his side. Rolfe watched grimly as the lad staggered up the incline to the lowered drawbridge, his leg and head bandaged. They stayed back in the trees, waiting. A small knot of men moved out of the thickets to the east, pressing close to the foot of the walls. Their arrival caused so little attention, Rolfe could have sworn there were no sentries on the towers. No challenge rang out as Rafe slowly crossed the wooden bridge. Once the lad was safe inside the walls, he would unlock the postern and admit the waiting party of soldiers. Belatedly, Rolfe wondered at his foolishness in approaching the castle in daylight instead of waiting for dark. Did he secretly hope they would give him a fight, the desperate action relieving his pent-up emotion?

"What's this?" he muttered, as the portcullis began to rise. Their welcoming reception was too good to be true.

When the iron grille was partway up, a woman dashed beneath the jagged teeth, her gray gown fluttering in the brisk wind. His heart lurched as he wondered if Marged had come here instead. But as the woman drew closer, he knew it was not she. This one was too slender, too fair for Marged.

"Welcome, welcome, good my lord," Alys gasped, tears spilling down her thin cheeks as she gazed at his beloved face. "We've eagerly awaited your return."

"Lady Alys, your warm welcome fills me with joy," Rolfe rasped, successfully hiding his disappointment. "We're weary from travel."

Dripping and wind-whipped, the surprised soldiers gladly clattered over the drawbridge into the bailey.

Alys stood wringing her hands, regretting that Rolfe had not sent advance word of his coming. The larder was stocked, but not with the delicacies she would have liked to offer him. Still, she must be grateful for small blessings.

To her surprise, when he had dismounted, he did not inquire after Marged. Had he done so, she could have told him little, for as yet she had received no word of her hated stepsister's death. Marged had simply never returned home. Alys hoped she lay forgotten in some overgrown gully, a nameless corpse, stripped by robbers long weeks ago.

Rolfe allowed Alys to escort him inside the Great Hall, aglow with firelight. His heart wrenched as painful memories from the past flooded back. Reminders of Marged were everywhere: her unfinished tapestry gathered dust in the alcove, her whelping greyhound bitch skulked in the doorway, her ivory chessboard, bearing a game half played, sat neglected in a corner.

"'Tis uncommon cold for June," he offered gruffly.

"It's uncommon cold all year round in this godforsaken place," Alys grumbled, her mouth twitching bitterly until she caught herself and added sweetly, "Now you're come, my lord, 'tis made pleasant as August."

Rolfe smiled in surprise at her remark. "When we've

supped, I want to inspect the garrison. Why were there no sentries posted?"

Alys colored at the accusation in his tone. "The soldiers provided by the King are a shiftless lot. They were inside sheltering from the rain. I thought I'd have to raise the portcullis myself, so reluctant were they to obey. I saw you coming over the hills."

Her explanation satisfied his curiosity about why they had passed unchallenged. Alys also seemed unaware of his recent imprisonment, or of his disfavor with the King. Marged must have kept her own counsel.

"Here, there's fresh pease porridge and roasted hen. Poor fare, I agree, but the best I can do at such short notice. Tomorrow, I promise, we shall feast," Alys assured him, waving away the serving wench so she might fill his cup herself. "Now, pray, my lord, tell me all your latest news. In this backwater we hear little beyond the state of the weather or the crops. We might as well be marooned on an island."

While they supped, Rolfe gave Alys an edited version of his adventures. At last, though he fought against the temptation, he could not keep from mentioning Marged. "You appear to be managing well as lady of the castle in Marged's absence."

"Aye, it's a role well suited to me," Alys assured him. "My stepsister's vanished again, leaving us to fend for ourselves. Without me, Bowenford would stand open to all and sundry. I've fought to maintain order until your return."

Rolfe sipped his wine. From her answer, it was apparent that Alys had heard nothing about her stepsister's uplifted status. Alys's ignorance suited him; he had no desire to discuss the painful subject of Marged and the King.

While he was inspecting the castle defenses, Alys hastened to her chamber to prepare herself for the evening's entertainment.

"When am I to be allowed to come down?" Joan demanded mutinously.

"Soon. Have patience," Alys snapped as she rummaged frantically in her clothes chest for something suitably impressive. "Here, I'll wear this tonight. Press it carefully."

Joan scowled as she accepted the fluttering emerald silk

gown decorated with silver spangles. "Is this all you want me to do, Lady Alys?"

"Mend the torn trimming—oh, and here's a loose bow on my silver slippers. Hurry, you wretch, don't just stand there. Later you must wash and scent my hair."

Choosing not to defy her mistress outwardly, Joan set about her despised chores. For some time, doubt about the sincerity of Lady Alys's intentions had gnawed at her vitals. All those festering suspicions had been revived when she saw Alys's bubbling excitement over Rolfe's arrival. It should have been she who ran to greet him. Rolfe was her lover. Lady Alys had promised that if she helped her dispose of her hated stepsister, he would be her reward. With narrowed eyes, Joan reviewed Alys's fluttering, giggling manner, silly as any maiden in the throes of first love. Such an untoward reaction to his appearance pointed to a conclusion Joan could no longer disregard—Alys wanted him for herself.

By nightfall, Rolfe had satisfied himself as to the strength of their position. Confidently announcing that he was the new captain assigned to Bowenford, he had proffered Edward's parchment in the dimly lit guardroom, displaying the royal signature before he quickly returned the parchment to its pouch. Thus he had boldly assumed command, placing his own men in positions of authority over Edward's lazy soldiers. Henceforth he would insist on strict discipline and sufficient sentries around the clock to safeguard them from surprise attack.

This necessary work concluded, Rolfe returned to the Great Hall.

Alys, attired in bright green silk, awaited him, plucking her lute and singing a pretty French love song. As the verses dragged on, her high, thin voice began to grate on his nerves and abruptly he signaled an end to her recital.

"That was most enjoyable, Lady Alys. I'd no idea you were so talented," he flattered her, swigging a great draft of mulled ale.

"Oh, my lord, such praise." Alys simpered, her thin cheeks flushed. She was already feeling lightheaded, for she had freely sampled the wine to which she had added a pinch or two of a potent philter promising to enhance a woman's charms. To Rolfe's cup she had added a new mixture, one assured to be the strongest love potion known. He was certainly amiable, but hardly amorous. She frowned, glancing at the dregs in the bottom of his cup. Perchance the mulled ale had diluted the effect.

"Welcome to Bowenford, Lord Rolfe."

Alys spun about, her eyes glittering with rage. How dare that little chit come downstairs without permission! How dare she speak to him!

"Thank you, Joan. I trust you've been happy here," he mumbled, finding the meeting difficult after what had been between them. Though he still found Joan appealing, with her full-blown blond beauty, he was not anxious to resume their intimate relationship.

Joan's brown eyes dimmed with tears of joy as she gazed at him. She was aware of Lady Alys's mounting anger, but she did not care. Rolfe displayed no outward signs of affection toward her. Likely he was saving more intimate greetings for later, not choosing to advertise their relationship before her mistress. Yes, Joan decided with returning confidence, that's exactly what he was doing. Tonight, when it was full dark, she would go to him. How beautiful would be their coming together.

"Being a maid is not to my liking, yet I tolerate it," she said aloud.

Rolfe nodded, turning aside to warm his hands at the fire.

Alys kicked Joan, grazing her ankle. "Get upstairs!" she hissed, beside herself with rage.

Joan hesitated, waiting for Rolfe to rescue her from Alys's temper. When he showed no sign of intervening, she reluctantly complied with the order. Later, she soothed herself, shuddering deliciously as she relived the delight of his arms, his kisses—then she would not even remember hateful Alys existed.

"More wine?" Alys asked sweetly, refilling his cup.

"The claret has a bitter taste."

"Meadowsweet. Perchance too much was added," Alys mumbled, her eyes downcast. In her eagerness to inflame his passion, she must have been too heavyhanded. In the future she would have to be more careful. Mentally she reviewed the sachets of untried potions hidden inside her sewing basket. Surely there was some magic formula there to bring him to her arms.

Wistfully she gazed up at him, finding his expression remote. His beautiful dark-lashed eyes glittered like lapis, his even teeth like pearls against his sun-darkened face. Alys gasped in alarm at the frenzied racing of her heart. How heavenly it would be when Rolfe welcomed her in love. All those hateful indignities she had endured in her husband's bed, the vile, sweating lust of his corpulent body, were meaningless now. This handsome man sped her heart and quaked her stomach until she felt as giddy as a betrothed maiden.

"Good night, Lady Alys. I'm growing weary. Tomorrow we'll talk."

Alys blinked owlishly, turned sluggish by the brew she had imbibed. Gathering her wits, she protested shrilly, "Nay, 'tis early yet. Shall I sing for you again?"

"Tomorrow."

"Perhaps a game of chess."

"No." Inwardly, Rolfe quailed as Alys's glance fell on Marged's ivory chessmen. "You're most kind in your efforts to entertain me, but tonight I find nothing more appealing than a clean bed and the hours to enjoy it."

Alys shuddered repeatedly when he smiled at her, fascinated by his firmly chiseled lips. How easy it was to imagine his mouth pressed against hers in the sweet intimacy of lovemaking. If only he had dallied longer before the hearth, giving her more time to woo him to passion. Yet this sudden talk of bed! Did it have a hidden meaning? Alys gazed up at him, her thin lips parted slightly in anticipation, her heart fluttering like a caged bird. If she was not mistaken . . . did he mean . . . was he suggesting . . . ?

"Your chamber's prepared. I saw to the arrangements myself," she breathed, her voice uneven.

Rolfe took her slender hand and raised it to his mouth. "Good night, Alys," he said.

She stared at him, her thoughts slightly muddled by the wine. He called her Alys. Usually he addressed her more formally as Lady Alys. By using her Christian name he had created a new intimacy between them. Her hand trembled in his, and she wished the moment would last forever. Had she not been a lady, Alys would have clung to his hand, suggesting by that eager handclasp all manner of promised delights.

"Good night . . . Rolfe," she whispered, his name like music on her lips.

Alys nearly swooned as she leaned against the table to watch him stride from the Hall. His broad shoulders were perfectly square beneath his worn brown doublet. And his tight-fitting hose displayed his long, muscular legs to perfection.

Alys sat abruptly. Her legs were trembling, and a curious heat stirred in her belly. Surely it was the wine that generated such lascivious thoughts—in the revealing light of day, she would have quickly discarded them as unseemly. As she admired Rolfe's body, her eyes traveling to his narrow waist, over his firm buttocks to his sinewed thighs, she had pictured him naked. Alys touched her hot cheeks in confusion. As was the custom, at times she had assisted her husband's guests with their baths. If she'd not had this experience to draw on, she would have thought all men to be hairy, spotty creatures crafted like a bullock.

"Are you done with me, Lady Alys?" Joan had returned, having heard Rolfe departing.

Alys flushed guiltily, ashamed to have been caught enjoying intimate daydreams of Rolfe's body. Did it show on her face, she wondered uneasily. Could silly Joan guess her unchaste thoughts?

"Of course not, you foolish wretch," she snapped, annoyed to have been interrupted at her game. "Think you I want to undress myself? Come, ready me for bed."

The two women ascended the tower stairs.

Alys found the narrow, twisting steps difficult to negotiate, and she paused frequently to rest. As she walked, jumbled pictures of Rolfe flitted through her mind, until she smiled like one possessed. With great difficulty, Alys finally negotiated the last bend in the stairs, stumbling on the hem of her gown as she entered her room.

Joan banged around in the carved chest, selecting brushes and scent flagons as instructed.

Had she been alone, Alys would have critically studied her body, anxious to see if she was beautiful enough to please him. As it was, foolish Joan hung about her every move, getting in the way, becoming a constant irritant.

"You clumsy fool!" Alys cried in aggravation as Joan dropped her brown velvet bedgown on the rushes. "I don't know why I ever thought you could be trained to serve me."

Joan glared at her mistress. "You forget, there's far more between us than is usual between mistress and maid."

Joan's pointed reminder made Alys catch her breath, and a wave of loathing swept over her. If it were not for Joan, matters would be far less complicated. Granted, in the past she had needed the girl, but she needed her no longer. By having the little whore in the castle, she must compete for Rolfe's attention. Joan was ten years younger than she, and blessed with a full-blown body, which even in her youth Alys had never possessed. Given half the chance, Joan would slip into his room.

"I've forgotten nothing," said Alys bitterly, her eyes glittering with malice in the candlelight.

"Rolfe's come back for me. And I won't stay hidden while you play the great lady to him."

Alys's cheeks stung, turning crimson. "How dare you speak to me like that! You'll do as you're told or, God help me, you'll be sorry."

So evil did Alys's countenance appear, Joan stepped back a pace, hastily crossing herself. "We share many secrets," she reminded Alys significantly, "secrets Rolfe would very much like to hear."

"Breathe one word of our secret to him, and you'll be food for the worms before sunset," Alys threatened her menacingly, the last vestige of benign intoxication flown. "I'm in charge of this castle and also of you. Nothing is to be done, or said, without my permission. Nothing. Do you understand?"

Joan swallowed uneasily. "I will speak to him," she declared defiantly. "You cannot prevent me. Then we'll see what he chooses to do. Matters are not up to you." With that, she fled from the room.

For a long time, Alys seethed before the hearth, imagining all manner of calamities befalling them if Joan dared reveal their secret plans. The mere mention of Marged's journey and subsequent disappearance, and Rolfe would be beside himself in rage. There would be no chance of wooing him then. His anger would blaze like an inferno.

A disturbing thought flitted through her mind. If she offered herself to Rolfe tonight, she doubted he would forego the pleasure. Likely it was what he hinted when he made a point of telling her how much he looked forward to going to bed. Alys smiled in wonder, remembering the expression in his blue eyes.

Her thin mouth set in determination, Alys slowly unbound her silver gilt hair, allowing it to float free about her narrow shoulders. Her beautiful hair was most calculated to charm a man. Disdainfully she flicked her small breasts; the warm touch made her shiver with pleasure. She was as small as a ten-year-old. He was sure to compare her unfavorably to the more bovine women of his acquaintance; both Marged and Joan were amply endowed. Even her hips were too slender, devoid of the sweeping curves men loved to fondle.

Annoyed with her own misgivings concerning her sex appeal, Alys stood up, letting her long hair fall around her. With her hair draped thus over her tiny breasts, he would never notice she was wanting. So long were her shimmering tresses, they even hid her meager flanks. She would offer herself to him surrounded by a silver cloud, acquiescent, yet eager to discover the secrets of love.

It was cold in the corridor, and Alys wished she had thought to bring a fur-lined cloak instead of her velvet bedgown. Clutching the brown embroidered collar close about her stringy neck, she hastened toward the guest chamber.

As she neared the room, Alys wondered at her own foolhardiness. It was still light. What if a servant saw her entering his room? And what if they did see her? Everyone would know soon enough when he claimed her openly for his own. As a woman she was virgin territory, awaiting the magic of a skilled lover. Without a doubt, Alys knew Rolfe de Bretayne was that man.

The door creaked as she pushed it open. A lone candle flickered beside the bed where he sprawled, sound alseep, his sinewy arms flung from the covers.

Alys closed the door quietly and set down her own candle

next to his. She could not decide whether to slip in bed beside him or to wake him first. She gazed lovingly at his face. He appeared younger in sleep. How she longed to stroke his lean cheekbones, to slip her fingers over his sun-bronzed skin and feel it warmly alive beneath her hand. She was spurred to action by the sudden fear that if she woke him, he might reject her.

With trembling hands she pulled back the heavy covers. Disturbed, Rolfe rolled over, muttering something in his sleep. Alys's heart pounded with fear. Now that she stood at his bedside, she was turned coward. If he woke and recognized her, she doubted she could go through with her bold plan. He stirred again, releasing his grasp on the quilts so that they came away easily. Alys turned back the covers, trembling as she kicked off her slippers. The black pelt spreading from his chest to his belly fascinated her. Unashamedly she glanced at the intimate part of him, which, in her ignorance, had caused her both qualms and pleasure. He was not aroused, yet the thick weight of his relaxed flesh told her no woman would be disappointed. Her jealousy surged anew when Alys recalled that both hated Marged and the sluttish Joan had stood where she stood now. They had intimately touched his magnificent body . . .

Steeling herself for action, Alys climbed into bed and pulled the covers over her meager body. She shivered with cold and fright; her hands were like ice. At last, when her hands were tolerably warm, she tentatively touched his thick black hair, surprised to find it crisp beneath her fingers. Pricklings of beard darkened his chin. Above his upper lip, the stubble formed a perfect mustache, and Alys smiled, bemused by the sight.

Rolfe moved, flinging his arm across her. Alys shuddered with delight. Not being as bold as some wenches, she did not kiss his lips, nor explore the secrets of his body. Such intimacies would come later.

"Rolfe," Alys whispered. "Rolfe, my love."

He grunted and withdrew his arm. Her abundant glittering hair fell about him as she raised herself against the pillows, slipping her shift from her shoulders to expose her small breasts. Wriggling, Alys thrust the garment over her hips, kicking it beneath the covers.

Again, Alys spoke his name. Rolfe did not stir. Seized by

a startling idea, which before tonight she would have dismissed with revulsion, Alys took his hand out of the warm covers and guided it through strands of silky hair to her breast.

A disturbing dream beset Rolfe. Even now, as he moved his fingers, the hard protrusion of a nipple pressed against his palm.

It was no dream! Rolfe's exploring hand encountered a soft nub of flesh, surmounted by a long, prominent nipple. He came fully awake. In the half-light from the flickering candles, his eyes slowly focused on the glittering cloud tumbling about his shoulders, spilling over the pillows to the floor . . .

"Alys!" he rasped in surprise. Fully awake now, he recognized the narrow, flushed face emerging from that shimmering bounty.

"Oh, Rolfe, love, I thought you'd never wake."

She tried to remold his hand about her breast, but he snatched it away.

"Get out."

Alys cried out in distress and clutched his shoulders, trying to pull him back to her, oblivious to his angry command.

"Listen, Alys, I've no wish to bed you. Go now, before you're discovered." Rolfe thrust aside the enmeshing silver-gilt cloud that found its way into his mouth, his eyes, snaring his fingers as he tried to disentangle himself.

"But you said . . . I thought . . . you . . ." she gasped in horror, falling back on the promise behind his words. Alys did not choose to admit she had sought him of her own accord, driven here by longing to discover that which she had never known.

"I never invited you or any other woman here. Tonight I haven't the need. So go, there's a good wench," he cajoled, his tone softening. "Go, before you're discovered and shamed. I'll never speak of this. It shall be our secret."

Alys gaped at him while she battled a tumult of mixed emotions. Tears spilled from her eyes, and her cheeks were hot with shame. Rolfe had rejected her! Here she had sat naked in his bed, his hand clasped about her breast. She had blatantly offered herself to him, and he dared refuse her!

Alys's eyes dilated to black pools in the candlelight. "Go?" she croaked weakly. "You want me to go?"

"Aye, 'tis no insult to you."

"No insult!" she shrieked, dragging up the covers to hide her nakedness. "Do you realize what courage it took to come here? And now you turn me down—you, who bed milkmaids and village sluts, who whore throughout Christendom—you dare turn me down! Me! A noblewoman of the blood royal—"

"Shut up, you idiot! Would you have the guards find you in so compromising a position? I don't need you, or any other woman. Can't you understand that? Whatever possessed you to think I invited you here?"

Icily mustering what little dignity she had left, Alys slid from the warm bed. She stooped, groping on the rushes for her bed robe, blinded by tears of humiliation. She felt the soft fur-edge of the velvet robe. To think he had turned her down!

"You bastard!" Alys hissed, dragging her bed robe high about her neck. "You bastard!"

Rolfe's mouth twitched in a grin, and he did not bother to hide his nakedness as he slid to the rushes. "Come, Lady Alys, such insults are unworthy of you. Get you gone while there's still time. I promise, in the morning I'll consider this naught but a dream."

She knew his words were intended to allow her a fragment of pride. But he lied. He would always remember she had come to his bed. This was a night neither of them would ever forget.

"May you rot in hell, you Breton bastard!"

"That, dear lady, is a distinct possibility." Rolfe chuckled as he propelled her to the door.

Her cheeks blazing, Alys averted her gaze from his magnificent nakedness. Humiliation smarted like fire through her veins, and she wanted to die.

"Good night, Alys. Sleep well." Rolfe made her a mocking bow, as assured as if he were clad in fine court raiment.

Head held high, Alys wrenched open the door.

"I'll always remember your kind thoughts," he said throatily, trying to master his amusement as Alys haughtily turned her back on him and hastened down the corridor. Still chuckling, he closed the door and returned to bed.

Numb with shock over what she had just witnessed, Joan drew back into the alcove, not wanting to be seen. She had been too far away to hear what was said. They were just two figures standing close, the wavering candle flame throwing entwining black shadows on the wall. There was no mistaking their identity: Lady Alys's silver hair fell in a cloak past her knees; Rolfe's muscular body gleamed golden in the light.

Joan leaned against the icy stone wall, fighting nausea as she desperately searched for a solution. All her hopes, her dreams, were shattered now that Alys and Rolfe were lovers. Loathing for her mistress flooded forth to fill the void. For every beating she had endured, for every harsh word, every humiliating act, Joan shook anew with hatred. Yet without money or position, she was impotent against her mistress's power.

One avenue of revenge alone remained, a vengeance so terrible she doubted even Alys had considered it. She would accuse her mistress of witchcraft. By merely possessing so wide a range of philters, charms, and poisons, Alys was condemned. Her treasured herbal would soon spark the constables' interest, for apart from innocent remedies for gout and indigestion, the book contained a lengthy section on poison and mood-altering potions, with special notations in her mistress's own hand.

On weak, shaking legs, Joan retired to her chamber. Tomorrow she would go to the local magistrate's house and denounce her mistress. Alys's hiding places were known to her, for she had taken her maid into her confidence, believing her evil secrets safe with a fellow conspirator.

Joan slipped outside at dawn, taking a wicker basket on the pretext of visiting Annie Bramble on her mistress's behalf. The soldiers waved her through the gate without question.

She broke into a run as she crossed the open land below the south wall. It was not likely that Lady Alys would be stirring so early, yet she dared not be discovered about her deadly errand. To safeguard her own life, she must ensure that Lady Alys was taken by surprise; her mistress was too clever to chance forewarning her.

By the time Joan reached the magistrate's house, the sun was already high. The new magistrate was a stranger, recently arrived from Hereford. When she was shown inside the magistrate's parlor, Joan found him booted and spurred, preparing for a journey.

"What is it, wench? Come, be quick about it, I must away," he dismissed tersely as he looked Joan up and down, mentally calculating the delicious payment he might extract from her.

"I've come to report my mistress, sir."

"Report her? Why, has she beaten you black and blue?"

Joan blinked back easy tears that filled her soft brown eyes. "She's beaten me often, but I never complained. 'Tis fear for my immortal soul which brings me here today."

The magistrate frowned, not anxious to waste any more time. "What do you mean, fear for your soul?"

"My mistress is a witch."

"Take care, wench, such grave accusations should not be made lightly."

"No, sir." Joan swallowed; then, fixing the well-dressed man with a trusting gaze, she said, "Long weeks I've wrestled with my conscience. Last night in a dream, the Virgin warned me about the powers of Satan."

"This sounds more a case for the village priest."

"Look." Joan drew back the cloth covering her basket, to reveal Alys's battered leather book, surrounded by packets and bunches of herbs. "I can't read, sir, so I don't know for sure. Pray tell me if this is a book of spells."

The frowning magistrate took the book that Joan had cleverly opened to a formula to render a man helpless for twenty-four hours. He peered intently at the spidery writing. The minutes ticked away while the magistrate examined recipes ranging from simple headache cures to a deadly potion containing death-cap fungus, guaranteed to kill its victim before sunset.

"Who is your mistress?"

"Lady Alys of Bowenford. Tell me, sir, are those writings evil?"

"Aye, they're vile and most condemning. Wait here."

The magistrate stalked from the room, his face grave. Joan could have hugged herself with joy. It would not be long before she would have the pleasure of seeing her mistress's terror when they came to arrest her for sorcery. With Alys out of the way, Rolfe would be hers again.

A priest and two constables accompanied the magistrate on his return.

"What's your name, wench?" the chubby priest asked after he had examined the herbal, hastily crossing himself as he encountered instructions for ensuring the birth of a male child.

"I'm Joan Vaughn, maid to Lady Alys of Bowenford."

Joan waited impatiently while the four men further examined her basket of herbs. If only Alys had made wax images to stick with pins, the evidence would have been conclusive. Unfortunately her mistress relied solely on herbal remedies to bring about her desires.

"Lady Alys wants the love of the captain of the castle," Joan announced loudly, freshly inspired. "I've watched her infuse his wine with love potions. She also mixes black powder in his food."

Her latest revelation made a definite impression on the authorities. "Will you lead us to your mistress?" asked the magistrate.

Joan quailed at the idea. "She suspects nothing. Would it not be better to catch her at her evil doings?"

"Granted, it would be preferable, but exceedingly difficult to arrange."

"So eagerly does she seek to inflame Lord Rolfe de Bretayne, she daily brews spells to win his love. He used to be the lover of her sister, Lady Marged."

When she mentioned Rolfe's name, the men became highly agitated; when she mentioned his relationship with Lady Marged, they positively bristled. Joan wandered away to the window to give herself time to think. Lady Marged's body must have been found. Why else would they react so strongly to her name? If she was questioned about the death, she must be careful in her efforts to implicate Alys in her stepsister's murder. Annie Bramble was old, but her memory was keen; she would soon reveal that it was Joan and not Alys who had bought the poison.

"How long has this man been at Bowenford?"

"He arrived yesterday. My lady has long awaited him."

"Did he come alone?"

"No, sir. He brought soldiers with him. They've recently come from the fighting in the north."

Again the men retreated for a private discussion. Uneasy twinges began in Joan's stomach as she reviewed this unexpected delay. Why were they so curious about Rolfe? Perhaps it had been ill-advised to bring his name into the story.

"Come, good wench, we'll visit your mistress together," suggested the priest.

His proposal made her even more uneasy, yet Joan was afraid to refuse. "You won't make me denounce her?"

"No. We merely wish to speak with her."

The magistrate's party rode swiftly to Bowenford. After several discarded plans, the priest decided they should speak at length with Lady Alys before reaching a decision. This was not what Joan had expected. Though the men assured her she would not be named as her mistress's denouncer, she had little faith in their promises.

To Joan's dismay, when they arrived at the castle, Rolfe was out hunting. The magistrate was also disturbed by this news. He decided not to speak to Lady Alys after all, only changing his mind after a lengthy consultation with the constables.

Alys stalked toward her unexpected visitors, ramrod-stiff, her hair severely braided beneath a snow-white whimple. When she saw Joan standing hesitantly in the shadows, she cast her an angry glare. Long hours ago her wrath had boiled when she could not find the little wretch. Alys thought Joan had gone hunting with Rolfe. Her unexpected arrival in the company of these strangers soon dispelled that idea. Whatever the reason for the wretched girl's absence, Alys was determined to thrash her soundly.

"Good morrow, gentlemen. I've ordered refreshment. What does my maid in your company? Has she offended some law?"

"Greetings, Lady Alys, we take pleasure in your hospitality. Nay, the wench has offended no one. She guided us to you because we wish to discuss with you a matter of some importance."

Alys nodded in understanding. She glared at Joan, waving her away.

Only too glad to escape, Joan raced from the Hall, anxious to return the basket of herbs before her mistress found them missing; the magistrate had kept the herbal.

Cups of spiced mead, with plump raisins floating on top, were handed to the honored guests.

Composing herself for the men's discussion, Alys picked up her embroidery hoop and went to sit in the window alcove. The magistrate and the priest followed her; the two constables remained at the table.

"Your maid told us Lord Rolfe has recently arrived at the castle."

Alys blanched at the mention of his name. Overnight her affection for the handsome object of her dreams had turned to loathing. "Aye, what of it?" she asked, her voice tight.

"Is he in charge of the garrison?"

Alys nodded. "He's had charge of our soldiers since he took Bowenford by force during last years's war."

"He's the same Breton knight who fought at Towton?"

"It's not likely there'd be more than one like him," Alys snapped, jabbing her needle into the white linen and pricking her finger.

The priest and the magistrate exchanged significant glances. "Has this man offended you, Lady Alys?" asked the magistrate at last.

"Offended, sir? 'Tis a polite way of putting it. He's naught but a ruffian, taking whatever he wills by force. Apparently, foreign mercenaries are all alike."

"Lady, you seem unaware of the price on his head."

"Price!" Alys gasped aloud, her face white as a sheet. "Set by whom?"

"The Crown. He's accused of treason."

"Then why is he still free? He simply arrived and established command."

"I'm told he's presently away from the castle. As he's aware of the order for his arrest, he'll try to evade capture. Do you know where he rides? And with what force?"

Alys swallowed the growing lump in her throat. Perfect revenge lay before her. Why did she hesitate? Surely she did not still cling to the palpitating wonder of his touch, his kiss.

Not now, not after he had humiliated her by his rejection. "Yes, I know where he rides. He has only three men with him."

The magistrate leaned forward, his florid face alight. "Will you lead us to him? There'll undoubtedly be a reward for you. King Edward's most anxious to apprehend him."

The words throbbed through her head as Alys stared unseeing at the linen altar cloth in her clenched hands. Pictures sweet and softening came to her mind: his mouth curved in a smile; his deep blue eyes assessing her with candor; his warm, muscular body, against which she had lain only last night, though it seemed a lifetime ago.

"Perhaps I could tell you where he is."

"Nay, you would have to show us. I'm a stranger to these parts."

"Father Damien knows the way."

"Ah, but the good father is troubled with . . . he has much pain in his backside," the magistrate explained in hushed tones, glancing toward the priest, who was looking through the window at the rolling green countryside.

"I've an excellent cure for piles," Alys proffered, eager to ingratiate herself with these influential men. "Perhaps I could give Father Damien my remedy."

"That's most kind of you, Lady Alys. Yet the remedy would not cure him in time to pursue the Breton."

The priest turned from the window. "You're knowledgeable in herbal remedies, then, my lady?"

Alys's confidence returned by leaps and bounds. "I'm most skilled at mixing simples, even though I say so myself. I can cure most ills, Father. I'll be only too glad to assist you. Wait here, 'twill take me but a minute. I keep a goodly supply of herbs on hand."

The priest and the magistrate again exchanged glances. "Very well, Lady Alys. That's most generous of you."

They watched Alys hasten through the hall, collecting a scullery wench to assist her as she went.

"Will she guide us?" asked the priest, when she was out of hearing.

"Believe me, Father, she'll come. Her spells mustn't have been potent enough. Such bitterness! The Breton must have spurned her. Yet one look at her stick of a body, and one cannot blame him." The magistrate grinned. "The young one's well worth considering, however—ah, Lady Alys," the magistrate said, turning to greet the returning noblewoman.

"Here, Father, the instructions are written on this paper," Alys said importantly. She was proud of her skill with herbs, considering it a vast asset that reminded them all she was of the highest intelligence.

The two men perused the written instructions, nodding in agreement; the handwriting was the same as the notations in that condemning volume.

"Do you have a cure for rheumatism, lady? My father's severely afflicted." Father Damien placed the packet of herbs and the instructions inside his vestments. "Perhaps you have a book of simples we might borrow, for such valuable knowledge should be written down."

Alys started in agitation at his suggestion. "My simples are family secrets handed down from my mother," she explained quickly. It would not do to allow her treasured book to fall into strange hands; certain notes and recipes could easily be misinterpreted. Her heart began an uneasy thudding as she added, "But I'd be only too glad to prepare a posset for your father. The herbs are easily obtainable, pussywillow being a most effective cure."

"Thank you, Lady Alys, you're most kind. Now, will you show us where this man hunts?"

Alys hesitated again, torn between spurned passion and a vestige of regard for Rolfe, which, however small, so far had prevented her from betraying him. But a movement beside the carved screen caught her eye. There stood Joan, dressed in poppy red, her blond hair piled high beneath a trailing headdress. At the sight, all compassion withered in Alys's veins. Rolfe had told Joan the secret he had promised never to divulge! Why else would she go gallivanting about the countryside? And now here she was, arrayed like a camp harlot, flaunting herself about the Hall as if she were the lady of the manor—a position that, in all probability, she soon expected to hold. Likely they had split their sides in amusement over his description of her pathetic attempts at seduction...

Alys spun about, her jaw clamped so tightly she could

scarcely speak. "Allow me to get my cloak. I'll willingly accompany you," she said.

Joan watched in amazement as her mistress swept past her, walking grim-faced between the priest and the magistrate. Surely she was not going so readily, without tears, without offering any defense. Unease pricked her. Had her mistress cleverly turned the tables by condemning *her* as the witch? After a few minutes' consideration, Joan smiled at her own stupidity. Had that been the case, they would have dragged her with them. Besides, she doubted that Lady Alys could contain her venom, had she played denouncer.

Joan turned about, her heart jumping with small irregular beats. What did it matter how Alys walked to her death? Soon Rolfe would return, the hunting over. How beautiful he would find her in comparison to skinny Alys, Joan thought, pulling her bodice lower to reveal more of her soft white breasts. She would not tell him where, or why, Alys was gone. Perhaps later, in a tearful, exceedingly careful manner, she would confide her unwitting involvement in Alys's plot to dispose of Lady Marged.

As if carved from stone, Alys rode silently along the riverbank. Rolfe had gone to take herons, for she had overheard his men discussing the proposed excitement. Little had they dreamed what further excitement lay in store for their handsome master!

"See, there's his party, beyond that stand of willows," Alys said, her voice high with tension. "Take care, he'll see you."

"Are you sure it's he? I've never seen the Breton."

"Oh, yes, it's he."

"Let us journey awhile along this path. Once around the bend, we'll cross the river and take him," suggested one of the constables.

Alys did not question what seemed to her a strange maneuver, her wits obsessed by hateful memories of spurned affection. All her pride had dissolved in a wave of humiliation, as well as her love and her hope.

"Will he be imprisoned?"

"After we've handed him over to the King's men, he will be theirs to judge."

They rode a long way in silence. The party seemed to be

turning farther away from the hunters. Alys still did not question their movements, preoccupied as she was with her own bitter thoughts. The men rode in close order, surrounding her. At first, Alys did not find even this maneuver strange, until she noticed they had left the river path far behind. She grew uneasy at the discovery.

"If we don't turn back, he'll give you the slip."

"Nay, lady, he hasn't the slightest idea we're on his trail."

The constable's sensible answer did not reassure her. "You must excuse me. I've important tasks awaiting. You suggested I'd be away less than an hour. We must have been riding for two already."

"First we're going to my house for papers," the magistrate explained, pointing his horse's head down a narrow road. "There more men await us. He may choose to fight to the death. And I'm a poor swordsman."

"Then you must go alone. I simply cannot be spared a moment longer. I've shown you where he hunted—'tis not my fault if you allow him to slip the noose."

"When I fashion a noose, lady, my quarry never slips it."

The magistrate's grim pronouncement sent fear prickling down Alys's back.

"What do you mean? He must be clear to Bowenford by now."

"We can take the Breton tomorrow, or the next day. He does not suspect."

"Then why have you brought me hither, wasting my time?" she demanded shrilly. Alys's mouth seamed to a tight line as she accused, "You've deceived me."

While she spoke, a small body of men rode past the church. "Here comes a special escort for you," said the magistrate.

Alys cried out in alarm as a constable seized her bridle. Confused, indignant, yet terribly afraid, she struggled against his superior strength until she thought her wrists would snap. "Where are you taking me? I demand to know!"

"You're under arrest."

"On what charge?"

"You've been denounced for witchcraft."

"It's a lie! I'm no witch!"

"This book says otherwise."

Alys's face advanced through several shades of color as she recognized her battered herbal. Only Joan could have presented them with her treasured book, for, besides herself, Joan was the only one who knew where it was hidden. Understanding shot through her in sickening waves. Joan had denounced her. The story about Rolfe had all been lies, concocted no doubt by that evil baggage. Being privy to the shameful truth of that night, Joan had known she would welcome an opportunity to avenge herself.

Black hatred filled Alys as she mouthed a terrible incantation, never before invoked against a mortal being, but learned long years ago at her mother's knee.

The magistrate was the only one who understood the French curse. Until now he had not been wholly convinced that Lady Alys was not merely a haughty gentlewoman, well versed in medicinal lore, but the evil content of her plea for aid from the powers of darkness removed all doubt. Swiftly the magistrate crossed himself, twitching his cloak away from contact with the witch's horse.

"Seize her! Bind her hands and feet!" he ordered.

"Thou shalt not suffer a witch to live," quoted Father Damien.

"Thou shalt not suffer a witch to live."

The chant was taken up by the party of armed men, who bound her struggling figure ungently to her saddle.

Rolfe turned for a final look at the rain-washed countryside. The sky shone so blue and cloudless, it was hard to believe yesterday had been a foul, almost wintry day. Such was the weather of these confounded reaches. His mouth tightened as he acknowledged a painful thought driven unbidden to his mind: 'Twas little wonder Marged loved this land. Such changeable weather suited her own mercurial moods.

"Let's return."

After issuing the gruff command, he spurred his horse, setting a course through the long, sweet meadow grass, spraying great showers of water as he rode.

It was gloomy indoors, after the bright sunlight. Rolfe threw down his gauntlets on the chest beside the hearth. Even in summer, a fire was a necessity in this frigid tomb of stone. Out of habit, he held his hands to the blaze.

"Lord Rolfe, there've been visitors while you were away."

"Visitors?" Rolfe handed Destier his cloak. "Who?"

Destier shrugged. "A priest and some petty official, accompanied by four henchmen."

Eyes narrowed, he asked, "Where are they now?"

"They left with Lady Alys, intent on some secret journey."

The news visibly relaxed him. "Perhaps she goes on a pilgrimage," he offered, concealing a smile at the thought. "We won't concern ourselves with that lady's strange choice of companions. Bring me some ale to quench my thirst."

While he stretched his legs before the hearth, quaffing deeply from a tankard of ale, he wondered about Alys's surprise journey. The mere presence of the priest suggested that she feared for the state of her immortal soul. Likely she went to cleanse herself of the wicked impurities of her thoughts. The vivid recollection of Alys's expression of outraged modesty, while she clutched the bedcovers beneath her chin, made him laugh aloud. For some unaccountable reason, the poor spinster had set her sights on him as the object of her gratification. He hoped he had not offended her too sorely, for she had been exceedingly hospitable toward him of late.

To his surprise, he found that Joan presided over the high table for supper. He bit back sharp words of rebuke. Why should she not be allowed to enjoy a brief hour of glory? If Alys returned unexpectedly and caught her at her play-acting, Joan's pleasure would be dimmed soon enough.

"Was the hunt enjoyable?" Joan asked politely as she welcomed him to the table.

"We bagged only a dozen birds. Yet the day was so fine, I didn't mind the poor catch."

Joan served him herself, carefully spooning a rich mixture into his earthenware bowl. She produced each subsequent course in the manner of a conjuror pulling a rabbit from a hat. The main dish was of saffron-stuffed roast heron—his own catch—reposing on a bed of spiced cabbage. A flaky-crusted mutton pie, swimming in rich gravy, followed. Cornets of sweet white bread, dipped in sugar and cinnamon, accompanied a white junket of thickened almond milk flavored with rose water.

"The meal was delicious. I'd no idea you were such an accomplished hostess," Rolfe complimented her after he had washed and dried his hands on a linen cloth held by a serving lad.

"I learned many arts before I came to Bowenford. Never was I intended to become a servant. Father raised me to be a gentleman's wife," Joan reminded him, a trifle too sharply.

"Then perhaps your lady can set about finding you a suitable gentleman on whom to practice your arts."

Catching her breath in dismay over his harsh tone, Joan seized Rolfe's hand. "Nay, let us not be angry. Not after so pleasant a supper."

He muttered a gruff apology. As yet his nerves were not well enough restored to afford polite conversation. "When the week's out, mayhap I'll be more pleasant company. Yorkshire's a goodly distance, and I'm not fully recovered from the ride."

"Come, then, it's much quieter and far pleasanter in the solar. I'll play the harp for you."

Rolfe was not eager to withdraw to the upstairs room, wherein he was sure Joan's undivided attention would be lavished upon him. Yet in payment for his sharp, somewhat sarcastic remark after so fine a meal, he felt he owed her something.

"Maybe for a half hour, then I must take me to bed."

His words brought an excited flush to Joan's rounded cheeks, but she made no comment as she led the way upstairs to the small adjoining chamber. All lay in readiness for this night of nights. A fire burned in the hearth, sweet with applewood, and she had requested rosemary to be sprinkled among the rushes.

He seated himself on the padded settle, accepting the brimming cup of wine she proffered. The dark wine was heavy and appeared sweet, but a bitter aftertaste coated his lips. Never had he drunk such strange wine as he was continually offered inside this castle, he mused, as Joan seated herself at the harp and began to pluck the strings.

Dozing, pleasantly lulled by the warm fire, the heavy wine,

and that tinkling, angelic music, Rolfe gradually relaxed. The needlework picture on the wall and the panel above the hearth were both Marged's work—Rolfe sat up abruptly, his jaw tightening. For a treacherous moment he had allowed himself to pretend it was Marged who soothed him with the rippling harp music, Marged who smiled sweetly at him, brightly arrayed in her scarlet gown, Marged whose red lips were parted, a thousand unspoken invitations in her eyes.

He stood. "Thank you, Joan, I've enjoyed your company immensely. Now I must retire—I can scarce keep my eyes open." It was a lie, but he could manufacture no more polite excuse.

"Nay, stay awhile. Take another cup of wine with me."

He hesitated, then sat down. "One cup."

She came to sit on the rushes at his feet. While he stared broodingly into the leaping fire, she must have unbound her hair, for he started in surprise to find the golden curtain spread over her narrow shoulders. Warning shot through him. Fool! How could he have been so blind? In her mistress's absence, Joan sought to seduce him. This solar, the gentle music, the heavy wine, were all aids to render him defenseless.

"Do you ever think about the past?" Joan asked, a catch in her voice.

And he did not mistake to which specific event she alluded. "That's dead between us," Rolfe growled, setting down his cup. "We both fulfilled a need that is long since gone."

"Mine's as green as ever," she whispered tearfully. "Oh, Rolfe, my heart beats as strongly for you tonight as it did then."

"You're a good wench," he muttered lamely, aware that his head was muzzy, his speech thick.

"Take me tonight," Joan urged huskily, kneeling before him and pressing her ample bosom against his knee. "I love you."

"No. That's all in the past."

"Rolfe, love, forget what's past. In this room there's no one to know, or care. Tonight we can love freely, without reckoning." When he stubbornly shook his head and moved to rise, Joan's face hardened. "Why? Surely to God you don't love Alys! She's little more than a padded bone. And her nature's as poisonous as her philters!"

"Alys! For the love of God, do you think I've no better taste than that?"

"Play not the befuddled innocent with me! I saw her slipping from your room in the early hours. You thought yourselves unobserved, but you didn't reckon with me!"

His head began to spin, and he steadied it with a shaking hand. "Christ, you saw!" His laughter erupted and he listened to the sound in surprise, marveling at the unfamiliar richness of the tone, as if he heard another man enjoying a jest. "Alys, the sacrificial virgin who swore me to secrecy . . . and you . . . you saw!"

Joan glared at him. "I find nothing humorous in it."

"Nay, wench, you don't understand, you don't understand at all," he explained brokenly, brushing away her enmeshing strands of hair. "Perhaps when she's recovered from her vapors, your mistress will explain the source of my humor."

Though Joan longed to scream at him that the hated Alys would never return, she bit back the revelation. In Rolfe's current strange mood, such an admission might turn him to anger. "If you don't love Alys, who do you love?" she asked, trying to hide her jealousy. "Am I not lovely enough to please you?"

"You're lovely and most pleasing, but I've no desire to bed you. My heart, God help me, belongs to another, and somehow I find my body curiously wanting in desire."

At his half-amused explanation, Joan drew back indignantly, unable to prevent spite from directing her tongue. "You must be a fool man indeed, to crave a dead woman!"

He blinked in bewilderment, hearing the venom behind those words. "Dead woman! You speak in riddles. Who is a dead woman?"

"Lady Marged's been dead these months past!"

Joan was amazed when he threw back his head with a great shout of laughter.

"The wine's more potent than I dreamed."

Joan stared owlishly at him, wondering at his words.

"Lady Marged's not dead. At this moment she probably writhes with royal Edward in his gilded bed."

"I don't understand!"

"My dear ignorant wench, our beloved Lady Marged has become 'Ned's black mare.' And, remembering his lusty appetites, I doubt sincerely that he'd be satisfied with a dead woman in his bed. No, the castle's mistress has risen to exalted status, Joan, love. Never again will she be an insignificant wench from the Marches—now she'll be known to posterity as the King's whore!"

The bitter words delivered, for never before had he uttered the truth aloud, he thrust Joan aside and strode from the room.

Crouched there on the sweet-scented rushes, Joan succumbed to a fit of hysterical weeping. She would not allow Marged to rise from the dead! Sooner or later, Rolfe's blood would boil for a woman; he could not help himself. All was not lost—she must have more patience, that was all.

She scrambled to her feet. Rolfe would be hers again. Why, tonight, had she a little longer to woo him, he would have yielded to her charms. The wine had worked on his humor, yet likely the weariness of his journey robbed him of sexual fire. This was but a temporary setback, for in the past Rolfe had never lacked for sexual need.

Frowning, Joan glanced in the wine ewer. Less than a cup remained. Alys had found a new hiding place for her aphrodisiacs, and Joan had been unable to find them. In time the hidden cache would come to light. But time was something of which she had little. If she could not woo him to her bed before his departure, she would lose him forever.

As she walked through the drafty corridors of Bowenford Castle, Joan fought against what she knew she must do. She had to buy more of the black draft from Annie Bramble. What if Alys had already implicated the old woman as her supplier, sending the constables to watch the hovel beside the Pontrilas road? Trembling with indecision, Joan stared up at the full moon shining through the arrowslits. Moonlight was created for the delight of lovers. How sweet it would be to lie in his arms, to have him whisper those treasured endearments once again. If she did not have Rolfe for her own, she would die from the pain! For so desperate a purpose, she could surely gamble one last time. Once Rolfe's passion was sparked, he wouldn't leave her—and she would have no need of magic potions.

* * *

The grim stone walls of her cell struck fear through Alys's heart. They appeared to live and breathe, moving closer to stifle her, speeding her pulse until she drew back in terror, scarcely able to breathe. She had never been courageous. It had only been during the past hour that she even dared to envision her probable punishment for witchcraft. Did they not burn witches at the stake? Alys shuddered and clutched her chest. She was a noblewoman, not some wild-haired, addled peasant; they would not dare inflict such a terrible punishment on one of her station. Though so far he had ignored her pleas to seek advice from higher authorities, the magistrate must yield. It would be unthinkable of him to take the law into his own hands and condemn her without trial. Such wise arguments usually bolstered her wavering courage, though today her depression remained unchanged.

Rattling bolts and jingling keys alerted her to the arrival of her jailor, accompanied by the magistrate. Alys sat ramrod-straight on her crude bed, hands steady and features composed.

"Good morrow, Lady Alys."

"How long will you continue in this stupidity?"

"You've forgotten we have evidence," the magistrate reminded her. "Until today, it's true, there've been few charges leveled against you."

"Until today," Alys repeated, her face like parchment. "What, pray tell, has happened to alter the situation? I can hardly be accused of witchcraft while I'm safe inside this foul cell."

"Witches knows no boundaries," interjected the jailor. "If you asks me, I says burn her at the stake, and the sooner the better."

Alys quelled the ruffian's zeal with a malevolent glare. The man crossed himself and staggered back, his fearful reaction affording her a measure of satisfaction. "Well, pray present your new evidence. You've no idea how eager I am to hear how someone's cow failed to milk, or how a stykeeper's brat went crosseyed."

"Several weeks ago a traveler succumbed to a violent illness and a local farmer was paid to bury him. Since that time the farmer's chickens have not laid. His cow's gone dry. A neighbor's wife miscarried her child. From all over the district we have reports of mysterious ailments attacking children."

"None of which have been caused by me!"

"Such calamities are common when a witch lives nearby."

"Blessed Mother, will you go to Hereford in search of evidence? Calamities always befall the peasants. 'Tis a natural outcome of inbred stupidity!"

"You cannot deny you mixed possets and potions for evil causes."

"I admit nothing."

"We have proof. And, failing your confession, we shall have sworn statements."

Alys smiled grimly. They would get no confession from her. "These sworn statements you threaten me with—would they be from a senseless wench who served me as maid?"

The magistrate did not try to conceal his knowledge. "One of the statements will be from your maid," he agreed.

"Ha! The wretch seeks to hide her own evil doings. Ask her who purchased spells and potions, who journeyed far afield in search of herbs. I assure you, it was not me. Joan Vaughn's your witch! My herbal has been in the family for generations. In former times, the mixture of poisons sometimes became necessary. You'll find nothing of necromancy in those pages."

"Are you suggesting the wench assisted you?"

"Not assisted—led me along paths at odds with my nature!"

"She cannot read. How can you accuse her of following the charms?"

"She lies! Test her, if you doubt me. The wench reads as well as you or I."

The magistrate and the jailor appeared greatly disturbed by her revelation. Alys hastened on, anxious to press her advantage. "Joan brought all the ingredients to the castle—dried adder's blood, powdered lizard, mouse claws—if you doubt me, I'll even tell you where the wicked creature bought them."

Moving closer, his face grave, the magistrate said, "If you lie to save yourself, it will not go well with you. How would a village wench have money to buy such things?"

"I swear on my immortal soul that Joan Vaughn procured

ingredients for spells and philters," Alys pronounced, her pale eyes glittering in the dim room. "As for money, she steals from me. There's a wisewoman living near the Pontrilas road. Ask her if she knows my innocent maid."

After a swift consultation with the jailor about the local wisewoman, the magistrate turned back to Alys. "The jailor says Annie Bramble lives next to the bridge. Is she the source of your supplies?"

Alys shrugged. "If she's the local wisewoman, then it's she. I don't know exactly where her hovel's located. She was someone Joan knew in the past."

"Why would your maid wish to accuse you falsely?"

Raising her head proudly, Alys pronounced in a clear voice, "For love of a man. Joan's jealous because she wants him for herself. That's why she accuses me of witchcraft."

After the magistrate had gone, Alys fell back against the wall, shaking in agitation. If only they would believe her. She did not know how befuddled the wisewoman might be, yet she must surely recall that no noblewoman came to her door seeking cures, unless Joan had bought off the old hag with the promise of gold.

The cool summer dawn was alive with birdsong when Joan hastened along the Pontrilas road, bound for Annie Bramble's hovel. Across the fields, ears of barley and corn showed lime-green against the black earth. The rolling meadows were painted blue with forget-me-nots. So hard had she run after she left Bowenford, Joan's breathing was still ragged. Tonight Rolfe would be hers! She shuddered at the delicious prospect. Perchance Annie Bramble had a more potent charm than she offered Lady Alys. Joan had never had much money to purchase the supplies, for Alys was excessively frugal in her habits. A gold ring set with precious stones should buy the strongest love potion of all.

When Joan arrived at the thatched hut, she found Annie Bramble sitting outside on a rickety stool, sunning herself. The old woman nodded a greeting, gesturing for Joan to go inside.

"What do you need this morning?" she croaked, her quavering voice high-pitched and indistinct.

"The strongest love potion you possess."

Squinting at the fair young woman, Annie Bramble pondered the request. "I've something from Spain, but 'twill cost you a pretty penny. I can't let it go for the pittance your mistress usually sends."

Joan smiled a triumphant smile as she produced the ring. "Here, will this be enough?"

The old woman took the glinting ring in her gnarled claw. "More than enough," she breathed, delighted with the offering. "Lady's getting desperate, eh, can't get the man in rutting spirit? Well, we'll soon remedy that. Mind—tell her only a pinch, don't want the poor sod taking half the women in the county, do we?"

While she waited for Annie to measure the potion, Joan's heart thumped with excitement. So powerful was this potion, there was no mortal way Rolfe could resist. Never would she reveal that she had charmed him to her bed. It would be her secret. Besides, once she was reestablished as his mistress, Rolfe would be so happy, Joan doubted he would care to know the details behind the event. It would be sufficient to have her, eager and loving, in his arms.

Within minutes, Joan was walking outside the odorous hut into the clear sunshine, the precious potion secreted in a hidden pocket in her skirts. As she hurried homeward, she stopped to pluck some purple comfrey for a beauty preparation she had found in Alys's herbal. Doubtless she would not need to enhance her beauty if the potion was as strong as Annie suggested, but an aid to seduction could not go amiss.

Joan had turned back onto the road, her arms laden with stalks of purple comfrey, when two men emerged from a nearby thicket.

"Joan Vaughn?"

"Yes."

"Maid to Lady Alys of Bowenford?"

Joan nodded, growing uneasy as she heard hooves clopping along the road. The magistrate and his constables appeared around the bend and her unease dissolved. They would not know she had visited Annie Bramble. Another half hour and she might have condemned herself.

"What have you there, wench?"

"Comfrey, sir. 'Tis an ingredient for beauty washes . . ." Joan's voice trailed away as she noticed the grim expressions on the constables' faces. "What do you want with me?"

"What are you doing so far afield? It's a goodly walk to Bowenford."

"The dew's good for my complexion. I often walk at dawn."

A disturbance behind the hedge took Joan's attention, and she blanched at what she saw: a burly constable was dragging forth Annie Bramble.

"Is this the wench?" the man demanded of the old woman, whose eyes rolled in fright. Annie nodded.

"Joan Vaughn, you were seen purchasing supplies for the vile art of necromancy. You are under arrest for witchcraft."

Joan wailed and shrieked, begging for mercy, trying all the wiles she could to resist arrest. Ignoring her pleas, the constables manhandled her to the horses, where they tied her across a saddle. During the struggle, the condemning potion fell from her skirts, providing conclusive evidence of her crime.

Tears streamed down her cheeks as she rode uncomfortably to jail, the sweet birdsong a mocking chorus in her ears. She need not wonder on whose word these men had lain in wait to spy on her. Lady Alys, grown desperate over her sentence, had sought to purchase clemency by implicating another in her crime. The fool! Didn't she realize the only clemency she would be allowed was a companion at the stake! Now they had three witches instead of one. The forthcoming spectacle of their deaths would add much glory to the magistrate's name, for the superstitious countryfolk would shower him with bounty in thanks for ridding them of a vile menace.

From inside her cell, Alys heard voices and the clanging of many hooves on the flinty road. A few minutes later she was surprised to hear Father Damien pronouncing some Latin rite, concluding the prayer with "May God have mercy on your soul," before the door opened to reveal a weeping, disheveled Joan.

"Here's your maid to serve you, Lady Alys," said the magistrate as he pushed the younger woman inside the cell.

Alys fell back in horror. No! Joan should be here in her stead. It was Joan who had caused all this! Joan! The pain in her chest became so acute she could scarcely breathe. Voices, faces danced before her as the iron band tightened. It had all been for nothing! Joan's arrest had not set her free. Now she knew that these hideous inquisitors with their evil, gloating faces were without mercy. Nothing and no one could save her now.

"The witch! See what ails her!"

Leaping forward, a terror-stricken constable yanked Alys upright as she toppled to the ground, and released her as she began to writhe, her mouth wide, gasping for air. Alys sweated profusely, her face crimson.

Stepping back, the men crossed themselves, afraid for their lives. Her face slowly paled to pinched gray as she stared at them, seeing them as devils with horns, as evil, carrion crows . . .

"She'll not outwit me!" bellowed the magistrate, coming to his senses as Alys jerked feebly on the straw-covered floor. "Revive her. We'll not be denied trial."

Reluctantly the men took her by the shoulders, propping her upright, surprised by the weightlessness of her body. One glance at her pinched face told them the witch's soul had fled. Alys was dead.

"Mother of God! She's cheated us at the last!" the magistrate declared grimly. Then, recalling that he still had two witches in custody, he rounded on Joan, his face a seething mask of rage. "You evil wench, you'll pay for your iniquities," he pronounced. "You'd best prepare yourself well. May God have mercy on your soul!"

The men left the cell; Joan remained behind, horror-struck.

After he had calmed himself with a draft of cold ale, the magistrate found his humor restored. He stood in the doorway, listening to birdsong and contemplating his next move. Three witches apprehended, two brought to trial, was achievement enough; to have a traitor sitting within arm's reach, a man sought by the King himself, was more good fortune than he had dared to hope. There were no limits to the glory he might achieve in this insignificant post.

Still smiling, the magistrate moved toward his horse. He would go home to sup and ponder his next move. Perchance he could arrange some trick whereby he could tempt the Breton from his lair. There was no hurry. First he intended to taste the luscious young maid—conquests of the flesh lay far closer to his heart.

seventeen

PEALING CHURCHBELLS ANNOUNCED the beginning of the summer's day.

Marged bowed her head as she knelt on the red velvet cushion in the dimly lit palace chapel, which was sharp with the smell of incense and candlewax.

A flurry of movement in the doorway announced the King's arrival. Today, Edward wore sumptuous purple cloth of gold lined with black velvet. His hair gleamed golden against the somber stonework as he strode down the aisle, nodding to Marged in greeting as he passed.

Throughout the brief mass she kept her eyes downcast, not anxious to encounter Edward's accusing stare. Again, last night, she had failed to respond to him with passion. Marged knew this was not the way to earn the right to visit Bowenford. Never before had she longed so intensely for the rolling green land of home. The teeming city stifled her. Though Edward had not officially placed her under arrest, she dared not leave London without his permission.

When mass was over, Edward requested that she join him in his chambers to break their fast with roast beef and ale.

"You look delightful this morning," Edward complimented Marged as she came inside the room. His gaze roved appreciatively over her apricot satin bodice, to where her smooth flesh swelled invitingly above the low-cut neckline, eventually coming to rest on her furred surcoat of embroidered lime brocade. When Marged stood within reach, Edward playfully tweaked the fluttering lime-colored veils on her heart-shaped headdress, tilting it askew.

"Your Grace!" Marged protested, clutching at her loosely bound hair as the headdress toppled off. It was to no avail. Edward relentlessly yanked free the black coils until her hair fell about her shoulders.

Her lack of enthusiasm for his teasing love-play turned him surly.

"Why don't you love me?" Edward demanded petulantly as he thrust a cup of ale into her hand. "I've done all in my power to make you happy."

He was in one of his difficult moods. She composed her features, not sure whether she would be best advised to appear meek or indignant. "You forget, it was not my idea to become your mistress," she reminded him bluntly, wadding soft white bread between her fingers as she spoke. Perhaps she should have told him a pretty lie. Lately she seemed unable to deceive him well. Edward was no fool; he readily saw through feeble deceptions, the discovery only heightening his anger.

"It's the Breton, God damn him! He invades our every hour!" Edward thumped the table, setting the cups jingling. "You foolish woman, why do you still moon over him?"

Marged gave Edward a stiff smile in reply.

He stalked the room, fingering the draperies and the chair cushions, restless as a caged beast. The sunlight flashed fire from a battered Celtic cross hanging on the wall. The Breton had presented the golden, jewel-studded ornament to him when Edward claimed England's throne. Moodily, Edward took down the object, fingering the dented gold, remembering the day he had gladly accepted this gift. The cross had been handed down for over four centuries in de Bretayne's family. During some past age, the Breton's ancestors had raided an English coastal village, where they desecrated the church before bearing their spoils home to Brittany. This ancient cross, which had once hung above an early Christian altar, de Bretayne had generously returned to its rightful land.

"He never went back to Brittany, you know."

The food in Marged's mouth turned to lead. "What?" she gasped, unsure whether she had heard right.

"I said, de Bretayne didn't return home. Your noble sacrifice was in vain."

Marged stared at him, her eyes huge dark pools in her stricken face. "Why did he not? Oh, Edward, you promised me."

He smiled when he heard the note of warning in her voice. Holding up his hand for silence, Edward said, "I'd naught to do with it. He simply ignored the grace period. They tell me he's since repossessed your home. Until I received that piece of intelligence, I was hard put to understand your mad desire to return to the Marches."

"I didn't know he was there."

"So you say." Edward regarded her closely. "Remember, any day I see fit, I can have him arrested. The terms of my pardon have run out."

Throbbing blood sped to Marged's face. "Please don't. We made a bargain . . . 'tis why I'm here still."

"You disappoint me. I'd thought you were still here because you bore me some affection."

"Oh, Edward, please, let's not begin again this morning. I'm here at your command. Long weeks ago you discovered you couldn't own my heart. What one has given away, one can no longer—"

"No, let's not begin again this morning," he snarled, seizing his half-filled cup and downing it. "I'm heartily sick of your feeble utterings about pure love. Though at the time I was angry with him, perhaps I've done the Breton a disservice. Never did he treat me as unkindly as you have, my lovely wench. His friendship was genuine from the start."

"That was not what Warwick had you believing."

Edward smiled grimly. "Ah, yes, dear Warwick—I've

learned to be more careful of my cousin Dickon's recommendations. In that respect, at least, you were right. Shall we invite the Breton back to court?"

Marged's gasp echoed in the room. "So you can arrest him?"

"I've no longer any desire to imprison him. You should know me well enough by now to realize I don't harbor vengeance. Though it's hard to admit, passion for you clouded my judgment. 'Tis not something of which I'm overly proud. Let it not be said of Edward that he treats his friends with malice—nor even his enemies. Bearing grudges I leave to my cousin. Would you like to have the Breton at court? He's a handsome devil, in great demand with the ladies. He would enliven our balls."

"You can't be serious!"

Edward banged down his cup. "I assure you, I've never been more serious."

"Be not so cruel to me!"

"Why? Have you not been cruel to me? Have you not withheld the passion of your body, steeling yourself not to respond to me? Have you not withheld affection until I'm nearly beside myself with anguish?"

"I never refused you."

"Nay, that's true. Yet to have you soft beneath me while you're roving God knows where in thought, is what I find hardest to endure. Yes, we'll have the Breton at court. Perchance when you set eyes on him again, you'll realize what a fool you are to breathe life into passion already dead."

Appalled by his suggestion, Marged gazed beseechingly at him, her eyes full of tears. "Is this how you intend to reward me—with pain and torment? Can he not go home to Brittany? Or can he not come to court after I've returned to Bowenford? You suggest I don't please you of late, therefore you must find little joy in my presence."

"You're mine! I won you, dearest Marged, perhaps only because I'm King, but win you I did. Don't you think I want the Breton to realize that? Don't you think I want to watch you together to satisfy myself that the fires are extinguished? Besides, sweet love, there are many wondrous fair creatures here at court. I'm not such a fool as you suspect. Here the Breton will find himself another soft armful, thereby ridding me of a constant irritant!"

On Michaelmas Eve, 1461, Rolfe battled his way along London's crowded East Cheap. He was constantly jostled by townspeople, accosted by raucous street vendors and molested by cooks' apprentices who attempted to lure him inside their establishments to buy fresh pasties and other delicacies. Long ago he had abandoned the effort to keep clean his Holland cloth sleeves; a dozen greasy hands had each left their mark as they grasped, tugged and beseeched the fine gentleman to sample their wares. He had left his lodgings at the Greyhound Inn, bound for Candelwick Street, and intended to choose material for an outfit to wear at Edward's welcoming ball on his return to Greenwich after his progress through England's southern counties.

Unable to resist a tray of exceptionally aromatic mutton pasties borne past him, Rolfe bought one of the savories fresh from the oven, so hot the steam seared the roof of his mouth. Lavender girls smiled at him, offering fragrant bunches of herbs to scent his coffers. Two burly rush-sellers, crying their wares, pushed past, slapping his face with the tips of their rushes, "fair and green."

This teeming thoroughfare was a different world from the sparsely populated Marches. London seemed to prosper under Edward's rule; the congestion of the streets told him that. Everywhere he looked he saw vendors on foot, on horseback, or in carts. The very air seethed with noise. Street cries, clattering hooves, men's voices, ever ready with loud oaths and bawdy sallies, all competed with cackling geese being driven to market, the chants of a party of mendicant friars, yelling children, squealing pigs, and yelping dogs. All London appeared to live in the street.

At the corner of the thoroughfare, a band of ragged minstrels played for coppers, the shrill notes of their shawms and pipes adding to the general racket. Farther along the cobbled street, a troupe of tumblers and jugglers cavorted among the crowd, earning shrill rebukes for tripping a worthy merchant and spilling a clattering heap of pewter pots to the filthy cobbles.

As he walked, Rolfe was wary of his purse, his hand never far from his dagger. Colorful and fascinating though it was, London teemed with vagabonds; cutpurses, thieves, and robbers lurked in the shadows or mingled with the crowds. On this bright morning, nimble fingers were as eager to relieve him of his money as if it had been night.

Picking up his pace, he crossed the street at the westerly point where East Cheap ran into Candlewick Street. For many days he had been debating whether or not to heed Edward's summons to court. His sense told him not to obey the command and leave himself open to arrest, yet his knowledge of the King's character assured him he could safely comply with the command. Warwick, who had sought to hold Edward beneath his thumb, was no longer the power behind the throne. Edward lacked neither wit nor intelligence; a man of action and determination, though much given to dalliance and pleasure, York's golden-haired giant intended to rule alone. Edward's unexpected summons suggested the young King had reconsidered his rash behavior, generated more by Warwick's guile and Marged's beauty than by any lasting resentment.

As always, when he thought about Marged, pain stabbed his heart. He had not inquired if she still danced attendance on the King, but he had no reason to think she did not. Though their inevitable meeting would not be pleasant, it was a penance he must face, for he brought her startling news from Bowenford.

The unexpected charges of witchcraft leveled against Alys and Joan had enraged him so much, he had risked seizure by storming the magistrate's house to demand their release. That was how he learned about Alys's death. The magistrate refused to yield to his demands to release the other two women. Rolfe barely escaped when the magistrate summoned constables to help take the fugitive captive. Without delay he left the Marches, slipping through the noose the wily magistrate had fashioned. Rolfe regretted abandoning Joan to such a terrible fate, but the very nature of her crime made it impossible to have her pardoned. These were the events he must make known to Marged. Remembering the constant friction between the stepsisters, he doubted she would shed many tears over Alys's demise.

"Good my lord, come forth to view my wares."

"Great cheap of cloth! Great cheap of cloth!"

As he turned into Candlewick Street, Rolfe was assailed by merchants and their apprentices clamoring for his trade. He swiftly abandoned his gloomy thoughts, needing all his wits to battle this effusive welcome.

Halfway along the street was a fine, gilded establishment, its overhanging upper stories gleaming with glass. The carving above the windows was gaily painted and magnificently gilded. This seemed a likely place. Rolfe's passage inside the shop was preceded by a bowing, groveling apprentice who would doubtless earn praise for his skill in enticing a customer inside.

The dark, vaulted shop was lined with shelves bearing hundreds of bolts of jewel-bright cloth, the bounty spilling over into a back room. Thoroughly bemused by this vast selection, Rolfe begged for more time to study the wares. The corpulent merchant, used to this reaction from his provincial customers, bowed and left him to his own devices. Out of the corner of his eye, however, he saw a towheaded apprentice dogging his steps, ready to pounce once he made his selection.

After almost an hour of walking back and forth through the cluttered rooms, examining cloths of varying prices, Rolfe selected a bolt of crimson velvet to be made into a doublet of the latest design. The draper urged him to trim the fine garment with cloth of silver. Rolfe succumbed to the man's suggestions, wincing when he learned the cost of his finery. Unused as he was to fashion, having worn leather jacks and plain doublets for most of his life, he was determined to hold his own against the plumed peacocks at Edward's lavish court.

The apprentice lad measured him, agile as a monkey while he darted about, crouching on a table to combat Rolfe's height, having him thrust out arms and turn his head. Rolfe's attention strayed to the open shop door, where sunlight speared the murky atmosphere to reveal dust motes and pieces of lint cavorting wildly through a sunbeam. His mouth went dry. In the doorway stood a beautiful creature lavishly gowned in deep blue velvet edged with narrow bands of ermine. At first he failed to recognize her, then a great, nauseating wave of recognition swept over him when he realized the woman was Marged. Not anxious to be seen, he moved deeper into the shadows.

Marged came inside the shop. Apparently she was a regular customer, for the beaming merchant ran forward to greet her, rubbing his fat hands in glee. A crowd of lackeys danced attendance on her, offering cups of wine, almond wafers, an upholstered chair for her comfort. Two liveried servants had accompanied Marged inside the shop; a third waited outside to hold the horses.

As he stared at her, Rolfe unconsciously licked his lips. God, she was even more beautiful than ever! Her face was finer drawn and perfectly tinted with cosmetics, making her appear more a work of art than a flesh and blood woman. Marged's features were devoid of their usual animation, as if she existed merely to be admired. Rolfe could not hear what she was saying to the merchant. He did catch some mention of the King and peach satin before the entourage disappeared inside a room reserved for important customers.

Rolfe passed his hand over his brow, wiping away a film of sweat. Now that he had finally seen her, he sincerely doubted his ability to carry off this grand plan. He was of a mind to decline Edward's invitation and take ship for Brittany rather than endure the ordeal of seeing her with her royal lover.

"Are you ailing, sir?" inquired the merchant solicitously when he noticed Rolfe's pallor while passing on the way to the back room. "You look most peculiar."

Catching himself, Rolfe grinned. "Nay, good man, it's more likely the shock of paying so much for a suit of clothes which turns me weak."

The merchant laughed heartily at his jest, and continued about his business.

Teeth gritted against the temptation to enter that private room and confront her, Rolfe turned resolutely toward the street. He even tried not to look at her waiting horse, gaily caparisoned in blue and silver, but his courage failed him. The dainty velvet saddle strung with silver bells, the dagged reins likewise adorned, all spoke of Edward's devotion. This milk-white gelding was nearly identical to the animal the King had given her to ride when she was last in London. The discovery did nothing to improve Rolfe's disposition, which, these past ten minutes, had turned decidedly foul.

Heedlessly thrusting his way along the crowded street, he headed to the nearest alehouse. He had already decided not to personally deliver the sad news from home. A letter would readily convey all he had to say about Alys. A letter would also relieve him of the agonizing torment of seeing her alone.

Since Edward's return from his progress through the southern counties, Marged had declined to attend court functions, pleading indisposition. She did not join the King for the Eltham Joust, nor on the royal barge traveling downriver to the Palace of Shene. The reason behind her sudden ill health was no great mystery to him: in their absence, Rolfe de Bretayne had come to court. Because he had much patience, strengthened now because he knew he would eventually triumph, Edward appeared to accept Marged's lame excuses.

There was one event however, he was determined she would attend. If she ailed, then he would have her brought hither on a litter, but come she would. De Bretayne had assured him he would attend his grand homecoming ball.

Marged watched the blustery wind whipping the first fading leaves from the plane tree in the yard below. All the bawdy gossip about Rolfe's popularity with the ladies, evinced by the bevy of lovelies who dogged his steps like lapdogs, brought her perilously close to experiencing her feigned illness.

This morning she had received word from Edward that she must attend tonight's ball. He had also instructed her to wear her latest gown.

Marged shuddered in distaste as she fingered the sumptuous peach satin gown draped across the chest. Lovely though the heavily embroidered creation was, when she wore it she felt like a whore. Likening her smooth golden skin to a peach, Edward frequently indulged his whimsy by ordering peach gowns of velvet, satin, and silk, each fitted to thrust her breasts up above the low neckline. So perfectly attuned was the shade of this particular satin, that from a distance her breasts appeared bare. To further heighten the illusion, an openwork design of pearl-embroidered pomegranates was centered over each breast. The fruits were tipped by an amber stalk, which, at a glance, seemed to be a bare nipple poking provocatively through the design. Edward had trembled with desire when first she modeled the gown. To his great annoyance she insisted on wearing a miniver-trimmed surcoat of peach velvet in an effort to disguise the illusion of nakedness. By his very ordering of this lascivious style, Edward proclaimed her station to his entire court. The daring gown seemed to say, "Behold my lovely, desirable whore."

With tightened mouth, she picked up the velvet surcoat. She intended to wear the overgarment tonight also, far too ashamed to flaunt the indecent gown in public. Yet even this garment did not hide the suggestive fashion as well as she would have wished, being cut too low in the bodice.

Long before Marged reached the thronged ballroom, it began to rain. The windows opening onto the gardens admitted gusts of cool, rain-scented air, relieving the banquet hall's smoky atmosphere. As she breathed deeply of the rain-washed sweetness, she was filled with poignant longing for home. She rapidly blinked away her tears. Edward would be angry if she did not appear gay and lighthearted. If she was to earn the right to visit Bowenford, she must make an extra effort to please him.

Flaring torches and dripping sconces lit the vast room with wavering light, making jewels wink with fire, washing sumptuous velvets in rippling colors. The old rushes had been swept away and the floor scrubbed; never before had the room appeared so bare. Because of her recent claims to indisposition, Marged had felt safe in excusing herself from the lavish banquet, arriving only in time for the ball.

On all sides, her presence was graciously acknowledged by Edward's laughing courtiers, who were splendidly dressed in rich fabrics laden with precious stones. Everyone was anxious to appear more splendid than his neighbor. As she passed, heads turned for a closer look at her luscious, provocative bodice. Self-consciously, Marged tried to pull the edges of her fur-edged surcoat closer together in an attempt to hide the exposure. It was useless. Lifting her chin high, her eyes burning with unshed tears, she walked proudly through the lofty hall, aware of the burgeoning gossip rippling as she passed. Even the gold chain strung with enamel roses of York—an exquisite diamond sun in splendor winking in the shadowed valley between her breasts—came in for its share of comments. The precious jewel was Edward's latest gift to her.

Tonight the King was splendidly attired in peacock-blue cloth of gold edged in gold satin and bands of ermine. His long, muscular legs were encased in silver hose that clung to his hips, revealing every detail of his form, for his glittering short doublet came barely two inches below his waist. Over doublet and hose, Edward wore an open pleated coat with gold satin sleeves. He wore a floppy peacock-blue hat pinned on the left side of his golden head and a glittering Yorkist device to match the heavy chain around his neck. Edward of York had been called the handsomest king in Christendom, and those who saw him tonight found it no idle boast.

Marged dipped a curtsy to her King, very reluctant to meet his gaze.

"At last," Edward breathed, raising her up. "I was afraid you were indisposed again."

Though his words were affable, Marged did not mistake the knife-sharp edge behind the remark. "I was unwell this morning—'tis why I did not come to sup." As she spoke, Marged looked him full in the face, challenging him to contradict her.

"It's no matter," Edward dismissed absently before he turned to receive a message from one of his nobles.

Moving leisurely amid the laughing throng of lords and ladies, Edward escorted Marged to a crimson-swathed dais banked with late roses, poppies, and purple Michaelmas daisies. Marged sipped a cup of spiced wine and nibbled a handful of sugar wafers while Edward lounged indolently beside her in his carved chair. A band of minstrels, wearing murrey tabards emblazoned with the arms of York, sang the latest French love ballads for their sovereign's entertainment. Though Edward appeared outwardly relaxed, amiable as a contented beast while he nodded to the words, Marged sensed a ripple of inner excitement passing between the King and his friends. The courtiers were watching her covertly, exchanging knowing smiles when Edward allowed his large hand to rest possessively on her shoulder. While the minstrels sang, his long fingers stole inside her embroidered neckline, sliding familiarly over the smooth globe of her upper breast. Though she hated this public fondling, Marged was too wise to remove the King's hand.

While still pretending to be absorbed in the minstrel's songs, Edward's bejeweled cronies shifted their attention to the east end of the room, where latecomers still drifted in. Eventually, Marged too was caught up in this undercurrent of expectancy. During the brief lull following the entertainment, she faced the carved screen, intently scanning the trickle of guests who sauntered beneath the banner-draped arch.

The sudden appearance of a tall, black-haired man dressed in brilliant scarlet velvet brought her bolt-upright on her cushioned chair. The courtiers, anxious to see Marged's reaction to the appearance of her former lover, leaned forward eagerly as Rolfe strode in.

Edward, while seemingly detached, also watched Marged beneath lowered lids, taking note of her pinched face, of the way she snapped the heads of the lavender stocks she carried, spilling a scented shower across her satin skirts.

Marged started to rise, but Edward pressed her back in her seat. "Nay, sweet," he said, "let him come to us."

"I have no intention of greeting him—" she began angrily.

"Enough!"

The warning in the King's eyes silenced her. Like one carved from stone, Marged waited for the man whose presence haunted her every dream to come pay homage to his King. Yet this knight was taking his own sweet time about the formality. Marged took vicious delight in the tension she saw mounting in Edward's face as Rolfe stopped to greet this person and that, gathering his own entourage of feminine admirers as he moved through the Hall.

The minstrels struck up a gay tune, couples hastened to take their places for the next dance, and at long last Rolfe reached the dais to bow before his King. Though since his arrival at court he had been daily prepared to confront Marged, until tonight he had been spared the ordeal. His heart raced and his stomach lurched; his palms grew moist as he looked full upon her, sitting at Edward's knee, beautiful, provocative, and totally out of reach.

"You do me great honor, Your Grace," Rolfe croaked, going

down on bended knee before Edward's makeshift throne. This position brought him level with Marged, but he did not look at her.

"Nay, 'tis I who am honored to welcome you back. I trust these past weeks you've freely enjoyed all the pleasures of my court."

"Assuredly, Your Grace, in full measure."

Edward laughed heartily; then, anxious to bring matters to a close, he half turned in his chair to lazily indicate the woman beside him. "You already know Lady Marged Bowen, but I doubt you've ever seen her looking quite as delectable as she does tonight."

Now Rolfe was forced to meet her gaze. Pain darkened his eyes as he looked into her lovely face. He could not help noticing Edward's beringed hand lying possessively on her shoulder.

"You are aware, Your Grace, that Lady Marged and I are old . . . friends?"

"Oh, certainly . . . very good friends, or so I've been told." Edward's eyes narrowed as he watched Marged's mouth tighten when Rolfe stood, graciously extending his hand to her.

"It's true, you're even more beautiful than I remember, Lady Marged," Rolfe complimented her as he barely brushed her ice-cold fingers.

"Thank you, my lord. We've not seen each other of late, yet I've heard much about your exploits."

He managed a slight grin at her constrained words, delivered as though through gritted teeth. "I trust they were exploits of great valor," he said.

"Nay, Rolfe, you wretch, no doubt they were exploits of great lustiness. Though I can scarce repeat certain stories to our lovely Marged, I assure you she's heard enough to question your vast reluctance to come hither. You seem to be enjoying to the full all available delights, which is exactly as I intended."

The bleak expression in Rolfe's eyes puzzled Marged.

"I suspected Your Grace would not dissuade me from amorous pursuit. Your court is world-renowned for its lovely women."

Edward smiled. "Aye, and this lovely creature outshines them all." Leaning forward, his grip tightening on Marged's shoulder, the King urged huskily, "Come, my love, let us lead the dance."

Rolfe backed away and bowed stiffly, purposely keeping his eyes averted from her painfully beautiful face. He was sure Edward's courtiers had not omitted one iota of information concerning any woman in whom he had shown interest. Tonight's uncomfortable encounter affirmed what he had long suspected. Edward, like a green lad eager to flaunt his conquests before his companions, ached to display Marged to him. The fact that Rolfe and Marged had been lovers must have greatly heightened Edward's satisfaction.

Women flocked around Rolfe, eager to partner him in the dance that opened to the general court when the King and his partner completed the opening measure. Without regard for identity, Rolfe seized the first shapely body he encountered, spinning the laughing fluttering creature into the whirling round.

Above the wench's head he saw Marged walking stiffly to the trestle table where the refreshments were laid. She downed a full cup of Malmsey before turning back to the throng, a smile fixed on her perfect features. He puzzled over her icy welcome as he mechanically followed the dance steps. Could it possibly be she still cared for him? Or was she enraged that he had stayed in England after she had made such a noble sacrifice on his behalf? Yet so beloved of Edward did she appear, there must have been little sacrifice to their bedding. This harsh reminder jerked him back to his senses.

The dance ended on a gay note, with an exchange of kisses. Bending back the fluttery creature in his arms, Rolfe planted a resounding kiss on her rouged lips, awakening an eager response he had not expected.

"I don't know your name, sweet," he whispered as he led the wench from the floor.

"You can call me Gillot, my lord."

Her breathless attitude revealed that she was his for the taking. By God, why should he live as celibate as a mealy-mouthed monk? Marged Bowen took her pleasure, and in no uncertain terms. Bedding the King could hardly be called a secret love affair.

He smiled down at the giddy creature encouragingly. He

barely noticed her eager, outthrusting breast spearing his velvet sleeve, for Marged was looking straight at him, her expression bleak. Sharp pain pierced his heart. After all this time she could still addle his wits and set his blood coursing with sweet desire . . .

"Come, Gillot, you can show me the Palace garden," he suggested in a harsh tone.

The invitation carried to Marged, who turned aside rather than meet his eyes. Anger hardened Rolfe's mouth, and he yanked the wench's arm, pulling her toward the open French windows.

"But, my lord, surely it's too wet outdoors," squealed Gillot in high-pitched protest.

"Nay, the rain's stopped. Flowers need rain to make them sweet. Didn't you know that, wench?"

Marged stood so stiffly, she thought her back would break. Did he deliberately flirt with the wench for her benefit? Angrily she thrust aside the softening thought. It was foolish to cling to such straws. Rolfe had known many women both before and after their love affair. Why should she suppose his interest in giggling Gillot Russell to be less than genuine?

"Come, sweet, dance with me," Edward invited huskily. Guilt at being discovered in such treacherous thought brought a blush to Marged's cheeks. Forcing her tight mouth into a smile, she said, "I'm tired, Edward. My throat's so parched, I must take a cup of spiced wine."

Edward, who had also watched the departing couple, offered to fetch the refreshment. This close to success, he could afford to be generous. When he returned with a brimming cup of wine, he found that Marged had retired to her chair amid the banked flowers. Though her face was parchment-white, her beauty was undiminished. Edward's heart lurched with a peculiar ache, a sensation far removed from his usual accelerating lust.

"Here, love," he offered gently, remorseful for having engineered the encounter that caused her such pain. "'Tis the finest vintage. See, I've brought you a raspberry tart with clotted cream."

Eventually growing tired of Marged's somber mood, Edward drifted away, a bevy of laughing beauties luring him back to the dance. Each woman present was eager to snare the young King's wayward interest. Marged had few illusions about the surface friendship of these court ladies. Without exception they aspired to change places with her. Many of them had probably already obliged Edward, whose capacity for lovemaking was boundless. Yet he had not chosen to honor them in the manner he had honored her. How ironic, she mused, as she sipped the spiced wine, she who had him for her lover did not want him, whilst they, who had him not, desperately craved his attention.

There were many times when she felt tempted to load her possessions on a sumpter and return to the Marches. Her courage usually failed her, vanquished by the cool breeze of reason when she considered her unique position at court. The very retention of her home was dependent on Edward's goodwill. Rolfe's life, too, was a pawn in the game. Though the King had assured her he did not intend to imprison him, she could never be sure he meant it.

Marged left the crimson-draped dais, warily skirting the shadowed reaches of the room. She had no wish to call Edward's attention to her departure. The freshness of the rain-scented garden beckoned irresistibly. Surely, by now, Rolfe and his woman would have found some private place to quench their thirst. Pain and bitterness brought a scowl to her face. Damn him! How fervently she had believed his vows of undying love. Yet, given one painful jolt, the fervor crumbled, as insubstantial as ash. That was what her love had become—ashes, smoldered beyond recognition, useless, cold.

The wind was chill, the dampness making her draw her surcoat closer about her exposed chest. In this hateful gown she would catch her death. Damn Rolfe de Bretayne! Damn Edward of York! Damn all men for their duplicity!

As Marged marched furiously through the formal garden, tears trickled down her cold cheeks. In surprise she brushed them away. She would not cry. Though she might rage about the outcome, she never once regretted saving that ungrateful bastard's life. But how dare he return to court! How dare Edward accept him! He should have been safe in Brittany long months before. It was to that end she had cast aside her pride . . .

Marged gasped and spun about as she felt an unexpected drag on her peach satin train. She cried out with shock as she beheld the broad padded shoulders and narrow waist of a scarlet doublet trimmed with silver. So distinctive was the clothing, she had no need to penetrate the gloom to identify its owner.

"Leave me!"

"No."

"Leave me! I command it!"

"Does dallying in the royal bed bestow the right to command?"

Nerves taut as steel, Marged slapped his cheek. "How dare you insult me!"

Rolfe seized her wrists, pulling them down, imprisoning her before him. "I'll do exactly as I please, lady."

"Haven't you always?"

"Not always."

"Forgive me. 'Twas a rare occasion I overlooked."

They glared at each other while Marged struggled in vain to free her wrists. Instead of releasing her, Rolfe tightened his grip until she gasped in pain and stopped her struggles.

"Why did you leave me for him?"

Eyes wide with shock, not believing what she heard, Marged could only stare at his faint image dancing before her tear-filled eyes.

"Answer me!" He shook her, spilling her tears.

"You're not owed an explanation."

"We'll stay here half the night if necessary, until I get one."

"Edward will come looking for me."

"But not diligently, if I know our handsome King. If he can't find you soon, he'll choose another."

Because his odious remark came very close to the truth, Marged's rage boiled anew. "Damn you! How dare you insult me! Isn't it enough to flaunt yourself with every bitch in Edward's court?"

"Because you limit yourself to the King hardly sanctifies the action."

"Think you I stay with him out of pleasure?"

"Yes—among other more obvious rewards."

"Perhaps you're aware of the reason you're free, instead of rotting above Micklegate Bar."

"I heard some most satisfying gossip that removed all doubt from my mind."

His snarled words chilled her blood. She blinked, going ice cold, shuddering in his grip. "You knew?" she whispered brokenly. "You knew, yet you didn't leave when you had the chance? Oh, why did you insult me by throwing away my precious gift?"

Approaching voices alerted Rolfe to a strolling couple. He pulled Marged with him, propelling her between the ornamental quince borders. Satisfied that they could not be overheard, he pulled her close enough so she could see his face in the murky light spilling from the ballroom.

"I waited for your return. Even when they told me you'd gone back to him, I waited. When I learned how you'd purchased my release, I waited still . . ."

"Why?"

"I thought, once the time was up, you'd leave him."

"It was too soon. I had to be sure you were safe. Though Edward's generally honest, Warwick is not. Craft and greed are attributes of his, or had you forgotten?"

"'Twas not with Warwick you slept," Rolfe growled, giving her an angry shake. "Edward had more to offer than I, I've always known that. Poor fool that I am, I thought our love to be true and the passion we shared would bind us for eternity. Now, no doubt, dear Edward shares the same magnificent gift."

Marged snorted in rage, trying to free her hands to strike him, but he gripped her wrists relentlessly.

"Hear me out, damn it! Don't revile me for doing what you yourself enjoy. Our generous King has even suggested that I might choose a suitable wife from amongst the nobility. I too recognize a bargain when I see it."

"I hate you!"

He gritted his teeth as her angry words sliced like hot steel. He had expected no less, yet the pain was still severe. She lashed out at him in retaliation because he had stripped away her lofty excuses for taking Edward as a lover. But the triumph gave him small pleasure.

"Though I'm not yet over the hurt, I don't condemn you for using your beauty to secure a place at court."

"That's most understanding of you, my lord. What other kind sops do you have to soothe me?"

"Damn you, Marged Bowen," Rolfe uttered through clenched

teeth. "No other woman ever made me so furious, yet so . . ." His muttered words faded before the sentence was complete.

Mentally, Marged completed his utterance. She raised her head, longing to see his face, to read the expression in his eyes. "So?" she prompted when he said no more.

He gazed down at her, tremors coursing through his body at her nearness. Emotion shot between them, drawing them close. She brushed against his fine court doublet, her draperies fluttering about his shoulders.

"So . . . terribly disturbed . . . after all this . . ."

Heavy footsteps crunched on the gravel walk. Whoever came from the Hall could not fail to see them standing here in a virtual embrace. A familiar broad shadow moved past the espaliered pear trees on the west wall, coming closer. Gold glinted on the man's peacock-blue velvet hat, dappled with torchlight.

Desperate to save Marged from Edward's vengeance, Rolfe had no choice but to inflict pain. The King would see them any second. Taking Marged in his arms, Rolfe swallowed, reluctant still to voice such cutting remarks. His gruff tone carrying through the garden, he said, "Your gown's so enticing—at first I thought you naked. 'Tis worthy raiment for our Ned's light o' love."

Marged gasped in shock, her heart fluttering close to her throat as he continued relentlessly.

"Aye, dressed like that, you make a right comely bawd. Do you think our generous King would object to sharing you with me one last time?"

Dragging her hands free, Marged struck him. Her legs quivered with emotion until she thought she would fall to the grass. "Damn you! Don't ever speak to me again!"

"The pleasure's all mine. Good night, sweet lady."

Marged swayed with shock as he bowed mockingly before disappearing between the dripping bushes. Then she cried out in alarm as a large hand touched her shoulder.

Edward said, "Too much wine spoils our Breton's chivalry. Ah, well, naught is lost, is it, love? Come, we must dance again. All the court's wondering where you are."

Thankfully, Marged turned into Edward's embrace, relinquishing herself to a gale of tears. Had Rolfe known Edward approached? Had he said those hurtful things to protect her from the King's anger? There she was again, snatching at straws. Angrily she dashed away her tears.

"Yes, it's growing cold outdoors. Besides, that boor's ruined my humor."

"Nay, sweetheart, have no fear. Your beloved Ned will soon restore the balance." Laughing, Edward swept her into his arms, spinning her about before he pressed a deep, searching kiss on her icy lips.

A few minutes later, Rolfe emerged from the dripping foliage, shaking moisture from his doublet. His face grim, he watched the two figures heading toward the lighted Hall, arms wrapped about each other's waist. "Now we're even, Lady Marged," he uttered through clenched teeth. "Your life for mine."

Then he spun on his heel and strode from the garden.

eighteen

AS THE ROYAL cavalcade approached Greyfriars Monastery from the south, the last vestige of morning mist lifted from the rooftops. The autumn sun made the copper gilt weathercock on St. Paul's steeple shine dazzlingly. At this early hour the London streets were virtually deserted. The occasional passerby gaped in awe at the richly dressed lords and ladies mounted on their sleek horses caparisoned in velvet and Spanish leather, without recognizing the golden-haired giant in the sad tawny doublet as their King.

The royal hunting party clattered through the cobbled streets, harnesses jingling in the morning quiet. Before they reached the northern gate, their racket was eclipsed by the peals of church bells tolling the hour, summoning all laggards from their beds.

It was at Edward's whim that this impromptu hunting party had been arranged. Daily his ministers pressed him to seriously consider an advantageous foreign marriage. Since his ascension to the throne he had also discovered that the state coffers were woefully depleted. And despite his overwhelmingly loyal reception in the nation's capital, Edward was disturbed by frequent reports of unrest from around the country, where dissident Lancastrians kept matters in ferment. His nineteen-year-old mind revolted against the pressure of constant battle between pleasure and duty. As was often to be the case in years to come, on this fine October day Edward chose pleasure instead of duty.

A pace behind the broad-shouldered King and his friends rode Marged on a milk-white gelding. Excitement stirred her blood, for she was eager to be free of the noisy city. And not only did she rejoice over the opportunity to ride into the countryside. This morning, Edward, in a most amiable mood in anticipation of the day's hunt, had promised she could visit Bowenford before the week was out.

To her relief, Marged had not seen Rolfe since that painfully humiliating incident in the Palace garden. Each time she relived what had promised such sweetness yet produced only pain, she shuddered.

She still chilled when she pictured Rolfe as he had been that night, so mockingly handsome in his fluted scarlet doublet, there was not a woman in the Hall who could take her eyes off him. Tears pricked her eyes as she forced herself to repeat his insulting words. Too much drink or not, his words had wounded her sorely. Her heart ached when she recalled her foolishness in thinking that former bonds of love would bind them forever.

Freshly determined to enjoy her final day in London, she thrust aside those painful thoughts. Now that they had passed beyond the city gates into the surrounding countryside, she became tinglingly aware of October's early-morning fragrance, a combination of damp earth, moss, and decaying leaves. On either side, the burgeoning woodlands were tinged russet and gold. How very different from the Marches was this land beyond London. Her spirits lifted and she quickened her horse's pace, pulling away from the others as they cantered across the browning land.

Edward noted her flight and chose to overlook it. He considered it safe for Marged to ride alone. Since de Bretayne's reprehensible behavior on the night of the ball, he was no longer a threat. This was the reason he had finally granted

Marged permission to visit the Marches. If the Breton's reaction had come to order, Edward could not have chosen better words with which to extinguish the last smoldering embers of her love.

When at last they set off about the chase, Marged was out in front. The autumn wind swept through her garments, uncomfortably chilly beneath these ancient trees where the light was as dim as night. Shouting and blowing horns, the excited hunters pursued their quarry through the sprawling woodland, driving the buck deeper into the forest. On her saddle, Marged carried a small hunting bow sheathed in murrey velvet and decorated with Edward's personal badge; it was his latest gift to her. Eager to get off a shot at the disappearing stag, she was startled when Balthazar, Edward's dog, turned abruptly in front of her, causing her horse to rear and land in a pit hidden by brush. The horse screamed in terror, and in a flash Marged was out of the saddle. She knelt to examine the shredded and bloody forelegs, while the huntsmen galloped past, ignoring her plight, their sights set on their King and his frightened quarry. Cursing them beneath her breath, Marged tried to comfort her injured beast, who had calmed somewhat and now stood snorting and tossing his head while blood puddled about his hooves, reddening the turf.

Loud crashing through the adjacent underbrush alerted her to the arrival of a rider. As she turned around, a large black stallion plunged from the thicket of elderberry and beach saplings, coming to a halt on the edge of the clearing. Relief was soon replaced by apprehension as Marged saw it was Rolfe who had come to her rescue. The rest of his small party gradually emerged from the trees.

"Are you injured, Lady Marged?" he asked in concern as he galloped to her side. When she shook her head, he dismounted and knelt to examine the horse's forelegs.

"Need he be destroyed?" Marged asked. "He's a good beast."

Their eyes locked as they knelt on either side of the frightened horse, whose white sides heaved tremendously while he suffered the pain of their examination.

"Possibly not. Knowing he's a gift from your beloved will doubtless give him added strength."

Marged's mouth set in a grim line at his sarcasm, and she said no more. She got up, patting the horse's velvety nose in comfort.

When Rolfe's examination was complete, he called for one of his body servants to bring a wine flask and cloth. Stiffly, Marged waited, gentling the gelding, watching as he washed the wounds and dried them in order to see the extent of the horse's injuries. The slashes below the knee proved not to be as deep or as numerous as expected. A smile of relief brightened her face and Marged slid her arms about the gelding's thick neck, giving him a reassuring hug.

Rolfe watched her actions unsmilingly, his heart wrenching at the need even to lay eyes upon her. God, would that he had already left for his promised reward—a lesser manor in Buckinghamshire—then he would not have needed to face her again.

"You'll need another mount. I'll have one fetched."

"Nay, all pleasure in the hunt's gone," Marged declined. "I'm turning back."

Rolfe strode to the small party awaiting him. "Go ahead, I'll join you later. If you don't hurry, you'll miss the best sport. Nay, pout not, Lilith," he admonished the plain but eager lady to whom Edward had suggested he plight his troth. Lilith Hardyng's father owned a goodly piece of Buckinghamshire.

"Are you sure you'll join me later?" Lilith inquired doubtfully. In the short time she had known this handsome, exciting Breton, on more than one occasion she had doubted his fidelity. Lilith stared hostilely at Marged, who waited beside the injured horse, her marigold skirts splattered with blood. The King's mistress presented a worthy temptation to so expert a womanizer. Lilith's frown deepened, and her budlike mouth pursed into an unlovely button.

"Of course I'll join you. Have you ever known me to abandon the chase?"

Lilith smiled tentatively, unsure of the exact meaning behind his statement. Blowing Rolfe a kiss, she reluctantly wheeled her mount about to follow the chase.

He waited until the party had disappeared between the tawny trees before he turned his attention back to Marged. With an oath he leaped to her side. "You fool woman, what are you doing?" he demanded as he saw her tearing strips from her silk surcoat to bind the horse's wounds.

"Bandaging his legs. What does it look like I'm doing?"

Rolfe muttered beneath his breath and hastily produced a linen cloth, which he tore into strips. In silence they completed the task, tightly binding the slashed flesh and partially stanching the flow of blood.

"You've ruined your gown."

"It doesn't matter." She looked at him so stonily that hot rage shot through his veins.

"Of course not—Edward's ever generous. I'd forgotten."

"I didn't ask you to stay. In fact, I'd prefer that you followed your sulky hunting companion. The way she gazes at you tells me she'll be devastated until your return. Is she your intended bride?"

"Edward encourages the match."

Marged snatched the reins from the ground and wound them around her wrist. "I'll take him to the closest village."

"I'll come with you."

"No! I don't want you to come with me!"

He ignored her protest. "The poor beast shouldn't be ridden. Here, you can ride with me. The stallion can easily carry both our weights."

When Marged would have stood her ground to argue the point, Rolfe seized her, his grip like steel. She gasped in surprise to find herself seated ungently on his saddlebow. A moment later he had mounted behind her. Clasping his arm about her waist, he tugged on his horse's reins, pointing the black stallion south.

Leading the injured beast, Rolfe headed along the leafy path in the direction of the nearest village.

"I could have managed by myself."

"You've no need to prove yourself to me. I already know you're as brave as any man," he retorted bitterly.

"What's that supposed to mean?"

"Anything you wish. Now shut up. I've no desire to quarrel all the way to Hampstead."

"Neither have I."

They completed their journey in a stony silence.

In the small hamlet beyond the woods, Rolfe settled the gelding at the inn before returning to London.

The sun was high and its warmth caressed her softly as a summer's day, yet Marged dared not relax her stiff shoulders. Rolfe's green and tawny doublet brushed her marigold habit. If she relaxed her spine another notch, she would be leaning against his body! She shuddered at the idea, not wholly sure it was an expression of distaste.

They clopped several miles farther in silence until, unable to bear this unnatural silence, Rolfe growled angrily, "Enough of this idiocy! Can we not at least treat each other like human beings? Considering what there's been between us in the past, I cannot believe this ridiculous formality."

"No, considering what's gone before, I'd have expected you to tumble me beneath the first hedge."

"Do you know naught but mockery?"

"Whatever insult I make can scarcely surpass your gemlike utterances, my lord."

"Always you speak in riddles. What utterances do you refer to?"

"The insulting speech you delivered in the Palace garden. Or did you think I'd have forgotten by now? Unlike you, I didn't overindulge in the wine cups."

"Nor did I."

Marged gasped, her cheeks flaming crimson. "You weren't drunk!"

"No."

Tears throbbed to the surface and she repeatedly tried to swallow them down. "That makes it all the more hateful."

"Listen to me, you fool woman," Rolfe cried, seizing her upper arm in a viselike grip. "Do you think I wanted to say those things to you? Do you think I could have said them, however drunk I was, had it not been necessary?"

"Necessary?"

"Aye, necessary! Edward was already on the path. He would have had to be blind not to see you in my arms. I insulted you to save your hide!"

"'Tis an easy thing to say now," she whispered, her voice choked with tears.

"Had you spoken to me before, instead of avoiding me, you'd have heard it a week ago."

The jogging movement of the horse kept pace with the throbbing hurt in her veins. Marged gulped and swallowed, trying to keep her pain silent. It was to no avail. Uttering a growl of anger at her continuing hostility, Rolfe wrenched her face around, his hand bruising her small chin. Through a blur of tears she gazed at his bitter features, set as if carved from granite, his mouth a straight line to match his scowling brows, his eyes dark with anger.

"Aye, tears," she managed through trembling lips as a look of surprise crossed his hard face. "Tears for all that was beautiful between us and is now faded and corrupt."

"You thought I meant to call you whore?"

"It wouldn't be the first time."

Rolfe hung his head, for he could not deny the charge. "You left me for him," he defended himself stubbornly, his voice harsh. "And that wasn't the first time, either."

"You know why I went to Edward. You also know why I stayed with him. God knows, you're the reason I'm there still!"

Not trusting himself with speech, Rolfe released her, noting the angry manner in which she flounced from his touch and straightened her garments. Never had this short journey to London seemed so many thousands of miles long. There was little he could say to remove the seeds of bitterness already sown between them.

At last they were through the city gate and jostling their way down the crowded thoroughfare leading to the Palace. Rolfe was exceedingly thankful when he finally relinquished his burden. He stopped to arrange for the gelding to be brought into the city. He knew Edward would wish it, for the blooded animal was valuable.

"Thank you . . . Rolfe. You needn't have put yourself out on my behalf."

He managed a tight smile in reply. "I've made arrangements for the beast's welfare. I can see how fond you are of him. Don't worry, he'll likely be back in harness before long, with no permanent harm done."

She nodded stiffly and turned from him before betraying

tears disarmed her. Those steps toward the stone archway to the courtyard seemed to last forever. As she walked, Marged was conscious of his gaze boring into her back; she steeled herself not to turn around.

When she finally entered the building, she stole a glance at the grassy mound beyond the wall, but Rolfe had already gone.

The court returned to the city in early afternoon, allowing ample time to dress for the grand masque at Greenwich Palace.

Upon his arrival, Edward sent Marged a note of condolence. She crumpled the paper into a ball and pitched it on the fire. She did not know if during the chase the King had been aware of her horse's injury. A disturbingly unpleasant feeling told her that even had he witnessed her dilemma, Edward would have dispatched one of his friends to assist her, rather than lose the buck he pursued.

Angrily, Marged swished about the room. Ever since she returned this afternoon, this vast stone palace felt as oppressive as a prison. Why did she stay in London, forever at Edward's beck and call? Tonight, if she wished, she could be on the road to Wales. It was not fair to feel hostility toward the young King, she decided at length. Edward was no ordinary man. Kings did not assist at accidents. She was expecting too much of him. While she pleased him, Edward had the power to grant all that she desired. He had already showered her with jewels, with sumptuous gowns, with a blooded horse; perhaps mansions, or entire estates, could be hers if she deliberately set out to please him.

Marged clenched her hands in an agony of longing as she stared at the trees tinged with copper, bronze, and scarlet in the misty distance. Beautiful though riches were, they were not what she really wanted. Her soul thirsted for the cold wind blowing off the mountains, for the fresh tang of the Wye and the wild tumult of Marcher storms . . .

She bowed her head and wept quietly for the ache in her heart. From out of a Marcher storm had ridden the one man capable of possessing her heart. Her deceiving mouth told such grand lies; her heart and blood alone admitted the truth.

* * *

Ghostly mist wreathed the Thames as the royal barges glided toward Greenwich. A cold wind blew off the water, making Marged nestle deeper into her marten-lined cloak. This final sumptuous entertainment, to which she had looked forward, now filled her with dread; Rolfe would be there. Yesterday her beautiful gown of rose damask edged in ermine had appeared so lovely; tonight she found no pleasure in it. If only she had not seen him again, perhaps she could have looked to the future in better spirits. During that endless nightmare journey this afternoon—constantly brushing against the hot strength of his body, feeling the touch of his hands upon her and his eyes boring into her very soul—the final delusions she had nurtured were destroyed. Too many poignant memories of what once had been between them flooded back. Now she must face a truth she had long denied; wherever she went, or with whom, Rolfe de Bretayne's disturbing presence went with her.

Greenwich Palace looked ablaze from the water. Liveried pages, holding flaming torches aloft, waited at the water steps to light the way for the velvet-canopied barges that slipped into shore where they disgorged their laughing, bejeweled passengers for the splendid royal revel. Twoscore trumpeters played a fanfare as the royal barge approached, bedecked with a gold-fringed canopy emblazoned with the royal arms.

Men knelt before the King on the steps, touching the fur-lined hem of his cloak. He greeted each man by name. Edward had the unusual ability to retain the name, rank, and district of each worthy presented to him, a talent that elicited beams of delight from those who were royally remembered.

Now Edward glanced about, and she shrank even farther into the shadows, knowing he looked for her. It had been his intention that Marged travel with him on the royal barge, but she had purposely tarried until she saw it pull away from shore. Now he must know she had already arrived, for his was the last craft to dock. She did not care. A new recklessness coursed through her veins. Tomorrow she would head west with the fresh scent of the mountains in the air. Before the week was out, she would be home. And never again would she leave Bowenford.

Inside the lighted palace, the vast rooms were alive with bejeweled velvets, gleaming satins, and soft, downy fur. Exotic perfumes mingled with the enticing smells of spiced dishes, smoke from the torches, and other less pleasant city smells, for the wind carried the stink of Fleet ditch.

Milling courtiers danced and drank, gossiped and gamed. Marged watched them, feeling totally detached, barely noticing when they spoke to her or tried to draw her interest in their raucous jests. Throughout the lengthy banquet, while she picked at the spiced meats washed down with choice wines of red and white, she was aware of one man alone. Rolfe, arrayed in his red doublet, his black hair gleaming like ebony in the torchlight, watched her from his place down the table. He was almost seated below the salt, being virtually level with the grand, castellated silver cellar. Tonight he was outranked by the multitude who bore grander titles, both inherited and awarded to them by a grateful monarch.

In a daze she gulped wine from her crystal goblet, clenching her slender hands about the twisted stem. Why did he stare at her so? God, did he seek to devour her with his eyes? After his afternoon's heated encounter, she would have thought all discourse between them was over.

Presently a great, gilded marzipan galleon in full sail was placed on the table before her, obscuring Rolfe from view. Only then was Marged able to breath a great sigh of relief and eat her gooseberry syllabub with a vestige of pleasure. The strolling minstrel's songs too became more entertaining.

From his grand carved chair beneath the gold-fringed canopy, Edward smiled at her, waving his hand in greeting before he jovially indicated the party of colorfully dressed mummers who were tumbling into the Hall. Marged forced a replying smile to her stiff mouth, while refusing to acknowledge the penetrating stare from another quarter.

While she watched a painted wooden galleon being wheeled into place, Marged's temples throbbed. Ten maidens, wearing gossamer-thin sarcenet shot with silver, floated across the room. When the curvacious damsels weaved before the battery of stout candles placed in front of the timber galleon, their garments became virtually transparent.

A gasp of excitement rippled about the bannered Hall as

men leaned forward, mouths agape, breath quickening as they watched the tantalizing view of rounded breasts and thighs.

The man to Marged's right offered her a bunch of grapes. Leaning across her, his drunken gaze lecherous, he plucked a frosted grape and placed it in her mouth, allowing his fingers to trail sensuously over her lips. Marged knew the nobleman only as Hal, one of Edward's favorites. Color flamed in her cheeks at the liberty he took, yet because of his high rank she refrained from rebuking him publicly.

Several braziers, giving off clouds of pink smoke, created a heady, perfumed fog that drifted to the rafters. From this billowing cloud appeared the likeness of King Neptune, standing on the galleon's deck, clad in a tunic of glittering iridescent scales, his trident at the ready. He delivered a lengthy monologue about the perils of the deep while the maidens danced through the pink smoke, singing softly, their white arms and legs wreathing sensuously to the background accompaniment of viols.

So strong was the smoke's spicy perfume that Marged's queasy stomach revolted. Excusing herself hastily, she bolted for the garderobe adjacent to the Hall.

In the chill stone room she retched miserably, overcome by a wave of disgust for the false gaiety of her life. Why had she stayed in London this long? She had been an utter fool to think that by her presence she was sparing the ungrateful Breton from the headsman's ax. He seemed well enough in Edward's favor, despite the fact that he had spurned her selflessly given gift. And now, because she had loved him so well, because she had never doubted his eventual understanding of her motive behind the action, she was locked in loveless servitude to England's King. Damn Rolfe for his arrogance in daring to insult her when she had cast aside her pride to buy his safety! Must she be cursed forever by loving and hating him at the same time?

When she felt sufficiently recovered, Marged went into the corridor and asked a servant to bring her a cup of water, which was mixed with wine, a necessary precaution to ward off ills from the tainted city water. As she sipped the sweetish liquid, Marged wondered what she should do. It was far too early to go back to Whitehall; the barges would not leave before dawn. Resting her pounding head against the cold stone wall, Marged closed her eyes in an effort to retreat from the throbbing ache in her temples. Fortunately the flaring torch lighting this corridor was at the corner, isolating her in a dim sea of oblivion.

Marged was not sure when she became aware of the hand on her shoulder. So locked in misery was she, she gradually grew aware of the touch as one who slowly wakes from sleep. Only when those firm hands drew her slightly away from the comforting support of cold stone, only when she encountered a solid bulk pleasantly scented with rose and musk, did she gasp aloud in surprise.

"Edward!"

"Nay, lady, sorry to disappoint you."

Eyes rounding in horror, Marged found herself looking into Rolfe's blue eyes, showing almost black in the shadowed corridor. So comforting had his touch been, in her confused state she had not known to reject it . . .

"Take your hands off me."

"No."

Marged gasped, her legs trembling beneath her sumptuous rose brocade skirts. "How dare you! I've merely to call the guard."

"I don't advise it."

Swiftly, Rolfe pulled her into a shadowed alcove, clapping his hand over her mouth as a servant bustled past, bearing a covered tureen.

"What ails you?" Tentatively he slackened his hand, ready to clamp it back if she attempted to call for help.

"Our afternoon misadventure filled me with disgust. 'Tis over that I'm sick!"

In the darkness he grinned at her explosive words. "I thought maybe our Ned had seeded your belly."

"Oh!" Marged tried swinging at him, but Rolfe deftly caught her wrist, pulling the back of her body against his chest again.

"A natural mistake. You must be more understanding."

"Why do you insist on seeking me out?"

"I don't know. 'Tis getting to be a bad habit of mine." He chuckled as he drew her closer to the heat of his body.

"You're drunk!"

"Just enough to provide the needed courage."

"Courage for what?"

"Can't you guess?"

A ripple of shock went through Marged's body. "I don't want to try."

He shrugged. She felt the movement against her back.

"Have it your way. Come, we've little time to lose," he urged conspiratorially as a servant recrossed the corridor, bound for the Hall.

Marged knew she should kick him, punch him, scream for assistance. Despite the deafening racket of the entertainment inside the Hall, surely a guard or a servant would come to her aid. She should scream for help—but she did not. That air of reckless abandon that had overcome her earlier this evening flooded back, wiping out every vestige of reason.

"Where are you taking me?" she whispered breathlessly, drawing back of her own accord as someone crossed the corridor directly beneath the flaring sconce.

"There are a hundred rooms from which to choose."

The wine. Yes, it must have been more potent than she thought, she argued desperately as she walked meekly with him into the darkness. Why was she doing this? She hated this arrogant Breton like poison. He was a rough mercenary, unschooled in gentle manners. Yet he was the only man she had truly desired in her entire life, the only man she had truly loved. Not handsome Edward with his crown and riches, nor any of those titled court wastrels who laughed too heartily and bedded far too many women, but this Breton from an unknown land across the Channel.

They passed a long window where bright moonlight spilled silver arrows across the floor. Marged stopped, shaking her head, trying to muster an ounce of reason.

"You're more beautiful than ever," he breathed sincerely.

She stared up at him. His face lay in shadow, the bulk of his shoulders throwing vast black shapes across the wall. A million disturbing thoughts seethed in her brain as blood pounding through her veins won a mad race to vanquish her last shreds of reason. Words formed on her lips, sensible protests against this boldness, denouncements of the sheer madness behind this folly, yet the only words she spoke formed a question she had never thought to ask him again.

"Do you still love me, Rolfe?"

"Oh, sweetheart, more than I ever did before."

His husky reply throbbed through her ears. It was a full minute before she realized what he had said. He did not move to take her in his arms, nor did she go to him. They stood apart in the moonlight, two statues locked in a secret world of pain and delight.

"I'm leaving tomorrow." Marged surprised them both with her flat statement.

"It doesn't matter. There are many hours before dawn."

Raucous laughter echoed down the corridor, shattering the spell. Marged shuddered and blinked, the courtier's hollow laughter affecting her like ice water trickling down her spine. She had been on the verge of going wherever Rolfe led, of doing whatever he asked.

"No," she said, finding returning courage. This was the man who had deserted her, who had insulted her, who had caused her grief . . . "Not now. It's too late."

His angry intake of breath sounded like hissing steam. In a flash he seized her and half-carried her with him. She cried out futilely, ignoring the ache of passion weakening her limbs. Her shrill cries bounced mockingly off the stone walls. Those who heard them considered the screams naught but loveplay from some fulsome maiden pursued by an amorous gallant, for the ladies frequenting Edward's court were scarcely virginal.

The first room they reached was unlocked. Rolfe thrust open the heavy wooden door, pushing Marged before him into the room. A startled maid leaped from her trundle bed, modestly clutching the bedcovers about her.

"Your lady's given me permission to use her room," he growled, flinging the girl a sovereign. "Go next door until I call you."

Protesting tearfully, yet making sure she retrieved the coin, the frightened maid fled without a backward glance.

"Be quiet," Rolfe commanded as Marged opened her mouth to scream. "I'm only doing what Edward himself commands."

"I don't believe you!"

"He told me to hotly pursue the lady of my choice, to woo her sweetly. But if that approach failed, he suggested I take her by force, saying the result by morning would be the same."

Marged could not dispute his statement. Those words perfectly reflected Edward's light philosophy. Hadn't he himself sought to take her at knifepoint in the walled garden at Choatesworth Manor?

Rolfe smiled cruelly. "Sound familiar? I meant no insult to His Grace."

"He thought you wanted that plain little baggage who hunted beside you!"

"Agreed—I cannot help the misunderstanding."

"He'll have you clapped in prison!"

"How will he know? Surely you don't intend to tell him."

Marged began to tremble as fear and excitement coursed through her veins. She knew that if she revealed Rolfe's actions to Edward, she might be denied her visit home—or worse. Edward appeared outwardly calm and gay, yet one was never sure when the famous Plantagenet temper might erupt. And of late she had not pleased him overmuch.

"You bastard! How sure of yourself you are!"

"It's strange, but your insults have a curiously familiar ring about them."

Though Marged glared defiantly at him, she was inwardly beginning to grow desperate. When Rolfe shot the bolt on the door, locking it, she darted to the far side of the room, her anger mounting as he dogged her every movement with ease. Finally tiring of the game, he grabbed her, ending her pointless flight.

"You should have learned by now that your strength is no match for mine."

Panic rippled through her limbs as she tried to resist him and found her resistance crumbling. "Do you intend to rape me?" she hissed, stiffening in his grasp.

Lazily he shook his head, his humor restored now that he was master of the situation. "Surely it won't be necessary."

Marged's mouth opened and closed soundlessly as she bit back the angry words.

"I thought not."

They stood toe to toe, his strong hands bruising her upper arms as their gazes locked. Though Marged fought against the reaction, she shuddered as she looked deeply into his eyes and recalled all those other times when delight and passion had turned their blue tint lazily soft.

"Don't force me to bend you to my will," he rasped, inclining her forward.

"You assume I still want you, but you're wrong!" Marged shouted.

"Am I? You always were a poor liar." Swiftly, Rolfe broke her final resistance, jerking her forward till their bodies pressed together. "Now tell me how much you don't want me."

Temper darkened Marged's green eyes and her nostrils flared wider, reminding him of a lovely, high-spirited mare. Her hand was raised to strike him, but Rolfe quickly vanquished her, pinioning her wrists behind her back.

Suddenly, without knowing why, Marged's full red lips began to quiver, her dark-lashed eyes started to fill with tears.

Now it was Rolfe's turn to shudder. "Dear God in heaven, I can't endure much more," he rasped, trembling as if possessed with an ague.

The sheer emotion in his anguished words took away her breath. Then Rolfe drew Marged from the rush-strewn floor, lifting her gently until she was positioned against that probing furnace of desire which leaped anew as their bodies met in intimate embrace. A sob escaped her lips as she finally relinquished her will to him. This was like a terrible, wonderful dream. Beyond his broad shoulders she saw the unfamiliar room with its massive furniture, the paneled walls burnished with flickering fireglow. Everything seemed unreal, and the most unreal part of all was the man who imprisoned her in his arms, his breathing shallow, his handsome face grim.

"Is this really happening?" she murmured, afraid she was dreaming.

"Aye, it's real."

"You love me still?"

"I love you still."

"Just like before?"

"No, far more than before."

Marged's surging blood screamed so loudly, her thoughts became a hopeless tangle. Words that made sense no longer came to her mind. Rolfe freed her hands. Reaching for his face, Marged sobbed deeply as she stroked his wonderful hot mouth, his lean cheekbones, recalling all the times she had delighted in the burning smoothness of his olive skin.

"Say all the pain's over, the hate—"

Rolfe silenced her ravings with his mouth. Like a bolt of lightning, emotion sped between them as their lips met. Shuddering, he let her down to the rushes, no longer able to stand upright and bear her weight.

"Nothing's changed," Marged gasped in wonder.

"Did you really think it would?" he asked, pulling her against him.

"Oh, yes. I lied so desperately to myself."

His smile was grim as he moved her to the great canopied bed with its tasseled purple hangings. "I know. So did I."

Marged gazed up at him, seeing his handsome features tenderly muted, the grim harshness dissolving before her eyes. Desire blazed in his blue eyes, which contrasted palely with his sun-bronzed skin. For the thousandth time she experienced a flicker of surprise at seeing such pale eyes within his dark face. Then all thought was eclipsed as he lay beside her on the embroidered counterpane.

"I don't care about tomorrow . . . or next week. Perchance I'm already dead," Marged raved as he pulled her close. "Oh, Rolfe, Rolfe, love me, please, please, love me."

His mouth came down hard on hers. Desperately she reached up, driving into his lips, his teeth, seeking his flaming tongue. Marged trembled as he plundered her mouth in symbolic union. No longer did she question her actions. She did not even remember that she had formerly declared hatred for him. All that mattered now was the heavenly pleasure of having him in her arms again.

His stirred manhood probed her clothing, creating an overwhelming wave of desire. Tears spilled from Marged's eyes as she tangled her fingers in his crisp black hair, dragging his face down to hers. She welded her mouth to his, letting the salty tears trickle between their lips to sting their bruised flesh.

She could barely contain her shivers of anticipation as he fumbled with the fastenings of her brocade gown, his fingers clumsy about the gold lacings. Aching with terrible desire, he could scarcely endure the suspense until her beautiful breasts were bared to his gaze. Though he tried to keep his touch gentle, he crushed her flesh, his fingers imparting pain with the pleasure.

Aroused to the point of barely feeling pain, Marged thrust forward into his eager hands, desperate to know again the inflaming caresses she had long dreamed about. When his mouth closed about her erect nipple, she cried out in a surging torment of desire.

He swept the rich brocade from her golden skin, slowly uncovering the perfection of her body. The memory of perfect curves, of the pulsing sweetness of her passion, had tormented his every dream.

Tears came to her eyes when she saw the sheer adoration in his face. Then it was Marged's turn to relive her own erotic memories; the intimate details of his splendidly virile body had haunted her days and nights. With mounting excitement she unfastened his lavish doublet, created in the latest fashion by one of London's master tailors; she cast the garment aside without a glance. His expensive lace shirt followed. As she ran her hands across his dark, matted chest, she sighed in sheer pleasure. She stroked his broad shoulders, smooth-fleshed and muscular, thrilling anew to the touch of his body. He was the most perfect creation of all. There was no need to gild such magnificence with costly court raiment. Reverently she kissed his flesh, drawing her mouth along the line of his shoulders, down his neck to his chest. When she reached his dark nipple she gently nibbled the flesh, thrilling at his sharp intake of breath.

"How much I've missed loving you," she whispered.

Rolfe's hands tangled in her flowing hair as he said, "Not nearly as much as I've missed loving you."

Growing impatient, Marged worked down his scarlet hose, deftly unlacing the points from his outer garments. She flung aside the doublet and shirt, trembling with anticipation as she forced down the gleaming scarlet fabric, which fit tightly as a glove to his smooth, high buttocks, and revealed the rippling muscles of his belly and thighs. At last the seat of his passion was unleashed. Shudders of desire swept over her as she gazed enraptured at his towering flesh, throbbing, thrusting toward her, silently beseeching. Heavily engorged with blood, his organ was so smoothly perfect, Marged could scarcely bring herself to touch him, almost afraid of her own mounting passion. When her fingers finally encircled his pulsating flesh, she gasped in delight. No other man could ever arouse her to such intense desire. Marged bent and traced the contours of his blazing flesh with her tongue. She bestowed butterfly-soft kisses, knowing he was fighting to endure the terrible delight of her caresses.

Rolfe wrenched her mouth away. Gripping her face between his hands, he croaked, "Sweet, it's more pleasure than I can stand."

His tormented admission made Marged smile. She was glad to have been able to give him pleasure beyond endurance. "How much I love you," she whispered as he enfolded her in his arms. And she sighed as she buried her face in the heated hollow of his neck.

He gently caressed Marged's smooth back, tracing his fingers along her spine, fully aware of the shudders rippling through her body in response to his touch. He laid her softly on her back, where he caressed the length of her silk-smooth flesh with his mouth and tongue, wanting to bring her to more heat than she had ever known.

Marged's breasts trembled with passion as Rolfe's hungering mouth sought out the secret places of her body. Flashes of heat seared every inch of her flesh. Eagerly she reached for him, capturing his velvety smooth manhood in trembling fingers, marveling at the sheer steel strength of it.

At her gasp of wonder, Rolfe smiled. It was hard to endure the pleasure of her hands; tension mounted unbearably in his blood until, like a dam bursting, he was swept into a heightened state of arousal. His caresses strengthened as he probed the blazing core of her passion. All the sweetness, the marvelous perfumed heat of that mysterious cavern, was his for the taking.

Marged shuddered beneath his probing hands as the aching between her legs became almost unbearable. "Love me . . . love me . . . love me . . ." she raved as his mouth swept from her shoulders to her neck, her lips.

Rolfe kissed her hungrily and positioned her on the bed, his actions instinctive, for he gave no conscious thought to the spreading of her silken thighs. He was thinking only of the sweet relief when he finally slid inside her. When he entered the furnace of her body, Marged's anguished cries of delight assured him he was eagerly received. Rhythmic shudders carried them dangerously close to fulfillment, though they both struggled to endure. Pleasure flooded her veins, nearly drowning her in ecstasy as Rolfe moved carefully inside her, trying to allow her as much delight as possible before she succumbed to the desire blazing between them.

Mouths locked, bodies welded close, grimly they approached the final stage. Great shudders wracked Marged's body as Rolfe repeatedly took her to the brink of fulfillment and drew back, forcing her to hold on to a fragile element of control that he himself found slipping away. Finally, when Marged thought she could not endure a moment longer, Rolfe reentered her, plunging deep, his burning flesh igniting a wave of emotion.

Marged screamed aloud in a frenzy of pleasure. Up she soared, taking Rolfe with her, rejoicing in the completeness of their union. Together they reached the pinnacle, experiencing more pleasure than ever before. They plunged into the abyss, falling, twisting over and over until they came down to earth, bodies softly fulfilled and aching with love.

{ *nineteen* }

MOONLIGHT SPLASHED THE Thames with silver when the royal barges pulled away from Greenwich Palace; long before they reached Whitehall, the moon had waned and dawn pierced the clouds with gilded spears of pink.

Marged sat beside Rolfe, aching to wrap her arms about him, yet not daring to display affection for him in public. Several of Edward's alert courtiers were already discussing the apparent reconciliation between the Breton and Edward's mistress; she could not afford to add fuel to their tales. Her heart sank as she pictured Edward's likely reaction to the gossip that would eagerly be relayed once they reached the Palace.

"I've watched many dawns come up, but none as lovely as this," Rolfe remarked gruffly, his eyes on the thinning clouds banked with gold.

Tears pricked Marged's eyes as a wave of weakening emotion swept over her. If only she could have disembarked on Rolfe's arm. If only she could have told Edward how much they loved and, begging his forgiveness, sought his blessing on their union. Those actions existed only in the realm of fancy. Bitterness tightened her mouth as she considered the probable outcome of such devastating honesty. Edward's towering Plantagenet rage would be aroused, and in its wake both she and Rolfe would likely be cast into the darkest dungeon.

"I promise this won't be the last sunrise we share," she vowed intensely, pushing aside her disquieting thoughts.

Hidden in the folds of her brocade skirts, his hand stole over hers. "Would you enjoy keeping Christmas on the Marches this year?"

"There's little likelihood of that."

"Don't be so pessimistic. You never know what the future will bring. I see you underestimate my guile."

"Take care, Rolfe, you underestimate your King."

He patted her hand in reassurance.

The barges were almost at their destination. Familiar timbered buildings huddled on the riverbank behind a forest of masts. The shallows seethed with small craft awaiting the coming day. Suddenly a multitude of pealing church bells clanged over the water.

"I've little to lose now," he declared with set jaw, once the carillon was over. "Without you, life holds little promise. Why shouldn't I take the ultimate gamble to capture the richest stakes in all Christendom?"

During the following weeks, Marged frequently repeated Rolfe's words to herself, taking comfort from the grim determination in his voice. Edward had sent Rolfe to Buckinghamshire to deliver some property deeds to a local lord, broadly hinting that while he was in the vicinity, he should speak his piece to Lilith Hardyng's father. Marged did not know what reckless plan he had in mind that chill dawn, but whatever it had been, she was powerless to prevent its being enacted. Rolfe took orders from no one. She could only pray he had sense enough not to take undue risks.

Today Edward hunted in the New Forest, anxious to take advantage of the fine October weather before he must turn to more serious tasks in preparation for Parliament's opening in November. At the King's insistence, Marged had delayed her departure for the Marches. She suspected that Edward too had secret plans fermenting in his brain, and her hopes for the future grew increasingly bleak.

Later in the month, when Rolfe arrived back at court, he rode in Edward's train. To her relief she saw that he was still a free man, therefore he must not have told Edward of their love for each other. A lump rose in her throat as she watched him ride under the stone arch into the courtyard, sun-bronzed and handsome in sapphire-and-white velvet. Tall black leather boots hugged his muscular legs; his silver rowel spurs glinted in the sunlight.

To Marged's great surprise, after Edward dismounted he slipped his arm about Rolfe's shoulders in a comradely manner. Then, heads bent in conversation, the two men entered the Palace. Unease stirred within her belly as she watched them together, as congenial as intimate friends. Edward would not treat him thus if he even suspected Rolfe of rekindling their love affair. Had Rolfe changed his mind about telling the King of his love for her? Marged bit her soft underlip, desperate to vanquish the niggling doubts that suggested Rolfe had probably succumbed to the lure of riches dangled before him by plain Lilith Hardyng's father. Assuredly, Edward welcomed the match—he was anxious to be rid of Rolfe's rival charms. Once Rolfe was married, Edward was convinced he could possess the fire in her body. And, personal desires apart, it would not be amiss to have a loyal man in Buckinghamshire.

Marged turned from the long window, hands clenched. She ached to know what Rolfe intended to do. Tomorrow she had planned to leave for Bowenford. She shuddered as she wondered if Edward would demand her services tonight. Since the masque at Greenwich Palace, he had not even kissed her. Marged would have been glad to let matters rest there.

Of late a new love had come into Edward's life, a smiling, buxom blonde who provided a stark contrast to Marged's dark beauty. Perchance this shapely creature would bring about her deliverance in the months to come. It was likely Edward would be occupied elsewhere tonight, for she had seen Jane's bouncy yellow curls protruding from under a page's hood.

Marged lit candles in the chapel, beseeching the saints to grant her freedom from Edward's bed. He had not given his final permission for her to leave. Uneasily, Marged wondered if that generosity was to be granted in person, after he was well satisfied. Bowing her head, she renewed her entreaties. Pretty Jane would never know what powerful aid drew her to her beloved's side.

Several hours later, as Marged was preparing for bed, she heard an unexpected commotion echoing through the corridors. Her heart plunged in her belly. Her prayers had been useless. The tramp of feet, the buzz of many voices all told her King Edward was honoring her with his presence.

The door flew open. There he stood, attired in a black-and-silver furred bedgown, his thick yellow hair gleaming in the flaming torchlight.

"Welcome, Your Grace," Marged uttered through stiff lips as she made him a deep curtsy.

"'Tis gratifying to find you expecting us. All of you may leave, we have no further need of you." Edward dismissed most of his servants, keeping with him only a valet and his favorite page, Hacket.

Marged grew uncomfortably aware of her heart thundering beneath her rose velvet bedgown as Edward crossed to the hearth and held his hands to the blaze. He smiled at her, his face relaxed, his humor pleasant. This observation plunged her spirits even lower. Rolfe had not spoken about their love, let alone asked Edward to sanctify that passion. Had he broached the subject, Edward would not be so amiable.

Nervously, Marged fingered the gold tassels edging the blue damask table cover while she waited for the page to pour their wine. The red-haired lad took the poker from the glowing embers and plunged its sizzling tip into the wine cups, heating the beverage before he handed it to his master.

"Thank you, lad. Now go, amuse yourself in a game of dice. We'll call if we need you."

The page bowed before skipping away to the adjoining dressing room, where the valet had already retired.

"Now we're alone."

Marged smiled sweetly, forcing the expression. "So we are."

"Do you still wish to leave on the morrow?"

"Yes. I'm already packed, though I await your final permission." Marged swallowed nervously when his brow furrowed. Did Edward intend to withhold his permission?

"I'll miss you, sweet. How am I to survive without your winning presence?"

"Nay, Edward, you'll be far too busy to miss me. Parliament meets soon. Then, before you know it, Christmas will be here will all its revels."

Edward glanced up sharply from his wine. "You'll return before then?"

"Well . . . I'd thought to spend Christmas at Bowenford. My tenants will expect it, this being my first year as their lady."

Though he nodded agreement, Edward scowled. "Yes, you're right, I suppose it's owed them. It's unwise to make the peasants too discontented."

"Exactly." Breathing a sigh of relief, Marged patted his broad shoulder, grateful for his understanding. "Edward, there's something I must tell you," she began, plunging ahead, though she realized it would be more prudent to hold her peace.

"After I've relayed my latest news, I'll hear you out. Now come, sit beside me." Edward patted the velvet-padded bench before the hearth.

Marged perched uncomfortably on the edge of the cushion, wishing he had allowed her to speak. Later she may not have sufficient courage to voice her treacherous thoughts.

"I don't intend you to take this ill," Edward prefaced as he slipped his heavy arm about her shoulders. "That's not the reason I'm giving you this news. I want to set your mind at ease once and for all." He hesitated a few moments, sipping the dregs of wine before he placed his cup on the hearth. "I've been matching a couple. A man who fought well for me, or to whom I owe favors, is sometimes given a bride in reward. In this case—"

"Rolfe!" Marged cried. She pleated her smooth velvet skirts to avoid looking into his pleased face. "Is it his marriage we discuss?"

"I've given my blessing on his union with Lilith Hardyng."

Marged swallowed. She already knew this news. "So I've heard," she croaked.

Peering closely at her, Edward seemed surprised by her apparent calm. "A date has been set for the wedding."

"Wedding?" she repeated hoarsely. "They're actually to wed?"

"During the festive season, so he tells me. He's been in Buckinghamshire, overlooking his reward and petitioning Sir Humphrey for Lilith's hand."

The news so stunned Marged that she could not even think. Like one long dead she stared at Edward, her eyes glassy in her white face.

"When he's wed, we'll both be rid of unpleasant memories. We can begin a new era. Perhaps then you'll come to me hot, instead of as cold as last night's supper." Edward's full mouth turned peevish when he considered all the disappointing nights these past months.

Numb with misery, Marged watched the firelight playing about his face, where triumph flickered keenly in his cornflower-blue eyes. Edward had won at last! Money, acceptance, an advantageous marriage—yet Marged found it hard to believe Rolfe had betrayed her for mere possessions. What other prize could Edward have dangled before her lover's eyes to make him finally close the door on their love? She had suspected there was something of the opportunist about Rolfe. Surely he did not think he could bed her while he was married to the Hardyng wench?

"I knew it would come hard. 'Tis best to make a clean break," Edward consoled her, studying her face. While he spoke, he fingered a ruby necklace inside his pocket, which he had brought to sweeten the truth.

"Is he at court?" she asked in a hoarse whisper.

"Yes, but I think it better you don't congratulate him in person. Go on your journey, enjoy the Marches, then return to us at Whitehall in time for the Yule revels. We'll send your people enough bounty to make up for their loss. Peasants appreciate commodities even more than they do pageants."

Edward slid his hand over her neck, folding back the collar of her bedgown to expose the honey-gold skin. Bending his head, he pressed his lips ardently against the smooth nape of her neck.

"Please, Edward," Marged whispered, tears throbbing to her eyes, "not tonight, not now."

He ignored her entreaty. Taking the gleaming necklace from his pocket, Edward placed the ruby circlet about her slender neck before stooping to kiss her again.

"There. It's a small token of my regard for you," he announced as he sat back to await her delight.

Desperately swallowing to enable herself to speak, Marged thanked him woodenly. Touching the cold jewels about her throat, she said, "You're much too kind, Edward. You needn't lavish me with gifts. You cannot buy me into your—"

"It's my pleasure to give them," he interrupted, not allowing her to finish speaking before he swept her into his strong arms. "Now, no more talk. You'll be gone tomorrow, and whilst you're away I will have to make do with wenches far less arousing. Come, love me this last time as if you meant it."

Edward seized Marged's hand and thrust it beneath his brocade bedgown. He was naked. Marged gasped as her fingers encountered the hot, throbbing surfeit of his manhood, fully aroused, eager to claim her.

"No . . . Edward . . . that's what I want to . . ."

"Enough!" He grasped her chin and forced her mouth to his, effectively silencing her protests. When their lips parted, aggravation knitted his fair brows. "You forget, dear lady Marged, I am your King."

And the mockery of those four words echoed in her ears as Edward bore her triumphantly to the curtained bed.

Heavy autumn mist obscured the tall steeple of St. Paul's and wreathed haloes about the russet trees in the park. All London glowered beneath the watery blanket, bringing perpetual night to the narrow, crowded streets.

Marged sat in the saddle, drained of all emotion. Her head throbbed with pain, the torment increased when she awoke to the memory of Rolfe's betrayal. How could he have deserted her for Edward's measly rewards? She had thought him too steadfast, too loyal, to have eagerly grabbed the bribe Edward dangled as temptingly as a carrot before a horse. Time and again, Rolfe had pledged his love to her, promising to find a way to keep them together. All lies! Lies! Those impassioned vows had meant no more than all the rest.

"We're ready, my lady," said the captain of the men-at-arms charged with accompanying her to Wales.

Raising her head, Marged stiffly nodded assent. Steely-eyed, afraid she would release her waiting tears, Marged drew on her gauntlets. "Very well. Let us be on our way."

The cold autumn wind sent dead leaves scudding over the grass as they traveled across the open heath beyond the city. The world seemed steeped in mist, the black hills somber shadows against a gray sky. Pink patches of herb Robert flourished beside the path, and the peppery sharpness of yarrow drifted from the roadside ditches. A deathlike hush, shattered only by the horses' clopping hooves, shrouded the country lanes.

When they paused to rest their mounts, Marged saw a sheltered clump of pimpernel, scarlet petals tightly shut, forecasting rain. They had gone less than a mile when the first cold drops splattered the bronze chestnut leaves overhead. Beneath this miserable cloak of mist and rain, Marged rode, head low, her vision restricted to the blurred patch between the horse's ears. These dismal surroundings mirrored the desolation of her heart.

From out of the uncertain light of late afternoon emerged a party of horsemen. Fearing robbers, Marged sounded the alarm. Her escort rapidly closed about her. When they finally came abreast of the riders who awaited them at the brow of the hill, Marged's hands went numb on the reins. A chill swept over her heart as she identified their leader astride a gleaming black stallion.

"Greetings, Lady Marged," said Rolfe de Bretayne.

"What do you want with me?" she demanded icily.

"I intend to ride part of the way with you."

Before she could protest his decision, Rolfe's soldiers descended from their grassy vantage point, fanning out to surround her small entourage. They brought with them two loaded sumpters and a stock wagon that had been hidden from view beyond a wood straddling the road.

Within the hour, as they clattered purposely west, the rain stopped and a pale sun struggled through the clouds to shed its feeble glow over the sodden countryside. Marged continued to ride in sullen silence, formulating speeches she dared not utter in the company of Edward's men. It was Rolfe who eventually broke the unnatural silence between them.

"For Christ's sweet sake, what ails you now?"

"You don't know?"

"I know only that you're sulking like a four-year-old."

Marged's eyes flashed at his criticism. "I suppose the news of your impending marriage was intended to fill me with joy?"

"I'd hoped it would."

She stared at him, stunned. "You must be mad!"

"Aye, I often suspect I'm somewhat deranged."

"You insufferable . . ." Words failed her. Marged spun about and charged for the spreading heathland, refusing to keep his company a moment longer.

The icy November wind cut through her habit as she galloped over the scrubby ground. She did not doubt he would pursue her to offer comfort with diverse lies.

"Hold!"

"Never!" she spat to the wind.

Marged careened over the spine of a low hill, plunging wildly down the other side, as reckless as if the devil himself pursued her.

"God damn you! Are you trying to break both our necks?"

Again she ignored his indignant bellow. She knew she could not long keep this pace, for the horse was growing tired beneath her, but as long as she was able, she would outstrip him.

Rolfe overtook her in a splattering shower of mud, his stallion skidding to a halt. He stood in the stirrups and grasped Marged's reins. Cursing beneath his breath, he leaned his weight on the leather and brought her horse to a standstill.

"Don't touch me!"

"Nay, for I've no wish to be savaged."

"You've no longer any right to mock me."

"Why not?"

"Because you're soon to be *her* husband."

To Marged's surprise, his anger visibly softened. A dawning smile lit his eyes as he whistled softly, "Mother of God! So that's it. I should have known." He managed to keep her flapping arms at bay. "Surely you didn't believe that claptrap?"

"No more! Haven't you lied to me, cheated me, often enough? There's no way you can slide out of this trap," she bellowed, making a supreme effort to free her horse's reins.

"Did Edward tell you I was to marry at Yuletide?"

"Yes. Surely you didn't expect him to keep your secret?"

"It wasn't a secret."

Marged sobbed in frustration when she could not budge his hold. "What possible excuse can you make this time?" she demanded, her green eyes flashing in her flushed face. "Silver-tongued with lies you've always been, yet this dilemma outwits even you."

"True, I'm to marry at Yuletide, lady—and so are you."

All the fight went out of her. She stared at him in horror, her vision glazing with tears. "What? Oh, Christ! Don't tell me Edward's parceled me off to the highest bidder."

Rolfe's anger subsided and his mouth twitched in humor. "Our Ned's as oblivious as a babe to the consequences of his actions."

Slumped in the saddle, Marged finally allowed herself the soothing relief of tears. What did it matter now if he saw her weep? What did it matter if he learned how sorely he had wounded her? She was surprised to feel the heat of his hand under her chin as he tilted her stubborn face.

"Mary, Mother of God, they always told me the Welsh were thickheaded, but I never expected this. Don't you understand what I'm trying to say to you?"

Marged blinked, the gold-flecked green glittering in the pale sunlight. "I'm not a total idiot! You're to marry Lilith Hardyng at Christmas."

His eyes were tender, the blue soft, iridescent. "Now that's a point I'll argue. 'Tis not plain, skinny Lilith Hardyng I choose to wed, you lovely halfwit—it's you!"

Shock speeded Marged's heart dangerously fast as she stared at him, unable to grasp what he was saying. "Edward said you were in Buckinghamshire to . . . to ask . . ."

"I went to view my gifted land."

"You must be out of your mind! He'll never give permission for us to wed!"

"Agreed. Therefore, I don't intend to ask it," he announced, chuckling at her shocked expression. "He told me to seek out the lady of my choice and make her mine. The fact we never actually established her name completely slipped my mind."

When he took her hands, Marged was trembling so violently, her teeth chattered. "Oh, Rolfe, love, no. We can't. He'll imprison you."

He ignored her tearful entreaties, pulling Marged toward him. The horses sidled against each other, snorting as he slid from the saddle, taking her with him. They stood on the wet turf, clinging to each other, hardly able to believe they were in each other's arms. Marged wept for all the pain of this past week, for her own lack of faith in him, her unspent anger unleashed in tears. She sobbed on his shoulder while he cradled her tenderly against him, only releasing her when he heard the sounds of approaching riders.

"Come, we'll put up for the night in the nearest inn."

Marged slid her arm through his, and they walked slowly back to their horses, who were cropping the watery grasses underfoot. Recklessly she turned to him, ignoring the watching soldiers as she pressed her mouth to his. Rolfe's proposed deception was treasonable. Edward would surely punish them severely. If he chose, the King could even order the death penalty—but she no longer cared. Whatever time she had left she would spend with Rolfe, even if she must die in payment for it.

On a gray December morning, Rolfe de Bretayne wed Lady Marged Bowen in Hereford Cathedral. Snowflakes drifted intermittently in the cold wind as Father Francis, an old family friend, performed the simple ceremony.

No one guessed the secret overshadowing the handsome couple as they embraced before the high altar gleaming with candles and gold plate. Not even the priest realized that the document granting royal approval for the wedding in Hereford Cathedral of King Edward's loyal subject, Rolfe de Bretayne, in this Year of Our Lord, 1461, had been granted on a falsehood. Many of those present were aware of Marged's former status at the court of their young Yorkist King, but they shrugged it off philosophically, deciding Edward must be rewarding the Breton's loyal service with the gift of his castoff mistress.

Oblivious to impending disaster, Marged hugged Rolfe's arm against her side as they walked sedately down the aisle of the lofty-naved cathedral. Marged's lustrous black hair hung unbound beneath a fur-edged headdress from which twin white veils streamed to the hem of her holly-green gown. She carried two red roses that had been presented to her by Master Henton, the armorer, in silent tribute to the fallen house of Lancaster, of which he was a lifelong supporter. He grew the fragrant blooms inside his warm parlor. Rolfe, setting little store by badges, had generously allowed her to carry the symbolic flowers.

They paused to kiss in the cathedral porch, two brilliantly garbed figures against the somber linenfold paneling. A handful of well-wishers showered them with dried rose petals, the colored petals whipping away in the wind to mingle with snowflakes. When Rolfe finally raised his eyes after the warm kiss full of promise, the blood froze in his veins. Standing in the shelter of the stone buttress was a group of men huddled in fur-lined cloaks. Even as their eyes met, Edward Plantagenet stepped away from the others, his face stormy.

"So this is how you repay my trust. You lied to me!"

Rolfe went to his knees, tugging Marged's velvet sleeve, nearly toppling her to the flagstones beside him as he wisely forced her to pay homage to her King. She stared up at Edward's angry face as one moonstruck, hardly able to believe what she was seeing. Fear rippled through her veins to chill her wedding-day bliss. Was she to be Rolfe's wife for only one hour?

"I asked your permission to wed in Hereford Cathedral."

"Aye, that you did—but not to *her!*"

"Mine was a sin of omission, not commission, Your Grace. You asked not my bride's name."

Teeth gritted, Edward glared in rage at the brightly clad kneeling figure. "You know, had you named her, Breton, I'd have withdrawn consent."

"'Tis why I did not name her. Long have we loved, Your Grace. Marged Bowen is the only woman I choose to marry."

"And you, kneeling silent as a fir tree, what have you to say?"

Marged swallowed, blinked, and finally forced her gaze to meet Edward's angry stare. "You know I've loved him since before I met Your Grace. Please, Edward, have mercy. Though you did me great honor, I pleased you not. My heart was already enslaved by another. Have mercy."

Stonily, Edward stared down at her kneeling figure, slender hands lifted in supplication, so achingly beautiful that moisture came to his eyes. She, whom he had desired for so long, had also deceived him. She had yielded up her body, but never once had he actually possessed her. Those wild Welsh Marches claimed her soul. Though he kept her within his luxurious palace, dressed in velvet and jewels, she rode the fierce wind sweeping the Marcher hillsides, ever beyond his grasp, always eluding him until he could have wept in vexation. He could not be happy with merely the shell of this beautiful woman. He had wanted to possess the fire in her blood, the beat of her heart, the surging in her loins . . .

"You dare crave mercy. Perchance you don't understand the consequences of deceiving your King?"

"I'm well aware of the gravity of my actions," Rolfe answered for her. He slid his hand into Marged's. "The guilt's mine alone."

Edward was gradually becoming aware of a gathering crowd chatting, staring, wondering at this strange tableau being enacted in the cathedral doorway. The handful of courtiers who had accompanied him on his passionate journey looked troubled, unsure of the next shift in their monarch's mood. When he left London, Edward had been boiling with rage at being duped. He had learned of their wedding from his soldiers, who, accompanying Marged to Bowenford, overheard her and Rolfe planning. As he thundered north, thoughts of vengeance seethed in his brain. Now, as he gazed at the kneeling couple, he discovered that his fury was spent.

"What a fool I've been. I thought it strange you chose to wed the Hardyng chit in Hereford. It's no longer a mystery why you did not invite me to your wedding."

"Your Grace, they're legally man and wife," offered a worried courtier who had been conferring hastily with the clerics who officiated at the ceremony.

Edward cursed beneath his breath and spun about, his fists clenched in renewed rage. He wanted to clap them both in prison. He was the King. The entire realm was his to command.

Such treasonable behavior could not go unpunished, or others would quickly put his leniency to the test. Yet, if he imprisoned them, he would gain nothing. If he killed the Breton and reclaimed Marged, he would get even less enjoyment from her body than before. Instead of emptiness, he would find hatred in her eyes . . .

A flurry of movement from the richly dressed courtiers attracted his attention. A slender page with a well-turned leg had stepped apart from the others. Edward would have looked away, had not the lad winked at him. Temper aroused by the page's impudence heated his face. He was about to step forward when the page impatiently unfastened his cloak, allowing the garment to drape open. A decidedly un-boyish chest was revealed. Edward's mouth gaped and his loins surged. The minx! Jane had come to Hereford against his wishes, disguised as a page boy! Sweet Jane was never cruel or distant; she always gave good measure of herself.

Rolfe got to his feet and raised Marged from the cold stones. He put his arm protectively around her as they awaited their King's final decision.

"You're a blackhearted rogue, Breton," Edward growled, spinning about and advancing on them. "But, by Christ, you fought right well for me on a dozen fields. Go then, enjoy your treacherously won prize. I never did own her—she's been yours from the start."

"Oh, Edward," Marged whispered, tears spilling from her eyes. She curtsied to him, then clasped his proffered hand, pressing her tear-wet mouth against it, oblivious to the bruising pressure of his many rings. "The saints will surely reward you for your charity."

Edward shook his head as he raised her to her feet.

"Nay, Marged, the saints rewarded me with you, and since that day I've had naught but anguish. Go in peace. Your husband awaits."

Rolfe knelt and Edward placed a beringed hand on his dark head to bestow his blessing. Abruptly the King turned away, his eyes seeking the voluptuous page who licked her full red lips in invitation, eager to be alone with him. De Bretayne could doubtless bring the Welshwoman to heat. Their shared Celtic ancestry, which bred such devious natures, likely provided the key to unlock passion. They were well suited to each other, he thought, glancing back at their dark, foreign beauty. Thank God, Jane was a typical English blonde with no yearning in her soul for mysterious, unfathomable things.

Their horses had been brought around to the cathedral entrance. Rolfe assisted Marged into the saddle, settling a fur-lined cloak about her shoulders before he mounted his black stallion and walked the animal over the cobbled forecourt to the royal party.

"Today you earned my lifelong loyalty," he said gruffly to Edward, finding it difficult to put into words the deep gratitude he felt. To allow them to go free after sorely wounding his pride had taken far more maturity than he had credited young Edward with possessing.

"I'll hold you to that vow, Breton," Edward said, forcing a grin. "By God, I'll hold you to it."

Impulsively, Edward reached up to clasp Rolfe's olive-skinned hand in his own large fair one. "Take this wild Welshwoman home to her beloved castle." He smiled after a moment.

Marged had ridden alongside them, and she brightened at the King's hearty suggestion.

"Thank you, Edward. Never before have you earned my respect as you have today," she said sincerely.

They parted on the cobbled forecourt. Edward and his party headed for the nearest inn to quench their hungers before heading south; Rolfe and Marged took the western road leading into the hills.

The small crowd gathered outside the great cathedral dispersed slowly, still not sure of what they had witnessed. The participants were all strangers, albeit magnificent strangers, but still unknown. As the good citizens of Hereford trudged home through a whitening mist, none realized they had just witnessed England's King, making one of the most selfless gestures of his reign.

Bowenford's Great Hall rang with music and laughter. This Yuletide was the first in many years that the vast Marcher castle had both lord and lady to preside over the festivities. Silken banners of red and gold hung from the aged beams; great boughs of holly, bay, and laurel festooned the walls and framed the window openings. Resinous smoke wafted blue-gray about the hammer-beamed roof, blackened by the fires of centuries. A great Yule log had been dragged in from the forest to heat the room; lit by fragments of last year's log, it blazed an orange inferno up the black, cavernous chimney.

This Christmastide, the March was peaceful. A Yorkist King was enthroned in London, but here, far closer to their hearts, their own Lady Marged sat in her rightful place at the high table, her soldier husband at her side. Strong, just, and most pleasing to behold, the Breton knight had readily been accepted as their new lord. All the tenants from the surrounding estate feasted within the Hall this snowy night.

Marged wore the dark green velvet gown in which she had been married, its low neck trimmed with vair, the white fur making a soft frame for her smooth, honey-gold flesh, which peeped enticingly above. Within the deep valley of her breasts nestled a gold Agnus Dei on a pearl-encrusted chain, a Yule gift from her bridegroom.

Rolfe sat beside her, his scarlet doublet a brilliant splash of color in the gloomy Hall. Never before had he appeared so handsome. A lump came into Marged's throat as she glanced at his strong profile outlined by leaping candleflames. At last he was hers. No longer need she hide her love for him.

It was strange to find Alys's chair empty. And though Marged felt a pang of guilt over her uncharitable thoughts, she was glad there were no abrasive influences left at Bowenford. She looked about the smoky Hall athrob with laughter and shining with merry faces. The resulting emotion brought her close to tears. These were her people. She had come home at last, and the man of her heart had come with her.

"Rolfe," she whispered, laying her head against his broad shoulder. "This is such a wonderful Christmas Day, I half expect to open my eyes and find it all a dream."

He pressed his lips lightly against her cheek. "It's not a dream, sweetheart. Though we took roundabout paths to reach it, together we'll share the destiny of this land."

"You aren't going back to Brittany, are you?" she whispered after a few minutes' silence, voicing a question that had haunted her for some time.

"Only to visit—or to fight, if my King wills it. Remember,

I owe our Ned my virtual soul in payment for you."

"Am I not worth it?"

"You used to insult me by calling me mercenary," he reminded with a grin, his hand whisper soft against her cheek. "This is the first time my good sword arm's been rewarded with a woman."

"And it's the most magnificent payment of all, isn't it?"

Playfully, Marged grasped a handful of his crisp black hair, lowering his face to hers.

"Assuredly. I most blasphemously liken it to discovering the Holy Grail," he chuckled, sliding his arms about her waist.

Their mouths met. All the noisy laughter, the Christmas sights and sounds, dissolved before the swift emotion of his ardent kiss. The promise of his mouth reminded her that tonight, and all those glorious nights to come, would be shared with her handsome lover. To call Rolfe husband seemed most strange. It was difficult to accept their lovemaking as a union sanctified by matrimony rather than a heady clandestine meeting, ended too soon by imminent departures.

"Pray God you don't have to fight very many of the King's battles," she whispered huskily, drawing away from him. "I don't fancy an absent husband."

"Why, sweet, I won't leave you behind. I'll take you with me, like the crusading knights."

Her laughing reply was drowned by a great shout echoing through the Hall.

The boar's head was carried forth with great ceremony. Brightly garbed pages danced before the enormous silver platter bearing the succulent, brown-glazed offering, its tusks gleaming, its mouth stuffed with a rosy apple. Mounded greenery encircled the platter; a rosy necklace of spiced crabapples was strung about the boar's neck. A lad bearing a silver pot of mustard headed the procession. Local carolers, singing in Welsh and English about the wondrous birth of old, filed inside the Hall, dressed in their best raiment in honor of their new lord and lady.

Marged gripped Rolfe's hand beneath the fringed red table cover, overcome with emotion at the sight.

The cook bore the steaming boar's head to the center of the high table, where it was set before Rolfe. A lengthy procession of servants wended their way between the lower trestles where the retainers had their boards, carrying a nonstop abundance of Christmas delicacies. Roast capon in mustard sauce, blood puddings, baked cod, flounder and sturgeon, glazed prettily with wine sauces. Coddling tarts, gooseberry flummeries, and platters of spiced dates . . .

From one of the lower tables, Rolfe's soldiers began a Breton carol. Rolfe's voice rang out as he picked up the old refrain his men were singing and he carried the verse alone, his rich baritone as sweet as any minstrel's lay. The Breton soldiers joined him in the chorus, standing with raised cups to toast the infant Christ.

Her eyes were misted with tears as Marged turned toward the crèche beside the hearth. It was fashioned from woven rushes from the Wye and timber from her own woodlands. Inside the straw-filled crib lay a carved infant brought by her mother from the Brecon hills many years before. It was a tradition at Bowenford that Eirlys's crèche be placed beside the hearth each Christmas. Though he could have denied her the right, now that he was master of Bowenford, Rolfe never questioned her customs, but merely accepted them, adding a few more from his homeland. Thereby they built a hallowed tradition to pass on to their children, who would come to treasure Christmas at Bowenford.

"Fill the cups and we'll drink a toast," he announced to the assembly, glancing about the room where a hundred shaggy heads nodded assent. When the cups were brimming and all faces were turned expectantly toward him, Rolfe raised his cup. Smiling down at Marged, he said, "I offer a toast to Lady Marged, my dearest wife. Long may she rule you in wisdom and love."

Marged's eyes misted as a great shout rang to the rafters. All within the Great Hall stood and raised their cups, old animosities buried in Yuletide fellowship as Welshmen, Bretons, and the King's own soldiers joined voices in joyous accord. At last she knew what it meant to be supremely happy. She was home at last in this wild, wooded land of rains and sweeping winds. And most wonderful of all, the handsome Breton, who had inflamed her blood to fiery heights, stood smiling beside her.